GIMME S'MORE

HOT CAKES SERIES

ERIN NICHOLAS

ISBN: 978-1-952280-09-2

Editor: Lindsey Faber

Cover design: Angela Waters

Cover Photography: Lindee Robinson

Models: Andrew Wilson, Kayle Berry

THE HOT CAKES SERIES

One small Iowa town.
Two rival baking companies.
A three-generation old family feud.
And five guys who are going to be heating up a lot more than the
kitchen.

Books in the series:
Sugar Rush (prequel)
Sugarcoated
Forking Around
Making Whoopie
Semi-Sweet On You
Oh, Fudge
Gimme S'more

ABOUT GIMME S'MORE

A friends-to-lovers romance that will make you melt.

Oliver's a dreamer who is always ready for the next big adventure.

Piper's the steady one who keeps his feet on the ground.

He's wildly successful, thanks to her always being there to catch him when he leaps before he looks. But she wants more. While he's as clueless as ever.

So she just gave her two weeks notice.

Ollie doesn't know how he'll survive without Piper. So for the next two weeks, he'll be sticking to her like the marshmallows on the s'mores she loves so much.

But does he want her as his assistant... or is there a sweeter spot in his life for the woman who's always had his back--and possibly even his heart?

1

───────

Piper Barry was in love with an amazing, brilliant, funny, good-looking man.

Who, at least twice a day, she wanted to smother with the stuffed dragon that sat on the corner of his desk.

Okay, maybe not *smother*. That was extreme.

But duct tape over his mouth? Oh yeah, she thought about that often.

"Is spit better than snot?" Oliver Caprinelli, that man—and her boss—asked her as she crossed his office to refill the water pitcher by the window.

"In every single context, yes." Piper was also aware that in any other workplace with any other boss, that question would be strange. Here though, not so much.

On her way back past his desk, she set the two folders and the manila envelope she carried in front of him. He was just one of her five bosses and the least likely to open those folders or that envelope. She put them down anyway.

"Grant said that a soda flavor called unicorn piss wouldn't sell well," Ollie said, almost as if he was thinking out loud.

He did that a lot. Thought out loud.

That never stopped Piper from chiming in though.

"And you think that calling it unicorn *snot* would make it sell better?"

This wasn't even the strangest conversation she'd ever had with Ollie.

"Wouldn't you assume that unicorn piss or snot tasted good?"

She wrinkled her nose. "No."

"Why not?"

"Uh, piss and snot."

"But *unicorn*," he insisted.

"I have never, not once, thought about the taste of unicorn... anything."

"Well, think about it now. Yes, good?"

What she thought was that working for Oliver Caprinelli would be a lot better if he didn't think out loud.

If he just sat there looking cute, things would be great.

"Why are we talking about unicorns?" she asked. "If you're adding something new to *Warriors*, you can do better. Unicorns are overdone."

The chances that this was about *Warriors of Easton*, the video game that Oliver and his four best friends had turned into the biggest-selling online game of the decade, was very good. It was nearly all Oliver thought about.

Ever.

Even when she wore her sexiest dresses. And the body oil that *all* of the other guys said smelled like spicy candy and that made them walk extra close by her desk every time they passed just so they could get a whiff. And when she worked late just so it could be only her and Ollie in the office after dark.

"It's not for *Warriors*," Ollie said. He still sounded distracted.

Honestly, he sounded distracted 90 percent of the time he talked about anything.

The man was a genius and his thoughts were always going

in a million directions. It was one of the things that fascinated her most about him.

And that made her think about picking up the dragon on his desk and stuffing it in his mouth. Trying to get Oliver's attention was hard enough. Keeping it was nearly impossible.

"What's it for, then?" she asked, pausing in front of his desk with the water pitcher.

She was able to study him as she waited for his answer. He was leaning back in his big leather chair, one ankle propped on his opposite knee. He was wearing dark gray slacks that went with the dark gray jacket he had tossed over the armchair that faced his desk. She wasn't sure where his tie was. She found his ties stuffed in drawers, suit jacket pockets, seat cushions, and file drawers—wherever he happened to be when it started bugging him, and he yanked it off.

His white linen button-down shirt was unbuttoned at the top, revealing tan skin and a hint of dark hair. The hair on top of his head was sticking up a bit in the back where he had a cowlick, and she made a note to schedule a haircut for him as she resisted the urge to brush that hair down. He also hadn't shaved this morning. He never grew a full beard or even let it get too scruffy, but once in a while there would be a day or two of growth. It made him look older and more intense. When he shaved, he looked easily five years younger than his twenty-eight years.

He was looking at the dragon on his desk, but Piper knew he wasn't seeing Spark. The plush dragon was one of the toys from the *Warriors of Easton* merchandise line. Spark was the one dragon in the game that couldn't breathe fire no matter how hard he tried.

Piper didn't know anything more about Spark than that. She didn't play the game and her awareness of it was limited to the things she'd handled as Oliver's personal assistant. That consisted mostly of keeping his appearances organized, answering emails, and dealing with the paperwork he had to do as one of the company's owners.

He had never cared about the business side of things much. He was the creative director. Still was, even though he and his four best friends who had owned *Warriors* under the umbrella of their company Fluke Inc. had sold *Warriors* to a larger gaming company last year.

Oliver continued to write story lines and develop characters for the game world.

But it was obvious that since they'd sold *Warriors* Oliver had been a little lost. His job hadn't changed a lot, but his friends were not involved with *Warriors* on the same level they had been and Piper suspected Ollie missed that intensely.

Warriors had always been a passion project for the five friends. It had taken off unexpectedly and they'd become accidental millionaires from it. But at its most basic level, it had always been something they did together and just had a good time with.

"Oliver?" she asked. "What's the unicorn spit about if it's not *Warriors*?"

He looked up at her and she could have sworn for a second that he'd forgotten she was there.

Even after working for the man for five years, that was still a little insulting. Especially when she was wearing one of her favorite pin-up dresses. It was bright pink, hugged her hips and breasts, and gave a little peek of cleavage without being inappropriate. She wore a wide black belt with it, black pumps with a big pink bow, black fishnets, and a black hair scarf.

She looked great. Sexy even.

And she would bet that if she had him close his eyes and asked him what color her dress was, he wouldn't know.

"Trying to come up with names for the sodas," he said.

She froze. Then straightened and narrowed her eyes. "What sodas?"

But she knew.

He frowned as if confused by her question. "The new sodas we're going to launch when I buy the soda company in Wisconsin."

"But you haven't bought it yet?" she asked. She'd thought he was over that idea. After she had told him it was a bad idea.

"We're meeting at the end of the week," he said. "It's basically done."

"I thought we talked about how this was a bad move," she said, trying to keep her voice calm. "I thought we agreed that you're bored now that Hot Cakes is doing well, and the other guys have all been spending more time with their girls, but that buying *another* new company is not the right move."

Honestly, Oliver had only gone along with the purchase of Hot Cakes because one of his best friends, Aiden, had been determined to buy it and wanted all the guys in on it. And because Ollie loved Hot Cakes' Fudgie Fritters.

He actually liked most of the cakes. Sometimes, he was essentially a fourteen-year-old boy in a twenty-eight-year-old man's body. He loved video games and snack cakes. And he loved hanging out with his friends.

He didn't, however, like soda. Interestingly. He didn't drink it. Claimed to not like it. But after they'd bought Hot Cakes and gotten it running well under their new management and had very successfully launched a new product and rebranded themselves, things had slowed down a little and now Ollie was feeling restless.

In part, because very few of the things they'd done with Hot Cakes had been *his* doing anyway.

Aiden had taken the lead, since the company was based in his hometown and buying it meant not only saving the town from losing its major employer, but also giving him a great reason to come home and be with the woman he was crazy in love with.

Dax had come along because Dax was always up for an adventure and was great with people. All people. In all situations. They'd needed Dax to help smooth things over with the disgruntled employees.

Grant had come along because he was the money guy. He'd never intended it to be a permanent move to the tiny Iowa town but, then he'd fallen in love with a hometown girl and now he wasn't going anywhere.

Cam was also from Appleby and had rekindled his relationship with his ex. Who just happened to be the granddaughter of the founders of Hot Cakes. The two of them had been the force behind the new product launch and its huge success, and everyone knew that their next new product, which was already in the works, would be just as big.

So that left Ollie just... being here. Being here with his best friends because he truly didn't have roots anywhere else and he could do his creative work for *Warriors* anywhere.

Which meant Piper was here too. She ran Oliver's life. She definitely helped all the guys and Fluke at large, but she'd been hired to be Oliver's assistant and he definitely needed the most... caretaking.

But now Ollie was bored. He'd been a little bored along the way since he'd had less direct investment, other than money, in Hot Cakes. But he'd enjoyed supporting his friends and brainstorming things like new snack cake ideas and names and the big launch event.

Now that was all over and he was looking for a new project.

Why? Why wasn't *Warriors* enough? He was the imagination behind that entire world. Everything that existed in *Warriors*, even now under new ownership, was because of Oliver. Why wasn't that enough?

And if he did have free time and had room in his brain for more, why couldn't he do something more meaningful than *soda*?

Ugh.

"I think soda lines up well with my brand," Ollie said. "Video games, snack cakes, soda." He nodded. "That makes sense."

"Your brand? What brand is that?"

"Oliver Caprinelli... let's have a good time." He paused and looked at her. "I'm working on a tag line."

Piper took a deep breath. "You need a tag line? Like you *individually* need a tag line?"

"I guess." He shrugged. "The guys are done with *Warriors* for the most part. And I'm more than Hot Cakes."

Piper wished she wasn't holding the water pitcher because she really needed to rub her forehead where a headache was starting. She had two types of headaches. The one right between her eyes, which came on quickly and she assumed had to with eye-rolling and frowning. She called those the *Ollies*. The ones that started in her neck and crept more slowly up the back of her head were the *Olivers*. They were tension headaches that came from stress and holding in all the *are you fucking kidding me?* that threatened throughout her days.

And she said some of them. She didn't have, or need, a lot of filter around her bosses. Which was great. They were more like brothers than bosses. They respected her, they *needed* her —and knew it—and they listened to her.

Except for Ollie.

"You're more than Hot Cakes?" she repeated. She agreed. But she'd never heard him say it and she was curious what he meant.

He swiveled his chair back and forth.

He was a big guy. Six-three, two-hundred-ten-ish pounds. He was wide and solid. He ran to keep in shape. In part because of that love of snack cakes and the amount of time he spent sitting and creating behind the computer.

He was wearing a custom-tailored suit that cost more than a lot of people's house payments in Appleby.

But he was pouting. And Piper wanted to put him in time out.

"I mean, I need something more to do," he said. "Aiden was the one who branched out into Hot Cakes. Grant's got his consulting business. Dax is running the nursing home. Cam has turned into a house-husband. What's *my* thing?"

The guys did all have pursuits outside of Fluke that they were enthusiastic about now. Projects and people that took up a lot of their time and energy. Additionally, the guys were all-in with their new relationships and the families and time that went along with those.

They were happy. Happier than Piper had ever seen them. And they were all still a unit. But Aiden, Dax, Grant, and Cam definitely shared a bond in being boyfriends and fiancés that left Oliver out.

Ollie was the only one who was still involved with *Warriors*. And he didn't seem to have another passion.

"So you're bored and your idea to branch out is soda?" she asked.

He shrugged. "Yeah."

Clearly he was very passionate about this new company. Piper rolled her eyes, making the jab of pain in her forehead worse.

"Oliver, you need to find something to *care* about," she said.

Like me, a voice said in the back of her mind.

She told that voice to shut the hell up. She and that voice had been over this before. She couldn't explain why she loved Oliver, but she did. However, Oliver would make her crazy.

Oh, and he wasn't interested. Clearly.

"I care about growing my brand."

"Oh my God," she exclaimed. "Your brand? You want your

brand to be video games and crap food? You can do better than that, Ollie!"

He lifted a brow. "Like what?"

He wasn't challenging her. He actually wanted her to tell him what he should do.

Oliver Caprinelli was a handsome, intelligent, charming-when-he-wanted-to-be,   funny-usually-accidentally-but-sometimes-on-purpose, crazy successful creative genius.

Who drove her insane.

It was all Aiden's and Grant's and Dax's and Cam's fault.

They'd all been enabling this man since they'd met him. They treated him like he was delicate. Like if they pushed him too hard or told him no, he'd lose his spark and wouldn't be able to create any longer.

They treated him like he was a spoiled royal prince.

Oliver had never had an idea that Dax hadn't said, "Hell yes!" to. He'd never made a mistake that Grant hadn't bailed him out of. He'd never created something Aiden hadn't been able to sell for big bucks.

Oliver had also never booked a hotel room or a plane ticket on his own and had no idea how to even use the Instant Pot in his hotel suite. Because Piper did those things.

But that had been her job. She hadn't enabled him the way the guys had.

It was really *their* fault he was the way he was.

But as she studied the good-looking guy who *looked* like a very successful functioning adult, she admitted that a lot of this was her fault too.

Ollie was bored because he truly had very little to do or take care of.

They'd all given him so much time and space to be creative that he had very little actually filling his days. Nothing *real* anyway. Nothing practical. His entire job was to sit down and imagine stuff.

He was good at it. It was definitely lucrative. There was no question about it. But yeah, it made sense that he was bored.

And, like everything else, she wanted to fix this for him.

"Oliver," Piper said, making her tone more placating. "You can do better than soda. If you want a brand"—she did *not* roll her eyes—"can't you come up with something more in line with *Warriors*? That's what people know you for."

He and Dax were the face of the company. They did YouTube videos, discussing the creation of the game as well as more in-depth conversations for fans about the world and the character arcs and what was to come.

People discussed the game as if it were a beloved television show or book series. They knew the main characters and cared about their development and what would happen to them. It rivaled the fans of Star Wars and the Marvel comics and movies. But it was a video game. So the fans could participate in the world. They could truly be a part of it.

"You don't think people drink soda while they play?" he asked.

She sighed. "Does it matter? Couldn't you buy a... gaming controller company or something?" She didn't love that idea either. How meaningful was that?

And yes, with that thought, she realized that she wanted Oliver to do something more *meaningful*. Not just because the world needed his creativity and intelligence, but because *he* needed to do more.

He didn't even care about this soda company.

"There aren't any controller companies for sale." He sighed and swiveled his chair. It squeaked when he went all the way to the right.

That squeak made her eye twitch. She was going to have to come in here and fix that later.

"There's one that wants me to endorse their controllers," he said, sounding completely disinterested.

"Okay." That wasn't great, but it was better than soda. Especially soda called unicorn snot. "Are you going to?"

"I don't like the controllers," he said.

"Oh well, then…"

"But maybe."

Piper blew out a breath. "You can't endorse a controller if you don't like it."

He shrugged. "Maybe I could do some commercials or something."

It wasn't that he liked the spotlight, though it would seem that way. He just liked to *do* things. He liked to travel and meet people and have projects. The gaming cons were fun for him because he got to go places and interact with people who were enthusiastic about things he was enthusiastic about. Dax actually did better on stage and engaging with audiences than Ollie, but Dax could pull Oliver out and make him relax and be charming.

"Oliver," Piper finally said firmly. "You should not endorse that controller and you should *not* buy that soda company."

"They're already coming on Friday."

"I can cancel the meeting."

"Nah." He swiveled his chair again.

The squeak made Piper grit her teeth. She was going to have a combo headache today.

"You're determined to go ahead with the soda?"

"Yeah."

He sounded *so* enthusiastic.

"And you're going to call one of the flavors unicorn snot?"

"Maybe spit. I haven't decided."

The biggest decision of his day was choosing between unicorn snot or spit.

She should *not* ask.

"What are the other flavors you've come up with?" she asked in spite of knowing that she didn't want to know.

"Troll blood."

She took a deep breath. At least there were trolls in *Warriors*. Maybe the labels could have something to do with *Warriors*. That was on brand for Ollie.

Ugh, he did *not* need to be a brand.

"Fairy dust," he said. Then he frowned. "But that's not good. Dust isn't liquid."

Piper just nodded. Honestly, none of this mattered. None of it was good.

"Dragon fire," he said.

"Fire isn't liquid either," she pointed out. She was on the verge of just laughing hysterically.

He nodded, frowning. "I know."

"You should just call *all* of them spit," she said. "Troll spit, fairy spit, dragon spit, unicorn spit. All different flavors and colors but similar theme. And," she said, on a roll now, feeling like she was going a little crazy, "you should add unicorns to *Warriors* in your next story. Then it all goes along with *Warriors* and *can* be part of your brand. In fact," she added, definitely feeling like she was about to crack. And that meant laughing uncontrollably, crying, or ripping the head off of Spark and strewing his innards all over Ollie's office. "You should talk to Whitney about making some *Warriors* snack cakes. Troll turds." She nodded. "Brown roll-up cakes. Or green. Is troll poop brown or green?"

She was breathing hard and her heart was racing.

Oliver, on the other hand, was still leaning back in his chair. He did, however, stop swiveling. And arched a brow.

"Don't be ridiculous," he said.

She laughed, sounding manic, but feeling a touch of relief. Ollie's bar for ridiculous was high but it was good there was a limit.

"We can't use *Warriors* on anything officially. We sold it off to Plus Gaming, remember?"

She stared at him. "Of course I remember."

"They own all the trademarks and logos and stuff." He sighed as if everything was just too much to bear. "So all of that is out. Though I guess I could still call the sodas troll and dragon spit and stuff. People might make the connection. We could put my face on the labels or something."

Piper opened her mouth to reply. Then snapped it shut. She started to reach for Spark. Then pulled her hand back. She pressed her lips together. Then pivoted on her heel and marched out to her desk.

She yanked open her middle right-hand drawer, lifted three folders out of the way, and withdrew the crisp piece of paper. She signed and dated it, then stomped back into Oliver's office. She laid it in the middle of his desk.

He sat forward. That made the stupid chair creak too and Piper pulled a breath in through her nose.

"What's this?" he asked.

"My resignation letter."

"Oh." He grinned and sat back again. "Okay."

She raised both eyebrows. "I'm serious, Oliver."

It was true that she'd quit twice before. But both times she'd done it verbally and once had been to Grant only. She *threatened* to quit about twice a month. It was her fault that he wasn't taking this seriously.

But a lot of Oliver's behaviors and attitudes were her fault.

Dax was the master enabler. Grant a close second. But she was easily number three. She could own that.

She could also fix it.

"I'm sorry," he said.

She tipped her head. "For?" She knew he had no idea what exactly she was pissed about. He *really* didn't know that she was, in part, pissed at herself.

"For upsetting you."

"But for *what*? Exactly?" she pressed.

He looked at her for a long moment. "For not liking your idea about the troll turds?" he finally asked. "It's not that I didn't like it. We just can't do it."

She sighed. He was going to need a little help here. Fine. She could explain this to him. Then she was leaving.

"You need to do *more*," she told him. "You need to do something important. You've been given every opportunity, and if you use your money and success and position to buy a soda company to make drinks for kids that are called troll spit, you are absolutely wasting all of it. And I can't be around to watch that."

He frowned. "I'm not wasting anything. I give money to charity."

"You do," she said. "But you randomly write checks to organizations. Those organizations appreciate it, I'm sure. But they don't really *mean* anything to you. They don't make you passionate. I know that Hot Cakes doesn't make you passionate either. I know you're here because of the guys. And *that* is awesome. Your friendships make you passionate. But *you* don't care about Hot Cakes. Not really. Hell, sometimes I'm not sure how much you care about *Warriors*. At least not as it is right now."

She felt herself frown as she said that out loud realizing that it was true. And that she was just now actually realizing that herself.

"I know that *Warriors* was your creation. Still is. But I think it's... not exactly what you want it to be. But instead of making it into more, you just keep doing the same thing with it. And I *don't* think you care about soda."

Ollie was frowning deeply now. "Does anyone *care* about soda?" he asked.

"I have no idea. It would be hard for me to imagine," she agreed. "But the point is, *you* need something to care about and I'm tired of you not looking for that. Not trying for that. I've been right here, for five years, supporting everything you've wanted to do—probably more than I should have—and made everything easy for you. I think that you need to figure out what you want and I think you need to work for it."

"Work for what?"

"For the things you want."

"What are those?"

She blew out a breath. "That's what you need to figure out, Ollie. You need to figure out what you *care* about. I think *Warriors* just happened to you. I'm not saying you regret it, but I do think you wish some of it was different. Hot Cakes just happened to you. That was all Aiden. And now, when you go looking for something of your own, you land on *soda*? And you want to call it troll spit? Come on. You're better than that."

Notably, he didn't argue with her about *Warriors* not being what he wanted it to be, nor did he declare that he loved owning Hot Cakes and thought that was incredibly important work.

"And you think everything is easy for me?" he asked.

"Yes." She laughed. "Very."

"So you think I'm..." He lifted a brow, as if challenging her to fill in that blank.

Well, she was ready.

"Entitled. Spoiled. Brilliant. A little lazy. Creative. Infuriating. One of my favorite people. And full of yourself."

He just sat blinking at her.

"And clueless," she added after a few seconds.

"Is that it?"

She shrugged. "I'm sure I can come up with a few more. Those cover the basics."

"You think I'm *lazy*?"

"I also said brilliant and creative."

He studied her, his eyes narrowed. "You also said one of your favorite people."

She nodded. "I did."

"So why are you handing me a resignation letter?"

"Because my contract with Fluke Inc. requires I write one. The contract, by the way, that none of you even remember that I had to sign."

She knew very well she could have gotten away with not turning that letter in. Sure, Oliver might have thrown a little fit and Cam might have dug into his paperwork when he had a tiny niggle in the back of his memory about a contract. But her bosses had become very dependent on *her* knowing all of the paperwork details about the business. If she'd told them she didn't have to write a letter, they probably would have believed her.

Which was why she couldn't do that. She'd never manipulate their trust in her.

"So you want to quit? Even though you just said you really like me and you know that I need to find something that matters to me? Don't you think I need you if I'm going to do that?"

She put a hand on her hip. Oh man, she'd love for this guy to need her. For more than booking plane reservations and writing emails and making sure he didn't eat room service every night at the hotel where they'd both been living for the past ten months. Not that she was complaining. They both had penthouse suites. The hotel room was nicer than her apartment in Chicago, and that had been really nice. The guys paid her well, what could she say?

"Why do you need *me* to help you figure out what you need to be doing with your life?" she asked, truly curious about his answer to that question.

"Because you know me better than anyone," he said easily.

Her heart flipped in her chest, then fell to her stomach. He wasn't wrong. She did know him. Probably better than he knew himself. But that was the problem. Oliver needed to get to know himself. He needed to figure out what he wanted. He needed to stop being dependent on everyone around him to tell him what he should and shouldn't do.

"This is all on you, sorry," she said.

"So you really are quitting?" He actually looked and sounded concerned now. Finally.

She nodded. "I am."

"You're really that pissed about the soda company?" he asked. "Fine. I won't buy it."

"No, Ollie, that's not it." She sighed. "Well, that's not all of it. That's just symbolic."

"So why are you quitting, then?"

"Because... I can't be in love with you and work for you. And the only one of those two things I can change is the working for you part."

2

The guys were going to kill him.

Ollie scrubbed a hand over his face.

They wouldn't be surprised, of course. But they were going to be pissed.

They'd all known that Piper quitting was a risk and that one day she'd probably wise-up and lose her patience and that would be it.

They'd also all known that when it happened there was a 90 percent chance it would be because of Ollie.

The other 10 percent chance was that it would be because of Ollie and Dax together.

And now it had finally happened.

If it came down to choosing between him and Piper, he wasn't sure he wanted to know how that debate would end up. Or how short the discussion would be before they decided they wanted and needed her more.

That was only one of the reasons he hadn't told them yet.

The other was because he was still processing the part where she'd said she loved him.

What was he supposed to do with *that*?

She wasn't just supposed to say that out loud right to him, was she? He had not been expecting that. The guys and their girlfriends had insinuated for a while now that Piper might have a crush on him but no, he hadn't expected her to ever say anything herself.

It was a *might have*. A *crush*. Okay, they were adults and maybe adults didn't have crushes exactly, but everything anyone had said suggested that it was just that Piper thought he was interesting at times and that she didn't hate spending time with him.

But a crush wasn't *love*. For fuck's sake.

And it had to be Piper?

Piper Barry was amazing. She was gorgeous. She was smart. She was capable. She could do anything. She was funny and sweet and sassy and tough.

She was intimidating as hell.

What was he supposed to do with her now?

What was he supposed to do *without* her now?

Well, the solution seemed pretty obvious. She'd basically given him the answer herself—*I can't be in love with you and work for you. And the only one of those two things I can change is the working for you part.*

So he needed to get her to *not be* in love with him anymore. Then she'd come back to work and all would be fine.

Now he just had to get her to realize she could do a hell of a lot better than him.

Of course, he'd been a pain in her ass for five years now. If that didn't do it, he wasn't sure what would.

He could get her an alpaca. She loved those things. He could buy one from Drew Ryan, the alpaca farmer north of town. Even though Ollie couldn't stand the guy.

But she was living in a hotel at the moment. The hotel manager, Stan, liked Ollie a lot and Piper's suite was huge, but he wasn't sure Stan liked him *enough* to let him put an alpaca in one of the penthouses.

And if Stan did let him get Piper an alpaca, that wouldn't make her fall *out* of love with him.

Though she would definitely think he was crazy to even think of it. That was run-of-the-mill Ollie craziness though.

Dammit.

He could... get arrested. That would remind her that he was impulsive and didn't think through consequences and did stupid shit. Often.

Getting arrested was *really* not hard to do. He and Dax had done it accidentally twice. Surely doing it on purpose would be even easier.

Of course, Bernie, the Appleby town cop, was a really nice guy and super laid back. If Ollie did something like streaking across the town park or hot-wiring someone's car, Bernie would probably think it was funny, laugh and slap Ollie on the back, and tell him to not let it happen again.

Well, shit.

He could punch someone in the face and get locked up for assault, he supposed.

Drew Ryan came to mind.

That would piss Piper off. She liked Drew, and Ollie hitting him would definitely not make her happy.

Yeah, maybe he'd see what Drew was up to and ask him to meet up for a beer or something.

Ollie started to pull his phone out, but then hesitated.

Piper wouldn't be the only one mad at him if he punched Drew though. Whitney and Dax and, really, all of his friends liked Drew.

And Drew might hit him back. And Drew might be a better fighter than Ollie.

That wouldn't take much.

Okay, so no streaking, stealing, or punching.

He could... hire a skywriter. They could write out... son of a bitch, what would he have them write? And how would he even find a skywriter?

See, this was the kind of stuff *Piper* did for him. She found the skywriters and helped him figure out what they should write.

Metaphorically, anyway. He'd never actually hired a skywriter.

Piper would definitely think a skywriter was over the top though. No matter what he wrote.

Ollie groaned and his head fell back against the headrest of his chair.

The guys were *definitely* going to kill him.

He dragged a hand through his hair. He needed to talk to her. He needed to fix this. Before the guys found out.

He shoved back from his desk and started for the door.

Fixing this meant convincing Piper that she was wrong to be in love with him.

He just needed to ask her how to do that.

A n hour later, he was standing outside her hotel room door.

"Piper! It's me!" He pounded on the door with his closed fist. Again. He'd already knocked. Then pounded. Now he was pounding again and wondering how much he'd have to pay the hotel manager, Stan, to get a key to Piper's room.

They had the only two suites on this floor so he wasn't bothering anyone else with his yelling. He could maybe get the heavy lamp by his window and knock her door down. That would probably bother Stan, but Ollie could deal with that later.

"Pi—"

Her door swung open in the middle of her name.

Piper stood there staring at him with wide eyes. "Somebody better be in the hospital or you'd better be bleeding from a major artery."

He heard what she said. But he couldn't process an answer. Because Piper was standing in the doorway in a robe, with her hair wrapped up in a towel on top of her head.

The robe was black. And silky. And short. Very short.

It wrapped around her and tied in the front, as robes did, and created a deep V between her breasts.

Her gorgeous, very generous—and did he mention gorgeous?—breasts.

Ollie was a little clueless—even he would admit that—but he wasn't dead. Which meant that he'd noticed Piper's very generous curves long ago.

The way she dressed would have made it impossible not to. Her dresses were bright and unusual and even the ones that didn't hug her hips and ass, caressed her breasts. She also drew attention to all those curves with big belts and bright scarves and other accessories.

The woman liked to draw attention to herself and he always happily gave it.

This robe was nothing like any of those dresses. It wasn't brightly colored. There were no earrings, no wedge heels, no bows. Just a lot of silk—both in the robe and the skin that stretched below the short hem.

He'd never seen her dressed like this. Not in any of the five years he'd known her. She was always put together, perfectly coordinated, looking kick ass, and untouchable.

Now she looked... very fucking touchable.

Except for the look on her face. And the way she propped her hand on her hip.

"Oliver," she said firmly.

His gaze lifted to her face. Away from her legs.

Damn, the girl had some great legs.

That shouldn't be a new revelation. She wore skirts and heels every day. He'd definitely noticed her legs before.

But there was something about this robe or her hair being up in a towel or the way she smelled or this doorway or... he had no idea, but this was different. Her legs had never looked like *this*.

"*Oliver*," she said again, snapping her fingers in front of his face.

"What?"

"*What*?" she repeated. "You're beating on my door, scaring the hell out of me, making me get out of the shower to come see what was wrong with you, and you're asking *me* what?"

He blinked at her.

"What's wrong?" she asked.

"You can't be in love with me."

She sighed and her hand dropped. "That's not how it works."

"Yeah, well, that screws everything up," he said crossly.

Everything had been fine that morning. Everything in his life had been fine. Normal. Easy.

And now Piper had quit, and she thought she was in love with him, and she was standing in front of him in a skimpy little robe, and he was noticing her legs and... everything was a mess now.

And Piper was the one who fixed the messes in his life, not the one who caused them.

"Sorry," she said, lifting her shoulder.

She didn't seem sorry at all. He frowned. "Can you put some clothes on?"

"No."

"Excuse me?"

"This is *my* room. I didn't invite you. You got me out of the shower. I'm going to go get back in there when you leave. So, no, I'm not going to go put clothes on while you stand here and tell me not to be in love with you."

"It's really distracting."

She looked surprised for a moment. Then, slowly, she smiled. A smile that made his heart thump and, at the same time, sent an *uh-oh* through his mind.

"Sorry," she said again.

She was definitely not sorry about that either.

"I just don't see why you want to be in love with me," he told her, resolutely keeping his eyes on hers.

He *really* wanted to look down. But he had a feeling she knew that and if he did he would somehow be admitting something he didn't want to admit.

"Well, I don't see why you wouldn't want me to be in love with you," she told him in the same tone he'd used.

"Because, apparently, you can't work for me *and* be in love with me. And I really need you to work for me."

She rolled her eyes. "Well, Oliver, maybe you think that's your choice because you've never really experienced me being in love with you."

"So this is new?"

"Not really."

"So I *have* experienced you being in love with me," he said.

She lifted a brow. "I haven't been acting on those feelings."

"So keep doing that."

She seemed to be considering that. Then she took a step closer. "No, I don't think I will."

He frowned down at her. Without her heels on, she was really short. The top of her head came to his chin. She usually *seemed* taller. Sure, it was probably the heels, but it was also just the way she presented herself. The way she walked, the way she stood, the way she talked and met everyone's eyes directly and took care of everything.

Now she was in a freaking robe with her hair up in a towel. She seemed shorter.

And now, hearing her talk about being in love with him, it seemed a little less difficult to believe.

Dammit. What the hell was that?

"What's that mean anyway?" he asked, feeling as grumpy as he sounded. "What do you mean you're going to act on those feelings now? Quitting? Leaving me? *That's* acting on being in love with me?"

She shook her head slowly and stepped closer.

He should step back. Part of his brain told him that. But a bigger part of him—like the entire rest of his body and brain—said *don't be a dumbass.*

She took the front of his shirt in her fist and pulled him down. And he went. Like a dumbass.

"It means doing things like this," she said softly.

Then she kissed him.

Ollie was shocked. Actually shocked. The idea of kissing Piper had never occurred to him before. The idea of Piper kissing *him* had *never* occurred to him.

But the shock was quickly replaced by thoughts like *damn her lips are soft* and *she smells so fucking good,* and, *of course, she's good at this too.*

He figured as long as their lips were pressed together, he might as well enjoy it for a few minutes.

So he cupped the back of her head, tipped his head, and kissed her back.

He realized that he'd surprised her when she made a little squeaking sound as her towel fell from her head. But she didn't pull back or reach to grab it. She grabbed the front of his shirt with her other hand in fact. And moved in closer.

The wet strands of her hair fell over the back of his hand, reminding him she'd just been in the shower, and he suddenly *had* to touch her robe.

He ran his hand from her shoulder down her arm to her wrist over the black silk. The warm black silk. Warm from her body underneath.

He really liked it. A lot. He moved his hand to her waist and stroked the warm silk there, back and forth over the dip. Then up and down over her hip.

Her hand ran up his chest to the back of his neck, pulling him even closer.

Well, okay. They'd already gone this far. It was going to be complicated when he let her go whether he backed her up against the door or not.

So he stepped forward.

She stepped back.

The door swung shut behind him and he turned her, putting her up against the wood. Both of his hands went to her hips and she rose on tiptoe with a little moan.

Oh, that was nice. He felt heat lick through him. He really wanted to put his nose against her neck. Did she smell the way she did because of her soap or her shampoo or some perfume she put on after her shower? If it was after the shower, then she wouldn't smell that way now would she? But he swore it was just *her*. And he wanted to run his nose all over her body to be sure. And while his nose was there, his mouth would be there too...

But he didn't want to release her mouth. Her lips were everything he'd never known he'd always wanted.

He tipped his head the other way, opening slightly.

She followed his lead. Enthusiastically.

Piper gripped the back of his head and stroked her tongue into his mouth, hungrily.

That little lick of heat in his veins intensified to a full-on punch to the gut and he felt himself press closer. His hand dropped from her waist to her thigh. Sure enough, her skin was as warm and silky as the material of her robe.

Her hands went to his lower back and she brought him against her. He pressed into her soft body and this time he was the one who groaned. His palm slid up her thigh and under the hem of her robe to the curve of her ass.

The naked curve of her ass.

He felt his body harden and tighten and he finally dragged his mouth to her neck, breathing deep as he squeezed the warm flesh.

Her breath rushed out as her head fell back against the door and he kissed down her neck to her collarbone as her robe gaped at the top.

Yep, she just smelled like this. This was just Piper. He was definitely willing to keep going to be *sure,* but he was convinced that her skin was just created to feel, taste, and smell like heaven.

"Ollie," she said softly, her fingers curling into his hair.

"Yeah."

"We need to stop."

He did. His nose was still against her throat and his hand still cupped her ass, but he stopped moving. He just breathed for a second. She didn't push him back but he felt her hands slide down his neck.

Finally, he lifted his head, leaving his hand right where it was under her robe.

She looked... mussed.

He'd never seen her look mussed. Her lips were pink. From his. Her hair was wet and curling around her shoulders. Her robe was falling off one shoulder, hinting at far more than the tease of cleavage he saw in her other dresses. If he tugged on the bottom of the robe that rested on the back of his wrist, he could expose one entire breast.

He wanted to do that so much it was shocking. Almost more shocking than the kissing in the first place.

But he didn't feel the panic he would have expected.

He felt a desire that he'd never felt before.

This was Piper. *Piper*. Kissing her should have been really weird.

It hadn't been.

"Why?" he asked.

"Because you don't want me to be in love with you."

Yeah, he really didn't. That seemed complicated. And like he was sure to mess it all up.

"But you *are*. Shouldn't you want this?" he asked.

She nodded. "Oh, I do." Then she pushed him back.

His hand slipped from under her robe and he sighed. "I don't get it."

"I know."

"Do I want you to explain it?"

"Probably not."

"Why I can't strip this little robe off of you and go for this thing that we both clearly want? I think I do."

She actually laughed at that.

"What?" he asked. She was *laughing*?

"You didn't even know you wanted this until I kissed you. You never would have kissed me first."

He tucked his hands into his pockets. No. He wouldn't have. Probably.

"And now you suddenly want this?" she asked.

"It was a really good kiss," he said with a shrug.

"It was."

"And you're sexy and sweet and smart and funny."

"Yes, I am," she said with a nod.

He had to admit, one thing he really liked about her was her confidence. He felt one corner of his mouth tip.

"You *really* should have wanted to do this before now," she said.

She pushed away from the door and he took an obligatory step back.

Watching her tighten the belt around her waist, he remembered the feel of her ass in his hand and her tongue against his. Yeah, he really should have wanted this before. Why hadn't he?

"I want it now. And you're in love with me. Seems like it's all going your way," he said.

She laughed and pushed him back far enough that she could open the door. "Um, no."

He looked at the open door, then back to her. "No?"

"I mean, sure, we could have some really hot sex," she said. "But if that's all I wanted, I could have seduced you a couple of years ago."

He opened his mouth to respond and then shut it, frowning hard.

She tipped her head, waiting for him to say something.

Finally, he brilliantly replied, "*What*?"

"Oliver, sex is easy. I could have kissed you some night when we were the only ones at the office after hours or one of the nights I dropped something off at your apartment that you'd forgotten. What just happened here could have happened a dozen times over the years."

"But?" he asked, feeling a rising sense of panic that he didn't understand.

"But I wanted more than that."

"You wanted me to be your boyfriend," he said flatly.

"Yes." She was clearly unmoved by his attitude.

"You couldn't have just said that?"

"Well, I've been trying to decide if you'd be good at it," she said.

"For how long?"

"About two years."

He blinked at her. "It's taken you two years?"

"Yes."

He stared at her. Piper was a very unique person in his life. She liked him. She admired him. She encouraged him and helped him do all of the amazing things he and the guys did with Fluke. But she was also... unimpressed. She didn't act like a single other woman he knew. At least not the ones who wanted to sleep with him. He knew women who wanted to date him because he was a good-looking—so he'd been told—millionaire. He knew women who wanted to date him because they were huge fans of *Warriors*. All of those women flattered him and fawned all over him and genuinely thought he was awesome.

Piper thought he was a pain in the ass.

She wanted him, evidently, and claimed to be in love with him. But it had taken her two years to decide if he'd be a good boyfriend.

And she was right to wonder about that.

Still, that rankled.

"So that's it?" he asked. "You're in love with me, but you're quitting your job, and you don't want to sleep with me?"

She nodded. "Yep. That's it."

"You're just going to... what? Work on getting over me, then?"

She shrugged. "Yep."

He scowled. "And you think you're going to be able to do that?"

"I really hope so."

Good. That was good. She needed to get over him.

He had no idea why that thought made his chest hurt.

"Will you come back to work for us if you can get over me?"

She looked at him, seemingly thinking. "Yeah. If I can get over you, I'll come back to work."

The pain in his chest intensified. He rubbed a hand over the spot. That was stupid. He *wanted* her to get over him. And to come back to work. For sure. The sooner the better.

He studied her, taking in the face, devoid of make-up, that was achingly familiar, yet seemed brand new tonight.

"Are you going back to Chicago?" he asked, his voice gruff.

She shook her head and he felt some of the tightness around his lungs ease.

"I have something I'm working on here."

"Like what?"

"Just something with Drew."

"Drew?" Ollie felt his eyebrows slam together. "Drew Ryan?"

Ryan owned a farm outside of Appleby with his brother, Dallas, and friend, Justin. They had alpacas, among other animals, that Piper seemed especially enamored with.

At least, Ollie had been telling himself it was the alpacas. Truth was, it was obvious Drew liked Piper.

Of course, everyone liked Piper.

Drew Ryan had probably thought about kissing her. Already. After only knowing her for a few months. Whereas Oliver had known her for five years and hadn't thought about it at all until tonight.

His gaze dropped to her mouth, and he rubbed the sore spot in his chest again.

Now he wasn't so sure he'd be able to *stop* thinking about it.

"Yes, Drew Ryan," Piper said.

"You think Drew Ryan will be a good boyfriend?"

She seemed to think about that for a moment. "Yes, he probably would be." She narrowed her eyes. "But not for me. See, I'm in love with someone else. He would be, at best, a rebound. At worst, a consolation boyfriend. That's not fair to him."

That actually made Ollie feel better which, he knew, made him kind of an ass. He'd rather she be alone? Really? A woman as amazing and passionate as Piper?

No. Probably not. Dammit. He didn't know. He'd never thought about any of this before an hour ago.

"Don't date Drew Ryan. Like anyone else but him."

"You need to go," she said, gesturing toward the still-open doorway.

"You're kicking me out?"

"Yep."

"But you're in love with me."

She let her head fall back and she groaned. "Yes. And I'm tired of talking to you right now."

"You're tired of talking to the man you're in love with?"

She gave him a look that said she was out of patience. He'd seen that look a number of times over the years. "Get out."

He stepped into the doorway, but paused. "You should have a boyfriend, Piper. If you want one."

"Yes, I know."

"You shouldn't write men off because of me."

Her brows went up. "I'm not."

He frowned. "But you said you didn't want Drew Ryan to be a rebound."

"Right. Drew's a friend. I don't want *Drew* to be my rebound."

"But you are going to find a rebound?" he asked, that chest pain back.

"Tired. Of. Talking. Good night, Ollie."

Then she closed the door in his face.

3

———————

The next morning, Ollie was the last one to enter the conference room.

On purpose, though, rather than because he'd forgotten the meeting and he no longer had an assistant to remind him.

He knew he had this meeting. He usually loved this meeting. He and his four best friends got together almost every single morning before going their separate ways to work, even though they were now not even all working in the same building.

He did not want to have this meeting this morning though.

He'd barely slept. He'd tossed and turned all night thinking about what Piper had said. And how she'd felt. How she'd tasted. How she'd sounded. How she'd smelled.

And now he was about to face his business partners, and best friends, without her. And without any caffeine or muffins.

Because Piper brought him coffee and muffins every morning.

And as pathetic as it was, he couldn't make coffee.

Well, he could. But his coffee sucked. Piper had the magic

recipe for exactly how he liked it. And he didn't know the right mix.

He took his seat next to Dax.

Thank God Dax was here. Dax wasn't an owner anymore, but he showed up for the meetings as a "consultant" and more as a guy who liked to start his day with his best friends.

And coffee and muffins.

"Oliver."

With a mental groan, Ollie looked across the table at Grant. "'Morning."

Grant lifted a brow. "What did you do?"

Busted.

"What do you mean?"

Dax snorted beside him.

Yeah, everyone knew that Ollie knew.

"Where's Piper?" Aiden asked. He was giving Ollie an I-know-you-screwed-up look.

"She's... not coming in this morning."

"You're in so much trouble," Dax muttered to him.

Yeah, yeah. And these guys weren't even his biggest problem.

"And why is she not coming in?" Aiden asked.

"Why do you assume I know?" Ollie asked.

"Because in the past when she's been sick, she's called me," Aiden told him.

"Maybe she just needed a day off."

Grant leaned in, his expression serious. "Did she?"

Well, yeah. But not just one day. He blew out a breath. "Fine. She quit."

Aiden and Grant both sighed.

"What did you do to her?" Grant asked again.

Kissed the hell out of her. Felt her bare ass cheek. "Piper loves me."

Aiden sighed and sat back in his chair. "Yeah, yeah. We all

love you, Ollie. But what did you do, or say, or not do, or whatever, that made her quit?"

Ollie shook his head. "That's what happened. I guess. She fell in love with me."

The other men all looked at one another. Cam leaned in. "Uh... she told you that?"

"Yeah."

"And"—Cam cast a look at the other guys—"what did you say?" He asked hesitantly, as if afraid of the answer.

"Hey, I tried to talk her out of it."

Dax gave a choked laugh. "How'd that go?"

"She kissed me."

The guys all froze.

Okay, that wasn't exactly the way it had gone, but those were definitely the highlights.

Grant, Aiden, Cam, and Dax all exchanged looks again. Ollie gave them a minute to let that all sink in.

"And"—Dax shifted on his chair and cleared his throat —"then what?"

"I asked whether she'd come back to work if she could get over me." He looked around the table. "She said yes, by the way."

Aiden rubbed the middle of his forehead. Grant seemed to be considering that. Dax snorted.

"And then?" Cam asked.

"Then she told me she was tired of talking to me and kicked me out of her room." He skipped the part about rebound boyfriends and Drew fucking Ryan.

Dax nodded thoughtfully. "And that leaves us..."

"Without Piper. For now."

Grant sighed heavily. "That's not acceptable."

"Well, I don't know what to tell you. She won't not be in love with me right now so... I've done what I can do."

Grant gave him a look that said *you're a dumbass.*

Aiden opened his mouth but then shut it.

"I..." But Cam clearly had nothing to add either.

"Dude," was all Dax said.

Ollie spread his arms out. "She has bad taste in men. What can I say? That's not my fault. I'm just sitting here, being me, and she fell in love with me anyway."

God, he was such a dick. But no one had ever been in love with him before. And he'd certainly never been in love with anyone. These four men were the closest he'd been and they were like brothers. They knew his limitations and they, thank God, also had each other, so the stuff he wasn't good at, someone else was. It worked in their personal relationships as well as their business partnership.

But, as Piper had said yesterday, all of that was in flux now. And yes, Ollie was feeling restless and kind of pissy about it.

All of the other men had interests outside of their business now. Fluke still existed but they didn't own *Warriors* anymore. Hot Cakes was fine, but that was definitely more Aiden's interest than anyone else's. Plus, he was all into helping Zoe with her bakery.

Dax had divested himself of his Hot Cakes shares and was running a nursing home now, of all things, and had become an instant family man, getting involved with Jane's dad and sister and stepsister. He'd even handled a bunch of stepmother drama. Grant had his side business in financial consulting and was all distracted by Josie and her new business. Cam was back together with Whitney and helping with her grandmother.

They all had other stuff going on, including being in love.

And Ollie was just here. The same as always. Which was more boring every day.

Now Piper wasn't here either. Everything was changing. It sucked.

He'd admit that coming into work this morning had felt off. Wrong. Bad. Not seeing her at her desk when he rounded the corner at the end of the hall, not hearing her morning greeting, not having her in the room now, picking up papers, delivering coffee and water. It wasn't the coffee and water that he wanted. It certainly wasn't the papers that he wanted. He wanted to see Piper.

Not seeing her behind her desk that morning had made him realize that he had always been eager to see what she was wearing, how she had her hair done, what bright colors she'd put together.

Then he'd immediately flashed to how she'd looked answering her door in her short robe with the towel on top of her head.

It had been like looking at someone new. Someone who maybe didn't have every single thing together in her life. Someone who could be caught off guard. Someone who didn't know every thought in his head before he had it. Someone he *could* touch.

Piper was too… much… for him usually. She was too good, too on top of things, too perfect. She didn't screw up, she didn't get things wrong, she didn't doubt herself.

She doubted *him* on a regular basis.

Why the *hell* was she in love with him?

He was scattered and forgetful and inconsiderate and messy.

"You need to fix this, Oliver," Aiden finally said. "We can talk to her. Try to offer her more money or beg her or whatever, but I don't think it will matter unless it's coming from you."

"Really?" Ollie asked, his annoyance with Piper falling for him spilling over. "Why would it matter if it comes from me? Either she falls out of love with me or I say 'yeah, sure, let's be in love and live happily ever after.' Those are the only ways to fix this."

"So say that," Dax said.

Ollie looked at his friend. "What?"

"Say that to her."

Dax was the most laid-back person Ollie had ever met. Ollie hadn't even realized how much he needed laid-back in his life until he'd met Dax. Dax had given him space, literally, in their dorm room to be messy and unorganized. He'd also given him figurative space to be unorganized and scattered. Oliver forgetting things and misplacing things had never bothered Dax. He rolled with things and living with him had felt like taking a huge, deep breath of refreshing, restoring air. *A breath of fresh air* had taken on true meaning for Oliver when he'd met Dax.

Dax Marshall had saved him. More than Dax would ever know.

So when Dax got serious, Oliver paid attention. Everyone did.

He looked serious right now.

"Ollie," Dax said, meeting his eyes directly. "If you're *not* in love with Piper, you're a complete moron. And I know that's not true. That woman is amazing. And she's good for you."

Ollie couldn't argue with any of that.

"It doesn't always work that way," Grant pointed out. "There's loving someone and there's being in love with someone. There has to be a spark. A chemistry."

Ollie looked across the table. Grant was studying him.

A spark. Chemistry.

He remembered every single thing about kissing Piper last night. Every touch, every inch of skin, every sigh and moan.

The spark wasn't a problem. But he'd felt it for the first time last night. Or he'd *let* himself feel it for the first time. Or something.

Still... not a problem.

"There's chemistry," he finally said simply.

"Then there you go," Dax said. "Go get her."

The conference room door opened and they all looked over hopefully.

Clearly everyone thought it was possible that Piper had changed her mind.

Except Ollie. He knew it wouldn't be Piper. And he rubbed his hand over the painful spot on the left side of his chest.

"Morning, everyone," Whitney greeted as she swept into the room. She stopped by Cam's chair and leaned over to kiss him, but then continued to her usual chair beside Aiden.

She took her chair, opened her folder, clicked her pen, and looked up.

She glanced around the table. "What's going on?"

"Piper quit," Cam said.

Whitney immediately focused on Ollie. "What did you do?"

He sighed.

"She's in love with him," Dax summarized. "Oh, and they kissed. But she threw him out before they had sex." Dax looked at Ollie again. "Wait, right? That's what you made it sound like."

Ollie nodded. He was feeling a really weird mix of miserable and horny.

Dax looked back at Whitney. "Yeah, she got tired of talking to him before there was sex. We were just telling him that he should go sweep her off her feet and marry her this afternoon."

Whitney had her phone pulled out and her thumbs were flying over the screen. Clearly, she was texting Piper. The women had become friends since the guys had taken over Hot Cakes. The two had a lot in common in their love for organization and hard work. Piper had confidence in spades where Whitney had needed to grow into hers a bit, but Ollie knew they'd been out on a few girls' nights.

He wondered if they'd talked about him. Then figured, if so, he wasn't so sure he wanted to know what had been said.

"I can't believe you kissed and she didn't tell me," Whitney said, almost to herself.

"Hey, Whit," Cam said.

She looked up at her boyfriend. "Yeah?"

"Maybe some advice? Like how Ollie can get her to come back?"

Whitney looked from Cam to Ollie. And frowned. "Oh."

"Just oh?" Ollie asked.

"Well..." She looked at Cam again and winced. "Not sure he can."

Ollie had been expecting that, but it stabbed to hear Whitney confirm it.

"There's *nothing*?" Aiden said. "An apology?"

"An apology for being him?" Whitney asked. She glanced at Ollie. "No offense."

"None taken," he said dryly.

"She's just..." Whitney sighed. "I don't know how much to say."

"Say it," Ollie said. "Whatever it is."

"She is in love with you," Whitney said, lifting her shoulder. "And she said she knew at some point there would be a time when she couldn't deal with being near you every day and not having more."

Ollie felt that painful area in his chest twinge.

"I'm not that great," he said.

No one at the table argued.

It wasn't that he thought they thought he was a bad person or a loser, but he wasn't exactly *charming* or anything. He wasn't particularly thoughtful or sweet. Lots of twelve-year-old boys thought he was pretty close to God because of *Warriors*, but even that he knew had a lot more to do with Dax and his online and conference personality than Oliver. Ollie's name was on the game as the creator, and that gave him a certain amount of notoriety. But, like all of the good things in his life, Dax had even given him that. Without Dax, all of the *Warriors* characters and stories would still just be scribblings in Oliver's notebooks.

"She said she'd come back if she gets over me. I guess we'll just wait for that to happen." Surely that wouldn't take long.

There had to be about a dozen better-than-him guys just waiting to ask her out.

As long as none of them were Drew fucking Ryan.

"Oookay," Whitney said slowly.

She didn't sound convinced. But she and Piper were new friends. It was possible that she didn't actually know how easy it would be for Piper to get over him.

"You're not going to go tell her you're in love with her, then?" Aiden asked.

He sounded resigned.

"Piper can do better than me," Ollie said.

Again, no arguments from around the table. They all looked worried, but no one jumped in to say, *you're the perfect man for Piper.*

Exactly. He would make Piper crazy. Not in a good way. Crazy like he had his mother.

"You need to go after her and either fall in love with her yourself or make her fall *out* of love with you," Grant decided.

"I'm not going after her for either of those things," Ollie said, feeling very grumpy. Dammit. This wasn't his fault. He'd just been minding his own business, being his usual fuck-up self, *not* kissing her, *not* noticing her breasts and eyes and legs—much—and she'd gone and fallen in love with him anyway. And *she'd* kissed *him*. This was not his fault. He hadn't done anything wrong.

Actually, he'd done everything wrong. All his usual things. He'd forgotten meetings and lost paperwork and blown off dinners and missed deadlines. As always.

Piper really did have bad taste in men.

"We'll just hire someone else to do all the Piper stuff around here," he said.

"Oh sure," Cam said. "We'll just hire someone to replace the woman who's been with us for five years, knows all of us better than our own parents, and knows and loves our business as much as we do."

"I only need someone who can get me coffee in the morning," Ollie said. Grumpily.

They all scowled at him. Yes, he was reducing one of their favorite people to a coffee-gopher. But they all knew he didn't really mean that.

Or did he?

Piper didn't help him with his *actual* work. The writing. The creating. That was all him. He did it alone. That was all his.

Sure, once it was done, Dax took it—well, now the other designers took it—and turned it into graphics and moving parts. Aiden and Grant and Cam dealt with the legal and business parts of everything that was necessary for his writing to turn into *Warriors of Easton*.

Piper booked him flights and hotel rooms and ordered him lunch and kept track of which documents needed his signatures and if there were calls and meetings he needed to be a part of.

But she didn't help him *write*, dammit. And that was the most important part.

Grant had initially hired Piper to babysit Ollie. Ollie was okay with that. He liked having people who would rein him in. He had no gauge for what was over the top and what was brilliant. Hell, most of the stuff he wrote into his scripts seemed over the top to him and ended up being called brilliant, so he really didn't know.

The guys were the guardrails for him. So was Piper. Piper looked things up like how much liability insurance would be if they brought in acrobats to ride unicycles across tight ropes at a town festival. Then she said they couldn't do it.

He was disappointed when people told him no, for sure, but

he was okay with it too. He knew they, collectively, were being creative but reasonable.

That's what he needed. Someone to keep him reasonable. And someone to make reservations and keep track of paperwork and run errands for him and yes, get him his coffee the way he liked it.

He pushed back from the table. "Let's get an ad out. Online. Newspaper. Tack it up at the bakery," he said to Aiden. "Whatever. However this works."

That was the kind of thing Piper would have done for them.

Grant gave him an annoyed but longsuffering look. "You going to be able to handle it if Piper comes in to train the new person?"

Ollie shrugged. "Sure. Why wouldn't I?"

She was the one in love with *him* to the point that she couldn't work near him anymore. Who got that worked up over *him*? Maybe she was a few bananas short of a bunch already.

And hey, Piper training the person would require zero input from him. She'd be able to tell the new person that if they *really* wanted Ollie's attention on something, they needed to print the paperwork in eighteen-point font and put it in a bright-red folder. She'd definitely be able to inform them he hated onions. On anything. She'd certainly mention that he couldn't work with music or conversation around him, but he also couldn't work *without* his white-noise machine on. Or Norah Jones music on. He didn't know why Norah worked for him, but she did. Something Piper had discovered.

But that could all be passed on to someone new. He turned on his heel and stalked toward the door.

"You'll have to tell her or him how you like your special coffee, Princess," Grant said dryly.

"Piper knows," he said, pulling the door open. "I've got work to do." As if he had a prayer of getting anything done with Piper on his mind and his severe lack of caffeine. He slammed the door behind him.

———

"Um, so I probably need to get back to work," Drew said suddenly, cutting off what he'd been saying.

Piper frowned as he focused on something over her shoulder. "What? Are you okay?"

"Yeah. I'm just about to become a third wheel," he said with a grin, lifting his coffee cup to drain it.

Piper looked over her shoulder. And felt her heart flip.

Ollie had just entered Buttered Up bakery and stood looking around. His gaze landed on her and their eyes met. He started in her direction immediately.

God, he looked good.

She wasn't the only one who noticed either. Several women in the bakery stopped and checked him out. He didn't seem to notice. He had homed in on Piper. She swallowed hard as her heart rate kicked up.

He was in a suit. No tie, of course—it was probably in his pocket. It was a dark navy blue. The button-down shirt under it was crisp white and unbuttoned at the collar. He looked hot and in charge and... on a mission.

Oh boy... She pivoted back to face Drew at their tiny round table.

"You don't have to leave," she said quickly.

For some reason, she kind of wanted someone with her when she talked to Ollie for the first time in over a week.

She'd never felt that way before. From the first day she'd met him, she'd been perfectly comfortable with Ollie, in every situation, whether they were alone or not. Sure, she felt butterflies when he smiled at her in a certain way—when he was fully focused on her and amused or pleased with something she'd just said. Sometimes she felt warmer when watching him squeeze one of his many stress balls with his big, wide hands, or when he licked his lips while eating or drinking, or when he linked his hands behind his neck and his shirt stretched over his abs and chest.

But she'd *never* felt anxious about being alone with him.

Now she did.

Of course she'd never gone over a week without seeing him at all. And she'd certainly never had a hot, deep, sexy kiss and his hand on her bare butt as the last memory of him.

Now it had been nine days since she'd kicked Ollie out of her hotel room and she'd been thinking about all of that every single day—well, mostly every single night—since then. She could still *feel* his hand on her ass if she let herself think about it.

She really tried not to do that.

"Oh, I think I do have to leave," Drew said. "He's never liked me much and he looks particularly... intent, right now."

Dammit.

"Stay."

"Nope." Drew pushed to his feet. "Hey, Oliver," he greeted as he pulled his ball cap back on.

"Hey." Ollie didn't sound friendly.

Ollie never sounded friendly to Drew. It made Piper roll her eyes every time. He acted jealous. Yet he acted shocked to think that she had feelings for him and *clearly* the idea of wanting *her* for something other than her fixing his stupid coffee perfectly —in a way he hadn't even known about until she'd done it the first time—had never occurred to him.

He'd wanted you during that kiss...

Yeah, okay, so he'd discovered he *wanted* her. But he didn't *want* want her...

She took a deep breath and focused on Drew. "Thanks for breakfast."

"Of course." He gave her a grin. "Talk to you later."

"Oh, you're leaving?" Ollie asked, pulling Drew's chair out and sitting down in it before Drew even answered.

"Yeah. Got some stuff to do."

"See ya," Ollie told him.

Drew laughed and headed out.

"He leave because of me?" Ollie asked.

"Yeah."

"He thought I was going to beat him up or something?" His tone was bored.

"I think he thinks you're weird," Piper said, sipping her coffee.

"I am weird," Ollie said with a nod.

"I know."

She'd missed him. And his weirdness. Drew was great. Nice. Polite. Reasonable. And not a bit weird. Weird drove her crazy but it was also interesting and fun. She'd always known that but this past week without it had been a bit boring.

That had not been a pleasant realization. The first couple of days had been great. Relaxing. No fires to put out. No strange research to do.

Then by day three she really wanted some weirdness. Some Ollie weirdness.

"Well, I don't care what Drew Ryan thinks of me," Ollie said, slouching in his chair and throwing an arm over the back. He was frowning.

Or, more accurately, he was pouting.

He looked ridiculous. He was huge in the tiny white chair with the wrought-iron back that swirled into a heart shape. And the pout on his face.

"I'll break it to him gently that you don't care about his opinion," she said.

"Don't talk about me with Drew Ryan at all," Ollie said, his frown deepening. "Better yet, don't talk to Drew Ryan about *anything* at all."

She thought it was funny that he always referred to Drew as *Drew Ryan*. She didn't bother to even comment on his ridiculous demand. She sipped her coffee again.

"Hi, did you want something, Ollie?" Josie asked, approaching the table in her Buttered Up apron.

Piper had to smile. She'd become closer to Whitney and Paige than to Josie, but she liked Grant's wife a lot. Especially since Josie could come over and ask him what he was doing here under the guise of waiting on him.

"I haven't had a muffin or good coffee in a week," he said, mostly to Piper.

Sulkily.

"So I'd love three muffins and a large coffee."

"Great." Josie scribbled that on her pad. "What kind of muffins?"

"Uh..." Ollie looked at Piper.

She just looked back at him.

"Which ones do I like best?" he finally asked.

"Seriously?" She sighed. "How are you not dead after a week of no one feeding you?"

"I've eaten," he said. "Just not any muffins. Or Parmesan chicken bake."

So sulky.

She cooked for him a couple of times a week. Each of their suites had a full kitchen but Oliver couldn't boil water, so when she cooked for herself, versus take-out or making do with salad or sandwiches, she took him half. His favorite was her meatballs, but he did love the chicken-and-pasta bake with the spinach and loads of Parmesan cheese.

"You don't know what kind of muffins you like without me telling you?" she asked.

"I know what I like. I just don't remember my *favorites*.

They're all good here." He gave Josie a smile, then frowned at Piper again. "I've been without *any* for a week so thought I should have my favorites now."

"You could have come down here and gotten your own. All week long."

"Was hoping my new assistant would do that. But so far, no go."

"You could *ask her* to do it," Piper suggested. She was going to help train this new girl, but they'd only hired her a week ago and Whitney was getting her settled. Whit said she would be great. Young, perky, organized, eager to do a great job.

Piper supposed she should start making a list of all the dumb extra things the girl would have to do for Ollie. Muffins and coffee at the top of that list.

"Grant said I have to give her a few days to acclimate before I start asking her for things."

Piper snorted. Grant had a point. The girl would be overwhelmed if Ollie went to her with his list of "needs."

But as Piper watched him sulking across the table from her, it occurred to her that he was far too old, successful, and intelligent to not freaking know what kind of muffins to order when he walked into a bakery.

And it was her fault that he didn't realize that.

"Cranberry orange, blueberry crumble, and caramel apple," she said to Josie.

"Got it." Josie turned away to get the muffins.

Piper pointed to the coffee station behind him. "You take a cup, fill it up, and put whatever you want in it."

He glanced over his shoulder, then back to her.

She leaned in, resting on her forearms. "Medium blend, three vanilla creamers, and one caramel."

He looked at her for three beats, then sighed, and got up to get his own coffee.

For the first time in five years.

She'd done that to him, Piper realized as she watched him get his coffee. She'd coddled him from day one. He was the genius of the group. He and Dax were both treated as if they had some kind of superpowers and needed special handling.

Dax milked that for all it was worth. He had gummy bears and bean bag chairs in his office, a Ping-Pong table in the break room, and just generally got away with goofing around almost constantly, chalking everything up to helping his "creative process."

She thought there was some truth to that probably, but over the five years she'd spent with these men, she'd observed them when they weren't putting on a façade too. Moments of frustration and moments when they were unsure. Arguments, flat-out panic a couple of times when things looked bad, and moments of pure joy and pride when things were really good.

The guys let Ollie get away with all kinds of crazy crap. They didn't always let him put his full plans into place because Ollie tended to think outside of the box, *and* the circle, *and* the triangle, *and* the octagon. He had wild and crazy notions and relied on the guys and Piper to keep him on track.

Maybe they did realize he was the softer of the personalities. But she wasn't sure their coddling was good. The guys didn't care if he blew off birthdays and meetings. They let him keep whatever schedule he wanted. They didn't get upset if one morning he called in to tell them that he was in New York and would be back on Thursday. If he said he'd just suddenly had the urge to be on top of the Empire State Building, they'd all just nod and say, "that's Ollie."

He got away with so much. Because of all of them. Because of her.

He returned to the table and took his chair, this time leaning forward onto the table, his coffee cradled between his hands.

"You look nice," he told her.

She looked down. She was wearing one of her usual office outfits. This was how she typically dressed. This dress was red with white polka dots. It had a halter top that tied behind her neck and a flared skirt that hit her knees. She had white wedge heels on and a big white bow sitting askew on her head.

"Thanks."

"I like those dresses. The ones you wear to work."

She smiled. So he had noticed. "Thank you." Then again, she'd never had his attention in those dresses the way she had the other night. She leaned in. "Better than the robe?"

His eyes met hers. There was definitely a flicker of heat there. "Yeah, better than the robe."

She lifted a brow. "I don't believe you."

"I like the dresses on you. I wanted the robe *off* of you."

4

Piper froze with her cup halfway to her mouth. She stared at him. She set her cup down. "Oliver, that was very..."

He just waited for her to fill the blank in.

"Sexy."

He looked mildly amused. "You sound surprised."

"I think I am."

"I can be sexy."

He could? Really? She found him sexy, but it had always seemed unintentional. She was attracted to things that she wasn't sure he was even aware he did. Like how he egged Dax on. How he said things just to get Grant to roll his eyes. The times he asked Aiden for advice just so Aiden could feel that he was leading the way. The "troubles" he'd had that he needed Cam to intervene in.

And his big plans and ideas—even when he was asking her to find out how much it would cost to rent or buy an actual circus tent—and the way he laughed and the way he appeared with Dax for their fans even though he didn't enjoy the spotlight.

And a million other things.

Josie returned with Ollie's muffins, setting the bag on the table. "I look forward to seeing more of you, Ollie," she said with a grin.

He sighed. "Until I can get this new assistant trained."

"Or you could keep coming in after that," Josie said. "We give special secret treats to our friends. But they have to come in in person."

Ollie gave her a little grin. "Like the special cupcakes you make for Grant?"

Josie blushed and Piper laughed. Everyone knew about the X-rated cupcakes Josie had made for Grant months ago. She'd even turned it into an off-menu specialty item in her side baking business. But she blushed every time someone mentioned them.

"Yeah, something like that," she said.

"That's all you had to say, Josie," Ollie said with a smirk.

"Okay. So... great." She smiled, then hustled away from the table.

"Yeah," Piper said.

He looked over at her.

"I know you can be sexy," she told him. He was very sexy when he didn't mean to be. Like when he said things he knew would make Josie blush. He didn't mean that to be sexy. Josie was very much one of his best friends' girl. But Ollie teased her because she was a friend and yes, Piper found that sexy.

"Yeah?" he asked.

"Yeah. I just haven't ever experienced you doing it with *me*. Directly anyway. Like the robe comment."

The corner of his mouth curled up. "Have I done it indirectly?"

"Every day," she said honestly.

They sat just looking at one another for several seconds.

"I miss you," he finally said.

That surprised her even more than the compliment on her dress and the comment about her robe.

She nodded. "I'm very hard to get over."

"And I'm mad at you."

"You're caffeine deprived."

"For that." He nodded. "And because I haven't written a fucking word in a week."

"That's my fault?"

"Entirely."

"That's ridiculous. You wrote for four years before you even met me."

"And it took me twice as long then and it was easier to write this stuff before there was such a big world with so many plots and characters." He scowled at her. "I can't find my character files."

She sighed. He could *never* find his character files and he never would. Even when they were in the folder in the center of his computer's desktop and labeled CHARACTER FILES.

"It took you twice as long as it does now?" she asked, shaking her head in disbelief. Ollie was not a fast writer.

"Yes. No one made me sit at my desk and I had no reward for getting shit done."

She fought a smile. She had implemented the writing sprints and reward system after reading about other writers doing it on Twitter. He had to write without doing anything else or getting up for twenty to thirty minutes. Then he got a five to ten minute break. And each time he got to his daily work goal, he got a reward. It was often food. He loved her cooking. But sometimes it was a game of Ping-Pong with Dax—if he hadn't managed to convince her he needed one during his breaks for his "creative process"—or a gab session with Cam. Again, if he hadn't taken a detour for one of those during his ten-minute breaks that often turned into forty-five minutes if she wasn't on top of him. And yes, she called them gab sessions.

The two men were gossipy as hell and could go on and on about the stupidest things.

"The office is distracting too," he said. "The new girl doesn't respect my need for Norah."

"So turn Norah on for yourself," Piper said.

Ollie couldn't work with any noise, except Norah Jones. Piper found Norah relaxing, herself, and one night when they'd been working late and she'd had Norah playing, Ollie had claimed to get more done than he had all week. They'd experimented and found Norah was magic for his concentration.

"I did." He looked grumpy. "It didn't work."

"Maybe you need her greatest hits album."

"I need you."

He said it flatly. It didn't sound sweet or like a compliment, for sure, but Piper's breath still caught. "Ollie—"

He suddenly shifted to sit forward. "I need to work with *you* around. So you need to get over me. But for now, here I am."

"Here you are?" she repeated.

"Yes. To work." He reached into his inner jacket pocket and pulled out a little notebook and a pen.

"What do you mean?" She watched him open the notebook and uncap the pen.

"I'm going to have to come to wherever you are to get any work done, I guess," he said. "Until you're over me." He narrowed his eyes. "How's that going? Are you there yet?"

She had to fight another smile. When she'd agreed that she would go back to work for Fluke if she got over Ollie, she hadn't been lying. If she wasn't in love with him, it would be easy to work there. She missed it already. But she wasn't expecting to get over him. Ever.

"Nope. Sorry. Still love you."

He sighed, very put-upon by the news.

"That's annoying, Piper."

It certainly was.

"And what if I don't want you to just follow me around?" she asked. "What if that will make it *harder* to get over you?"

He frowned. "I guess I can go sit at another table and hope that being near you is enough."

She shook her head. "You don't actually think just being in the same general vicinity as me is what helps you write." That was stupid. He was just pissed that he wasn't getting his way and shaken that she'd finally walked out and dumped his world upside down when all of them worked so hard to keep his world so steady and easy.

"Look, I've been sitting at the same desk, listening to Norah, trying to write the same scene for the past week and can't. The only change is you. And the coffee."

"You're being a baby."

He shrugged, unconcerned. "There are millions of people expecting this new installment in two months. Designers and marketing people who need this to put food on their tables. I don't care what it says about me that I need to be near you to produce. I just can't gamble on it or try new things right now."

Or ever. But she didn't say that out loud. Ollie wasn't good with change and "new," it was true. And yes, it sounded dramatic, but he wasn't wrong about the people depending on him. His world—his words—made a lot of people happy and kept a lot of people employed. And it was impossible to ignore that she missed him and liked the idea that he wanted to be near her to work. Begrudgingly maybe, but still.

He wanted her to get over him? Well, she wanted him to fall for her.

Seemed that being together was the best way for one of those things to happen.

But that didn't mean she was going to let Ollie totally get his way.

She was sure that was going shock him.

"Fine." She pushed back from the table and stood. "Come on then."

"Wait." He frowned. "Where are you going?"

"Well, you didn't think I was going to be sitting at the bakery all day, did you?"

"I..." He sighed. "I have no idea what you're doing if you're not with me," he groused.

"Of course not," she said with an eye roll. "But you're about to find out." She lifted her bag from the floor by her chair and slung it over her shoulder. "Just give me a second to change and we'll go."

"Change?"

"My clothes."

He straightened. "You're going to change clothes?"

"Yes."

"Why?"

She tipped her head, narrowing her eyes. Why did he care? "Because this dress and these shoes aren't appropriate for what I'm going to be doing."

"What are you going to change into?"

She frowned. "Jeans and a t-shirt. If that's okay with you?"

He frowned too, but he was studying her dress. "I'm not sure." He seemed to be saying it to himself rather than to her.

"You're not sure if it's okay if I change my clothes?" she asked.

He sighed. "Do I have a choice?"

"Not even a little."

"Then I guess it doesn't matter."

She started to respond, then shook her head. This was a ridiculous argument. "I'll be right back." She started for the back of the bakery where Zoe and Josie said she could use their private powder room to change. She turned after two steps though. "You only like me in these dresses?" she asked.

He sighed and didn't look at her. "I didn't say that."

"You've never seen me in jeans before."

"I'm aware."

She and Ollie spent a lot of time together but, again, they were both workaholics. Even their after-hours time was generally spent at the office, so, in office clothes. When she did take food to him or dropped things off at his hotel room or apartment, it was always when she was still dressed for work.

She wasn't sure why that was.

Okay, she *did* know. She loved how she looked in her dresses and heels and she'd wanted to look good for him whenever she saw him.

As ridiculous as that was when it came to "impressing" a guy who was not detail oriented. Which was a nice way of saying that she often had to tell him the date on the calendar and the mailing address of the hotel—his *home* for all intents and purposes for the past ten months—at least once a week.

He wasn't stupid. Far from it. But he was a dreamer.

Which was a nice way of saying that he could be a flake.

"So why do you *not* want me to put jeans on now?" she asked. This was such a dumb conversation.

He finally looked at her. "Just do it," he said. "Let's see what happens."

Oookay. Well, she'd never argued that he wasn't weird.

She changed into the faded, worn jeans and the tee she'd tucked into her bag. She slipped on simple tennis shoes and pulled her hair up into a high ponytail.

But she couldn't resist adding a scarf around the base of the ponytail.

It was bright blue and matched the sparkly words on the front of her t-shirt that said *Feminism is my second favorite f-word.*

Yes, the shirt had sequins. She wasn't exactly an *outdoorsy* girl. She just knew that her heels didn't combine with the dirt out on Drew's farm very well. Because she'd worn her heels out to the farm before and that had been a big mistake. Partly because it was hard to walk over dirt in heels. Partly because there was more than *dirt* out there on Drew's farm.

She added some lip gloss, spritzed her perfume on her neck, and then left the bathroom.

Ollie was halfway through his second muffin by the time she got back to the table.

Piper couldn't help but smile. She was sure he had missed them. But damn, what a baby.

"Okay, you ready?"

He looked up.

And immediately started choking.

She watched him as he coughed. He reached for his coffee and took a drink. He seemed fine for a moment. Then he took a breath and started coughing again.

He didn't need the Heimlich. Thankfully. She could have done it, but he was a big guy and it would have been difficult. But he got to his feet, bending at the waist to cough hard.

"Good lord!" Josie exclaimed, appearing next to Ollie. She handed him a glass of water. "Are you okay?"

He shook his head but took the glass, downing it in three gulps.

The entire bakery was looking at them now.

He lowered the glass slowly, took another breath, coughed once. Then swallowed.

"Are you all right?" Josie asked again.

"Yeah." He nodded. "I guess."

"Okay." She took the glass from him.

"What was tha—" Piper's question was cut off as Ollie took her arm and steered her toward the door.

He marched her to the door and swung a right when they hit the sidewalk. He directed her into the alley that ran between the bakery and the antique store next door. It was wider than a usual alley. There were twinkle lights strung between the buildings overhead and benches and planters full of flowers along the cobblestone-paved pathway that ran from Main Street to Railroad Avenue.

"Oliver, wha—"

He stopped and backed her up against the side of the bakery.

"I really like the dresses you usually wear," he said. His voice was gruff.

Totally confused, she nodded. "You've mentioned that."

"I think I should only spend time with you when you're wearing those."

Annoyance slammed into her. "Is that right?"

"That would really be better."

"Well, I suppose if I really cared what you thought about how I dress, I'd take that into consideration."

What an ass. She pushed him back. And spread her hands down her t-shirt. It molded to her breasts and the V-neck highlighted her cleavage. Much as her dresses did.

She wasn't thin. She didn't have a tight ass. She liked *every-thing* they made at Buttered Up. But she liked how she looked in this tee and jeans and in all of her dresses and Oliver Caprinelli could fuck right off if he didn't. Plenty of men liked curves, and just because she'd been stupid enough to fall for her flaky, self-absorbed boss didn't mean she couldn't get over him. Probably. Maybe.

"You don't care what I think about your dresses? And jeans?" he asked.

He actually seemed confused.

He was *a lot* of work. But, as she had for the past five years, Piper couldn't let the moment pass without trying to help him understand. She knew she and the guys were his gauge for what was normal. Kind of, anyway. And she knew that part of her job, even if no one had given it conscious thought, was to help keep Oliver on this side of weird as much as possible.

"I didn't even know I was going to see you today," she said, working to keep her tone conversational rather than exasperated. "How does what I'm wearing today have anything to do with you?"

His gaze dropped and traveled up and down her body. She felt her heart rate pick up and told herself to calm down. Oliver was studying her because she'd just asked him a question. He wasn't trying to be flirtatious or sexy.

"Okay, maybe not today specifically," he said, bringing his eyes back to hers. He looked confused. "But you said you're in love with me. Doesn't that mean you want me to like how you look?"

That being in love with him confession had really been a mistake, she realized. He was obsessed with it. Which was amusing on one level. Maybe Ollie had never had a woman tell him that before. Or maybe he was just that shocked that she felt that way. But on another level, it was annoying. It had made him uncomfortable. He certainly hadn't said that he felt the same way. Yet he had to keep bringing it up.

"I guess I would like to think that you like how I look in whatever I wear and that you would like me because of a lot of things other than how I dress."

"But attraction is about physical appearance," he said. "And how you dress is part of that."

She put her hand on her hip. "Attraction is about a lot more than that."

He frowned. "So, your attraction to me is not about how *I* look?"

Piper sighed. Patience. This man took more patience than anyone she'd ever met. "It's not *just* about how you look."

"What's it about?"

What was going on? He needed reassurance? From her? Why? "You want to know why I'm in love with you?" Might as well put that right out there.

"I would like that. Yes."

"Why?"

"Because I really don't know."

Piper felt her heart squeeze at that. Wow. He was hardly lacking in confidence. Sure, they sometimes had to pull him back on his big, crazy, circus-tent-level ideas, but he knew his value to the company and his friends. He knew he was brilliant. Sometimes *that* was the problem, honestly.

"Your creativity."

"Everyone thinks I'm creative."

"Well, you are."

"So is Dax."

"Yes."

"Are you in love with Dax?"

"No."

"Then that can't be it."

She couldn't help but smile. "You're going to argue with me about what I love about you?"

"It just needs to make sense," he said.

"It does?"

"It's a huge complication, Piper," he told her without a touch of amusement. "It at least needs to make sense if it's going to mix everything up."

Ah. Well, she wasn't so sure that love *made sense* all the time. But she knew this man. He'd created an entirely fictional fantasy world and then pulled millions of people into it with him. Things in *Warriors* were fantastical, but they made sense according the laws of the world. The world, and laws, he'd created. Of course, he could also add to those laws any time. Didn't want gravity for a particular plot point? Then suddenly a certain part of the planet didn't have gravity. If someone questioned him in a meeting about it, he was ready with explanations that sometimes went way back to the very first version of the game. Or sometimes he'd just say, "we never said the *entire* planet had gravity." It really depended on his mood.

She often got the impression that Ollie's biggest frustration in life was that the real world had rules that he didn't agree with and couldn't change.

He was not going to appreciate her telling him that love didn't always make sense or saying things like *the heart wants what the heart wants.*

"Okay, you're right, it's probably not your creativity," she said. She'd long ago learned to pick her battles with Ollie.

"Then what is it?"

"Your dedication to the company and the guys."

"They make me very rich."

She lifted a brow. He was not dedicated to his friends and their company because of the money. Why was he so damned grumpy today?

"You don't care about the money," she said.

"I don't? The private plane I happily use, the penthouse suite I currently occupy, the custom-tailored suits I wear would all seem contrary to that statement."

Yeah, he was going to argue with everything she said. Oliver didn't care about the money.

The private plane was, actually, more practical at times. And the guys didn't use it every time they traveled. And they shared it with another company anyway.

The penthouse made sense, considering he'd been living there for ten months now. It was more like an apartment than a hotel room, really, and in the beginning anyway, he hadn't known how long he was staying in Iowa. Now it seemed he was considering staying for good since the guys all were. But he hadn't made the decision to look for an actual apartment yet.

The custom-tailored suits... well, okay, he really did like those. He could have easily gotten by wearing jeans and his geeky t-shirts, like the one that said *I'm sorry for what I said while I was gaming.* Or his favorite *I paused my game to be here.* They had an entire line of *Warriors* apparel as well. He so rarely met with anyone but fans that he really had no need for the suits. But he liked them.

And he looked damn good in them.

"I love that you would do anything for any of your friends," she said. "You make up problems for them to solve because you know they need that. I love the way you fully embraced Whitney becoming a part of the company and finding herself. I love the way you encouraged all of your friends in their relationships with their girls even though it was going to take them away from you."

He didn't have an immediate argument for those. He just stood looking at her.

She looked back.

"I'm not a total ass," he finally said.

"I know."

"So you love me because I'm not a total dick," he said. "That's kind of a low bar."

She sighed. He was such a pain in the ass. "Okay, brace yourself, Oliver."

He actually straightened slightly. He frowned. "For what?"

"For the *truth*. I can't totally explain *why* I love you, but I can tell you how I know that I do."

Suddenly he looked worried. "Never mind. You don't have to do that."

"Oh yes, I do."

"No, really—"

"I love how I feel when I hear your voice first thing in the morning—the way it makes my heart lift."

He seemed to be frozen, except for his throat when he swallowed hard.

"I love how I feel when I hear you laugh—the way it makes my stomach flip," she said. "I love how I feel when you actually focus on me, *really* focus, and listen to me—the way my chest feels warmer."

She didn't get his full focus often, but when she did, it was powerful. And she had noticed that it was easier for her to get his attention than it was for anyone else. That also made her stomach flip.

Right now, she had that full focus. He was staring at her. His jaw looked tight and he was clenching his hands at his sides, but he wasn't moving or speaking.

"I love how I feel when you talk about *Warriors*—the way your voice gets more excited, the way your eyes light up—it makes me feel like I just swallowed a drink of hot chocolate. I love listening to you and Whitney brainstorm. It makes me just want to giggle... and try to make it all happen. Even the acrobats. And you know very well that I usually would *not* want to make acrobats happen."

She took a breath. She probably shouldn't admit the rest of this but, she was on a roll now.

"About two years ago, I started to realize that I was trying harder to make your crazy ideas happen. I now have to *make* myself pull *you* back. Because I really just want to make you happy."

He pulled in a long breath.

"And," she added before he could say anything, "since we've come to Appleby, I've watched you watching your friends falling in love and I see how happy it makes you. I know you wish things could stay the same, but you want them happy even more. Seeing you so happy for your friends shows me how much you truly love them and that makes me love you more."

She swallowed. "And yeah," she said. "I do love how you look. I love your hands and your eyes and your hair and your smile and your body. I want to get naked with you and have hot, dirty sex with you all night long every night." She took a breath. "And yeah, I do care how you think I look in my dresses *and* in my jeans. And that's how I *definitely* know how I feel about you. Because I never really care what people think of me. But I care what *you* think. The guy who can't even remember if he ate lunch some days."

She blew out a breath and straightened, waiting for him to say or do something.

Finally, he said, "I have a hard time attaching to people and forming relationships."

She felt her lips curl. Then she laughed.

He scowled. "I'm serious."

"How long have you been telling yourself that?"

"What do you mean?"

"Oliver, you are incredibly attached to Dax, Aiden, Grant, and Cam. And, maybe you haven't noticed, but you're attached to me too. And you're getting attached to Whitney. I think Jane and Josie and Zoe are getting pretty close too."

"Well..."

She smiled as he trailed off. "Well... you're full of crap."

"Dax..." Ollie tucked his hands into his pockets. "Dax made me attach to him."

She laughed again. She understood what he meant. Dax was very difficult to not like. "He forced you to be his friend?"

"He made it impossible to ignore him and then... impossible to not like him." There was a smile teasing Ollie's mouth.

Yeah, that smile, especially the reluctant ones, made her stomach flip.

"And the other guys?"

"Dax brought them in and before I knew it, I had this group of friends." Ollie shrugged. "I didn't do much. Mostly tried to stay out of their way."

She knew the story of how *Warriors* had come to be. Oliver and Dax had been assigned to be roommates at the University of Chicago. They were a year younger than Cam and Aiden. One night Aiden and Cam had been passing by Ollie and Dax's room. There had been a bunch of guys gathered in their room and Aiden had stopped to see what was going on. They'd been watching Ollie and Dax play a new video game. As soon as they'd realized that Ollie and Dax had *created* the game, they'd shooed everyone else out of the room and had kept the game under wraps until they could develop it further and trademark it and get all of their ducks in a row. Which was where Grant, a guy Aiden had met in one of his business classes, had come in.

Grant had understood the business side. Aiden had been more of the marketing and networking guy. Cam had researched trademarks and incorporating and contracts and had handled the paperwork long before he'd headed to law school. In fact, Piper had learned from Whitney that Cam had gone to law school *because* of the guys and *Warriors*. It was kind of the puzzle piece that had been left and he'd wanted to be a part of it, so that had determined his direction.

Dax and Ollie, in the meantime, had kept working on the game. Ollie wrote the story lines and developed the characters, and Dax brought them to life on the screen, taking Ollie's words and making them first into pictures and then into moving graphics.

But Piper didn't believe that Ollie didn't "do much" and had just stayed out of the way. The five men she'd worked for over the past five years loved each other. They were like brothers. Oliver included.

"Ollie, they need you," she said.

He scoffed.

"They do. Dax needs someone beside him when he jumps out of airplanes and wades in the fountains in Rome."

"He could have found a hundred guys to do that with him."

She shook her head. "Come on, Ollie. You guys, together, have created a place where you can all be who you are. You make sure Grant has some fun and doesn't take everything so seriously.

You validate Aiden and give him a place to really shine. You give Cam people and something to protect, which is one of his best strengths. And you keep Dax safe even while he's being... Dax."

"How do you know Dax isn't keeping me safe?"

She smiled. "You keep each other safe."

He just sighed.

"Fluke is where you all belong, where you all *fit*, and it wouldn't be what it is without any one of you."

"But they've all found other things," he said.

Right. The thing he'd created, that had brought them all together, that had been their initial bond, that had kept them together for nine years, was still there. But they were all moving on. Not entirely, but they weren't all living and breathing Fluke anymore.

She knew that bothered Ollie. And she understood it. It had bothered her a little too. She'd been afraid that Fluke was breaking up. And it was true that it had changed. But what she'd learned over the past few months since the guys had fallen in love and found other places and people to put some of their passion—they kept coming back together.

They met every morning. For sure. Sometimes more often. They saw each other socially too. But those morning meetings mattered the most. They didn't have to have those. Dax wasn't a part of Hot Cakes, officially anyway, and Cam often joined via Zoom because he was at the house with Didi, Whitney's grandmother. But they still all found themselves gathering together, even if it was for only fifteen minutes, every morning whether it was necessary or not.

Because they needed each other. They needed to touch base, to start their day from their foundation. No matter what else changed in their lives, where they'd started, together, still drew them.

"You need something else too," she told Ollie. "You feel like this because you're the one that hasn't added anything new. You need somewhere else to put some energy too."

"Like dating you?" he asked, his eyes narrowing.

She rolled her eyes. "I will not be tricking you or talking you into anything, Oliver. I've put it all out there. What you do with the knowledge of how I feel is up to you. But you could do a lot worse than putting some energy and time into *me*," she said.

He sighed. "Yeah. Probably."

A little more enthusiasm from him than that would be nice, but he was adjusting and she knew that took time.

"I do think you could use a change of pace, though," she told him.

"Like what?"

"You want to work wherever I am? That's fine. I can get you set up."

He looked suspicious.

He should. He was starting to figure out that Piper-lets-me-get-away-with-almost-anything time was over.

This was going to be very different from what he was used to. But it might be good for him. And at least she'd have him around. For a day or so before he bailed.

"Let's go." She started toward the front of the bakery and her vehicle.

"Where are we going?" he called after her as she kept going.

"You'll see."

She was probably enjoying his worry far too much, but she was definitely grinning when he finally joined her in her small, fully-loaded SUV, with the custom neon-blue paint job.

Hey, her bosses at Fluke Inc. had paid her very well.

And as she turned north on the highway and Oliver realized where they were headed and groaned, she rolled her eyes and reminded herself that she'd earned every penny.

5

———————

She was taking him to Drew Ryan's farm. For fuck's sake.

And she was wearing jeans and a t-shirt. A t-shirt with sparkles on the front that drew his eyes directly to her breasts and the V-neck that showed the smooth, creamy upper curves of her breasts.

He had no idea what the t-shirt said. He was aware that the sparkles were in the form of letters, but he hadn't read them. Why would he look at the words when those glorious breasts were right there?

He'd managed to make it past those curves to the ones of her hips and ass in those jeans though.

Blue jeans. Denim. Faded, worn, molded to her body, denim blue jeans.

If someone had asked him if Piper Barry even owned a pair of jeans, in any color, he would have said no. But damn, she not only owned them, she wore the hell out of them.

Why was she wearing jeans and a t-shirt?

Why did her wearing jeans and a t-shirt make him so crazy?

He could have chalked it up to him being muffin-less for the past week. Or just missing her for the past week. Or being generally grumpy about everything for the past week because he'd been sleeping like shit and unable to get a damned thing done on his script.

But none of that explained why she'd made him crazy in her robe the other night.

He knew what it was. But he didn't want to admit it.

As she turned in at the sign that declared them to be at the Ryan Alpaca Farm, Ollie let out a little growl.

She glanced over. "You okay?"

"I've just had my fill of Drew Ryan for the month."

"You saw him for about three minutes."

"Yep."

She laughed. And kept driving.

No one took his dislike for Drew Ryan seriously. But it was serious. It was stupid. But it was serious.

Drew was a nice guy. He'd never done a thing to make Oliver think otherwise.

Even the day he'd started really hating the guy, Drew had been nice.

That was a lot of why Ollie hated him. He was nice. Normal. Very capable of having normal relationships and remembering things like birthdays. And that it was Wednesday. And March.

Ollie and Piper had been out at the farm looking at animals that Drew said would be great for a petting zoo at the big cake-tasting event Hot Cakes was putting on. Everyone had told him that a circus theme was too much and that they couldn't bring in a tent and acrobats, but that they could have bouncy houses and a petting zoo. That had been a pretty uncool substitute in his opinion. But Piper had wanted to go along to look at the animals and getting out of the office always seemed like a good idea, and before he knew it, Drew had Piper holding baby goats and petting alpacas—standing *way* closer than he needed to for either of those activities and making her laugh—and Ollie had said no way to the petting zoo.

Then Drew had put his hand over Piper's as they brushed one of the alpacas and Piper had looked up at Ollie and said, "come on, Ollie, please?" and somehow they'd ended up with alpacas, a pot-bellied pig, goats, and an emu, of all things, at the cake tasting.

Much to Whitney's chagrin.

Yes, he was jealous of Drew Ryan. And how much he seemed to like Piper and how much Piper seemed to like *him* and how *normal* Drew was—did it get any more normal than a guy named Drew Ryan who was a farmer in Iowa, for fuck's sake?

Yes, he was aware of his jealousy.

He was clueless at times, but he wasn't an idiot.

"Do you come out here every day?" Ollie asked Piper grumpily as she pulled up in front of one of Drew's barns.

"Yep," she said, shutting off the engine.

He looked over. "Really? Every day?"

"Well, since I don't have a job anymore anyway." She started to get out.

"Are you and Drew Ryan sleeping together?"

He realized that he'd made a big mistake one second before she swung back to look at him, her eyes flashing.

"*What?*"

"Nothing."

"No, that's not a nothing. I told you the other night that Drew and I are friends."

"Yes. And that you don't want him to be your boyfriend. But that doesn't mean you don't have a friends-with-benefits thing going on," Ollie pointed out. Stupidly.

"So the only reason I might come out here every day would be for sex?" she asked, her voice tight, her eyes narrow.

"Well, you're not exactly farm material."

That was true, dammit. The woman dressed in pin-up dresses and heels every damned day. She wore long fake eyelashes and did her nails and matched her hair accessories with her belts and shoes. How was it possibly an insult to point out that she didn't exactly exude an outdoorsy, muck-around-with-animals vibe?

But it seemed that it was an insult.

"I find it fascinating," she said after a moment during which Ollie was pretty sure she'd counted to ten, "that you think you know me so well."

"We've known each other for five years," he said. "We've spent a ton of time together."

"Yes. And I know exactly how to make your coffee and order your burgers and all the different places where you stick your neckties when you get sick of them, and that, for reasons I still haven't figured out, if I use my shaped sticky notes you *never* see the notes, but if I use the plain old yellow ones you do. But you know nothing about me, Oliver."

He thought about that. Then asked, "You have sticky notes that are different shapes?"

She made a noise that seemed like a muted scream and got out of the car, slamming her door hard.

He scrambled out his door as well. "Wait! I just asked a question."

"I have notes that are flowers, lips, high heels, coffee cups..." She pulled in a breath. "Yes, I have sticky notes that are different shapes."

He'd never noticed that.

A fact she was clearly aware of.

She turned on her heel and started for the barn.

"I know that blue is your favorite color," he said, hurrying after her. Damn, for a short woman, she could move. "I know that—"

She stopped and spun and he nearly plowed her over. His hands went to her shoulders and hers went to his chest.

He realized he was breathing hard as he stared down at her.

"Everyone knows blue is my favorite color," she said. She pushed on his chest and stepped back.

He didn't want to let her go. But he did.

"It doesn't hurt my feelings that you don't know details about me, Ollie," she said, her voice quieter. "I was your assistant. It was my *job* to keep track of details about you."

Exactly. That was exactly why all of this was so frustrating. She'd been *paid* to put up with his weirdness. She'd *had* to be there, no matter how nuts he made her.

Now... she could just walk away from him.

"I don't know Grant's favorite color," he said.

"Does Grant have a favorite color?" Piper asked.

"I don't know. I just... what I mean by that is, it doesn't mean anything that I don't know details," he said. "I don't do details. It's just me. It's not... you."

She sighed and nodded. "I know."

And she did. She probably knew him better than anyone.

"My point is," she went on. "You don't get to say things like I'm not farm-material or act all freaked out when I wear jeans or assume that I'm coming out here because I'm sleeping with Drew as if you know me so well. You don't."

"You're right."

"I'm not sleeping with Drew. Not that it's *any* of your business. But it's not a friends-with-benefits. It's just *friends*. And that's because of *me*. And you. Drew has asked me out. I said no. Because of how I feel about you. So now, *please*, for the love of God, shut the hell up about Drew."

Shutting the hell up seemed like a really good idea.

Every time she talked about how she felt about him and being in love with him, it made his chest tight. Not in a bad way, but in an I-want-that way. And that scared the shit out of him.

He would make Piper crazy. He already made her crazy. They would last about five minutes. And, just like she'd said back at the bakery, she would be very hard to get over.

Very likely impossible.

"Yeah. Fine. Tell me what you are doing out here," he said, changing the subject.

He was definitely curious about what she was doing out here at the farm every day. Especially if it had nothing to do with Drew Ryan and her having sex.

Even if it *did* involve her in blue jeans.

At the barn, she grabbed the handle and pulled, sliding the big door open.

Inside it looked like… a barn. Or what Ollie would have imagined the inside of a barn would look like.

It was full of stuff like tools and machinery and was dirty and dusty.

Again, not the type of place he would have pictured Piper, but he wisely kept his mouth shut about that this time.

She headed for the beat-up green pickup that was parked near the door.

She looked back at him as she pulled the driver's side door open. "You coming?"

"We're driving that?"

"We are," she told him with a smirk.

If she was thinking that he wasn't the outdoorsy, barn-type guy either, she'd be right.

Of course she was thinking that.

He rounded the front of the truck and climbed in. "Why can't we take your car?"

"Because it might get muddy," she said, starting the pickup. "And it doesn't have room for all of that." She gestured over her shoulder with her thumb.

Oliver pivoted to look into the bed of the truck. It was filled with stuff. Most of which appeared to be painting supplies. Buckets of paint, a ladder, brushes, a toolbox, and miscellaneous other things he vaguely recognized but had never used himself.

"You're painting something?"

She nodded, grinning, and maneuvered the truck through the door and around the side of the barn, pointing it toward one of the fields.

There was a path through the long grass but not one that was evident until they were on top of it.

"What are you painting?" They were clearly heading away from the house and other buildings around Drew's property.

"A cabin," she said simply. Then she added, "Well, more than one, but today, obviously, just one."

"A cabin? What kind of cabin?"

"A cabin," she said with a shrug. "Like a... cabin. A small, house-type structure." She glanced at him. "What other types of cabin are there?"

"Well, there are log cabins," he said. He didn't really know much about cabins. Or anything about cabins except what he'd seen in movies and read about in books. "Hunting cabins. Mountain cabins."

She looked amused. "This is a camping cabin."

"What's a camping cabin?"

"A cabin that people stay in when they're camping," she said, grinning as they bumped along over the very uneven path. "You've surely seen movies about kids who go off to summer camp."

"Well, sure." He couldn't recall any titles or plots but he had a general image of cabins clustered around a lake and kids dressed in matching t-shirts doing things like canoeing and archery and making s'mores around campfires.

"That's what these cabins will be," Piper said.

"Camping cabins? For kids?" he asked.

"Yes."

"Really?"

She looked at him. "Yes."

"And you're painting them?"

"I'm helping. Just like I helped build them. Well, except the first one. That one was already there. We just fixed it up a little. It was Drew's grandpa's hunting cabin. But we built the rest. I helped."

"When did you do that?" It was March. It had been cold and snowy for much of the past three months. Even he knew that wasn't building weather in Iowa.

"Last fall."

"Huh." He definitely noticed that she and Drew seemed friendly but he'd had no idea she'd been spending so much time out here. He didn't like it. But she'd asked him to stop talking about Drew.

That didn't mean he wasn't going to stew about it though.

"We started talking about it after I helped get the farming program going with Sunny Orchard," Piper said. Sunny Orchard was Dax's nursing home. They'd set up a program with Drew where they brought residents who had farmed or enjoyed gardening and animals out to the farm a couple of days a week to give them some activities they'd loved and missed. It was actually pretty cool. And one of the reasons Dax told Ollie he should lighten up about Drew.

"We built a greenhouse," Piper went on. "And had such a good time that one night when we were sitting around talking about other ideas and Drew mentioned the cabin and brought me out here to see it."

"Drew just casually brought you clear out here to see his hunting cabin just the two of you, just as friends," Ollie said. Hey, *she* was the one that had brought up Drew's name, not him.

"Well, Drew didn't think we should just be friends," Piper said casually. "That was the night he kissed me."

Ollie felt his hands ball into fists. That made his gut tighten and he actually saw red. "He *kissed* you?" he ground out.

"Yep," she said cheerfully.

Cheerfully. As if his heart wasn't somewhere down around his knees and he didn't want to put Drew's head through the first wall he saw.

He could definitely get arrested for the pummeling he suddenly wanted to give Drew Fucking Ryan.

"But you're just friends," Ollie said.

"Yep." That was also pretty damned cheerful. She cast him a glance. "That was also the night I told him I was in love with you so we could only be friends."

"And he just said, 'oh okay, that's fine'?" Ollie asked, somehow getting the words past his tight jaw.

"Pretty much." She lifted a shoulder. "Drew's a good guy."

"Hey, Piper?"

"Yeah?" Even that sounded cheerful. Like maybe she was enjoying his obvious jealous rage.

Yeah, yeah, he was jealous.

So what.

"How about *you* shut the hell up about Drew Ryan?"

She gave a little snort-laugh and yeah, she was enjoying this. But she said, "Okay." She paused but in the distance a cluster of buildings came into view. "But," she said. "I did help design these cabins. And the entire idea of making this into a kids' camp was mine."

He stared at her. He was surprised. He'd admit it. She could be mad about that if she wanted to be. It was true.

She shot him a glance. "You weren't expecting that, huh?"

"You starting a kids' camp and actually helping build it wouldn't have been in the top twenty-five things I would have guessed you'd been doing in your free time," he said honestly.

"And full-time since I quit my job."

Right. She'd been working out here full-time. On Drew Ryan's farm. In blue jeans. While Ollie had been stuck in a coffee-less office unable to write a fucking word on his script.

Awesome. Just awesome.

A minute later, they pulled up in front of a building that, sure enough, looked like a cabin. It was basic. Four walls, a roof, a few windows, and a front door with a single step up from the ground.

He looked around. There were five others just like it. They were clearly new. Only one exterior was painted. It was a bright blue that matched her car. He'd guess Piper had picked the color. The six buildings were arranged in a circle around a large area of dirt and grass. At the very center was a fire pit surrounded by rocks and wooden benches. About a hundred yards away to the east was a stream, a tributary of the small river that ran past the property and eventually fed into the Mississippi. There were trees about two hundred yards to the north and a vast grassy field to the west and south.

"This is all Ryan's property?" Ollie asked as Piper shut the truck off.

"I thought we weren't talking about Drew."

He honestly didn't even like her saying Ryan's name. "We're not."

"Okay." She seemed to be fighting a smile.

"Why a kids' camp?" Ollie asked.

She looked out the windshield at the buildings. "My younger brothers have always loved camp. It's been so great for them. They've met amazing friends, people who are like them and who helped them understand that no matter what they're into, they can find a place to belong. But they also learned about people who are different from them and how easy it really can be to find something in common with everyone at least on some level. They learned about teamwork and putting others first and how rewarding it can be to help others." She sighed. "Just a bunch of really great things." She looked over at him. "My brothers were—are—wild boys. They're awesome. Smart, good-hearted, kind, but wild. Camp was so great for them when they went. And they loved going back every year.

So, when Dr—when *we* were talking about things to do with a big area of land that was *not* plant or animal based—"

She laughed as if she and Drew had some private joke about him not wanting any more plants or animals, and Ollie frowned. He didn't like her having private jokes with Drew Ryan. But more, he didn't like that he had no clue that Piper had younger brothers.

"We just thought maybe this would be the perfect place for a camp." She shrugged. "Maybe it won't work, but if we want to give city kids a taste of rural living, then there's no place like this. They can come see a real farm, get up close to animals they would never see in their usual lives, meet kids from different backgrounds."

"You're going to bring city kids here?" Ollie asked.

She finally looked over at him. "Yeah. I mean, why would we bring small town or country kids here?"

"So this isn't for Appleby kids?"

She shrugged. "This *is* Appleby. How would it be fun for Appleby kids to come here?"

"I just..." He frowned. He had so many thoughts swirling in his head.

Piper had helped *build* these buildings. Drew had seen her in those blue jeans. She was starting a kids' camp. She had younger brothers. Who had grown up in the city. Which meant she had too. He knew she was from Chicago, but he didn't know she'd grown up there. And that bugged the shit out of him suddenly. Almost as much as it bugged him that Drew Ryan had seen her in those blue jeans.

It also bugged him that they weren't doing something here for Appleby.

And why did he care about that?

This wasn't his hometown. They'd helped save the biggest employer when they'd kept Hot Cakes open. That was enough good-doing for Appleby, wasn't it? He supposed Aiden and

Cam, and yeah, even Grant and Dax since they'd fallen for born-here-will-die-here girls, had just made it a habit to think that everything was about making this town better.

This was Piper's thing. Well, and Drew Ryan's thing. They could do whatever they wanted with it.

"Where'd you get the money for this?" he asked, getting out of the truck when she did and following her up onto the porch of the cabin they parked in front of.

"Drew and Dallas donated the land," she said. Dallas was Drew's brother. "We've done some fund raising for the rest."

"Have the guys helped?" Ollie asked. He was going to be pissed if Aiden, Grant, Cam, or Dax had given her money for a project he hadn't even known about.

Why, he couldn't really say. The guys could spend their money on whatever they wanted to, of course, and they certainly didn't have to tell him about it. And Piper could talk to them about whatever she wanted to. Including pet projects that she needed donations for.

It just bugged him to think that he was the only one who hadn't known about it. And that she hadn't asked *him* for money.

"No," she said as she pushed the cabin's door open and stepped inside. "I've funded some of it and we've gotten a few grants and some private donations."

"You've funded some of it?" Ollie repeated, watching her walk to the middle of the room.

It really was just a box. It was just one big room with windows in the three walls besides the one with the door.

She turned to face him. "Yes, I've funded some of it."

"You have that kind of money?" he asked.

That was *none* of his business.

But she laughed. "My bosses have been very generous." She propped a hand on her hip. "Four of them realize that my job responsibilities with the fifth are worth quite a bit."

Ollie rolled his eyes, but he didn't argue. He wasn't surprised to hear that Grant and Aiden—he knew they were the ones that had decided on Piper's salary—were willing to pay big bucks for her to babysit him.

"I don't have a lot of expenses, other than my wardrobe. And my car. And Grant's taught me a lot about investing," she said.

That was one of Grant's specialties. He even taught seminars about it. He taught single women—specifically single moms and widows, but really any single women—to manage their finances so that they would be financially independent and never in a relationship because of money.

He was glad Grant had helped Piper. Piper needed to be independent. She didn't need to lean on anyone, especially any guy.

Especially him.

But there she was, standing ten feet away, in blue jeans, looking hot as hell, and supposedly in love with him.

How was he supposed to ignore that? *Any* of that?

He shoved a hand through his hair and looked around. "So you also got other people on board," he said.

"I've met a lot of interesting people through my work with Fluke," she said. "I've been thrilled with the number of people who have been willing to listen to my ideas and who have been interested in helping out with the funding."

"That's impressive," he said.

"Is it?" She tipped her head.

"Of course."

"You don't even know that much about it."

"You're always impressive, Piper."

She didn't respond to that. She just kept standing there, looking like sex. He felt the growing urge to take the five steps that separated them, so he tucked his hands in his pockets and made himself turn around, pretending to study the room from another angle.

"So what is this going to be?"

"One of the sleeping cabins. We'll put bunk beds in here. Some cubbies for personal belongings. But this is basically it."

"Where are the bathrooms?"

"We built a separate building for toilets and showers. It's finally been warm enough for them to turn the water on this past week."

He turned back. "Wow, primitive."

She smiled. "I think having to get up in the night with a flashlight and walk to the bathroom, worrying about serial killers and tigers along the way, was very character building for my brothers."

"I didn't know you had brothers."

She opened her mouth and he braced himself for her to point out that he didn't really know shit about her.

Which was true. It had been on purpose. But it was still true.

Getting close to Piper would have been trouble. She'd been hired as his assistant, paid to put up with him. That was a much simpler scenario than getting close to her, liking her, and then worrying about driving her crazy. It would have messed with his head. And probably his heart. As seemed more obvious every second he let himself think about kissing her the other night.

She didn't say that though. She just nodded. "Four. One set of twins. All younger than me. Wild and crazy. Handfuls, all of them. Especially together."

Four wild younger brothers. He smiled at that. "Makes some sense why you're so good at dealing with all of us."

She nodded. "I grew up wrangling them. I knew I'd be good at it as soon as I met you guys." She shrugged. "Actually as soon as I read Grant's job description. I was supposed to just be *your* assistant initially. Coming off of my four brothers, having just *one* to keep track of sounded really good."

He'd known that Grant had hired her just for him. He'd been insulted for about thirty seconds when Grant had said he was hiring Ollie an assistant. Then he'd realized it was perfect. An assistant was exactly what he had needed. What he still needed. But dammit, not just any assistant. He needed *Piper*.

"What did the job description say?" he asked.

"That he was looking for someone who was energetic, incredibly organized and detail-oriented, had a sense of humor, and was patient beyond all expectation. Someone who was open to working strange hours and doing a variety of tasks from errands to event planning. Who could deal with no two days being alike."

"It didn't mention that you'd be babysitting a twenty-something-year-old man-child with picky eating habits, zero attention span, and hyperactive tendencies?"

He couldn't believe he'd just said all of that. He *never* pointed those things out about himself. They were facts and the people closest to him knew them well, of course, but he didn't talk specifically about those issues. Ever.

"No," Piper said. She paused, then added, "Those all came up during the interview though."

He couldn't help a small smile. "He gambled on telling you up front what you were getting into and you still taking the job?"

"Wasn't that better than me finding out after the fact?"

"I would have bet the other way."

"What's the other way?"

"You taking the job and realizing how charming and funny and interesting I was before finding out that I'm..." He trailed off on purpose, wanting her to fill that in.

"*A lot* of work?" she asked.

He grinned. "Yeah."

She regarded him thoughtfully. "That would have turned out okay too."

"Yeah?"

"Yeah. You are charming and funny and interesting."

"And a lot of work."

"Definitely."

"I'm glad you stuck with it as long as you did."

He hadn't been expecting to say that. But he realized it was true. And losing her was exactly what he'd figured would happen eventually and why he'd tried not to care and, well... he'd screwed that up. And that's why he was so damned crabby since she'd walked out.

Her expression was soft when she smiled this time and she looked sincerely touched. "Me too."

"Really?"

She nodded. "It's been good."

"You could come back."

"I know."

He shouldn't want her to come back. Being around her every day knowing that she was in love with him would be torture. And now that he'd kissed her—or she'd kissed him, or they'd kissed, or whatever—he'd want to kiss her at work. Constantly. Okay, maybe not *constantly*, because she wouldn't be wearing blue jeans. Or her short bathrobe. She'd have her regular dresses on. That would help. But he'd want to kiss her a lot.

And he'd want to fall in love with her too.

"I think this is going to be better," she said.

"What is?" he asked, feeling the grumpiness start to build again.

"Us not working together. But spending time together."

She started toward him. But he didn't move when she got close. She stopped in front of him and tipped her head to look up at him.

"I can write out here?" he asked.

"Sure, in the finished cabin. It's fully furnished. It's painted inside and out. There's electricity and the kitchen is all hooked up. The Wi-Fi isn't great, but that's probably a good thing. Then you won't get distracted. We have to use the bathroom building for toilets and sinks and stuff, but it's just right there." She pointed to a long, tan brick building behind the blue cabin.

A separate building for the bathroom. This was... interesting.

"I could really drive you crazy, you know," he said. "Just the two of us working out here together." But for some stupid reason his heart *thunked* hard at that thought. Being alone with Piper all day sounded pretty amazing. Alone, clear out here, away from, well, everything. Yeah, that sounded damned good.

She shrugged. "Maybe. Or it could be better than ever."

"How so?"

"Well, for one thing, I don't work for you anymore," she said with a little grin. "So I can tell you to shut up and fuck off if you bug me."

6

———————

Her response was sassy and teasing. And it made him want to kiss her. As if he needed anything else adding to that.

"You already tell me those things. Even if it's not in so many words. You even kicked me out of your hotel room the other night when you were tired of talking to me."

"Yeah, I guess I did."

"Even after a really hot kiss."

Now why had he said that? As if he needed reminding of that. He needed to *not* think about that.

Her eyes heated and her grin grew almost sly. "Yeah, I did. So this will be fine."

Ollie couldn't look away from her mouth. And then he couldn't stop thinking about how her lips had felt on his. And then he couldn't stop thinking about how her body had felt against his and how she'd sounded and tasted and smelled.

This was what happened to him all the time. He'd be on one train of thought and then something would distract him and he'd lose all track of what he'd been doing.

Of course, this particular train of thought was making out

with a gorgeous woman who he really liked and who really liked him, in spite of knowing him very well. So, it wasn't quite so strange that he'd get distracted just now, he supposed.

"This is where I'm going to be, so if you want to be with me, you have to be here too," Piper said. She tucked her hands in her back pockets.

He really wished she hadn't done that. The position thrust her breasts forward and the sparkly writing on the front of her t-shirt caught the sunlight, making it even harder to not look at it.

It was *literally* a shiny object pulling at his attention.

"Ollie?"

He closed his eyes. "Yeah?"

"I said, this is where I'll be. So if you need to be with me to get your writing done, then you need to be here too. And I think it might be good for you."

His eyes opened. "Good for me how?"

"The fresh air and sunshine won't *hurt* you and getting away from the office could be good," she said. "And when you get restless and fidgety, instead of playing Ping-Pong or distracting Cam, you can go for a walk by the stream or you can help me paint or plant flowers."

"You make me sound like a kindergartner who can't sit still for story time."

She just lifted a brow.

Okay, sitting still wasn't really his strong suit. It made being a writer difficult, for sure. He had to write in sprints. He could focus and write for about thirty minutes at a time. An hour if he was really on a roll. Then he needed to get up and do something. Technically, pacing would have been enough. Or twenty push-ups. Or jumping jacks. Those were the things his therapist suggested. He only needed about ten minutes of break time before he could get back to work.

Instead, he usually took a walk. Which took him past his

friends' offices. Which meant he usually popped in to see what they were doing and to chat, and an hour later or so, he'd make it back to his office for another thirty-minute sprint.

It wasn't efficient. He knew that. He knew he shouldn't leave his office.

But knowing it and doing it were two different things.

Plus, when he was messing around with Cam, it meant he went by Piper's desk. And it meant that after about forty-five minutes she'd start coming in and nagging him to get back to work.

Huh.

He'd always rolled his eyes at that. And of course, dragged his screwing around out for another fifteen minutes or so. But now that he thought about it... he'd liked knowing that Piper was keeping track and that she wouldn't let him mess up his *entire* day.

Once Cam had stopped coming to the office as much because he was hanging out with Whitney's grandma so Whit could come to the office and be her kick-ass corporate self, Ollie had missed Piper's nagging. And his productivity had slowed.

That was probably why he'd started going into Whitney's office and "brainstorming" with her.

Whitney was awesome because she would get going on big ideas just like he did. The whole gang had to work to reel them both in. Whitney was almost more fun than Dax.

Dax always said, "sure" whenever Ollie proposed a plan or adventure, but Whitney added to the plan. He knew she'd deny it until the day she died, but the acrobats at the cake tasting had actually initially been *her* idea.

"Manual labor during my breaks, huh?" he asked Piper. More importantly, activity *with* Piper. In blue jeans.

The damned truth was that for the past week, even though Whitney was still in the office, Ollie had been bored and grumpy. He could have blamed it on the fact that Dax and Cam weren't around anymore. They were *way* more fun to hang out with in the middle of the afternoon than Aiden and Grant. Mostly because Aiden and Grant liked to actually *work* in the afternoon.

But he knew the truth was that Piper was gone.

Dax had been gone for months now. Cam had been in and out for a while too. Yes, he'd missed them, but he could have gone down to Dax's nursing home to hang out—and play Ping-Pong—or over to Cam's place. He could have played Ping-Pong with *Didi*, Whitney's grandma, and had cookies over there.

But no, he hadn't gotten truly grumpy until Piper was gone.

Awesome.

Feeling that way was one thing. Realizing it and admitting it to himself was something else. Now he was screwed.

Piper misinterpreted his sigh as annoyance over the manual labor she was suggesting.

"Oh, come on," she said. "It will be great. It's routine stuff. Like the painting. Once you're doing it, you just... do it. You can think and plot and work through your story lines. But you'll also be moving and working. I think it could be the best of both worlds. The planting will be the same. We'll be putting in grass and some bushes. That won't take a ton of brain power, so you can use the time to think about what you're working on."

Ollie studied her for few ticks. "I didn't realize you'd paid that much attention to how I work."

"Well, you have been my full-time job for the past five years."

He nodded. "And I didn't even know you had brothers."

She lifted a shoulder. "I was paid to pay attention to how you work, Ollie."

Right. That's what he'd liked about the set-up. She was there, taking care of him, putting up with him, for money. Good money. Great benefits too. He didn't have to worry about annoying her or making her nuts. It was her *job*.

Now it wasn't.

What if he drove her nuts now?

But he didn't have a lot of choices here.

His options were to leave and *not* help her out here. To leave and go back to the office and work on his stories at his desk and pace the hallways and maybe actually do a few jumping jacks —he'd never really given those a chance—and not see her. And not drive her crazy.

And probably not get any writing done.

And leave her out here in her blue jeans with Drew Ryan.

Or to stay. And potentially actually write. And paint. And plant grass—whatever that entailed. And bushes. And see how long Piper tolerated him without a paycheck coming in.

Well, hell. "Okay, let's do this."

She grinned and he nearly groaned.

She really was so damned beautiful, and she looked genuinely *happy*. Because of him.

"Okay. I'm painting the outside of this cabin today."

"Bright blue again?" he asked.

"Yellow, actually. They're each going to be a different color."

She stepped around him, the sparkles catching the light again, and he looked up at the ceiling.

"You started with your favorite though," he commented as he turned to follow her.

"Oh, because that cabin's mine," she said. She looked over her shoulder at him.

"Yours?"

"Yeah. As the camp director."

"You'll be staying out here when camp's in session?"

"Definitely. And for the next two weeks."

Ollie tripped over... nothing. Just his own feet.

"You're *staying* out here this week? Like *tonight*? You're not driving back and forth?"

"Dubuque is a long way and it seems like a waste of time

and gas to go back and forth just to sleep. Plus, I think it will be so fun to camp out here and see what it will be like while we finish the buildings and grounds up, and I get plans in place. We'll wait a little bit to start hiring staff, but we want to start training them on weekends in April and May so we can start camp in June. So I'll be out here a lot anyway."

She was going to be running a camp. That was so... weird.

But who was he to judge weird?

"You're staying out here alone?" he asked.

"Well, I was going to be," she said. "But now you're here."

He tripped again and nearly fell down the one step outside the door.

"I am?" he asked.

"Sure. I mean, I guess you can drive back and forth to Dubuque but that's a long way and just think of all the... writing... you could get done out here."

There was something in her tone that made him narrow his eyes. She sounded... tempting. Yeah. That was exactly how she sounded.

Like she was going to try to seduce him.

Which would work.

Absolutely.

But she'd want him to fall in love with her in return and he didn't want to do that. Because he wouldn't be good at it.

Of course, she should know that. Of all people, Piper should know that.

So if she seduced him and he fell in love with her and she stayed in love with him and he messed it all up, then it was really her fault in the end, right?

"Where will I stay?" he asked.

"In the cabin with me," she said as if it was obvious.

He supposed it was. He wasn't exactly the type to sleep outside under the stars, and the other cabins weren't finished. Or furnished. Though he could fix that with a phone call.

He eyed the truck. He should drive back and forth to Dubuque. Or he should drive back to Dubuque and fucking stay there and save him and Piper both some heartbreak.

That short robe was probably in her bag.

But it was a long way to Dubuque.

And he needed to write. And he sure as hell couldn't do that at the office. Apparently.

"I thought you wanted to get over me."

She turned and regarded him with a hand on her hip. "I did. When that seemed like the only option."

His heart squeezed. "And now there's another option?"

"Yep."

"What's that?" But he knew what she was going to say.

"Having you all to myself. Just us. Together. Alone."

See, that should sound creepy. She had him out here in the woods in a secluded cabin. No one knew he was here. She could tie him up and make him write, like that woman in *Misery*.

But, as difficult as writing was for him sometimes, Piper wanted something a lot bigger, and more complicated, from him.

"And then you'll get over me," he said. "If we spend all this time together, I mean. That should definitely help with that." It would be so great if that were true. But his stupid chest hurt now that he'd said it out loud.

Piper tipped her head and gave him a soft smile. "I don't think that's what's going to happen, Ollie."

He swallowed. "What do you think is going to happen?"

Why couldn't he just shut up? Why did he keep talking? Why couldn't he just ignore all of this? Deny it? Like he'd been doing for the past two years since the guys had started hinting that Piper felt more for him?

But he didn't. He asked the damned question.

And she, of course, answered it.

"I think you're going to fall in love with me."

Yep, there it was. The shoe he'd been waiting to drop. The nail in the coffin. The gauntlet thrown down.

So it made no sense that his heart kicked against his ribs and he felt a rush of adrenaline. Sure there was the "oh shit, man, you're going to screw this up so badly" thought that went racing through his head. But his heart wasn't listening.

"You're pretty cocky, you know that?" he finally managed.

She nodded. "Yeah, well, you can't even look at me in blue jeans without almost choking to death, so I think there's something there."

There was something there, all right. A huge freaking mistake about to happen.

But hey, she was going in eyes wide open, right?

"You think you know what you're doing?"

"Dating you? Yes."

His eyes went wide. "Dating me?"

She nodded. "Yes."

He looked around. "This is dating?"

"Spending time together. Getting to know each other. Seeing if we're compatible." She paused. "Physical intimacy." She lifted a shoulder. "That's dating."

"I... but... we..." He scowled. She had to call it *physical intimacy*, didn't she? She'd totally done that on purpose. Obviously his body heard *hot dirty sex* but that wasn't how his head heard it. It wasn't how she'd meant it either. Intimacy was a whole other thing.

Not what he had at Comic Con, that was for sure.

And Piper knew it.

People thought she had her hands full dealing with him, but they had no idea how much trouble this woman had the potential to be for him.

"You could have had 'physical intimacy' with me the other night," he said dryly, knowing that she was going to deny that.

She laughed. "I could have had hot sex against my hotel room door the other night."

Yep, called it.

"Would have been good," he felt compelled to say.

She nodded. "Too bad you annoyed me by talking."

He almost laughed at that. "I wasn't talking when you stopped things."

"But I remembered the talking you'd done *before* the kissing."

"Which talking was that?"

"The part about you not wanting me to be in love with you."

He blew out a breath. "The talking and annoying you thing is *sure* to happen again. And you can't send me back to my room if you get tired of talking to me out here," he pointed out.

"Hmm, that's true."

"What are you going to do in that case?"

She studied him, a gleam in her eye.

A gleam that should have made him nervous.

Instead, it made him hard.

"I think if you start annoying me out here, I'll just have to come up with some other way for you to use your mouth."

Oh, that short robe was definitely in her bag.

Awesome.

And dammit.

***

She was now officially dating Oliver Caprinelli.

At least, she'd just informed him that she was and he hadn't said no. So that made it official.

Piper couldn't help grinning as she went to the truck to retrieve the painting supplies.

Okay, so he was kind of stranded out here. They were about six miles from Drew's house and Drew's house was about nine miles from Appleby. But there was cell reception out here. Ollie could have called one of the guys for a ride. Or just asked her to take him back to town. He could have just said no about staying out here. He could have told her this was all stupid.

He hadn't said any of that.

This was going to be *great*.

She'd often thought that if she could just get him out of the office, away from the computer, and away from the other guys, that Ollie might actually *see* her.

She hadn't thought that at first, of course. The first year of her employment, she'd just been his—well, *their*—assistant. A lot of her daily duties had focused on Ollie and making sure he got the business stuff that he hated done on time. And that he remembered meetings. And that he ate. Basic things like that.

But it hadn't taken long before the guys had realized she was very capable and that Ollie didn't take 100 percent of her time and effort and they'd started asking her to do more for them all.

She'd loved her job. The guys were friendly and funny and creative and intelligent and no day was ever the same as the last. She was paid well and had amazing benefits and had been made to feel essential to the company from day one.

By year two, she'd considered them all friends. Brothers almost. Okay, very much like brothers. She was used to herding rambunctious, smart, funny boys. These guys were just older than her biological brothers. And she couldn't ground them. Still, it hadn't been that different than dealing with her brothers, really.

She'd gotten to know Ollie, Grant, Aiden, Cam, and Dax by then and was not only good at taking care of them, but enjoyed it. She liked ordering their lunches just the way they liked them without even having to ask. She liked introducing them to new things—a new sandwich shop or a new brewery—that she knew they'd like and then having them rave about what great taste she had.

She liked doing little things like booking a massage for Aiden at a hotel when he traveled and getting a text telling her how it had been just what he needed. Or emailing a suggestion for a Mother's Day gift to Grant and having him tell her she'd nailed it. Or making sure Dax and Ollie saw posts from fans, like the eight-year-old boy who'd been diagnosed with leukemia and wanted, more than anything, a phone call from one of them. They'd both called him, at the same time. She'd cried listening to the call outside their office door and then when she'd seen their faces afterward.

But it was year three when she'd realized that, somewhere along the way, she'd fallen in love with Ollie.

It had snuck up on her.

She felt love and affection for all five of the men that were her bosses, but it wasn't until Dax and Ollie were comparing— i.e., bragging about—their fan mail and Dax was crowing about how he was the only one who got emails from women their age that Piper realized she'd been deleting all the emails from fangirls to Ollie. Not the young ones. Girls age eighteen and under got through. But anyone older? Yeah, they were trashed. But come on. Twenty-two-year-old women didn't need to be writing fan letters to a man about a video game. Didn't they have more important things to be thinking about? Doing? Weren't there real men in their lives they could flirt with?

Of course, that didn't explain why all of Dax's emails were forwarded. Not the ones that said his seventh level of the ice cave was crap or he'd completely screwed up the design for the sea elves. Because the people writing *those* emails needed to get a life too. But the letters from the girls telling him how wonderful he was? Yep, those got forwarded. The ones where the women got really specific about the dirty things they'd like to do to him got forwarded with "Regarding your magical staff" in the subject line.

Oops.

She'd confessed. To Dax. And told him to shut up about his own fan mail because it was making Ollie feel bad. Dax had smirked and said that she could just send Ollie's messages through and he'd feel fine. Piper had said that wasn't an option. Dax had laughed, knowingly.

And Piper had been faced with not just the realization that she was in love with Ollie but that she wasn't the only one who had realized it.

"So I'm going to need a few things if I'm staying out here," Ollie said as he joined her at the back of the truck.

He'd shrugged out of his jacket and, she assumed, tossed it on the front seat. He was rolling up the sleeves on his dress shirt now and she stopped to watch.

After his thick, long fingers had rolled one sleeve up to his elbow, she lifted her gaze from his muscular forearms to his eyes. He was watching her with a bemused expression. Like all of this was really weird and he wasn't sure how to feel about it.

"Do you want me to call someone to bring some things out here?" she asked, lifting two buckets of paint. She was sure Whitney and Cam would go to Ollie's hotel room and get him a bag. She could meet them in Appleby to pick it up.

Ollie grabbed a bucket full of brushes. "I can go get my stuff."

She had to admit, she wasn't sure he'd come back. But she said, "Sure. Okay." She turned toward the cabin.

"Piper."

She looked back. "Yeah?"

"I came to the bakery to find you."

She stopped and turned. "I know."

"So the chances of me coming back out here are probably pretty good."

He'd known she was worried about that. Huh. But she nodded. "Because you need to write."

"Yeah."

Right. "You should go now," she said. "Keys are in the ignition."

"I'll go later." He carried the supplies to the side of the cabin.

"Why later? Why not now?"

"Why now? Why not later?" he countered.

"You're not dressed for painting." She let her gaze travel over the dress shirt, suit pants, and leather shoes.

"I can write in this though."

The script. Right. They were dating, but he was in it for the word count. At least in part. At least for now.

She blew out a breath. "Fine. You should go now because later, you'll have a better idea about what this is going to be like and you might change your mind."

7
———————

Ollie gave her a half grin. "You said the kitchen in the cabin is fully functional, right?"

Piper rolled her eyes but couldn't help her smile.

The home-cooked food and his writing. She did have two pretty powerful reasons for him to stay.

He'd always been a sucker for her food and she loved cooking for him. She loved cooking in general, but there was something about Ollie, even back before she'd fallen in love with him, that had made her think that he hadn't been nurtured much. Or something. All of the guys liked her cooking and were complimentary about it, but Ollie *loved* it. He especially loved when she made stuff just for him.

Of course, she'd also mentioned sex. But that was, interestingly, *not* one of his top two draws.

While he'd clearly been all-in on that the other night in her hotel room, it was obvious that calling it "physical intimacy" had freaked him out. She'd known it would. She'd done it on purpose. He needed to know what she was expecting here. She wasn't a convention hookup. She wasn't some woman who had just met him and thought he was hot and wondered what it would be like to bang a millionaire on his private plane. She *knew* him and she wanted a damned *relationship*.

She wanted to sleep with him. Very much. But she was beyond being able to have just a fling with him. If they tried a relationship and it didn't work out, that was one thing. But if they just hooked up and never tried for more, she'd always wonder. She'd always want it.

"Homemade chili and cornbread for dinner. Ghost stories and s'mores around a campfire tonight," she said.

"S'mores. Of course."

He chuckled and Piper felt heat swirl through her belly.

God, she loved when he laughed. He wasn't as jovial as Dax. He wasn't as outwardly friendly and outgoing as Aiden. But he wasn't as gruff as Cam—before Cam had gotten back together with Whitney—or as serious and stoic as Grant. He fell nicely in the middle.

His laughs were easy and natural but not a given.

Piper wondered for a moment if Cam and Grant's grins and laughter affected Whitney and Josie the same way. Did it feel as special to them as Ollie's did to her? Did it turn them on the way Ollie's did her?

She made a note to ask the women next time she had a chance.

She squatted and started opening paint cans. She handed him a stir stick and pointed to the can she'd just opened. "Stir that up."

She watched him crouch and start stirring as if something was going to jump out of the can and bite him. She reached over and grasped his wrist. He glanced up at her and for a moment they just looked at each other. Then she pressed so the stir stick went all the way to the bottom of the can and she circled his hand with hers. "*Stir* it," she said.

She let go of him, reluctantly, and he followed her direction, stirring deep into the can.

She turned to her own can of paint, pushing the thoughts of how big and solid his wrist and hand were. And how hot his skin was.

"Speaking of food, what have you been eating this past week?" she asked.

He sighed, heavily. Dramatically. "Pizza. Subs. Cam finally took pity on me and brought me some leftovers from his mom's the other night."

"And I'll bet they've invited you over for dinner at her house at least twice," Piper commented, watching her stir stick swirling through the sunshine-yellow paint, instead of looking at him.

"They have."

"But you didn't go."

"Nope."

She and Ollie had both been invited to Maggie McCaffery's. A few times. Maggie had a big group dinner at least once a week at her house. It had always been Zoe and Josie and Jane. Aiden and Cam had, of course, joined them when they'd been home visiting. Long before Aiden and Zoe were anything more than friends.

When Aiden had come home to stay, he'd become a fixture. Of course. He was like one of Maggie's own children. Then Dax had started going to dinner with Jane. Then Grant with Josie. Actually, the way Piper understood that story, Grant's first appearance at Maggie's dinner table had led to his and Josie's first hookup.

Cam had not only become a regular again at his mom's table when he'd moved back, but he'd brought, first Whitney's grandmother, Didi, then Whitney with him.

It was a full house now.

But Piper and Ollie had never gone.

Piper because her only goal at the end of a workday was to head to her hotel room, get out of her heels and Spanx and be *quiet* and *alone*. She was an extrovert, for sure, but working for five brilliant men kept her busy and on her toes. Literally. She loved her work outfits and she loved getting *out* of her work outfits. Plus her room was twenty minutes away in Dubuque, unlike Aiden, Cam, Dax, and Grant, who had started shacking up in Appleby as soon as their pretty girls batted their eyelashes at them.

"Why don't you ever go to the McCafferys' for dinner?" Piper asked as she stretched to her feet.

She knew her reasons, but she wasn't sure about Ollie's. Sometimes it was because he stayed at the office long past mealtime. But that wasn't always it. And she wondered if sometimes he stayed late at the office to have an excuse not to go to dinner.

"Not my thing," he said, also straightening with his paint bucket in hand.

"Not your thing?" She laughed. "I happen to know that dinner is very much your thing. Especially when it's home-made. And by an amazing cook." All of the McCaffery women were legends in Appleby. Zoe and her grandmother more for baking and Maggie for cooking, but they were all rumored to be magical in the kitchen no matter what they were making.

Ollie shrugged.

"Come on. You know you'd be welcome there. Why don't you go?"

He sighed, stirring the stick around in the paint. "I don't do mothers. Or fathers. And now that they've added a grand-mother too? No thanks."

Piper widened her eyes. "You don't do mothers, fathers, or grandmothers? What's that even mean?"

He lifted his head. "It means that I'm not good with families."

She studied him. "This is related to what you said about not attaching to people?"

"Yeah."

That was all bullshit. He did attach. Completely.

But she knew he didn't mean to.

And he didn't attach to new people.

She'd been watching him for five years. At first to learn his habits and preferences so she could be a good assistant, then because she was in love with him. So yeah, she'd seen him with his friends, a lot, and with people he didn't know well. He was friendly, but he held himself back from anyone new. He'd come to Appleby with every intention of being a really good boss and wanting to learn what their employees wanted and needed. Then he'd realized that things were not as happy and easy with the Hot Cakes factory as the guys had all hoped, and he'd been completely relieved when Aiden and Dax had stepped in to lead the way and fix things.

In fact, it was Jane, Dax's fiancée, who had approached Ollie in his office when he'd been the first of the new owners to show up at the factory. She'd demanded to know their plans and had laid out the problems and Ollie hadn't been able to respond to any of it.

But he hadn't needed to. Aiden and Dax were there almost immediately, taking care of things so Ollie didn't have to.

All of that was one of the reasons that him getting close to and brainstorming and enjoying working with Whitney was so amazing to see.

But as Piper stood studying him, she realized why he was comfortable with Whitney. It was partly that the woman was a big thinker and they got each other going creatively. But it was also because Whitney hadn't had many friends. She'd been very lonely when they'd all showed up to take over Hot Cakes. She'd been working for her family and generally getting overlooked. She'd given up a lot of other relationships, including one with Cam, to be a part of her family's business and they'd subsequently pushed her aside.

Ollie felt comfortable with Whitney because she had also had some trouble attaching.

Huh, maybe there was something to that attachment thing.

"Well, the chili tonight will be amazing," she told him, letting him off the hook when she really wanted to dig deeper. But she always had this conflicting urge to push him—make him do more, talk more, try more—and to protect him.

"I have no doubt."

Well, at least he had no doubts about her food. That was something, she supposed.

She went to grab the ladder.

Ollie was beside her before she'd even lifted it out of the truck bed. "Where do you want this?" he asked.

She pointed at the side of the building. He carried it to the spot and propped it against the side.

They didn't talk as he made sure the ladder was set securely and she poured paint into a tray, selected a brush, and climbed up the ladder. The cabin had been primed over the weekend and she was excited to get some color on another building out here. She'd been thinking about this project for months. The paint, furniture, and landscaping was going to start making it look *real*.

"Who helped you with all of this so far?" Ollie asked from below her.

She looked down.

"Drew."

Ollie rolled his eyes. She smiled and reached up, dragging her brush back and forth over the wooden slats.

"Dallas, too," she said. "Justin has been out a few times. We've hired a few kids from town that the guys have had help out at the farm from time to time. We're thinking about hiring a few more. And bringing them on as camp counselors."

"You could have asked us, you know." He sounded grumpy again.

Piper laughed. "Oh sure. I was going to ask Aiden and Grant and Dax and Cam to come out and help build and paint cabins."

"Why not?"

She looked down at him again. "My millionaire, suit-wearing, gaming sensation bosses? Really?"

"I never would have expected you to be out here on a ladder painting cabins at a camp that you've set up and plan to run. In blue jeans," he added, almost as an aside. "People can surprise you."

"Okay, fair enough."

She realized her starting a camp might seem weird. It seemed nothing like the work she'd done for the past five years for Fluke. But it wasn't really all that different, honestly.

Her superpower was taking someone else's idea, any idea, and forming it into a workable plan and then organizing every detail until it all fit together like a completed thousand-piece jigsaw puzzle.

Managing something like a summer camp with multiple schedules and activities and supply lists for a couple dozen kids and counselors at one time? Oh yeah, *that* she could do.

And now that she was unemployed, she had plenty of time on her hands. She wasn't good at just sitting around, so she'd turned her full-time attention to the camp.

She could also admit, at least to herself, that she kind of wanted her brilliant, creative genius boss and the object of her affection, to be impressed with the camp and her plans.

She rested her elbow on the top rung of the ladder. "Why do the blue jeans bother you so much?"

His eyes dropped to those blue jeans. Or rather to her ass in the blue jeans.

"They're not you."

"They're very much me," she said. "They're just not the me who you know."

He looked up again. "Yeah."

"And it, what? Upsets you?"

"Not really the right word."

"Then why do you seem so upset by it?"

"Because I guess I was thinking that you would be the person who would stay the same."

She twisted more on the ladder to look down at him. "What do you mean?"

"Aiden is all into expanding Zoe's business, Dax is running a *nursing home*, Grant is now living in a tiny town where they've named an ice cream sundae after him, and Cam is basically a stay-at-home husband who takes care of Whitney's grandmother and bakes cookies all day."

Piper thought about all of that. Then she nodded. "Okay. I see what you mean. Your four best friends—"

"My only friends."

She frowned, but okay, he had a point there too. "Your friends," she started again, "all have lives and interests that are pretty different now than they were a year ago. But they're the same people."

"Kind of."

But their relationship with Ollie wasn't the same. They didn't spend as much time all together. He and Dax hadn't traveled anywhere together since they'd all come to Appleby. They hung out, of course, but the other guys cut the time short now because they were all eager to get home to their girls.

"Well nothing I'm doing is that different," she said. "Just because you've never seen me in blue jeans before doesn't mean it's new." She turned back to the painting.

"This whole camp thing is new," he said, his tone frustrated. "You painting cabins and making s'mores and wearing short robes—"

She turned quickly to snap at him over mentioning her clothes *again*. But the move made her wobble on the ladder and she gasped, dropping the paintbrush and gripping the ladder rung.

The next thing she felt was Ollie's hands steadying her. By grabbing *her*, not the ladder. More specifically grabbing her ass.

She sucked in a breath at the contact and froze.

The wobble had been relatively small. The ladder was still again and she was completely safe.

But his hands stayed on her butt.

She counted to ten. Then counted to ten again.

"Oliver?" she finally asked.

"Yeah."

"I'm good."

"You really are."

She huffed out a laugh. She wasn't sure what he meant by that, but it had sounded complimentary. She looked over her shoulder. "I think you can move your hands."

It took him a second, but he looked up and met her gaze. "Do I have to?"

She wet her lips. "I mean, I'm not *upset* with your hands there."

He took a breath and then slowly lifted his hands and stepped back. He tucked his hands into his back pockets, his gaze moving over her from her face to her ass and back up.

"So you *do* like the jeans?"

"I hate the jeans," he said with a frown.

"That's not how it seems."

He sighed. "In five years of knowing you, I've never touched your ass. Now, within a few hours of you being in those jeans, I have."

"Well, don't forget that you touched my ass in my robe the other night too," she said, feeling annoyed by how annoyed he seemed by the ass touching that she'd rather enjoyed.

"Oh, I haven't forgotten about that," he said. "Holy shit,

Piper, I've been thinking about that, and everything else, every day since."

Okay, that was enough of this. She climbed down from the ladder—she didn't have her paintbrush anymore anyway—and faced him squarely, her hands on her hips.

"And was it so terrible?"

"It was fucking amazing," he said, seeming frustrated.

"Then why do you act pissed off and *scared* that I might make a move?"

"Because…" He narrowed his eyes. "Because I don't think you will make a move." He took a step toward her. "I would be *fine* with you making a move. *Please* make a move. But do it now. Before I—"

She was barely breathing suddenly. "Before you what?" she pressed.

The muscle along his jaw tensed and he was clearly gritting his teeth.

"Before you *what*, Oliver?" Piper asked. Dammit, he wasn't chatty. He didn't share a lot. He wasn't open and didn't say everything that came to mind the way Dax did. But she *was* going to hear this.

"Before I *do* actually fall for you."

She searched his face. There were emotions swirling in his eyes but she couldn't name a single one.

"I know you think that's what you want," he said. "But I think it's going to ruin everything."

Her heart did a back flip in her chest.

"I don't want to just sleep with you, Ollie," she said. "I do want that," she added, so he was *clear*. "But I want more than that. I want to date you."

"I don't date."

"You do too." But she frowned as she said it because he didn't really. In the beginning, when she'd first taken the job, he had, but it had been a long time. She knew he had hookups at the conventions he and Dax went to because the guys gave him shit about it. But she didn't hear about women in Chicago. Of course, she'd just assumed that he didn't talk about them with his friends. She certainly didn't *want* to know, so she didn't dig either.

"I don't. I never have," he said.

"I sent flowers to at least two women when I first started working for you," she pointed out. "And I know I picked out a birthday gift for one."

He nodded. "You did do those things. And it made things very complicated for me when I tried to explain to them that we were not dating and my assistant had sent those mistakenly."

"But..." She trailed off. Okay, she remembered the one she'd sent the birthday gift to calling the office the Monday after and sobbing in her ear, trying to get a hold of Ollie. Ollie had refused to take her calls. He'd also refused to tell Piper why. And that had been early in her career with Fluke Inc., before she would have made him tell her. Or gone to Dax to find out what had happened.

"Oh," she finally said.

"Yeah. Oh."

She narrowed her eyes. "Did you stop dating women in Chicago because you were afraid I would send them stuff?"

He sighed. "Do you really want to talk about my dating life and habits?"

"Yes, actually."

She wanted to know everything about him. And it wasn't as if she thought he'd been living like a monk. Lord, she kind of hoped he hadn't. No, she didn't need details or names and photos of the women—though she knew from conversations she'd overheard that some of those photos would be of women dressed up as fairies and princesses and such from *Warriors*— but she wanted him to have some experience. Because when she finally got him naked, she wanted him to know what he was doing.

"I did, for a while," he said. "The women who could track me down at the office and go through my assistant to make dinner plans and could mention things like their birthdays and our two-week anniversary of meeting." He gave her a look.

Yeah, one of the women she'd sent flowers had done exactly that. She'd called and said she wanted to know what time Ollie would be done with meetings on that Thursday because it was their two-week anniversary and she wanted to do something special. Piper had, stupidly, found that kind of sweet and since Ollie had been out of town, she'd sent the woman flowers. From him, of course.

Apparently, that had been the wrong move.

"You could have told me to not do that," Piper pointed out.

"I didn't realize that I needed to go through a whole list of things you *shouldn't* do," he said. "I kind of thought we could just stick to the list of things you *should* do and anything that wasn't on there was a shouldn't."

"But after I sent the flowers... you never yelled at me for that."

He shrugged. "You were trying to be nice."

"Still, that *was* pretty presumptuous of me."

"It was."

"But you didn't say anything because I was new and you were trying to be nice to me. You just broke the girl's heart... blamed it on me behind my back, of course... but let me go on thinking I was doing a great job."

He smiled. "Something like that."

She returned his grin. He would tell her to knock that shit off now. Probably loudly. Yelling it from inside his office out to her desk with a "dammit, Piper!" Because they knew each other now. He knew she could take that and she would have rolled her eyes and told him that he should be nicer to the women he dated.

She might have even sent a bigger bouquet the next day just to mess with him.

"I hate to break it to you, Ollie, but you already know me pretty well. And you like me."

His smile died. "Yeah. I do."

A horn honking broke into their moment.

They both pivoted to see two pickup trucks pulling up behind theirs.

Dallas Ryan got out of one, and three teenagers—Matt Porter, Tanner Sanders, and Landon Summers—got out of the second.

"Hey," Piper greeted them. She was going to have to hope that she and Ollie would have more time to talk later. If he decided to stay. "You guys are early. I figured since it was the first day of spring break, you'd have other stuff going on."

"We goofed around this morning," Matt said with a grin. "But then we figured we could get more work done if we got out here early."

"You mean, you realized if you came out early, you could get more hours in and earn more money," she said. They were being paid by the hour.

Matt nodded. "Yeah. We were kind of hoping you'd let us work more hours all week."

Piper nodded enthusiastically. "I will absolutely let you work more hours."

"Awesome."

She laughed. "Ollie, this is Matt, Tanner, and Landon."

"Hey," they all greeted one another in typical guy fashion.

"And I wanted to check on the showers since you're staying out here for several days this time," Dallas said. "Figured I could put some painting time in too."

"He knows you're staying out here?" Ollie asked low enough for only her to hear.

She nodded. "Figured someone should know where I was."

"I should have known."

She rolled her eyes even though he couldn't see her from where he was standing just behind her. "When have I ever told you where I was?"

He didn't answer. Because they both knew the answer. Never.

"Well, great. Definitely hoping for hot water in there," she told Dallas.

"Can do," he answered.

"We'll go prime building four," Matt said.

"Great," Piper told them. "That's perfect." It didn't really matter where they started. There was plenty to do. She loved that they didn't need a lot of direction though.

The younger guys grabbed supplies out of the back of the truck and started for the cabin furthest away.

"So I'll check the plumbing. Then do you want me to start painting building three or do you need help here?" Dallas asked.

Ollie moved in closer behind her. "We've got this one."

Dallas didn't smile but Piper could tell he was amused. Dallas was a great guy, just like his brother. He hadn't flirted with her or asked her out the way Drew had, but she knew he genuinely liked her. He also didn't seem all that surprised to see Oliver here.

Which was interesting, because when she really thought about it, *she* was surprised that Ollie was here.

"Okay, great," Dallas said. "Then, I'll just be over there." He inclined his head toward the next building. Let me know if you need anything."

"We won't," Ollie said firmly.

Dallas looked at Piper. She just shrugged.

As he turned and started toward the bathroom and shower building, she faced Ollie. "We won't?"

"It's just painting and putting in grass and bushes, right? It'll give me a chance to go over some plot points in my head."

"Oh, you did hear me say all of that?"

He nodded. "I'll admit I was distracted by your breasts in that t-shirt, but yeah, I heard you."

She was startled by his admission that he'd been checking her out.

She looked down. "You know, this t-shirt doesn't show anything off that my dresses don't show off. Those are fitting across the bust and show cleavage."

He nodded. "I guess."

But he thought she should wear *those* when they were together. He'd said as much back at the bakery. She didn't know exactly what that was about, but she did know that he'd been thinking of her as his assistant, and maybe friend, for five years while she'd been wearing those dresses and he'd almost choked to death when she put this t-shirt on.

"So seriously, what's the deal with the jeans and t-shirts?"

His gaze dropped to her breasts. Which, of course, responded by getting tingly and hard-tipped. "The sparkly words, I suppose."

She didn't think that was it at all. She believed him when he said he didn't date and she knew that most of his hookups, at least over the last couple of years, had been mostly at conventions.

"I don't think it's the sparkly words, Ollie."

His eyes came back to hers. He saw something in her face that made him sigh. "You're going to tell me what you think it is?"

She smiled. "Sure."

"What if I don't want you to?"

"What do I do when you don't want me to schedule Zoom

calls with Dan and Doug?" Dan and Doug were the execs who now owned *Warriors of Easton.* The guys Ollie more or less worked for now. He hated Zoom calls with them. He hated all calls with them actually.

"You do it anyway."

"Exactly."

"Okay." He crossed his arms. "Why do you think that I am completely distracted by your breasts in t-shirts and your ass in blue jeans but not in the hot, knock-out dresses you wear every day?"

"Wait, you think my dresses are hot and knock-out?"

"You're a gorgeous woman, Piper. You wear the hell out of those dresses. You look like a freaking pin-up model from the forties. Every man who sees you nearly trips over his tongue. Of course I think they're hot."

She stared at him. "But you don't have any trouble with staring and not putting your hands on my ass when I wear those."

He shrugged. "I know. And you were about to tell me why that is."

Right. She did have a theory about that. Maybe even more so now that he'd admitted to having noticed them. And liking them. But being able to resist her in those.

"I think those dresses are like costumes," she said. "They put me into a role. I'm playing a part you know how to react to when I dress like that. You can just say, *oh she's my assistant and I'm not supposed to be attracted to her.* When I dress like that, you can put me in that compartment. But when I'm in t-shirts and jeans, I'm real. I'm just a woman and there's no specific compartment and so you can't ignore your reactions to me then."

He just stood looking at her. Piper let him process all of that.

Finally, he nodded. "I think that's exactly it."

"Really?"

"Yeah. Makes sense."

"Oh. Okay."

Well, she had to admit that helping him with these insights was a lot easier than she'd expected. He was easily accepting these observations.

"And don't forget the short bathrobe. Definitely a real woman in that. Didn't have time to compartmentalize my reaction to that."

She would never be able to forget his reaction to her short bathrobe. She wet her lips and nodded. "Being caught by surprise was part of that too, I would imagine."

"Probably."

"If you'd been expecting the robe, would you have kissed me?"

Because as much as that kiss had been torturing her, she would have really hated *not* getting it.

"*You* kissed me."

"You totally kissed me back. And then some, Ollie."

He cleared his throat and Piper enjoyed thinking that he was replaying all of that in his mind.

"Yeah. I'm thinking that the short robe and you starting it would have led right where it did whether I'd been expecting it or not."

She grinned. "Noted."

He arched a brow. "Did you bring your short robe along for camping?"

"I did."

He sighed as if that was a terrible answer.

She laughed. She really liked that Oliver was attracted to her and was being open about it. Even if he found it inconvenient.

8

———————

"Okay, you are *not* dressed for painting and even though I appreciate your willingness to help, I can't have you ruining your pants or shoes," Piper said, after she'd confirmed his worst fear as if she'd just told him that the sky was blue.

She had that robe in her bag.

Her wearing that short bathrobe in that secluded cabin where the two of them would be spending the next several days...

Who was he kidding? It wouldn't matter if she were wearing footie pajamas around that cabin. He wanted her. And camping out with her was the best worst idea ever.

"Ollie?"

He met her gaze. "Yeah?" He hadn't been studying her breasts. Or her ass. He'd been looking at her shoes. Which were not sexy. They were tennis shoes. Very basic gray-with-white-laces tennis shoes. As different from the heels that she normally wore as she could possibly get.

And he was completely turned on.

"I said, you should go write," she told him, obviously repeating herself.

He really should.

At least he could get work done on his script. If he was going to lose his heart and then lose this woman, he could at least leave this campground with his damned script finished.

"Yeah." He scrubbed a hand over the back of his neck. "Okay."

She stood watching him as his gaze dropped back to her shoes.

She had that short bathrobe in her bag.

Big deal. He was turned on by canvas tennis shoes.

"You all right?" she asked.

Nope. Not at all. He was about to sleep with and fall in love with a woman who was a sticky-note loving, multiple-calendar-having perfectionist.

That was a terrible idea.

He appreciated that she thought she knew all his quirks and could love him anyway, but he knew better. They put in long hours at the office sometimes, but it wasn't twenty-four-seven. His forgetfulness and messiness and disorganization made her work life more difficult, but that wasn't the same as making her home life chaotic. As his assistant, she could clock out from the frustrations. As his girlfriend, or more, there was no out.

Except breaking up with him and leaving, of course.

Kind of like his mom had. His mother had traveled more and more over the years as he'd grown up, needing to escape from the way he made her crazy.

But he wasn't sure he had a choice here. He wasn't going to be able to resist Piper so he just had to show her what being with him would really be like and brace for her change of mind.

Of course, the kissing in the meantime would be nice.

He realized that this situation was a lot like realizing you were plummeting to the earth *after* you'd already jumped out of the airplane. At this point, the only true choice was to pull the ripcord on the parachute. He was going to hit the ground eventually. Might as well try to enjoy the fall. And make the landing as soft as possible.

"Okay, I'm going to go write," he finally said.

"Great idea."

He gave her a little smile. "There's coffee in the kitchen?"

"Keurig," she said with a nod. "You use the little pod things in that."

"Got it."

"And the creamer is in the fridge."

He lifted a brow. "You have the vanilla and caramel creamer?"

"Yes."

"But you didn't know I'd be here." He frowned. "Did you?"

She looked like she was trying to decide how to answer that. It honestly wouldn't surprise him if she told him that yes, she'd known he'd end up out here.

But she said, "That's how I drink my coffee too."

"Medium blend, three vanilla creamers, and one caramel?" he asked.

"Yep."

Realization slowly dawned. "That's how I started drinking it. You made it that way for me one time because that's how you like it."

"You actually took *my* coffee one day and drank half of it before I realized," she returned with a grin.

He felt his mouth curving in response. "Huh."

"Yeah. Huh."

"So I guess I'm good with the coffee situation."

"Guess so."

Suddenly he felt that maybe he was good with a lot of situations here.

He made his way to the bright blue cabin, suddenly

inspired to get to work on the script again. He really did think that just being in the general vicinity of Piper was going to help.

Along with the good coffee.

The three guys that had arrived with Dallas were working on the cabin next to the blue one. They'd gotten about half of the one side painted, but they were doing a lot more talking and laughing and messing around it seemed. At the moment

He stepped into the cabin and immediately took a deep breath.

It smelled like her. Sweet and spicy and, dammit, comforting. That scent made him feel like everything was going to be okay.

He was in trouble.

But your script will be done. At least there's that.

Yep, at least there was that.

He was going to have to deal with being heartbroken while his four best friends were madly in love, but whatever. Actually his *five* best friends. Whitney was in love too. But she and Cam were in love with each other. Did that still count as five friends in love? Yeah, probably. He'd have to see five people all the time who were sickeningly happy and planning their futures with their soul mates.

Ollie rolled his neck and got his thoughts reined in. This was what happened. He'd need to focus on a task and something else would come to mind and he'd spend ten minutes pondering details that had nothing to do with what he needed to get done.

He looked around Piper's cabin. It was not just fully furnished. It was downright cozy. It looked like a place someone spent a lot of time. There were even throw pillows. He frowned. How much time did she spend out here? She was at the office every day, of course. She put in long hours. But it was possible she spent weekends here. Or even some weeknights, he supposed. There were at least a couple of nights a week she was at the hotel. He knew only because she brought him dinner. But they didn't see each other every night. It was very possible she spent some nights out here. In Drew Ryan's backyard.

She doesn't want Drew, he reminded himself.

But Drew had kissed her.

She didn't want Drew because she thought she was in love with Ollie. She was going to get over that. And maybe once she was over him she'd change her mind about Drew.

Ollie felt himself scowling at that thought.

He crossed to the coffeepot. Caffeine was always a good answer.

He found the coffee pods and got his cup brewed and the creamer mixed in the way she'd instructed. Taking a sip, he had to admit that swiping her coffee that morning over two years ago had been a really fortunate accident.

He went to the little kitchen table and pulled out a chair. He looked around again. The place was downright homey. It wasn't fancy like the hotel rooms he and Piper had been living in. But this was very Piper. Which was an odd realization.

Polished and stylish had always been his impression of her. But he was realizing that was on the surface. Which was, of course, as far as he'd let himself look. She knew how to use every piece of technology there was. She knew everything about every social media platform, old and new. She could multitask like a champ. She could sweet talk anyone into anything. She could also tell someone to fuck off—essentially, not literally—all the while smiling and making that person feel like she was being completely respectful and professional.

But within five minutes inside her cabin, Ollie knew that had been a part of her costume. She'd said that's what her dresses and heels had been to him and she was right. Those outfits had given him an image of her that allowed him to put her into a specific box in his mind. A do-not-touch box.

This place was more *her*. Like the blue jeans and tennis shoes and damned sparkly t-shirt.

The cabin was full of bright colors. The walls were a soft yellow, the hardwood floors were covered with multicolored braided rugs, and the furniture—a sofa, love seat, and over-stuffed chair—were a basic light blue but covered in pillows and throw blankets in a variety of shapes and colors. The coffee table held books and two coffee cups, also in different colors. Even the kitchen was a riot of colors. There was a simple white wooden table with four chairs, but the chairs each had a different color cushion. The dish towels were a rainbow of colors as were the dishes. Everything was simple, but colorful. Practical, but fun.

Ollie was so caught up in thinking about all of that, he was startled when Piper came through the door.

"You don't have your computer."

He was sitting at the table, one ankle propped on his opposite knee, his cup halfway to his mouth. He blinked at her.

"Ollie?"

"Yeah?"

"You don't have your computer. Do you?"

He did not. It was in his car. Back at the bakery. He'd planned to plot in his notebook at the bakery to see if being near Piper again helped his creativity and productivity. If it had worked he would have gone to his car to get his bag. But she'd whisked him off to the woods and he hadn't thought of the computer.

Of course he hadn't.

"I don't."

She looked around. It probably seemed that he'd been sitting here daydreaming.

Because he had been.

"Are you going to just write longhand?" she asked.

He did that from time to time when he was stuck. "Sure."

"Where's your notebook?"

In the inside pocket of his jacket. Which was outside in the truck.

He took a drink of his coffee.

She put a hand on her hip. "You don't have your notebook?"

"I haven't started yet. I was mentally preparing," he told her.

She shook her head, clearly not buying it, and crossed to the coffee table.

Hey, he would have eventually realized he needed to go get his notebook.

She moved a couple of books and then turned with a laptop. "You can use my computer. All your stuff is in the cloud. I can get you to it from here."

Oh yeah. Maybe they weren't *clear out* in the woods. "That'll work too, I guess."

It would be great actually. He hated retyping his longhand notes. But sometimes when he got stuck, his brain would start working again if he changed up how he was writing.

She grinned at him as she set the computer on the table and leaned in to type her password in. He caught a whiff of her scent and his body tightened.

"You know, I might need to work in sprints today," he said.

"Good idea." She turned the computer toward him, then leaned on to her forearms on the table. "You can set a timer on your phone."

"And I might need some incentive to look forward to."

"You can come out and help me paint for your breaks."

"I was thinking of something *fun*."

She laughed. "Like what?"

"Like..." He wrapped his hand around the back of her knee and ran his palm up the back of her leg. "Maybe you could reward me for working hard."

Her breath caught and, dammit, there was going to be

heartbreak, but he couldn't help but love the effect he had on her.

"Reward you, huh?"

Their mouths were only a few inches apart with her leaning in like this. "Yeah."

"What kind of reward would most motivate you?"

Her voice was definitely breathless.

He grinned. "How about fifteen minutes of making out for every twenty minutes of work?"

She swallowed and her gaze dropped to his mouth. "A kiss for every half hour of work."

And she was still pushing him. He gave her a slow grin and dragged his hand up to the curve of her butt. "How about ten minutes of making out for every twenty-five minutes of work?"

"Five minutes of making out for every half hour," she countered.

"Five minutes of making out for every twenty minutes."

"Deal."

He squeezed her ass. Then he slid his hand up her back to cup her head and brought her in, relishing her little intake of air. He leaned to brush his mouth over hers on his way to her ear. "You know I'll be a terrible boyfriend, Piper."

She let out a shaky breath. "Are you going to prove me wrong?" she asked softly.

He kissed her neck, breathing in her scent, then sat back and looked at her. With regret that surprised him, he said, "Probably not."

She blew out a breath that seemed frustrated. But she didn't argue.

"I need to go paint," she said.

He nodded. "And I need to get to work."

"Okay." She straightened away from the table. "See you in thirty minutes."

He grinned and gave her butt a little swat. "Twenty minutes."

She was smiling as she went out the door.

He took a second to watch her go. In those jeans. With that ass he'd had his hands on three times now.

Playful, sexy Piper was definitely new.

And he liked her way too much.

On top of already liking her way too much.

Dammit.

He tried to work.

He really did.

He made more coffee. He turned on Norah.

Still, he only got three paragraphs written. Which was, admittedly, more than he'd written in the past week. It still wasn't enough.

But holy shit, the kids working on the cabin next door were distracting as hell.

"You're dead, man!" someone yelled.

Laughter erupted right outside the window in the living room area of Piper's cabin.

"You'll have to catch me, asshole!"

"I'll catch you and make you regret that!"

Ollie rubbed his forehead. The boys had been shouting and laughing, playing their music loud, banging the ladders against the cabin, and just generally being loud and annoying for the past twenty minutes solid.

He was going to make someone regret something.

He was out here in the woods with a woman who was messing with his head and who was, in exchange for him offering up his heart and ego, supposed to be helping him *write his fucking script.*

But these guys were making it impossible.

Something hit the window, making him jump—and that was it.

He shoved his chair back and stomped to the door, jerking it open. He stalked out onto the porch—Piper's cabin was the only one with a porch—and looked around.

One of the kids had just ducked around the side of the cabin they were supposed to be painting. He heard shouting and laughter behind his cabin and then one of them came skidding around the corner.

"Hey!" Ollie shouted.

The kid jerked and stopped, turning to face him.

"What the *hell* are you doing?" Ollie demanded.

The kid—Ollie thought this one was Landon—looked around. "We're just... messing around."

"Aren't you supposed to be working?" He looked toward the cabin. It was still only about half painted on the side he could see.

But the brushes were now strewn across the stubby grass and dirt. The pan of paint had been overturned, the ladder lay on its side, and now as he studied Landon, he noticed streaks of paint down the kid's shirt and jeans.

"Do *not* tell me you were throwing paintbrushes at each other," Ollie told him, scowling.

"We... uh..." Landon looked around again. Clearly hoping for allies.

There weren't any.

"So not only are you not working, but you're wasting the paint and ruining the brushes. *And*"—Ollie added when Landon's mouth opened—"almost breaking my window."

He didn't know a lot about guys this age. He'd been one, of course. But in high school Ollie had not been the type to hang out and goof around with buddies like this. It was probably why he and Dax did a lot of goofing around now. He had lots of fans this age though. Still, he interacted with them online or at conventions. Where Dax was the one who did most of the talking.

Yelling at them was on the don't-do-that list though, he was pretty sure.

"We're just taking a break," Landon said with a shrug. But his face was a little red. "No big deal."

Ollie sucked in a breath, trying to be cool. "I'm trying to work in here," he said, tipping his head toward the cabin. "Your break's been going on for a while. You should get some work done. Since that's what Piper's paying you for."

The kid nodded. "Yeah. I know." He straightened slightly and glanced at the cabin behind Ollie. "You're working out here?"

"Trying to."

"Like on *Warriors* stuff?"

Ollie lifted a brow. "You know *Warriors*?"

The kid laughed. "Uh, yeah."

Okay, so a lot of people, especially people this kid's age, knew *Warriors*. Ollie just wasn't used to running into those people on a typical day in the midst of his usual activities.

He gave an internal eye roll at that thought. Nothing was typical or usual about this day or these activities. He was at a *camp* and in the midst of developing a crush on his ex-assistant.

Then again, that didn't feel new. It was. It had to be. Didn't it? But it didn't feel new. It just felt... dangerous.

"What kind of work on *Warriors*?" Landon asked.

That pulled Ollie back to the fact he was having a conversation. It wasn't as if his thoughts didn't wander—all the time—but man, they got off track even more easily when it came to Piper it seemed. And that was saying something.

"A new script," he told the kid.

Landon's eyes went wide. "No way."

"Yep."

"Like—" Landon glanced at the cabin again. "You're just sitting in there writing a new episode?"

"That's how it works." He'd love if there was some other magical way that happened. But no, he had to sit his ass in front of a computer and *make it* happen.

"That's... cool."

"It really might be." No guarantees. First drafts often sucked. "If I could concentrate."

Landon nodded. "Right. Sorry, man."

The kid actually seemed sheepish now and that made Ollie feel like a dick. It wasn't as if he and Dax hadn't done exactly what these guys were doing. Many times. Just abandoned the work they were supposed to be doing to jack around. For no reason other than they wanted to. He was certain they'd "distracted," i.e., annoyed the hell out of, a number of people over the years. People who had been unfortunate enough to be given the room next to theirs at a hotel. People who had had the bad luck of being seated in front or behind them on an airplane before they'd had a private jet. People who had been trying to enjoy those fountains in Rome that they'd decided to go wading in.

And he and Dax were grown-ups.

Okay, they were adults. By age. They weren't exactly grown-up.

But these were kids. Teenagers out of school early, outside in the nicest weather they'd had in months.

He sighed. "It's okay. No problem."

"No, seriously. I'm sorry. We love *Warriors*. We can be quiet." Landon looked toward the cabin they were supposed to be painting. "I mean, we can be *quieter*."

"Yeah. I..." Ollie blew out a breath. "Tell you what. Give me twenty-five minutes. We'll all just focus, and get some work done. Then I'll need a break, and I'll give you the signal, and you guys can blow off some steam then for a bit. How's that sound?"

"Yeah." Landon nodded. "We could do that. I think."

"Twenty-five minutes," Ollie said. "We can all focus for that long." If he could, these guys could.

"Sure. Yeah."

"Okay." Ollie turned to head back into the cabin, but he pivoted back. "I'm setting a timer. The rules are, work solid for the twenty-five minutes. No breaks, no distractions. See how much you can get done. If you get distracted before the timer goes off, we have to start the twenty-five minutes over. Deal?"

"Sure. Deal." Landon nodded. He looked sincere.

"Okay."

Ollie stepped into the cabin. And sighed. Holy shit. He'd just talked a bunch of kids into work sprints. He'd laid down *rules*. For someone else. What was happening to him?

It had been an hour and nine minutes.

Not that she was counting.

Okay, she was totally counting.

Piper had given Ollie more than the twenty minutes he'd said he was going to work because she'd thought maybe he'd gotten on a roll and didn't want to interrupt him. But an hour and nine minutes? Ollie had never done anything straight for that long. Honestly. Not even Ping-Pong.

As she approached the cabin, she realized that it was quiet. Not Ollie-must-be-hard-at-work quiet. But this-isn't-right quiet. There was no Norah playing, for one thing. But she realized that she should have heard noise from Matt, Landon, and Tanner over here too.

How had she not realized that the boys weren't making any noise several yards back?

She was distracted. By Ollie.

Who was *not* watching the clock and counting down the seconds when he could come claim his "reward" from her—and stop working. Apparently.

This was an interesting-but-kind-of-annoying role reversal.

She poked her head into her cabin, but Ollie wasn't there. Somehow she'd known he wouldn't be.

She looked around from the front porch.

The ladder and painting supplies were beside the next cabin where the boys had been working. There were streaks of paint on the scraggly grass—mostly weeds—and dirt between the two cabins, oddly, but the entire side of the cabin facing hers was painted, and it looked like they'd gotten a good start on the front as well.

So where were they now? They would have had to come past her to get back to their car if they were going to leave, and she knew they would have said goodbye.

Just then she heard a faint shout. She crossed to the end of the porch and peered around the edge of the cabin but didn't see anything. She heard another shout though. It sounded like it was coming from the trees behind the cabins. They were about a football field away, down by the stream. Had the kids gone down there for some reason?

They were seventeen and eighteen. She hardly needed to babysit them. She didn't know if they knew how to swim, but she could assume the guys, having grown up in Appleby, had been around the streams and the river all their lives and were being safe.

No, the reason she headed in that direction was because she was suddenly sure that they were with Ollie.

And *that* she felt the need to check up on.

As she got closer to the trees, their voices got louder, and the sounds of the nearby stream grew.

"Yes! Finally! Awesome!" someone—she thought it was Tanner—cheered.

"Come on, you've got two more."

That was Ollie.

Piper picked up her pace now that she knew for sure he was there with the kids.

"You've got this, Landon! Jump!" a voice, she was pretty sure was Matt, called.

She found a narrow trail into the trees and followed it down a slight incline. A few yards later, she came out at the edge of the stream. On the other side were two of the teens and Ollie.

Matt, Tanner, and Ollie were standing on the ground looking up. She followed their gaze. And her mouth dropped open.

Landon was balanced on a large branch that was about ten feet off the ground. He was clearly getting ready to jump to a branch that was across a space of about three feet.

Piper frowned. It was a long jump, but if he missed that was a decent fall. It wouldn't do any major damage, probably. But he'd be bruised.

"What is going on?" she demanded.

Everyone swung to look at her as she approached, including Landon, who wobbled on the branch. He grabbed ahold of the branch above him, keeping his balance.

"Hey," Ollie greeted. "Landon's almost done."

She looked around. "What are you guys doing?"

Matt gave her a huge grin. "Ollie's got us doing an obstacle course during every break. He adds on to it each time. This time we're doing the branch jumps," he said, indicating Landon and his position overhead.

"Obstacle course?" she repeated. Of course it wasn't a simple walk down to the stream. Not with Ollie involved.

"It's been awesome," Tanner told her. "We work for a while, then we get a break. We just took a hike down here the first time, but then Ollie had the idea to make it into an obstacle course." He pointed to her side of the stream. "We take a running jump onto that rock," he said, indicating the huge rock in the middle of the running water. "Then we jump to the bank. We crawl through the grass, duck under those branches"—he pointed to some shorter trees with branches that hung to the ground in a canopy—"roll to a stand, climb that tree." He then pointed to a tree two trees behind where Landon stood. "We walk across those branches, and now he needs to jump to that tree and swing down."

Piper followed Matt's finger. There was a long rope hanging from a high branch in the tree in front of the one Landon was balancing on.

She looked at Ollie. "You climbed up there and tied that rope?"

"Yeah." He seemed confused by her question.

Of course he had.

She put a hand on her hip. "You're spending your breaks with these guys instead of with me?"

He looked up at Landon. "Yeah, we've been..." Ollie trailed off as he looked back to her, and realization dawned. "Oh. Right. Well, they..." He stopped and cleared his throat.

He'd forgotten. Piper shook her head. Wow. He'd forgotten that she'd agreed to make out with him during his breaks if he focused during his writing sprints.

She'd been upstaged by an obstacle course in the woods with three teenage boys.

She probably should have been hurt or annoyed by that, but honestly... that was exactly in character for Oliver.

Ollie started for her. He jumped to the rock in the middle of the stream, then to the bank on her side of the water. When he was standing right in front of her, he met her eyes and said, "I'm really sorry, Piper."

She sighed. "It's okay. If I'd known there was even a possibility of an obstacle course out here, I would have known I wouldn't see you for a couple of hours."

He gave her a sheepish grimace. "The guys were messing around and distracting me, so I made a deal that if they worked while I wrote, then we'd take breaks together. I thought getting them out here and active and having fun would be good so they would really concentrate on the work when they were at the cabin."

"You had them doing sprints with you?" she summarized.

"Basically."

"Probably a good idea."

That seemed to surprise him. "Yeah?"

"Obviously. They got a lot done," she said.

"They did," he agreed. "Landon especially works better in sprints. He can focus for about twenty minutes on one thing, then he needs to do something else. He can get a lot done, but he needs variety and some structure."

She smiled up at him. Did he realize how much Landon sounded exactly like Oliver himself? "Did you get any writing done?"

He nodded but slowly. "I worked through some things. I've got the scene sketched out. Mostly."

So no, he hadn't really gotten any writing done. "But it's progress?" She actually really did want him to be able to write better out here with her than he did at the office without her.

"It is," he said. "I'm definitely ahead of where I was when I started today."

"Okay. Good."

"You're not going to tell me this is dangerous for them?"

She frowned. "Do you think it's dangerous?"

"I... no. Not really. They're eighteen. Athletes. Relatively bright. And I did everything before I had them try it."

"I think it's okay," she said.

He narrowed his eyes. "Really? I mean, the rock's slippery. Or they could roll in poison ivy. Or they could fall out of the tree."

"So they might need to dry off or get some calamine lotion or an ice pack," she said. "I mean, we *might* need to get some X-rays or a splint, but I don't think any of this will hurt any more than them getting hit in football practice or even some of the stupid shit I'm sure they do on their own."

He still didn't seem convinced.

"What?" she asked.

"You just seem like the type to be concerned about something like this."

"Do I?" she asked. "Or am I the one who forwards your insurance information to the ER in Miami because you lost your wallet and then calls all your credit cards to cancel them... because you lost your wallet? And am I the one that buys you the best heating pad on the market and leaves it on your bed so you see it first thing when you get home from urgent care? And am I the one that reminds you to take your pain meds on time so you can keep the pain under control?"

"You... are," he finally said.

"Exactly. I don't get worked up about bruises and stitches, Ollie. Those are called consequences. I learned a long time ago with my brothers that I could *tell* them not to do something stupid a second time, or I could let the broken rib or torn meniscus remind them."

"Wow." He lifted both brows. "That's harsh."

She laughed. "You clearly know there are risks here. You just spelled three out to me. If you don't want to have to put calamine on for a few days, then don't roll in the grass. I don't need to tell you that."

He moved in a little closer. "Would you help me put the calamine lotion on?"

Now she lifted her brows. "Gladly. Though it's very possible you'd get"—she glanced behind him—"caught up in something else and not even remember that you're... itchy."

"You're mad that I forgot I was going to spend my breaks with you."

"Not mad," she corrected. "Just... horny."

His eyes widened at her answer. She was pretty sure it was the "horny,"not the not being mad. "Really?"

"Are you asking if I've been working and thinking about the chance to make out with you during your breaks and getting excited about it?"

He nodded. "I am."

"Yes, Ollie. I definitely want to make out with you."

"I can take a break now," he said, reaching out.

But she stepped back and shook her head, fighting a smile. This was also a *consequence*. "I need to get things cleaned up and dinner started."

"Dinner?"

"Yes, Ollie. It's almost five, and the chili and everything will take an hour and a half."

"It's almost five?"

She smiled, her heart squeezing. She had no idea why his inability to keep track of anything was so endearing, but it was.

Okay, she had an idea. It spoke to the caregiver in her. She wanted to take care of him. She didn't care that he didn't keep track of the time, because she did. She was always aware of what time it was. It was second nature to her.

It also just *worked*. *They* worked. They fit. They balanced each other out. And she loved that.

Keeping track of time and meetings and details was something she could do for him, and for the company, that was important, something she was good at, something she could contribute. Because the stuff Ollie did? She definitely couldn't do that.

When he lost track of time it was because he was doing things like creating and brainstorming and entertaining. All things she wasn't good at. She'd sat in on brainstorming sessions with the guys before and ended up mostly just taking notes. She could absolutely weigh in on *their* ideas. She knew an amazing idea—and a horrible idea—when she heard it. She could make any of their ideas happen. She knew how to research, reach out, network, and negotiate to make things happen. But just starting with a blank page or a "so what should we do?" just left her sitting there with nothing.

She sometimes got the impression that Ollie and the guys were in awe of her ability to juggle multiple tasks and keep everything running. Yeah, well, she was in awe of *their* ability to just make stuff up, create things out of thin air, sit down with a blank screen and twenty minutes later walk out with a whole new world that hadn't been there before.

Maybe that was romanticizing it—and making it sound simpler than it was, of course—but it seemed pretty magical to her. And she didn't even play the game. She just knew of it.

She didn't have a total lack of imagination. This camp was, hopefully, proving that to her. She could come up with fun things too. But even as a kid, when she'd "played pretend," she'd pretended to be things like a teacher or a mom or a doctor or a scientist. Real things. Things she knew existed. She'd never pretended to have magical powers. She'd never pretended to be a cursed princess.

Of course, she'd also spent a lot of time babysitting and playing with four little boys. There had been a lot of dirt and tree climbing and poison ivy—*real* dirt and poison ivy and yes, broken bones and stitches—in her life as a kid.

Which was fine. Definitely.

But she sometimes wondered if her imagination switch had been turned off at some point.

Whereas Ollie's seemed turned on and the dial pushed all the way to HIGH.

She marveled at that. Even when it made him absent-minded and messy.

"It's almost five," she confirmed. "Dinner's at six thirty." She started to turn to walk back to her cabin.

"So I should..." Ollie said.

She smiled, but then hid it when she turned back. "You should get the boys back up to the cabin to clean up and get them to head home."

"Oh." For just a second, he looked disappointed.

Of course he was. She was sending his playmates home for the day. "They'll be back tomorrow. All day," she told him.

He definitely brightened at that. She laughed and shook her head.

"You could head to Dubuque and get the stuff you're going to need to stay out here for the week," she suggested. She really wanted him to stay. And, dammit, if having this obstacle course to look forward to during his work breaks would make it more fun out here, then she was fine with that.

He didn't even glance at the boys before he nodded though.

"Yeah, I think I'll do that. Maybe even get enough stuff for more than a week."

"Hey, Ollie," Dax answered on the third ring.

Ollie had him on speaker in the car as he drove back to Dubuque. "Hey. You at McCaffery's?"

He could never keep track of which night his friends all got together at Cam's parents' place for dinner. He knew it was once a week. Or more. It seemed like they were always getting together. And yes, as Piper had pointed out, he knew he was always welcome. He just didn't like the big family thing.

"I am," Dax said. "You okay?"

"Yeah. I just thought I'd call and let you all know that I'm with Piper."

Dax paused. "With Piper? You mean like physically at the moment or emotionally and spiritually or what?"

Ollie frowned. "Physically."

"So physically as in sexually or just you're in the same phys-ical location at the moment?" Dax asked.

Ollie sighed. Everyone thought *he* was difficult, but seriously, Dax Marshall could be such a pain in the ass.

"Actually, neither. At the moment," Ollie said, "I'm on my way back to Dubuque by myself right now, but I've been with her all day, and I'm going back out there tonight."

"Okay. Good," Dax said.

"I didn't actually answer your question, you know," Ollie said.

"Which question?"

"Any of them. About if I'm with Piper physically, sexually, emotionally, or spiritually." Whatever the hell being with someone spiritually meant.

"I just assumed you were going to be with her in all the ways," Dax said.

Ollie started to reply. Then he frowned. "We're camping."

"Oh." That seemed to give Dax some pause. "Well, that's... interesting."

"She's starting a camp for kids. She's painting the buildings and stuff."

"Yeah, Jane told me."

Ollie scowled. "You knew?"

"I knew she was working on a project with Drew Ryan on his farm that was going to be some kind of weekend camp for kids," Dax said.

"Why didn't you tell me?"

"Drew Ryan," Dax said simply.

Okay, that was a decent point. It was no secret that Ollie was not a fan of Drew Ryan.

"And because we don't talk about Piper."

"We talk about Piper," Ollie protested.

"We don't talk about how you feel about Piper."

"You know that I feel... good... about Piper." Ollie frowned.

That seemed like a very inadequate description of how he felt about Piper. Even before the blue jeans. "And we talk about her all the time. She's our executive assistant. Hell, our last two morning meetings have been almost entirely about her."

"Because she quit, and we can't function without her."

"We've been functioning without her for a week," Ollie said.

"Sure," Dax said, and Ollie could hear the grin in his friend's voice. "That's why you stomped into Buttered Up this morning and sat sulking at her table until she agreed to take you to camp with her."

"That's not exactly how that happened," Ollie said. But it was kind of how it had happened.

Dax chuckled in his ear.

"How did you hear about that?" Ollie asked. "Never mind." Of course he'd heard it from Josie. Or Zoe. Or from Jane, who had heard it from Josie or Zoe. Or he'd heard it from Grant or Aiden, who had heard it from Josie or Zoe.

Living in a small town was also turning out to be a pain in the ass. At least if he wanted to have any secrets.

"Grant," Dax said, in answer to his question.

As if it mattered.

"I need to write," Ollie said simply. "I can't write at the office without her. So I'm going to be wherever she is until I hit this deadline."

"Well, I have to say that your turning into a reclusive writer living in a cabin in the woods really doesn't require much of a stretch of my imagination," Dax said agreeably.

His tone absolutely indicated that he didn't believe for one second that writing was the reason Ollie had gone looking for Piper.

"Is it really reclusive-writer-in-the-woods stuff if Piper and four teenage boys and fucking Drew and Dallas Ryan are here too?" Ollie asked.

Dax chuckled. "Probably not."

"And you agree that Piper will make sure I'm working."

"Of course she will."

"So this makes sense."

But him being with Piper made sense for other reasons. She made him feel good. She made him feel like he was brilliant and worthy and... safe. Which wasn't very manly, but didn't everyone need to feel safe sometimes? Like they could screw up and it wouldn't be the end of the world? And she thought he was brilliant and worthy without even being a fan of *Warriors of Easton* and with knowing all of his faults and flaws.

The women who thought he was brilliant and adored him at conventions, adored him from afar. That was completely different.

His friends thought he was brilliant and loved him, but some of their perceived "brilliance" came from the fact he'd created something that had been wildly successful for all of them. Sometimes he thought they forgot that Aiden could sell anything to anyone or that Dax was the one who took the stuff Ollie put on paper and made it "real". Dax could turn anything from a rough draft into something even better.

But Piper didn't have a true affinity for *Warriors,* and she definitely wasn't observing him from afar.

Her adoration was real.

That made his heart kick.

Could she *actually* be in love with him?

"Your camping for two weeks with Piper makes sense if you're going to start dating her," Dax said.

Ollie focused on his friend and their conversation again.

Dammit, they were dating. Kind of.

"Yeah, well, it won't surprise you to know that I already screwed that up."

"Oh?" Dax asked.

He did not sound surprised.

"I blew off a... meeting with her earlier." He was such a

dumbass. How had he forgotten about the promise of a make-out session for getting his work done?

But something niggled in the back of his mind. Had he forgotten it? Really?

"On purpose?" Dax asked.

"No." Not exactly. He hadn't thought *Oh, I'm supposed to go make out with Piper, but I'm going to mess around with these guys instead.* "Not consciously anyway."

Dax didn't comment on that.

Ollie wished he would.

"Was she mad?" Dax asked.

"No." She really hadn't been.

She'd been horny about it.

Ollie felt his body respond to that. Just as it had when she'd told him. Horny. He made her horny. He liked that. A lot. Except that it, like everything else when it came to Piper, intimidated him.

That was definitely not manly or alpha or whatever the fuck it was that women wanted in the men who took them to bed.

He didn't worry about that with his convention hookups. They didn't know the real him. Talking didn't matter with them. At least not about things other than *Warriors*. And *Warriors* was the one thing, the one place—fictional though it was—that Ollie felt completely in control and on top of things.

Because he could make shit up there. If something didn't make sense, or he didn't remember something about how things were *supposed* to work, he just changed it. He needed it to rain to make something in the story work? Then he made it rain. He needed someone to be able to fly because that was a lot easier than figuring out how to get them to the top of the mountain any other way? Then he put a flying spell on them.

Well, *he* didn't. He had a goddess do it. Of course.

His convention hookups totally went along with all of that.

Goddesses and out-of-the-blue rainstorms even in a desert? No problem.

He really liked people who just went along. It made his life a lot easier.

A lot easier than the people who thought 10:00 a.m. meant 10:00 a.m. on the dot. Or who thought that 9:57 a.m. was even better. People who would put sticky note after sticky note on his desk reminding him about his ten o'clock meeting every thirty minutes starting at seven o'clock. People who would come into his office at 9:59 a.m., see that he wasn't ready, and would turn the computer on for him, log-in, set a cup of coffee by his mouse, and point to the screen with one eyebrow up. While her breasts and ass were looking amazing in a fitted little sweetheart sweater, wide shiny leather belt, and skirt that clung and made her hips wiggle when she walked.

Ollie scrubbed his free hand—the one not on the steering wheel—over the back of his neck.

Obviously, he'd noticed Piper at work before. *Everyone* noticed Piper everywhere she went. But in those skirts with everything perfectly ironed and coordinated and not a piece of lint or a stray thread to be found, she'd seemed untouchable. And he'd abided by that message. He hadn't touched. He put it out of his mind completely as a matter of fact.

Which was why his friends' hints and insinuations that she had feelings for him had annoyed the shit out of him. He *needed* to ignore all of that.

Because her reminders and sticky notes and turning his computer on and getting him coffee *had* made his life easier.

Well, it had made it easier to not miss video conference calls anyway.

He really hated those conference calls.

He'd much rather be making it rain in the desert.

Still, he had to be on those calls, so Piper had made his life easier in that he hadn't had to deal with the consequences of missing those calls.

Yeah, he'd been intimidated by Piper, and now, even in blue jeans, even wanting her with an intensity that completely shocked him, he was intimidated by the idea of making out with her, of having a relationship with her, of getting closer to her and being her boyfriend.

Because he was going to be really terrible at this.

"So you didn't blow anything off on purpose, and she wasn't mad, so no problem," Dax said.

Ollie sighed. "But she should be mad, right? I mean, she shouldn't have to put up with that from the guy she's dating."

"Oliver," Dax said, his tone more serious. And really, just his use of Ollie's full name indicated that he was about to say something important. "Piper Barry knows herself and she knows you. I don't know that you could surprise her at this point."

Ollie shook his head. "I really have no idea why she wants to be with me."

"None of us deserve our girls," Dax said. "I don't know why Jane wants to be with me. But I'm fucking grateful she does. And I do know that being with someone doesn't mean never messing up. It just means that when you realize it, you try to make up for it."

Ollie thought about that. "So instead of avoiding her, I need to try to be worth the aggravation when I *am* there."

Dax chuckled. "Something like that." Then he said more seriously. "I can tell you that, while it's sometimes annoying not knowing if you're going to show up for dinner on time, or at all, when you are *there*... when we're wading in Roman fountains and jumping out of airplanes and up onstage at Comic Con, there's no one else I'd want to do those things with."

Ollie was surprised by the jab of emotion in his chest. "Yeah?" he asked.

"Of course."

"Not even Jane?"

"I'm madly in love with Jane," Dax said. "But some people are in our lives to eat strawberry pie with, and some are in our lives to jump out of planes with. I need you both, man."

Ollie knew it was absolutely not alpha-manly—yes, he spent too much time on fan forums where they discussed things like that about fictional characters—to be touched by another man telling him that. But he was.

"Thanks," he told Dax.

"Definitely. But you've got your skydiving partner," Dax said. "You really need to have a strawberry-pie partner."

"You think?"

"Absolutely. You don't know what you're missing."

Dax had been more of a convention-hookup, women-loving playboy before he'd met Jane than Ollie ever had been. Probably in part because Dax did like to actually *talk* to people.

"I don't know about strawberry pie," Ollie said after a moment. "But can I substitute s'mores?"

10

———

Piper realized she was humming while she cooked.

But, dammit, the guy she was in love with was on his way back to camp out with her for the next week—or more—and give this thing a chance.

Kind of.

He was coming back because she refused to return to the office, and he'd made progress on his script, and he now had a playground and new friends to goof around with.

Still, he was coming back to camp. With her.

She just couldn't help feeling pretty damned optimistic. He was so going to fall in love with her.

She'd gotten all of her painting supplies put away when the guys got back from the stream. Landon was walking upright, with no assistance, so she assumed he'd made the jump from tree to tree without mishap. She'd come inside to start cooking as they cleaned up from their day's work and the kids had headed out. Then Ollie had asked Dallas if he'd take him back up to the house. He'd asked her for her car keys, said he'd fill her car up when he got back from grabbing a bunch of clothes and toiletries from Dubuque, and had kissed her on the top of the head.

He'd kissed her on the top of the head.

That was the stupidest thing to be thrilled about but... that was a dating thing.

It certainly wasn't something you did to your assistant. Well, not your professional assistant that you didn't think of as anything more anyway. And it wasn't something you did to someone you were just hooking up with at a weekend convention.

Top-of-the-head kissing was something you did to someone you were dating.

At least in her mind.

She frowned as she stirred the chili.

Then she reached for her phone.

She dialed Paige's number without even hesitating.

Paige was a self-proclaimed commitment-phobe.

Who was now living in Louisiana because of a guy she was crazy about.

Of course she claimed she was just there temporarily, having some fun, taking a break from Appleby and her nosy, determined-to-marry-her-off family, having hot sex, for sure, but nothing more. But Piper had seen the way Paige looked when she talked about Mitch.

There was something more there. Piper would bet her favorite t-strap sandals with the cherries on the toes on it.

She wondered if Paige had figured that out yet though.

She also wondered if Paige had kissed Mitch on the head yet.

Or, at least, how she'd feel if he kissed her on the head.

"Hey!" Paige greeted after the third ring.

There was a lot of noise on her end of the line.

"Hey, is this a bad time?"

"No, why?"

Piper heard a door slam and the background noise dropped significantly.

"Sounds like you're at a party."

Paige laughed. "Oh, that's just dinnertime. It always sounds like that here."

"Wow."

"I know, right?"

"So not really a break from the big-family thing you had here?"

"Well..." Paige paused, "it should seem the same, I know," she said. "It's a big family, and everyone is always around and in each other's business, but it feels different here."

"You're *not* engaged to Mitch yet, then?" Piper teased.

Paige laughed again, and honestly, Piper wasn't sure she'd heard her friend this happy. She hadn't known Paige long, but the other woman had always come across as more snarky and sassy than carefree or... well, happy. Not that Paige had been bitchy, but she'd had a lot of expectations put on her in Appleby, and it had seemed that she had been in a constant state of rebellion.

"I'm not," Paige confirmed. "But I am having fun here."

"I'm so glad."

"So what's up with you?" Paige asked. "I'm glad to hear your voice. I miss you."

Piper smiled at that. They hadn't spent years together, but when Piper had started taking classes at Paige's yoga studio, they'd bonded pretty quickly.

"I miss you too," she said. "I actually have a question for the only other anti-relationship person I know."

Things were even quieter on Paige's end of the phone now as if she'd gone into another room or walked away from the group of people she'd been with. Piper heard a birdcall and she could have sworn water lapping.

"Where are you?"

"I walked down to the dock," Paige said. "It's so different here, Piper." She sighed. "They're all loud and bossy, and it's hot here already and it's only March. There are real live alligators roaming around, and holy shit, these people eat spicy-as-hell food. But it's really... nice."

"Maybe you're not as anti-relationship as you once were?" Piper asked.

That gave her some hope. If Paige could come around, maybe Ollie could too.

"I don't know about that."

"Oh." Well, so much for that theory.

"I have a lot to work out there," Paige said. "But tell me what *you're* talking about. I know you're not talking about *you*. So I assume you mean Ollie?"

Piper sighed, stirring her spoon through the chili. "Yeah." Paige knew how she felt about Ollie. Well, everyone did, more or less, but Piper had actually confided in Paige. Paige knew she was in love with him and wanted more.

"What did he do? Or not do?"

"He kissed me back when I kissed him."

There was a long beat of silence on Paige's end. Then she said, "Well, holy shit, that's awesome, Piper!"

Piper nodded even though her friend couldn't see her. "Yeah. It was. It was hot and he was all in on the kiss. I mean, I was the one who pulled back and said no to it going further."

"But..."

Piper pictured Paige's confused expression.

"*Why?*"

Piper actually chuckled. "Because I want *more*. I want it all. And he wasn't going *there*."

"Oh well..." Paige was clearly thinking about that. "I mean, that can lead to more."

"Is that what happened with you and Mitch?" Again, Piper felt the bubble of hope rise up. She probably needed to talk to *Mitch* and see what he was doing to convince her beautiful, stubborn, skittish-about-love friend to give him a chance. But hearing Paige's perspective—which was more like Ollie's perspective—was probably also helpful.

Paige sighed into the phone. The sound was a bit wistful and a bit *oh yeah*. "It sure didn't hurt," she finally said. "I mean, making me want more of that certainly played in his favor when he wanted me to come to Louisiana."

Piper stirred her spoon through the thick soup without seeing it. "Hmm," she said out loud.

Paige laughed softly. "Yeah, I'm not telling you *not* to sleep with him. But Mitch also refused to let me make it only about that."

"How did he do that?"

"By not letting me push him away. By being around. By not letting me forget about him. By being... him."

She stopped, but Piper had the sense that she was thinking through her answer, and Piper stayed quiet, letting her gather all her thoughts.

"The thing is, he's being so patient," Paige finally said. "He lets me know all the time that he wants me, but there is something undeniably sexy about someone who is content to just be with you and who likes you, wherever you're at in figuring it all out, who will just take whatever you can give."

Piper repeated that in her mind. Then she groaned. "I just have to be patient?"

Paige laughed. "While also letting him know that you want him."

Piper chewed on her bottom lip. "Is Mitch going to win you over eventually?"

Paige sighed. "I guess all I can say right now is that he's going to make it incredibly hard to leave in the end. Harder than it's ever been."

Piper felt her stomach twist. "Ugh, why did I call you? I should have called head-over-heels-crazy-in-love Whitney."

Paige snorted. "You called me because you wanted someone who would tell you that you need to respect there could be a very good reason Ollie doesn't want to or can't commit."

She knew that. Dammit. "Maybe I called because I knew I'd need Mitch's number, so I'd have a friend to call when we were both sitting at home with broken hearts."

"Maybe."

Paige didn't laugh that off and that made Piper frown. "You really might break that guy's heart?"

"I don't want to," Paige said. "But I guess? Maybe? But I was honest with him going in."

Piper knew that too. Paige was very up front and Mitch had still wanted her to come to Louisiana. "Ollie has been too."

"Then you're going in at your own risk."

"Yeah."

"Is that why you haven't slept with him?" Paige asked. "Because you know he could still walk away, and if you sleep together, you'll be even more devastated?"

Piper thought about that. If she had, it had been subconsciously. But finally, she said, "No. When I kicked him out of my room it was because I fully intended that to be it and I was going to work on getting over him."

"And now?" Paige asked. "Why aren't you sleeping with him now?"

"Because he's not here at the moment."

Paige laughed. "Is he coming back?"

"He is." That she knew for sure. Now. Because of the kiss on the head.

"And what about then?"

"Well, does sleeping with Mitch make it harder to walk away?"

Paige was quiet for a couple of seconds. "I was going to say that you can't sleep with him hoping that will make him want to stay. You can't use sex that way. But—"

"But?" Piper asked when Paige stopped.

"I guess the sex with Mitch does make it harder to think about leaving. And…" She blew out a breath. "That's never happened before. The sex hasn't made a difference before."

"So it's not just about orgasms."

"Nope," Paige said, not even pretending to laugh that off. "I'd want to hang out with him even if he wasn't the best I'd ever had. And I guess, in this case, that makes the sex important. If we *hadn't* slept together, I wouldn't realize that. I wouldn't realize that this is not just a friendship, but it's also not just a fling."

Piper was surprised. "He's the best you've ever had?"

"For sure. And I think it's because of the liking him thing." Paige actually sounded a little confused. "I mean, it's absolutely all of his, ahem, attributes and skills."

She said it lightly, and Piper could perfectly picture the mischievous grin she was wearing. It was a Paige Asher staple.

"But I think what makes him better than all the rest is that I really, truly *like* him too."

"Man, I hope he's way out of earshot," Piper teased. "You'd hate for him to overhear all of this."

"Oh, you have no idea."

"Thanks for the insight, babe," Piper said. "I know why I called you. You always give it to me straight."

"Always," Paige said sincerely. "And I'll be here if all of my advice ends up sucking and you get your heart broken."

Piper appreciated that her friend was acknowledging that could still happen. She wasn't sugarcoating things. Or saying she had all the answers. She was just being honest about what she knew and felt.

"Can I come to Louisiana if I need to get away?" Piper asked.

"Oh, honey, yes," Paige said, taking on a bit of a Southern accent, making Piper laugh. "They have moonshine down here that will take away all your bad memories—hell, some of the good ones too probably—not to mention stripping the paint off your walls." She laughed. "And there are definitely some hot Louisiana boys who would be happy to be your rebound."

Piper smiled but her heart was already rejecting the idea of being with anyone else. Ever. Ugh, she was in so much trouble.

"I can't imagine ever wanting anyone else," she confessed.

Paige sounded sympathetic when she said, "Well, then, you can just play with the otters. You can't be unhappy when you're playing with otters."

"Otters?" Piper asked.

"Oh yeah, they have this swamp boat tour company, Boys of the Bayou," Paige said. "But they're starting this otter encounter on the side, too. People can pet and play with and feed otters. They are so cute. In fact, they're starting this whole petting zoo on the side. It's hilarious, because they're calling it Boys of the Bayou Gone Wild, but it's otters and alpacas and goats and rabbits and stuff. Nothing very wild at all."

Piper smiled at the affection she heard in her friend's voice. "It sounds like you like it there."

"I'm doing otter yoga," she said. "We do yoga while otters run around. It's super distracting and nothing like cat yoga, but yeah..." Her voice softened. "I do like it here."

"I'm really glad. Even though I miss you and could *really* use some girl time."

"Well, I'm just a phone call away," Paige said. "And I'm only here temporarily."

Uh-huh. Piper wasn't so sure about that.

She heard the sound of a car outside and looked out the window over the sink in the mini-kitchen. Her heart flipped. Ollie was back.

"I'm gonna let you go," Piper said.

"Oh, did your man finally get back?" Paige asked.

Her man. Yeah. Well, he was for now. He was willing to have campfire dates. Paige had said that there was something really sexy about someone who was willing to just be with you where you were. She could do that.

"Yeah. I think I need to show him what this can be."

"You do," Paige agreed. "Make it damned hard for him to leave next time."

"Wow, from the commitment-phobe queen?"

"Who would know better how to do this?"

"Exactly," Piper said with a grin.

They said goodbye and disconnected just as Ollie came through the door.

"Piper? I—" He saw her and stopped. Both walking and talking.

"Hey."

"Holy shit."

Piper snorted. She looked at the stove, then down at herself. "What?"

She was wearing the flannel from that afternoon, but it was on top of a white tank top and a pair of cut-off gray sweatpants.

Ollie tossed his duffle to the side and swung the door shut. He shoved a hand through his hair and shook his head.

"The normal-girl thing is still catching me off guard," he said.

Piper laughed. "Well, get used to it. I'm not cooking in any of my work dresses, no matter what you say."

He seemed to have gotten over his initial surprise. His gaze went over her again. From the high ponytail she wore to her bare feet. Slowly. Twice.

"I'm not sayin' I don't like this look. I'm just still adjusting to what it does to me."

Piper let her gaze travel over him as well. She didn't see any super-obvious effect, but she liked the idea that he was a little rattled.

Just having him in the cabin with her was making her heart beat faster.

"I've always really liked you in suits," she said. "But you do very nice things to jeans and Henleys too."

The corner of his mouth curled. "I'm also getting used to us saying things like that to one another."

She shrugged. "Yeah. It might take some practice. But I think this is good. Normal, *real* stuff." She gestured toward the table. "Like dinner. It's ready."

She dished up the chili and cornbread muffins and lettuce salads she'd made and set them on the table as he washed his hands at the sink and took a seat.

This definitely felt intimate to her. Different.

She'd cooked for him several times. And she loved when he told her how much he liked it. They'd eaten together. Lunches over their desks. Even a few lunches and a couple of dinners at restaurants. One had been pizza at nearly midnight after they'd put in a sixteen-hour day. One had been a nice dinner at an upscale Chicago seafood restaurant celebrating the sale of *Warriors of Easton* to Plus Gaming Ltd., the company that had bought the guys out just over a year ago.

That dinner had been with all the other guys too. She'd been surprised, though touched, they'd included her, in fact. And she'd spent the evening feeling a little sad about the whole situation. She'd suspected Ollie had been less than ecstatic as well.

The sale had resulted in a lot of money for them all, of course, but she wasn't so sure that Ollie had been ready to give *Warriors* over to someone else. She also had the impression that he was a little hurt the other guys had been so enthusiastic about the sale.

She tried to shake that off as she took her seat at the table with him.

This was a first. A meal she'd prepared that they were going to eat together. Just them. In an isolated cabin in the woods. Alone. After having admitted their attraction, and shared a scorching kiss.

She already wanted more of this.

And he hadn't even taken the first bite.

"Did you want to sell *Warriors*?"

"This is amazing."

They both spoke at the same time.

Ollie looked up at her. "What?"

Piper tucked a foot under her butt. "When Plus Gaming came to you guys, what was your first reaction? Did you want to sell?"

"Why do you ask?" He took another bite.

She should let him eat. But now, for some reason, she really wanted to know this. Maybe because she really wanted to know *him*. Or she wanted proof that she already did know him.

"I got the impression when we went to dinner that night, all of us, to celebrate, that you weren't as happy as everyone else."

He swallowed his bite and wiped his mouth with his napkin. Then he met her eyes. "I wasn't."

She nodded. "Then—"

"I got the impression you weren't either."

She lifted a brow. "I wasn't."

"Why not?"

She tore off a piece of her muffin and ate it, thinking about how she should answer that. It was none of her business what the guys did with their company. She shouldn't have had an opinion one way or another. But after she swallowed, she answered honestly. Because that's what she wanted from him.

"I was afraid I wouldn't have a job anymore. For one thing."

He smiled slightly. "I was a little worried about that too. For me."

"You thought *you* wouldn't have a job?"

"It's not like I'm really qualified to do anything else," he told her.

"What was your degree in?" She should know this and was surprised to realize she didn't.

"I have a basic business degree."

"You do?" She leaned in. "You *hate* business. Everything about that side of things. Getting you to fill out forms or look at a spreadsheet is like pulling teeth."

"I didn't say I liked it or was good at it. You asked what my degree was in."

She grinned. "How'd you even pass enough classes to get that degree?"

But she answered with him when he said, "Grant."

He nodded. "He pulled me through."

"He made you do it."

"Yeah. I was going to drop out. When the game took off, I figured what did I need a degree for?"

"You were going to drop out? Seriously?"

"Lots of very creative and successful people don't have college degrees."

"Okay. But... you really didn't want one?"

"I didn't like school." He was stirring his chili and took a bite after he said that.

She didn't have trouble believing that, actually. Sitting still, studying, showing up to things at specified times, doing things the way other people thought he should... none of that was really Ollie.

"Why didn't you do graphic design or computer science like Dax?" she asked. "At least you would have liked that."

He actually laughed at that. "I wasn't good at the business stuff, but I *really* sucked at the computer stuff."

"Really?"

"Yep. They thought about having me take the classes Aiden had so he could help me, but he was doing more management stuff, and it was a lot of public speaking and group projects. Definitely not my thing," he said. "They thought maybe I should follow Cam, but he just got a basic English degree once he decided on law school, and there was no way I was going to do all that reading."

She was staring, she knew. "They all got together and decided which degree you should get?"

"I was going to drop out," he repeated. "They all said no way, that they'd get me through somehow. So we sat around and decided what would make the most sense."

"You mean, what would be the easiest."

He leveled her with a look. "Yeah."

She had not known any of this. But now that she thought about it, she really could see how Ollie would have hated school.

"But you really thought you wouldn't have a job if you sold?"

"We made it a condition of the sale," he said. "Well, Cam did. That was him and Grant. I had to continue on as creative director and head writer or no deal."

Damn, she really liked those guys. "They were looking out for you."

"Always," he agreed. "So, like I said, I'm not qualified to do anything else."

She studied him as he ate. She took a few bites too.

"So what was the other reason you didn't want us to sell?" he asked after a bit.

"What?"

"You said you were worried about your job *for one thing.* What was the other?"

She lifted a shoulder. "It just felt sad. Like what brought you guys together was ending. And…" She bit her lip.

"What?" He was watching her now.

"It bothered me that you seemed bothered," she told him.

He put a piece of cornbread in his mouth and chewed, looking at her. Then he asked, "You weren't happy because the other guys were happy?"

She shook her head. "I like the other guys. I'm glad when they're happy about things. But—" She leaned in. "I'm in love with *you*. So your feelings matter more to me than theirs do."

Something flickered in his eyes. She'd told him she was in love with him before, but it seemed like each time she said it, he was less surprised. Maybe it was sinking in. Maybe eventually he would start liking to hear it.

Maybe he'd eventually say it back…

She straightened. She couldn't get ahead of herself here. Paige had warned her that she had to respect that he might have very good reasons for how he felt and that he might still walk away.

She wasn't going to hold back her feelings from him, but she had to not expect to get all those same feelings in return. That wasn't fair to either of them.

"Do you regret it?" she asked. "Selling?"

He set his spoon down and rested an elbow on the table, leaning in. "We're going to do this intimate, share our feelings, get-to-know-each-other thing, huh?"

Her heart tripped. She wanted this. "Yes."

"Okay, then… no. Not regret. Exactly. I miss it. I wish we could have stayed the way we were forever. But Dax, Aiden, Cam, and Grant are like brothers to me. I would do anything for them. They wanted to sell so I said yes. And I would do it again."

She saw his sincerity. And heard it. And she wanted to hug him so badly she almost came out of her chair.

"Do you feel like they didn't respect *you* or your friendship?" she asked. "It was your creation. If you didn't want to sell, then—"

"No." He cut her off firmly.

"No?"

"Those guys have given me more friendship than I've ever given them back, Piper," he said, his voice a little rough.

She looked into his eyes, studying them, thinking about the five men she knew and had observed, together and individually, over the past five years. "You didn't tell them you didn't want to sell."

"No."

She reached out. She couldn't help it. She laid her hand on his arm. "You are a good friend, Ollie. You love them. They know that."

He snorted. "I blow off birthdays. I forget to check my texts. No one would dream of asking me to pick them up from the airport or water plants while they're out of town or anything like that."

Well, all of that was true. Still, she squeezed his arm. "They love just being around you. You make them happy. They like *you*. Not the things you do… or don't do… for them. They're grown men, who happen to be millionaires. They can all get rides from the airport and hire people to water their plants."

"You're missing the point on purpose," he said.

"I know." She took a breath. "I'm just saying that it's not just about that kind of stuff."

"Well, good, because I can guarantee that I will forget to send you flowers on Valentine's Day."

She worked to focus. He was making a point. But, of course, her mind went off on a Valentine's Day—*that's months and months away. He thinks we'll still be dating by then? Woo-hoo* —tangent.

"I can get my own flowers when I want them, Ollie," she

said, with total composure. That was also true. She didn't need him to send her flowers. But would it be nice? Of course.

"Again, you're missing the point. On purpose."

"Okay," she acknowledged. "Well, I do think that if it's a day like that, one that stays the same all the time, is clearly marked on every calendar, and is widely advertised in every medium, that perhaps, you could *try* to remember it."

He nodded. "What I *should* do, is hire a really competent assistant who could take care of things like sending flowers on appropriate holidays for me."

"Getting flowers that were actually sent from someone else because you couldn't, or didn't, remember doesn't mean anything."

"It does if the other person doesn't know that they're from someone else."

"But I would."

"Another reason this will probably not work out between us."

She blew out a breath. "Another reason that we should probably just stay away from flower deliveries."

"Another reason you should come back and just be my assistant."

"You mean be someone who coddles you."

"Yes."

"No." She squeezed his arm. "Come on, Ollie. You can do better. You know you can."

He didn't say anything to that. She had the sense that he wanted to argue, but he just dug back into his chili instead.

Sometimes Dax drove her crazy with his talking. But she doubted Jane ever had to wonder what was on her fiancé's mind.

They finished eating, and Piper had a rock in her stomach the entire time.

Was forcing, or even cajoling, Ollie to try this relationship thing with her what she really wanted? Of course not. She wanted him to want this.

But there was something about the story he'd told about selling *Warriors* just because the guys had wanted to sell that was niggling at her.

He would do anything for the people he cared about.

Even the stuff he didn't want to do. Stuff he didn't like. Stuff that made him uncomfortable. He wasn't the manipulative type. He didn't do things to get people to do things for him in return. So she didn't believe he was just here to get his script finished. She also didn't believe that he hoped this made her realize she was *not* in love with him so that she'd come back to work. He had agreed to stay at the camp because she wanted him to. Even if he didn't like it.

She thought about that as they cleaned up from dinner.

They didn't really talk. Nothing more than, "Where should I put this?"

"Second cupboard," type of stuff.

But they cleared the table, stored the leftovers, and did the dishes together.

And the entire time, Piper's mind spun.

Oliver was the brains of *Warriors of Easton*. Well, he was the imagination. Grant and Aiden were the brains, she supposed. At least when it came to the business. Cam was the muscle. Metaphorically, anyway. He protected the brand and the trademark, took care of the contracts, covered the legal aspects. Dax was the artist, the one who brought it all to life, but he was really the heart. He was the one who interacted with the fans and brought the enthusiasm and color—literally—when it came to the game graphics to *Warriors*.

Oliver was the imagination. The creator. The... god. Really. It all came from him first. Without him, there would be no characters or magical lands for Dax to draw and color. There would be no franchise to protect and expand. Or sell.

Warriors of Easton was *Ollie's*.

But the guys had taken it over, grown it, and then sold it.

Oliver had gone along with that.

She surreptitiously watched as he dried the bowls. He'd just gone along with that. Why?

Because he would do anything for the people who mattered to him.

He put friendship and relationships and love ahead of everything else. Ahead of business and money.

And now he was out here with her. At a campground. Agreeing to help paint buildings and finding a way to get her other hired hands to be more productive and even willing to sit around a campfire with her and make s'mores.

She didn't need flowers from this man. She didn't need him to remember that it was Valentine's Day. She didn't need him to remember details. She was a master at details. She was almost *too* good at details.

She wanted to be a part of Oliver's big picture. And if he needed to be with her to write, maybe she already was.

"You ready for our date?" she asked, holding up the bag of marshmallows she'd laid on the counter.

He looked from them to her. "Our date?"

She laughed. "Campfire and s'mores time."

"That's a date?"

"Well, it's not a business meeting."

"We could talk business."

Piper remembered what Paige had said. "Okay. We can talk business. But I'm having *s'more* than that." She grinned at her own pun, gathering up the s'mores ingredients and grabbed a blanket from the back of the couch.

"Our previous business meetings were just missing s'mores?" he asked, following her out of the cabin nevertheless.

"Every get-together of any kind can be improved with

s'mores," she said sincerely. "Wait until you try the bourbon-infused marshmallows I have on order."

"Damn, you're serious about s'mores," Ollie said.

She turned and pinned him with a gaze. "When I want s'more, I want *s'more*."

He gave her a little smile. "Noted."

She tossed the blanket over one of the benches and set the marshmallows, chocolate bars, and graham crackers on the stump that acted as a little table between two benches.

Drew and Dallas had built the wooden benches a couple of months ago, but because they'd been in the midst of the coldest part of the winter in Iowa, they had yet to be used. They'd been made out of tree trunks carved out with chainsaws, sanded just to where they weren't too rough to sit on, then finished to withstand most of the elements.

The benches circled the stone firepit. Each bench was about as long as a love seat, which meant three or four kids could sit together, depending on the size of the kids, but only a couple of adults.

Piper chose the middle bench, and Ollie sank down beside her. She was pleased he hadn't taken a separate bench. She'd brought a cookie sheet along and set it on top of the stone edge of the firepit. She spread the s'mores ingredients out on it so they could be easily assembled as the marshmallows toasted.

She'd also purchased special marshmallow roasting sticks. They were extra long, metal, with multiple prongs at the end, and colored plastic ends. She could, of course, have the kids—and Ollie—toasting marshmallows on actual wooden sticks they picked up from the campsite, the way God had intended it, but these seemed safer, and more sanitary. They even came in a little rack that they could keep out here by the firepit.

She handed one with a green handle to Ollie.

He put three marshmallows on the end of his and then looked at her.

She just looked back. She loved just looking at him. She loved being here with no desk between them. Toasting marshmallows was the only task on either of their to-do lists for the evening.

They'd been alone together at the office a number of times, but while she'd been tempted to kiss him several times, there had always been the he's-your-boss thing hovering between them.

That was gone now.

Her gaze dropped to his mouth.

"Piper?"

"Yeah?"

"Don't we need a fire?"

She could just lean in and put her lips against his. She really thought there would be plenty of fire, then. But she nodded. "Yeah."

She turned toward the firepit and dug into the pocket of her shorts for the little box of wooden matches.

"I bought easy-starter logs at the store, but I can teach you to build a fire from regular wood and sticks if you want."

She leaned over the edge of the pit, rearranging the logs a bit, then struck a match, lighting the bottom log.

"Ollie?" she asked. He didn't answer, and she looked over her shoulder.

His gaze was fully on her ass.

She smirked. "Hey, Ollie?"

"Yeah?"

"Do you want to learn to build a fire?"

"I really prefer watching you do it."

She straightened and turned to face him. "See? This date is going well so far."

His gaze climbed to her face. Slowly. Taking his time as he went from her hips over her stomach, breasts, and mouth on his way to meeting her eyes. "It's the clothes."

She gave him a knowing smile. "Not just the jeans and the bathrobe, then?"

"The real-girl clothes. *Any* real-girl clothes."

She propped a hand on her hip, feeling the warmth of the flames building behind her. Paige had also said the sex made it harder to think about walking away from Mitch.

"You don't think you would want to kiss me right now if I was wearing one of my regular dresses?"

"I want to fill my hands with your ass. I didn't say I wanted to kiss you."

"Ah." She stepped closer to him. "That's true."

He straightened but spread his knees. She stepped between them. "Well, Oliver," she said. "I'm very happy to have any part of you on any part of me."

"Oh yeah?" He lifted his hands without hesitation and cupped her ass in his big palms.

The warmth licking down her legs and through her stomach had nothing to do with the fire behind her.

"Yeah," she told him.

He squeezed. "I like these shorts."

"They don't make you want to kiss me at all?"

"Well..."

Then he shocked the hell out of her by leaning in and pressing his lips to her stomach.

Her tank top was between her skin and his mouth but damn, it didn't seem to matter. Her nipples tightened, her inner muscles tightened, and she sucked in a little breath.

He looked up, and his gaze zeroed in on her hard nipples. The tank was fitted and thin enough that there was no way to miss them. They grew even tighter with his attention on them.

"Pull your shirt up, Piper," he murmured as he squeezed her ass.

Oh Lord yes. They didn't need to talk. They'd talked at dinner. That was enough. She didn't even think about *not* complying. She raised the hem of the shirt, preparing to shrug out of her flannel and strip the tank off entirely. But she'd only lifted it past her belly button when Ollie put his mouth against her again.

The feel of his hot mouth on bare skin, *any* bare skin, sent shock waves of lust through her body. She lifted a hand to the back of his head, his name coming out as a husky whisper, *"Ollie."*

Then he made her knees nearly buckle by dragging his mouth back and forth, abrading her skin with the stubble around his mouth and along his jaw. Goose bumps broke out and spread like fireworks bursting from that point of contact.

She gasped.

Could she orgasm from the simple touch of his mouth on her *stomach*?

With this guy? It was possible. It might be a little embarrassing, but she wasn't sure she cared at the moment.

He lifted his head and looked up at her. "How about some s'mores?"

She blinked down at him.

She wasn't sure she'd ever wanted to kiss someone more. His lips were right there. His eyes were on hers. She had his complete and total attention. She'd experienced his full focus a few times in the past. It was always short lived, but when it happened it was potent.

"Piper?" he asked.

"Yeah?" She was vaguely aware that she sounded distracted.

"S'mores?"

Oh, she wanted some more all right.

She would really love to make *him* into a giant, real-life s'more. She could wipe melted chocolate and marshmallow on his lips and lick it off. She could smear melted chocolate and marshmallow on his—

"Piper?" He added a pinch to her ass this time as his mouth tipped up into an incredibly sexy smile.

Her eyes went to his. "What?"

"S'mores." It wasn't a question this time.

She blinked. "Yes." She wanted s'mores. *On him.*

"Good grief, is this what it's like to talk to me all the time?" He actually nudged her back as he grinned.

She blinked again and tried to focus. Was this what it was like to... She shook her head. Then thought about his question. "Yes," she said truthfully. "It's very much like that."

He chuckled. "That's gotta be annoying."

She stepped back, took a breath, and took her seat next to him. "Well, if you were zoning out because you were thinking about the things I was just thinking about, I would be *very* forgiving about your distraction."

"Oh?"

She nodded. "If you wanted to cover me in melted chocolate and marshmallow and lick it all off, you could daydream all day long."

His eyes heated, and Piper felt her lower stomach tighten. Wow.

"That's what you're thinking about?" he asked.

"Yep."

He didn't say anything to that, so she stuck two marshmallows on the end of her stick and extended it toward the fire. She acted completely nonchalant, but the truth was, her heart was pounding so hard in her chest, she was certain Ollie would be able to hear it.

"But we're getting to know each other too," he said, also reaching to get his marshmallows into the edge of the fire.

"Right."

"You realize *that* could be counterintuitive."

"As in, getting to know you could turn me *off*?" she asked. Did he really think that? But it would make sense why he didn't really date. He didn't let women know him beyond what they already did—he was handsome, rich, and the talented, successful creator of *Warriors*.

"Exactly."

"But I already know you." She turned her marshmallow to toast the other side. "This is more about you getting to know me. And that's only going to make you want me more. No matter what I'm wearing."

She understood the theory that her clothes were making him look at her differently and getting her out of the mental box he'd put her in, but it annoyed her a bit too. She definitely wanted to get to the point where what she wore didn't matter.

It hasn't even been a day. You've been in love with him for two years. You have to give him time to catch up.

"I have ADHD."

It took her a second to pull herself out of her thoughts and to realize what he'd said. She looked over at him.

He met her eyes. "I have ADHD," he said again.

She paused. How should she respond? It was clear he thought he was laying a big reveal on her.

Finally she said the only thing she really could. "I know."

11

____

Now it was Ollie's turn to blink at Piper. Then frown.

He shook his head. "I don't mean *I'm a little ADHD* as in I have a hard time sitting still and paying attention. I've actually been diagnosed. I was diagnosed as a kid, but I didn't grow out of it the way some do."

Piper realized she needed to tread carefully here. He was sharing with her and she *loved* that. This was not something he likely talked about often. Or ever. But she nodded again. "There are a lot of adults with Attention Deficit Hyperactivity Disorder. Sometimes they get diagnosed as adults, actually."

His frown deepened. "Right. I've always known I had it though."

She nodded and waited for him to go on.

The smell of burning sugar hit her then, and she glanced at the fire. Her marshmallows were charred, black balls on the end of her stick.

"Crap!" She pulled her stick back and knocked it against the side of the firepit. The burned balls of sugar fell into the pit. She sighed.

Ollie pulled his stick back.

His marshmallows were perfectly toasted. Dark brown but not burnt. They'd be crisp on the outside and gooey on the inside. He slid one off the tip of his stick with his fingers and held it out to her.

She leaned in and took it from his fingers with her mouth. Her lips closed around his fingertips, and she added a drag of her tongue to be sure she got it all off.

His eyes were locked on her as she sat back, licking her lips.

He lifted his fingers to his mouth and licked them as well.

Heat curled through her stomach at the sight.

She didn't miss the detail that Ollie had paid enough attention to toast the perfect marshmallows while she'd gotten distracted and burned hers to a crisp.

"Thanks," she said, her voice husky.

"My pleasure." His voice was low, and the spot on her stomach he'd kissed tingled.

She wet her lips again. She didn't want to skip over the conversation about his ADHD. That was important. It was important that he was sharing it.

But, *damn*, she wanted to kiss him so badly.

"I looked up ADHD in adults about three years ago, Ollie," she told him. "I've known for a long time that's what was going on."

"You never said anything."

"Why would I say anything?"

"Did you wonder if I knew?"

She thought about that. "I assumed you knew," she said. "I'm not sure why, but..." Little bits of memories came back to her. "Actually, I do. I think it was the way that you always knew that you could just throw ideas out and everyone else would mold them into doable plans or would reel you back in if you got too over the top. I think it was your self-awareness about that. And how self-deprecating you always are about your distractibility and how you don't know *how* to organize things but that you know you need them organized. When I would find something that really worked, you always seemed relieved. Like when I started using the red folders for the *really* important stuff. You seemed happy to have that little extra bit of help."

He nodded slowly. "I was. I was just really happy to have *you*."

"No," she said, holding up a finger. "You can't guilt me. You don't *need* me, Ollie."

"I do."

"You don't need *me*," she said, emphasizing a different word. "I'm not saying that you're not a little better off with some help, but it doesn't have to be me. I don't do anything that someone else couldn't do. And I think you could do more if you tried."

His shoulders tensed, and he looked into the fire instead of at her.

She frowned. "Come on, Ollie. You became really dependent on me. You could do more."

"I told you that I've been dealing with this all my life. I definitely know what I can and can't handle, Piper."

"You don't even use the calendar app on your phone."

"Do you know how much shit gets loaded in there?" he said. "Every fucking little thing. Then when I pull it up, there's so much to look at, I can't make sense of any of it."

"Every fucking little thing? Like the meetings you need to be at and dinners with your best friends and the release dates for the new *Warriors* packs? Those are all important." She smiled even as she shook her head.

He nodded. "But the releases will happen whether I know about them or not. And my friends are used to me missing dinners. So I focus on what I can. Like the meetings I always have to be at."

"You don't even put those on your calendar," she muttered.

"Because I have *you* to remind me, and you're a lot nicer to look at than my calendar."

She snorted. "That was a very half-assed compliment."

He lifted a shoulder.

"Okay, so I get that you have a lot of stuff that *could* go on your calendar and that gets overwhelming. But someone else could definitely keep track of your meetings for you."

"Probably."

"So hiring someone else was a good idea," she prompted.

"Probably."

"What's the problem?"

"She's not you."

"That's... nice. But it doesn't have to be me. You can see me every day," she said. "I *want* to see you every day."

He sighed. Heavily. "I'm like this outside of work too, Piper." He finally looked at her again. "At work, your job is a little easier. Believe it or not. Organizing my schedule. Getting me where I need to go when I need to be there. Keeping my paperwork in order. And you're getting paid to deal with my nonsense. Outside of work, it's a lot more... chaotic. It's stuff like where I put stuff in the house and getting to social engagements on time and remembering the details about something we discussed last week. And you won't be getting paid for that."

Ah, so he didn't think she would find dealing with all of this worth it when it was personal.

"Is that why you don't have many personal relationships with women? You don't think they'll put up with all of that?"

"And it's a lot of work for me," he said. He shrugged. "It's easier to just worry about myself."

"There are ways to cope. Strategies."

"I know."

"You're not willing to do that?"

"I've tried some things. Like medications. I took those as a kid. I stopped in college. Then went back to them. Then stopped again."

"Did they work?"

"Yeah. They helped me focus so I could get through classes. But..." He shrugged. "I felt dull. It made me less creative. Everyone noticed. And I hated it. I know that I can be a lot and over the top, but I wasn't myself on the meds, and I've chosen to deal with the ADHD other ways. Like by hiring you."

She laughed softly. "Grant hired me."

"Well, I became friends with a guy who would hire an assistant for me," he said with a small smile.

"Good strategy."

"Exactly." He was quiet for a long moment. Then he sighed and focused on the fire. "I'm telling you this because you are the most stubborn, persistent woman I know, and you know me well enough to probably wear me down over time anyway."

"Uh, thanks?"

"And I really wish it could be different with you," he said. "I do. For the first time. So I'm going to tell you what's up because I actually don't want you to think I'm just a selfish dick. Other women, I don't care so much, but with you, I... want you to know that I've actually given this some thought."

Piper felt her heart squeeze as she studied his profile. He looked so serious. And she heard every word. He really wanted her to understand whatever he was about to explain. That mattered. She knew he didn't spend a lot of time explaining himself and that she was important enough to him for him to go into this, whatever it was, meant a lot to her.

"Okay." She wanted to hold his hand. But she resisted. She linked her fingers together and tucked them into her lap.

So she was startled when he reached over and took her hand, lacing their fingers together and resting them on his thigh.

Her eyes wide, she stared at their hands, waiting for him to go on.

"I was an only child," he said. "My mom really didn't like being a mom." He took a deep breath. "She has OCD. It wasn't diagnosed officially until I was about ten, but she had problems with it before that, obviously." He looked over at Piper. "I drove her crazy."

Piper frowned. "But—"

"I mean literally. I made her symptoms, including her anxiety, way worse. I was hyperactive. I couldn't sit still. I couldn't keep track of my stuff. I didn't follow through on things." He sighed. "I was her worst nightmare."

Piper arched a brow. "She was your *mother*. I'm sure she didn't feel that way."

"Oh, she did." He gave a little laugh that was devoid of humor. "She told me every day that I drove her crazy. At one point when I was a teenager, she said she would be so much better off if she hadn't had me. It was hard enough dealing with her OCD tendencies, but when she had a messy, loud kid, who couldn't follow directions or pick up his shit, it made it ten times worse."

Piper frowned. "You have to be kidding. What a bitch." She quickly slapped her other hand over her mouth. "I'm sorry." She dropped her hand. "Ollie, I shouldn't have said that."

"She couldn't help it."

"*You* couldn't help your stuff either."

"But like you said, I didn't really try."

Piper almost groaned out loud. Dammit. She had kind of said that. Or she'd maybe said pretty much that.

"You're very organized, very put together," he said, looking at their hands instead of into her eyes. "I imagine that someone like me could drive someone like you crazy. Like really crazy. I mean, I know I do. But Dax does too, just not to the extent I do."

"I don't have OCD, Ollie," Piper said, squeezing his hand.

"When I say crazy, I don't mean *crazy*." She cringed. "Should we be calling it that? I mean, it's a true disorder. I shouldn't make light of it."

He shook his head. "We both know what we mean. We're not being disrespectful. It's not as if we don't take mental illness seriously."

She took a breath. That was true, she supposed.

"I already drive you crazy. At work."

"Just the run-of-the-mill crazy," she said gently. "I get exasperated at times, it's true. But I knew going in that you needed extra help for organization and scheduling. That was my job."

"Exactly," he said with a nod. "It was your job. You knew going in what it was going to be and you were paid for it. That's not the same as dealing with it on a personal basis at home."

Piper thought about that. That was actually a fair point. She could understand why he thought that. Why he was convinced that if she wasn't being compensated for putting up with him, that she might not want to stick around when he was difficult.

She ran her thumb over the back of his hand. "Maybe, back in the beginning, the job description and money made it all... better. But, Ollie—" She looked over at him and waited for him to meet her eyes. "I'm in love with you. That gives me infinitely more patience."

He sucked in a breath. He did seem to be getting used to her saying she loved him. At least he didn't stare at her as if she had three heads and had announced that she ate puppies for breakfast. But hearing the words still appeared to affect him each time. She hoped so. She hoped his heart *felt* it every time.

"My brothers are *a lot*," she said. "They are loud and fight and make huge messes. I'm not trying to trivialize your stuff, but, yes, they make me batty, but I also love them and would do anything to help them navigate the world and be happier and safer and successful."

"My *mom* loves me," he said.

Piper swallowed hard at that. Yeah, his mom loved him. Surely. She *should have* anyway. But Piper did know, or at least she suspected, that they weren't close.

He didn't go home for holidays. If he called home, it was from his apartment or hotel room late at night, because she'd *never* heard him on the phone with a family member. She never put calls through from his mother, like she did from Maggie for Cam and Aiden, or Grant's mom, or Dax's mom. She'd arranged for Dax's mom to join him at a convention in Chicago two years ago. She was a Master Warrior Enchantress in *Warriors of Easton*. She'd met Grant's mother a few times in their offices since she lived in Chicago, and she'd stopped by to go to lunch with her son. She'd met Grant's sister as well. All of the other men had relationships with their families, at least on some level, that were involved enough so eventually their executive assistant had at least spoken to them.

She'd never met or spoken to or even sent a gift to Oliver's mother.

"How is she now?" Piper asked.

He shrugged. "The same. Dad said she did get better when I moved out."

Piper swallowed the little growl that threatened to crawl up the back of her throat.

"Do you not go visit?"

Ollie was from Chicago. When their offices had been there, she'd assumed he'd gone home to see his parents from time to time.

"As little as possible."

"Why?"

"It's easier on her."

"Even for short visits?"

He sighed. "We will occasionally get together for dinner. Out. At a restaurant. But I often show up late. And once I missed the meal altogether."

"They should know to tell you to be there an hour before you should actually be there," she said.

He nodded. "Like you do."

"Yeah, like I do." How would *parents* not learn how, and try to, compensate with their child?

"That bugs my mom. She's very... exact. If we say dinner at eight, then we should all be there at eight."

"Then your *dad* should tell *you* seven and her eight," Piper said, her exasperation clear in her tone.

He gave her half smile. "Well, we both drove my dad nuts."

Piper shook her head. It really wasn't *that* hard to make adjustments. "Look, Ollie, the thing is, kids aren't supposed to make adjustments and make things easier on their parents. It's supposed to be the other way around."

He just shrugged. "It wasn't at my house."

She didn't like Oliver's mother. That might be a problem at their wedding, but Piper would deal with that then. She was *not* going to get over disliking the woman who'd made Ollie feel like there was something wrong and, worse, unlovable, about him.

"How did you know I have ADHD?" he asked.

"I read about it," she said.

"But why did you think to read about it?"

"I was just observing some of your... behaviors. Initially, I thought you were just kind of a spoiled prince who liked having someone do everything for him." She nudged him with her shoulder. "Which you are and do."

"It's pretty awesome."

She smiled. "But over time I started realizing there were times that you did things on purpose and there were things you didn't. I don't know, I guess I just started noticing that you honestly seemed completely incapable of remembering meetings. There were some that I knew you really did want to attend. But you even forgot about those."

He nodded.

"So I started reading. I thought maybe you'd had a concussion, or you had some neurological disease. I came to ADHD, and other symptoms fit. I started observing you with that in mind and it completely fit." She lifted a shoulder. "It also helped me with ideas for how to help you."

"Like what?"

"Giving you one thing to do at a time. Prioritizing what I needed from you. Cutting down on the distractions. Keeping your office clean and organized."

"I thought that was because *you* are a neat freak."

"I do like things neat, but I read that it would help you to keep things decluttered. It would help you focus and not feel overwhelmed."

"I do like when you clean my desk."

She laughed and shook her head. "I know." She paused. "I also really tried to just be honest with you. About when you were pushing my buttons. When you were pushing other people's buttons. When you were being impulsive. When you let something go or missed something."

"I like that too." He ran his thumb up and down her index finger.

Piper was certain he had no idea that the simple touch caused a riot of hot butterflies to swoop through her belly. She didn't mind it. But she was amazed by the strength of the sensation.

"But I wasn't honest about knowing about the ADHD," she said. "I guess I didn't know who knew, if you were open to talking about it, if that was something I should mention to my boss."

He looked over.

They were sitting shoulder to shoulder, holding hands. But she felt as if they were now leaning in closer.

"I was your boss, kind of, in the beginning. But it's been a long time."

"What do you mean?"

"We're friends, Piper. Don't you think?"

She smiled softly at that. "Yes. But you've kept the boss thing pretty firmly in the way of getting too close. I mean, we spend time together and I know you very well. But you don't know me. We've never held hands before." She squeezed his hand.

"Because I didn't want to lose you."

Her heart tripped. "You thought you'd lose me?"

He gave a short laugh. "I *have* lost you. Exactly the way I was afraid I would." He looked at her. "You quit."

She had. She wet her lips and nodded.

"At least it took five years. I honestly figured you'd be out way before this."

"But you don't have to lose me," she said. "I just want *more*."

"Yeah." He didn't sound thrilled, that was for sure.

"Now that you know that I know about the ADHD, that doesn't make you feel better? That doesn't give you more confidence that I could really stick around and not get scared off?"

He shrugged. "I realized, quickly, that I needed you. The guys did too. You really do make everything better. Organizing me, for sure, but the business had grown out of our control by the time Grant hired you. You came in and made everything better immediately. Again, getting paid to put up with all my crap was really different than dealing with it personally. I didn't want to get too close because I didn't want to mess up the work relationship and I—" He dragged in a long breath. "I didn't want to have my heart broken."

"You thought I would break your heart?"

"It would definitely hurt to get close to someone and have them decide you're too much work."

She frowned. She needed to reassure him that wasn't going

to happen with her, but she had to dig a little here first. "Is that how you think your mom feels about you?" That was an appalling thought.

"She's happier and healthier when I'm not around," he said.

Oh yeah, she hated his mom. A lot.

"Ollie."

He didn't look at her.

Piper sighed. "Oliver."

He sighed too. And still didn't look at her.

She wasn't going to argue with him about how his mom felt or treated him or what she said. Piper didn't know. Maybe his mom was misunderstood. Maybe she was awful. Likely she was somewhere in between all of that.

But Piper could absolutely argue with him about how *she* felt.

Piper rose and moved to stand in front of him, their hands still clasped. "Oliver."

He looked up reluctantly.

"I'm very sorry that you feel that your mom is better off without you. But I can *promise* you that I am not. And will not be. I want you. I know that I'm going to have to help you keep things decluttered. I know that I'm going to tell you to meet me an hour before I want you somewhere. I know that my life will be ruled by sticky notes and alarms and that if I want flowers, I'll have to send them to myself. But I *know* that. I'm going in eyes wide open."

His fingers tightened around hers, and she wondered if he was even aware of it.

"In spite of the fact that you thought we should have alpacas at a baking competition and that you thought you should name a soda Unicorn Snot, I still want to cover you in melted chocolate and marshmallows."

Even in the dim light, she could see his eyes flicker with emotion at that. She knew some of it was desire. But she also suspected at least some of it was affection. Knowing that she liked him in spite of his quirks, mattered. That mattered to most people. Being loved in spite of the things that people most disliked about themselves meant a lot.

It was important that she really knew all of his quirks.

"*You* were the one that arranged for the alpacas at the baking contest."

"Only after you said no because they were Drew's, and he was flirting with me that day."

"You're wearing me down," he finally said.

"Thank God."

"In less than twenty-four hours."

"I'm very good."

"Do you see why I've been afraid of you?"

She laughed. "You haven't been afraid of me."

"Oh, yes, I have." But he tugged her forward.

She went. Very willingly. She stepped forward. Then with another tug and his other big hand on her hip, she slid into his lap, straddling him.

Her breath caught in her throat. "You have nothing to be afraid of, Ollie. I'll take very good care of you."

He gave her a crooked grin at that. "You're good at *everything* you do, Piper. I have no doubt that I'm in very good hands."

She definitely wanted him in her hands.

She took his face between her palms and leaned in. "You okay so far?" she asked with her lips just above his.

His hands went to her ass and brought her up against him more fully.

He was hard.

She was surprised. And very pleased. And immediately turned on.

"I'm okay," he told her.

"Then here I come."

She pressed her lips to his.

His fingers curled into her ass, and he gave a little groan as she licked her tongue along his bottom lip. He opened under her kiss and their lips melded fully. He met her strokes with his own.

Her body melted into his. She wrapped her arms around his neck, pressing close, her breasts against his chest, his body heat warming her. His hands ran from her butt up her back, bringing her against him even more firmly as they tasted each other. She ran her hands into his hair. He stroked up and down her spine.

When his hands dropped to her butt again, he dragged his palms down the outsides of her thighs. His hands on her bare skin sent hot prickles of sensation down her legs to her toes.

She ran her hands down his sides to the bottom of his shirt and then under the edge and onto the bare skin just above his waistband.

He groaned, and she wiggled in his lap in response.

She pulled back to look down at him. They were both breathing hard. He was watching her, his gaze intense, his full focus on her. She shivered. His full focus was heady. In part because it was unusual. She could get used to getting it this way, that was for certain.

He wet his lips. "I'm never going to be the one that stops this," he told her, his voice gruff.

"Good."

"I thought you didn't want this."

"I most definitely want this." She certainly hoped they were talking about sex.

"Your hotel room—"

"That was when sex was all you were offering."

He swallowed. "You think I'm offering more now?"

He was here. She'd realized this was out of his comfort zone, that this was different. But before he'd told her the full story about how he avoided spending a lot of time with his mom so he didn't bug her, and before he'd admitted that he'd kept from getting closer to *her* so that he wouldn't make her "deal" with him when she wasn't being paid to do so, she hadn't realized how big this really was.

Yeah, he was offering more.

"Ollie," she said, looking right into his eyes. "I want it all. Can you give me that? For two weeks?"

He didn't answer immediately. But finally he said, "I'm not sure I can help it."

And she fell just a little more in love with him.

"But—" he added.

And she almost groaned.

"You've agreed to keep me around for the full two weeks."

Dammit, she wanted to hug him so tightly. And cover him in gooey, warm chocolate and lick it all off. Slowly. And thoroughly.

Yeah, naked hugging. With chocolate. That's what they needed to do.

"Promise," she said, never meaning anything more.

"So are you going to toast the marshmallows, or am I?" He ran his hand up and down her thigh.

She was feeling pretty soft and melty herself at the moment. "I'd really like for you to keep your hands where they are, doing what they're doing," she said, shifting on his lap to reach for the stick he'd been using.

He groaned as the shifting brought her against the hard ridge behind his fly and she gave a little lusty sigh.

"I was thinking about doing more with my hands," he said. He slipped one under the bottom edge of her shorts, the pads of his fingers skimming the band of her panties where they crossed her hip.

"I'm all for that," she told him. *Yes, please.* She'd been thinking about Ollie's hands on her for so long, this felt surreal. *Really*, really good. But surreal.

She tossed the marshmallows he'd toasted previously into the fire and grabbed two new ones. She stuck them onto the stick as he slid his palm up her, under her shorts and panties, to cup her bare butt.

Somehow she managed to get the marshmallows into the edge of the fire while his fingers stroked back and forth over her skin.

"Now you have to *focus*," he told her huskily. "Don't want those to burn."

"I'm *really* good at concentrating." Her voice was a little breathless.

"Yeah, yeah. But you're cocky about it." He ran the pads of his fingers back and forth over the curve where her butt met her thigh. "And I'm feeling kind of cocky about the idea of making you lose your train of thought."

"Hmmm," she said, letting her eyes slide shut, soaking in the feel of his touch. "You can try."

Screw burned marshmallows. She didn't care about the marshmallows. But if he wanted to play, she'd play.

"I want those marshmallows gooey enough to cling to your nipples."

Her eyes flew open. He was watching her with a hot gaze and her nipples *loved* the idea.

She did care about the marshmallows after all. Very, very much.

She glanced over her shoulder and rotated the stick.

He chuckled.

God, she really did love teasing with him like this. She had never experienced a naughty Ollie. Not sexy naughty anyway. He'd been *naughty* a few times. Like ending up in jail in Rome. And Vegas. But Grant had mostly dealt with those.

Impulsiveness was part of the ADHD. She hadn't known that initially, of course. She'd thought Ollie truly was a spoiled, rich guy who thought he could get away with anything. But it had all fallen into place when she'd realized that his brain processed things differently. Like the inability to think through to consequences.

Of course it didn't help that he had a best friend who always said, "Hell yes!" to Ollie's impulsive ideas. Like jumping on a plane to Madrid because he wanted to see how much of his high school Spanish he'd retained.

"They look good."

She looked at him. "What?"

He arched a brow. "The marshmallows, Piper. They look good."

She jumped and pulled the stick from the fire.

He chuckled. "I don't know why you get so exasperated with my trouble concentrating. It's pretty cute when you do it."

"Because your trouble concentrating isn't because you're thinking of me sucking on your nipples."

His smile died, his expression growing intense. And hot. He squeezed her butt. "If I *was* distracted because of that, it would have been okay?"

She gave him a little smile. "It would have been better." It had never been not okay. Not entirely. She'd understood. Did she sigh when she'd reminded him of a conference call, and then he still dialed in late? Yes. Did she roll her eyes when he asked her where his character biography folder was on his computer for the third time? Yes.

But she was never so frustrated that she'd thought about quitting.

Falling in love with him had been the cause of that.

And now she was starting to think that she might need to go back to work.

Would someone else take care of him as well as she did? No way.

But she wanted more from him than their work relationship. Could they have more? Could they be involved personally *and* work together?

"The marshmallows are going to get too cold," he said, lifting one hand and plucking one melty white mass from the end of the stick.

He lifted it to her mouth. She parted her lips, but he simply rubbed it over her bottom lip. Then brought her down for a kiss, running his tongue over her lip to lick the marshmallow off.

They kissed deep for several long moments. In one part of her mind it seemed dreamlike to be kissing Ollie and to have him kissing her with such hunger. But in another it felt so right and so natural, and so *good*, that it seemed as if they'd done it before. Maybe in another lifetime.

"Lift your shirt," he said against her mouth.

Yeah, she could definitely think about work and where they went next *after* this.

"The marshmallow will be too cool now," she said, dragging her mouth from his far enough to speak.

"Not this one."

He pulled his arm back to reveal a toasted marshmallow on the end of a stick.

Her mouth dropped open, and she looked from the stick to the fire to him.

"You *toasted a marshmallow while we were kissing*?"

He gave her a cocky smirk. "Guess I *can* multitask if the tasks are both really fun."

12

Piper narrowed her eyes even as she smiled. She shrugged out of her flannel and stripped her tank top over her head. She was wearing a bra so she wasn't entirely naked, but the way his eyes heated and his smug grin dropped away, she felt as if she was.

"Let's see that multitasking," she told him.

"Take it off." His gaze was on her bra. He took the marshmallow from the stick and bit into the very end to reveal the melty inside.

She shivered with desire and anticipation. She'd imagined kissing Ollie. She'd imagined him naked—yes, she'd ogled him in the office and no, she wasn't apologetic about it. But she had never, not once, imagined them making out with marshmallows.

She liked it.

A lot.

Piper reached behind her for the hooks on her bra. She let the plain white garment fall down her arms, then tossed it on the grass beside them.

She had big breasts. It was a fact. They made for amazing

cleavage in her dresses. They gave her great curves. They didn't, however, give her tiny scraps of lace and silk for bras and lingerie.

She didn't care.

Oliver didn't care either, it seemed.

He lifted a hand, almost reverently, to cup one.

She let out a long sigh as he palmed it. He had big hands, so he was definitely able to "handle" her. And he did. So well. He kneaded, running his thumb over her nipple. Piper let her head fall back, arching closer.

"Yes, Ollie."

"You're so beautiful, Piper." He said it softly, huskily, almost as if he was awed.

She wondered if he was feeling the same combination of this-is-so-surreal and this-is-so-so-good.

"Thank—" She felt the warmth on her nipple, and her head came up.

Ollie was rubbing the melty marshmallow over the hard tip of her right breast. He spread the sticky white sugar in bigger and bigger circles, watching as if he were painting a masterpiece.

Then he lifted his eyes to hers as he popped the marshmallow into his mouth. He gave her a sexy half smile before lowering his head and licking her nipple.

She gasped as heat flooded through her, turning her insides to a melty marshmallow consistency. Her hand went to the back of his head as he licked and sucked. She loved having her nipples played with and appreciated a lot of pressure.

"Harder, Ollie."

He didn't ask questions. He sucked hard, sending an arrow of lust straight to her clit. "*Yes.*"

She wiggled in his lap, pressing closer to his cock. He seemed to like that idea because he shifted on the bench, pressing up against her as well.

She wanted more of that.

Reaching between them she ran her hand down the length behind the denim fly.

He hissed out a breath against her breast.

Yeah, she liked affecting him. She also *really* liked touching his cock. The guy was big all over. She'd known he would be. Proportionately it just made sense. He was tall and had big hands and feet. But she was happy to know she'd been right and *very* happy to be proving it by touch.

Sight was next. And some more feeling. With other parts of her body.

She ran her hand up and down, pressing and squeezing.

But it seemed that Ollie's multitasking had gotten disrupted because he was resting his forehead against her chest, breathing on her breast, but the licking and sucking had stopped.

"Ollie?"

"Yeah?" His voice was tight.

She grinned. "You okay?"

"Never been better."

Well, that was very nice.

"I was a little better when your mouth was busier," she teased.

She felt him smile against her chest.

"I got distracted."

She rubbed him. "Let's practice the multitasking."

He gave a little groan. "Maybe it would be easier to focus if we talk through it."

"You can't suck and talk," she pointed out, squeezing him.

His voice was thick when he said, "I can stroke though."

Stroking nipples was okay too, she supposed. "If you also pinch and squeeze—"

But she wasn't the only one who got completely distracted

when he ran his big hand down underneath her butt and then forward to cup her through her shorts.

"Ohhh," she said on a long exhale. "Got you."

He grinned up at her. "Yeah."

She squeezed him. "Yeah."

His eyes narrowed, and he shifted her on his lap, moving his hand so his fingers could slip under the loose edge of her shorts. His fingers stroked over the hot silk of her panties between her legs, and her eyes nearly crossed.

She squirmed, wanting to press closer to his fingers but not able to get a lot of leverage perched on his lap the way she was.

"I need to move."

"Why?" he asked.

"I need to..." She frowned. "Get closer. Get naked."

"Be in charge?" He lifted a brow.

She bit her bottom lip. Then nodded.

He gave her a slow smile and stroked his fingers over her again. "I don't think so."

"But—"

He pressed against her clit and she sucked in a quick breath.

"While I agree that most things go better when you're in charge..." He slipped his finger under the elastic edge of her panties suddenly bringing the knuckle of his middle finger against her clit and rubbing gently.

Piper gasped, and she completely forgot about anything but that part of his body and that part of her body being against each other.

He nodded. "Yeah, I've got *this*."

"You're pretty cocky," she said. But the breathlessness took any sass right out of her tone.

He rubbed again. "Yeah. I am."

He should be. He'd found her clit, through clothing, no less, without an ounce of coaching. Now he was applying the perfect amount of friction and pressure to have her hovering on the edge of orgasm already.

She did *not* want to know how he was this good with clits.

"The idea of making you come apart, of making your in-control, in-charge attitude shatter, is the most addictive fucking thing I've thought about in a very long time," he told her gruffly.

That sounded so damned good. "I'm in."

She wasn't the type of woman who needed control *all* of the time. She was type A, for sure. She knew what she was good at. She prided herself on being organized and getting shit done. But she was fine with other people doing their things too. If someone else could do something better than she could, she was happy to let them. Hell, she'd *recruit* them for the task.

It was *very* possible that Ollie would be better at giving her orgasms than she was. And she was *super* okay with that. That couldn't be said for every guy she'd been with.

Ollie's hand went to the back of her head, bringing her down for a deep kiss as he turned his other hand so that he could slide a thick finger into her.

"Oh, *damn*," she said against his mouth.

"You're tight," he said gruffly.

She nodded. "Been a while."

He slid that finger out and back in, deep. "How long?"

She couldn't have lied even if she'd wanted to. Her brain was all about *this* moment. What was going on here with this man. Screw multitasking. "Two years."

He paused. Yeah, she'd figured that'd get his attention.

"Two years?" he repeated.

She kissed him, running her hand over his face, loving the feel of the scruffiness of the start of his beard against her palm. "Two years," she confirmed.

"Because of me?"

She was so glad he'd put that together. He was starting to believe it. Or at least understand that she believed it.

"Yeah."

He started to pull back to look at her, but she clasped him closer. "Keep going," she said softly. "Please, Ollie."

He gave a groan. Of surrender. And moved his finger. In and out, slow and deep at first, but as she moaned and gasped and pressed closer, he picked up the pace. He also kept up the magical friction against her clit with the pad of his thumb.

It had been a *long* time. At least a long time since someone besides her had done this. And this was *Oliver*. The one man she wanted doing this to her.

It didn't take long for her to start climbing toward that delicious orgasm crest.

Then he returned his mouth to her nipple. Maybe because she'd taken her hand from his cock, or maybe because he just knew she needed that too, or maybe because *he* couldn't help it. He sucked hard.

And she went over the moon.

She came hard, gasping his name.

He brought her head down again, kissing her as the pleasure coursed through her. He kept holding her and kissing her as the waves became ripples and then quieted entirely.

He withdrew his hand from her shorts and wrapped his arms around her.

Piper buried her face in his neck, hugging him close.

"I really like s'mores," he said.

She giggled into his neck. She loved this part of his body. His skin was hot, and he smelled so good. He was solid and strong, and she could feel the rumble of his voice as she heard it.

"We only got to one third of the s'mores so far," she said.

"Still, best campfire I've ever been to."

She lifted her head to look down at him. "How many camp-fires have you been to?"

"This is my first," he admitted.

"They don't all go this way."

He chuckled. "Maybe a good thing at a kids' camp."

She grinned at him. "I like having this camp to ourselves."

"So far anyway."

"Don't do that."

"Do what?"

"Assume I'm going to end up *not* liking it."

He was quiet for a moment, but he did smile. "Orgasms have to help increase your tolerance level for crazy."

She leaned in and kissed him. "For sure," she said when she lifted her head.

"And I was thinking," he said, his hands going to her hips and bringing her against his cock again. "Maybe I should get as far ahead as I can before I do anything annoying."

"Hmm." She wiggled happily against him. "Not a bad idea."

"How do you feel about campfire s'mores sex?"

"Never had it, but it sounds like something right up my alley. How about you?"

"You know I'm the adventurous type."

Adventurous. Sure, they could call his impulsiveness and inability to think through to major consequences "adventurous."

"Okay, then." She reached for his shirt and started unbuttoning.

He shrugged out of it as soon as the last button let go.

Oh, she'd been waiting for this. She kind of regretted that they were in the dimming light now that she had Ollie's chest and abs on display now, but what she couldn't take in with her eyes, she could certainly work on memorizing with her hands.

She ran her palms from his neck down his shoulders to his

chest, then down either side of his abdomen, to the waistband of his pants. "These have to go too."

"I'm not going to get mosquito bites in bad places, am I?" But he was already nudging her back so he could stand.

She got to her feet, eager to watch him strip. "Too early for mosquitos." That was very fortunate. "At most, you might get a little chilly." It was still March after all. Typically, she needed a jacket or a blanket over her lap if she sat on her balcony after sunset.

"Don't think that's gonna be a problem," he told her as he bent to untie his shoes and toed them off, kicking them to the side and then tossing his socks in the same general direction.

Tonight, she'd brought a blanket out but hadn't even thought of using it. The fire, combined with Ollie's body heat and the way he jacked hers up, had been more than enough. Now, though, as his hands went to the button and zipper of his jeans, she reached to spread the blanket out where he'd be sitting again. The bench had been sanded and finished, but she didn't want to risk any splinters in sensitive areas either.

She quickly straightened, though, not wanting to miss a moment of him getting naked.

He watched her watching him as he pushed his jeans over his hips. He shoved them to his ankles and kicked them to the side. Then his thumbs went to the waistband of his boxers.

"Let me," she said, stepping forward.

"You've got some to get rid of yourself," he said, looking at her shorts.

She stripped the shorts and her panties down, stepping out of them.

Ollie froze, staring at her.

She propped a hand on her hip, letting him look. She was curvy, but she'd never been worried about her body, even with sex. The men she was with were into curves and having places to put their hands and plenty of surface area to kiss and suck and lick and stroke. Guys who weren't simply weren't her type.

Ollie seemed to snap out of his stupor a moment later. He dropped his boxers and sat back on the bench. "Come here."

She couldn't though. She was busy staring herself.

Yep, big. She'd been right.

And gorgeous.

Her whole body responded to just the sight of him. She knew, and agreed, that women weren't typically turned on by sight as much as they were by thoughts and ideas and words. But, damn, the sight of Oliver Caprinelli sitting in front of her, totally naked, by a campfire, wanting her... she was one big toasted marshmallow.

"Piper." His tone was low and firm.

She swallowed. He didn't use that tone with her much. But he had a few times. Usually when he was out of patience with her nagging him about something. Or when she was going on about something that he'd long ago lost interest in.

Now it seemed he was out of patience. But this was definitely not a frustrated "Piper". His voice was husky and needy.

"Come here," he repeated.

She took a step forward, but she swiped a piece of chocolate before coming to stand between his knees. She put it to her lips, licking the end and then sucking it into her mouth, letting it melt on her tongue.

"You sure you want to do this like this? Out here? Sitting by a fire?"

"I've imagined it sitting up," she said, sliding into his lap. "Straddling you."

He was clearly surprised. "Yeah?"

"I'll admit it was in your office chair in my daydreams though."

She leaned in and kissed him, tangling her tongue with his, letting him taste the chocolate. His tongue stroked hers, his hands squeezing her hips. Her breasts pressed into his chest, her nipples beading at the contact.

"Just daydreams?" he rasped against her lips, running his hand over the curve of her butt and between her legs where she was still hot and wet from before.

She moved against his hand, wanting his fingers deep again.

"Oh, the night dreams were either me spread out on your desk, bent over your desk, or straddling you in the bean bag you sit on in Dax's office," she told him.

He gave a mixed groan-laugh as he stroked over her clit and then dipped a finger into her pussy. "Damn, I want to do all of that."

"Good. But I'm really loving the campfire thing," she said.

"Yeah?" His finger pressed deeper.

She nodded even as sparks of pleasure danced along her nerves. "I'll admit I'm not very spontaneous. Office sex seems very in my wheelhouse, you know? Bean bag chairs notwithstanding."

He added a second finger, stroking her a little faster. She reached between them again, now circling his bare cock with her hand.

Again his breath hissed out and a "holy fuck" rumbled up from his chest as she stroked up and down his length. He was hot and hard, and just touching him like this made her ache deep inside in a spot she wasn't sure she'd ever been touched.

"Office sex does seem like you. In your office dresses. With the heels still on. Skirt hiked up."

She nodded. "Even though a lot of those skirts wouldn't go very high."

"But I like you being spontaneous." He pressed his fingers deep and circled her clit with his thumb.

Her inner muscles contracted around his fingers. "Oh God, me too."

He gave a dark chuckle and lowered his mouth to her

nipple. His mouth sucking on her while stroking her while she had his cock in her hand was enough to start her climbing again. But this time she wanted it all.

"Condom?" she asked.

He froze.

She sighed.

Dammit.

Why would Ollie think of a condom? Coming out to a campfire? He hadn't known what to expect out here. *She* hadn't known what to expect. She'd hoped they'd kiss. She had *not* expected to need a condom.

But if she was going to date this man, she was probably going to have to be in charge of condoms. He wasn't the plan-ahead guy.

Which made her pull back to look at him. "Oh my God, you use condoms with the women you hookup with at cons, right? Please tell me you do."

He frowned. "Of course."

She lifted both brows. "Of course? Oliver, I love you, but you are not the most prepared person I know."

He sighed. "Are we really going to talk about other women right now?"

"I think now is a really good time for this, yes. Actually, we might be a few moves past when we should have done that." She even took her hand off of his cock. The cock that may or may not have been covered in condoms with all the fairies and princesses who had wanted to get up close with his magical staff.

He also withdrew his hand. Which was probably good. Probably. It was hard to feel that way about it, honestly.

"When I... meet women at cons," he said. "Which," he added, "is not as often as you apparently think it is."

She rolled her eyes at his choice of the word "meet" and

decided not to press on the issue of how often "not as often" was.

"I always take them back to my room," Ollie said. "Then I don't have to worry about not having what I need."

She felt her mouth drop open. "You take them back to your room? Oliver!"

"What?"

"These are total strangers! It's bad enough you're hooking up without knowing them at all, but you're letting them know where you're sleeping? What if they're crazy stalkers?"

He ran a hand through his hair. "Well…"

She pushed back and got to her feet, grabbing her flannel and pulling it on. "Well, what?" she asked, planting her hands on her hips.

"Grant gets us private security when we go to cons. So if anything gets weird, the security guys take care of it."

Piper pictured big, muscled guys positioned on either side of Oliver's hotel room door, in dark suits with earpieces in, standing guard while he had his latest "meeting" with a magical elf from *Warriors of Easton*.

She stared at him. "You make it sound as if that's happened."

"Only once."

She tipped her head.

"Okay, twice. Unless you count the twice with Dax. Then it's four times. But only twice to me."

She knew what she was getting into, she reminded herself. Mostly anyway. She'd known about the other women. In theory. She'd *chosen* not to find out details. So she couldn't really be shocked. Or angry, of course.

She and Ollie hadn't been dating. He was a grown man— regardless of how he acted sometimes. He got to choose when and how often he had sex and who he had it with. It wasn't as if he'd been cheating on her. And she didn't *actually* know how many convention hookups he'd had. He and Dax were both big talkers. All the guys were. They loved to give each other shit and joke and tease. For all she knew, the stories she'd overheard about princesses and magical staffs had all actually been *one* princess and one weekend.

So she was going to let all of that go. She'd dated other men. Some of them very temporarily and superficially. In other words, she'd had a couple of hookups herself.

That was all in the past.

"Do you have condoms in the cabin?" he asked.

She blinked at him. "No."

Why would she have condoms in the cabin?

"Are you on the pill or anything?"

"No." She hadn't been involved with anyone in two years. If she had been, she would have started the shots again that she'd used before. And she would have been using condoms. But why would she be buying and packing condoms now? "And," she said, as she really thought about his question, "I wouldn't be having sex with you without a condom even if I was. You've been having sex with strangers at Comic Con!"

"People at Comic Con don't automatically have STDs, Piper," he said, reaching for his boxers and pulling them on.

"Of course not," she conceded. "But—"

"And I *always* use a condom."

She swallowed. Okay. Good to know. "But with me you wouldn't? If I was on the pill or something?"

"Of course. If you said it was okay."

"Ollie?"

He looked up from pulling his jeans on.

"What are you talking about?"

"I completely trust you," he said. "There's no way you would do anything that wasn't safe for both of us."

That was nice. And annoying. "Well, that's true," she said. "But it would be nice if we could say the same about *you*."

He frowned. "I would never hurt you. On purpose."

"I know. But—" She sighed. "You need to think about the fact that you've probably had more partners than I have, and you've probably known them less well than I've known mine, and you and I have never had this conversation before, so it's appropriate that I be wondering about how you've handled things with the other women you've been with. Especially when I've just found out that you've brought them back to your hotel room without thinking about how unsafe it might be for them to know where you're staying."

"I was totally safe," he said, clearly irked. "I had security. And condoms." He yanked his shirt over his head.

"Okay." She believed him. "Well, we don't have condoms now, so I guess... we can't do anything more right now."

He just stared at her.

"What?"

"You're serious?"

"Well... yes."

"So now what?" He seemed confused.

"Bedtime."

"I don't have a bed."

"You'll have to sleep in mine."

"With you?"

"I'm not sleeping on the floor or the couch, and you're too big for the couch," she told him.

"But no sex."

"No. Sex," she said firmly. Good Lord.

"I've never slept with a woman I haven't had sex with."

"You *sleep* with these total strangers you take up to the hotel? You actually fall asleep? You're actually *unconscious* with them in your room?" She shook her head and started for the cabin. "For God's sake, Oliver. They could rob you. Kill you. Take a million naked pictures of you and post them all over the internet." She swung back. "Have you checked for naked photos of yourself on the internet?"

But her gaze darted past him to the firepit behind him.

That was still on fire.

She'd left the fire burning.

And her clothes over there. And food, which could attract animals.

She closed her eyes and drew in a breath. He'd completely distracted her.

Dammit.

They couldn't *both* be distracted and letting things go.

"I. Had. Security," Ollie said as she sighed and started for the firepit.

"Did they keep the women's phones when they went into your room?" She doused the flames.

"Well..."

"Exactly." She gathered the s'mores supplies and her clothes. "You or Dax need to scan the web for naked photos, Oliver."

"Fine. You're probably right."

She went back into the cabin. He was right behind her.

"In my defense, it's kind of gentlemanly that I didn't just assume we'd need condoms tonight," he said. "Right?"

Piper snorted. If she wasn't concerned about him being naked on the internet where all of those *Warriors* hussies could ogle him and drool over him, and she wasn't completely feeling hussy-ish herself, she might find that gentlemanly.

"You were in Dubuque tonight," she pointed out. "*In* your hotel room. You could have easily grabbed condoms when you were grabbing your toothbrush."

"Are you under the impression that I have condoms in my hotel room?"

She set the s'mores ingredients on the counter and turned to face him, holding her clothes in front of her. "Yes."

"Why would I have condoms in my hotel room in Dubuque?"

She narrowed her eyes. "Are you *not* using condoms in Dubuque? Oliver, I swear to God—"

"I haven't had sex since we got to Iowa!"

She stopped and stared at him. She shook her head. "*What?*"

"I haven't needed a condom since we got to Iowa," he said. He shoved a hand through his hair. "I don't have condoms in my hotel room, Piper."

Okay, he still could have stopped and gotten some at about a hundred stores between there and here, but that was not the point right now. It wasn't at all what she wanted to focus on. "You…"

"I haven't been fucking other women just down the hall from you," he said, meeting her eyes. "Jesus, Piper."

"Because there aren't any gaming cons in Dubuque?" she asked.

"Because you were just down the hall," he said.

"Why does that matter?" Her heart was in her throat now. She wasn't sure why she *needed* the answer to that question so badly. She did not think it was because Ollie had been harboring secret feelings for her all this time. She knew that wasn't what he was going to say. But she still wanted to hear his answer. So much.

He didn't want to answer. It was clear on his face. He swallowed hard.

"Oliver? Why does it matter that I would have been just down the hall?"

"Because you might have run into them when we came back to the room or the next morning."

That would have killed her. But he hadn't known that. "So?" she prompted.

He tucked his hands into his back pockets and tipped his head to look up at the ceiling.

"Ollie?"

"Because you might not have liked them." He looked at her again. "And you wouldn't have liked that I didn't remember their names, or that I wasn't on my way out to breakfast with them."

"I would have known all of that from running into them in the hallway?" she asked, bemused.

"Well, after you ran into them and invited them into *your* apartment for coffee, probably with *my* caramel creamer, you would have known more about them than I did. Then at work later that day, you would have asked me about them, and I wouldn't have known anything, and you would have been disappointed in me. Or if you didn't see me right away and didn't realize all of that, you would have sent them flowers from me and screwed the whole one-night stand up for me." He lifted a shoulder. "So I didn't want to take them back to the hotel."

Piper felt her heart pounding. Not in a good way. "You could have gone back to their places."

"This from the woman who is appalled that I took strangers up to my room at conventions?" he asked. "Going back to their places would have been even stupider. They could have a whole backyard full of dead bodies."

She almost said *what about another hotel?* but stopped herself just in time. She was thrilled he hadn't been with any other women in a long time. Why was she suggesting ways he could have been banging the women of Dubuque, Iowa?

She wet her lips and asked the question she didn't want the answer to.

"You haven't brought any women back to the hotel in Dubuque because I'm hypercritical, and you didn't want me to judge your dates?"

He frowned. "No. I didn't want you to judge *me*."

"You?" she asked.

"The fact that I wouldn't know her name or where she worked or"—he blew out a breath—"how many brothers she had."

Piper's heart squeezed. "I'm not upset that you didn't know that about me, Ollie."

"I am." He shrugged. "I told you, I don't attach. It's on purpose. I don't like disappointing people. I wouldn't have *wanted* to know how many brothers any of the women I've slept with had. I honestly didn't really care where they worked." He gave a little wince. "I probably should have known all of their names. But," he went on, "with you it feels really weird that I didn't know that very important big fact about your life."

She had to admit there was something nice about him wanting to know more about her than he did about all of the other women.

"I'm sorry I've given you the impression that you disappoint me sometimes," she said. "That's not..." But she didn't finish the thought.

She supposed she did sometimes get disappointed. And that was completely *her* fault, not his. He'd never made promises to her. He'd never tried to be anything other than who he was. He'd never confessed about his ADHD before, but he'd acknowledged his weaknesses and accepted her help for them. He'd never promised to try to fix them. He'd paid her to put up with his "quirks" and had been less than enthusiastic about the idea of her taking them on without that incentive.

"That's not how a friend should make another friend feel," she finally filled in. "I really am sorry."

"But you totally would have given a woman coffee if you found her by our elevator some morning," he said, the corner of his mouth tilting.

"I would have," she agreed. "Walk of shame solidarity."

"You've done a walk of shame?" He looked very interested in that.

"Maybe once. Or three times," she said.

"Did the assholes give you coffee?" he asked, clearly amused.

"Nope."

"Fuckers."

"Right?"

They were both smiling now.

She moved to stand right in front of him. "You've never made a promise to me that you haven't kept," she said.

He lifted a hand, brushing her hair back over her shoulder. "I've been late to more meetings this year than some people will be in their entire careers."

"But you never promise to be on time."

He nodded. "I know myself."

"And you never promised those women breakfast the next morning. Or even coffee. You can't feel bad about that. And I can't judge it."

He studied her eyes. Finally, he said, "Okay."

"Okay."

Then she took his hand and led him toward the bed.

"This is going to be very hard," he said, watching as she shrugged out of the flannel and pulled her shorts and tank on, without a bra or panties.

Yeah, hard, she thought as he stripped out of his t-shirt and jeans. Hard abs, shoulders, chest, back... cock. He was definitely still hard there as well. Definitely. Obviously. He slipped under the covers with her in only his boxers.

She turned on her side, switched off the bedside lamp, then snuggled her ass right into his groin—his *hard* groin—and pulled his arm over her.

"Well, maybe next time you won't forget the condoms," she finally said.

He nuzzled her neck and took a deep breath.

"I promi—"

"Nope," she said loudly and firmly over him. "Don't you dare use the P word in regard to condoms, Ollie. That's serious. You *can* disappoint me by forgetting the condoms after you promised not to."

She felt him smile against her hair. "Fair enough."

13

———

Ollie took a deep breath. Then another.

Slowly he opened his eyes.

Was this heaven?

The air was cool and smelled like bacon. And pancakes. He was lying on something soft. He could even hear the sizzle of the bacon.

It had to be heaven.

He had never woken up like this before. And he wanted to. Forever. Even if it meant he was dead.

But then he heard a soft, "Dammit, son of a bitch."

And he smiled.

He was somewhere possibly even better than heaven.

He was in Piper's bed.

And she was in the kitchen making breakfast.

The only way that could be better would be if she were still in bed.

And they had condoms.

As he stretched and turned toward the sounds and then opened his eyes, he decided that there was one more good thing about this cabin—it wasn't very big. She was about thirty feet away, cooking, in only a pair of panties and another fitted tank top with spaghetti straps.

He grinned.

This was real life. But this *had* to be what heaven would be like too.

He watched her as she cooked, feeling his whole body stirring.

But not just his cock. His freaking chest felt tighter and warmer too.

His attraction to her had surprised him in the beginning. Not because he didn't think she was gorgeous and funny and brilliant. But because he'd, apparently, locked any thoughts of a relationship or even sex down tight.

But once she'd been in his lap and he'd touched, tasted, seen, and heard her, he'd been addicted.

He could really be screwed here.

But as she turned, saw he was awake, and gave him a huge, bright smile, he decided that he didn't care.

This wouldn't be the first time a big idea had occurred to him and he'd just rolled with it, consequences be damned. And Piper was one of the people who helped him with those consequences when things went sideways. If she was right here beside him, then everything would be fine.

"Morning," she said as she approached the bed.

Fuck yes. Breakfast in bed. With Piper. How could this be a bad idea?

"Morning."

"Morn—"

There was a knock on the door.

Piper sighed.

"Who is that?"

"Probably Drew."

Of course it was.

She handed him his plate and then started for the door.

"Piper."

She glanced back. "Yeah."

"Get dressed first."

She glanced down. "Oh. Pants. Right."

Did he hate the idea that she might have just gone to the door like that if she'd been here alone? Yes, he definitely did.

She pulled on yoga pants that were draped over the arm of a chair and started for the door again.

Ollie sighed. "Piper."

"What?"

"Get. Dressed."

Her breasts looked amazing in that tank top. Without a bra. And there was no fucking way he was going to let Drew see that.

She rolled her eyes and reached for the flannel shirt she'd been wearing last night. On second thought...

Ollie set the pancakes and bacon to the side—with a definite twinge of regret and a longing look—and flipped the covers back. He got out of bed and headed for the door.

"You're not going to get dressed?" Piper asked.

He looked over at her and her expression that was half amused and half I-want-to-see-how-this-goes.

"If Drew wants to get a good look at *this*," he said, waving a hand down his body. "He's free to gawk all he wants. But *that*"—he pointed at her—"is mine."

Her eyebrows shot up even as he felt a flip in his own gut. What? That was *his*? That was pretty damned possessive for a guy who didn't want attachments or anyone having expectations of him being able to meet any kind of decent-partner standard.

But she didn't comment on it.

Neither did he. Because he had no idea what to say.

He was not sharing her with Drew Fucking Ryan. That was really all he knew.

He pulled the door open. "What the hell do you want?" he asked.

Drew did, in fact, take in the sight of Ollie in his boxers only. From head to toe.

"My eyes are up here, Ryan," Ollie told him.

He met Ollie's gaze. "Good morning."

Damn, the guy's grin was annoying. "Was about to be. Then you showed up." Drew didn't know that all Ollie had been on the verge of getting in bed was bacon and pancakes. Because he didn't have any condoms.

But it wasn't as if he couldn't have had some fun with Piper and the maple syrup without the condoms...

"Well, we can come back later," Drew said. He leaned to the side so Ollie could look past him.

Matt and seven other teenagers, five boys and two girls—including Jane Kemper's little sister Kelsey—were standing out by two trucks and a car.

"There's more of them today," Ollie said unnecessarily.

"Word about the *Warriors* being written out here—and something about a kick-ass obstacle course—spread," Drew told him.

"You think the obstacle course is kick ass?" Ollie asked.

"I'm just repeating what I've been told." But Drew was grinning.

"Hi, guys!" Piper ducked under the arm Ollie had braced on the doorframe. "Hey, Kelsey!"

She'd gotten dressed. At least she'd put on a bra. And blue jeans.

Ollie sighed even as his body decided she looked just as hot in those as she had in just her tank top and panties. He shifted, so he was standing behind her and his sudden hard-on was hidden from their audience.

Of course, that put her front and center. Her smile was big and genuine, and Ollie had to admit he'd been *really* good at compartmentalizing Piper into the *assistant-only-don't-fuck-this-up* box in his head. Because that smile? That made him want to press her up against the side of the cabin and kiss the hell out of her.

"Hi, Piper. Matt said you all needed some extra help out here," Kelsey said with a grin.

Piper laughed. "Did he say that, or did he say there was a kick-ass obstacle course and free food?"

Kelsey nodded. "He mentioned both of those things too."

"Where do you want them?" Drew asked Piper.

Ollie gave in to the stupid urge to put his hand on her shoulder as the other man talked to her. Obviously, he'd spent the night with her. Did he really have to stake his claim? It seemed that she'd shared with Drew how she felt about Ollie when she'd turned Drew down for the date he'd asked her on.

After he'd kissed her.

Out here at this campground.

Ollie moved his hand to cup the back of her neck. Yeah, he needed to stake his claim.

He couldn't see Piper's expression, but he saw Drew's. The other man definitely got the message. Though he didn't look upset so much as he looked entertained.

"You guys can finish up cabin four," Piper said to Matt. "And another group can start on cabin six." She looked at Drew. "What do you want to do?"

"I'm going to start on the interior of cabin two, but can't stay long. Justin's gonna come out later and finish up."

Piper nodded. "Okay. Thanks."

"You've got it. See ya later." Drew gave her a wink.

Ollie knew that was for *his* benefit, but he still frowned at the other man.

Drew headed for his truck with a chuckle.

Fucking guy.

"They're going to be here all day?" Ollie asked as he watched the kids getting supplies out of the truck bed and start for the cabins.

"Guess so."

"Do they come every Saturday?"

She looked up at him. "It's not Saturday. They're on spring break, remember?"

Ollie sighed. Right. It just seemed like Saturday. Or something. Honestly, it didn't much matter to him what day it was. He worked every day. And his friends worked every day. And his editor worked whenever Ollie sent him stuff. So his schedule wasn't really dictated by the day of the week. But he was aware that one of his issues with doing things on time and the way other people wanted him to do things was that very inattention to details like what day it was.

"Is it still March?" he asked dryly.

She nodded with a grin. "Yep. Got it in one try." She looked over to where the boys were spreading drop cloths over the ground beside the cabins. "Thanks for motivating them to get out here early and to bring friends."

He shook his head. "I didn't."

"I think you did. They weren't all here before yesterday."

Huh. "I didn't really do anything."

"You focused them on the work but made it fun," she said. She turned slightly so she was facing him more fully. "And I'll bet they're hoping for some insider info about *Warriors*."

He glanced at the kids. Based on what they'd gotten done yesterday, with the extra hands and hours, they could get a lot done today.

With more people, they could add on to the obstacle course. They could do it in teams. Maybe every time they completed a side of a cabin, he could tell them something about the new adventure he was writing. Maybe they could even help him past the part he was stuck on. Normally, he batted ideas around with Dax. Aiden if he was really stuck or Dax wasn't around. But these kids played the game. At least Matt and Tanner and Landon did. He'd bet they could brainstorm the shit out of a new adventure.

He felt his heart kick. New people involved could mean some fresh ideas. This could be great.

Piper laughed, and he looked down at her.

"I lost you there for a second, didn't I?" she asked.

"No, I was just thinking about…" He sighed. "I was thinking about asking them for some brainstorming help."

She looked surprised but nodded. "That could be great. Are you stuck?"

He'd been stuck for months. "A little."

"Dax hasn't helped?"

"Dax has been really busy."

Something flickered in her eyes. "Aiden? Cam? Grant?"

"Busy, busy, and busy," he told her. But he smiled. "And Cam and Grant kind of suck at the mystical, fantasy stuff."

She smiled too. "I can see that."

"It'll be okay."

She pulled her bottom lip between her teeth, clearly thinking.

"What?" he asked after a second.

"I was going to offer to help, but I'm not good at that stuff either."

He frowned. "You are. You're incredibly creative." He wondered why he'd never asked her to brainstorm *Warriors* before.

She shook her head with a laugh. "I'm not. I can tell when an idea is good or bad. I can tell when something in a plotline makes sense or where you need to make some magical spell or exception to gravity or something, but I couldn't come up with the stuff in the first place."

Now that she mentioned it, Ollie realized that she'd always been very quiet during group brainstorming sessions. Piper being quiet was unusual. Those didn't happen all that often, of course. Usually only at the beginning of a new adventure script because everyone liked to have an idea where *Warriors*, as a world and product, was headed next.

For Dax, it helped him start planning graphics. For Aiden, it helped when he'd talk to their marketing team and contacts. He'd know just enough to get them all excited about what was coming. He and Grant could also get started on possible additions to their line of merch, and Cam could get ready for any new trademarks they might need.

Of course, none of them did any of that work anymore, so Ollie had been on his own with a lot of it. Well, he'd been teamed up with the people in those positions for Plus Gaming. But it hadn't been the same. At all.

Their knowledge of the game was limited, and their passion for it was driven by the bottom line rather than a true love for the world they'd created.

"I'd love to talk to you about it," he said. If they were doing this dating, share-everything thing, maybe that was something they could do. He'd love to have someone to bounce ideas off of.

"I..." She was biting her bottom lip again.

Ollie lifted a hand to her face and freed her lip with the pad of his thumb. He stroked back and forth across it. "You what?" he asked.

She winced and looked at his left earlobe instead of into his eyes. "I probably wouldn't be much help. I don't play *Warriors*."

He looked at her, dropping his hand. He was a little surprised, he wouldn't deny. It wasn't as if being a gamer was at all required in her job description. Her job had a lot do with the game in a general sense. She kept them all going so that they could keep *Warriors* going. But she didn't contribute directly to the game.

"You don't play regularly? You're not really into it? Or you've never played?"

She winced again. "I've never played."

"Really?" He couldn't decide if he was just surprised or if he was a little hurt or if it didn't really matter at all.

"Really." She finally met his eyes. "Do you hate me?"

"No." Of course he didn't hate her. "I'm surprised though."

"Because I'm in love with you and am thrilled that you're taking an interest in the camp and getting involved but find out that I'm not similarly interested or involved in your big professional passion?"

He thought about all of that. "Yeah." That pretty much summed it up. "I mean, I guess, working with us all this time and everything, I guess I would have thought you'd be at least curious."

She nodded. "That makes sense. But"—she blew out a breath—"I've been horribly jealous of that game."

"What?"

"When I first came to Fluke, I was a little curious, so I read about it, but gaming isn't really my thing, so I just never tried it. Then after my crush on you started, I hated how hard it was to get your attention when you were caught up in the game and... the women." She sighed. "I hated the women that got your attention because they were into the game, and so I just got stubborn and decided I was going to get your attention anyway." She gave him a little grin. "That turned out to be a lot harder than I'd expected."

His chest tightened at that. He lifted a hand and brushed her hair back. "I'm a dumbass."

She nodded. "Sometimes."

He gave her a little grin. "Why do I love that you can tell me that without hesitation?"

"I don't know. You're a little weird."

But she said it with such affection in her expression that Ollie felt warmth spread through his chest, and he bent to kiss her. It was a soft kiss, nothing like the heated kisses from last night, but it twisted his gut and heart up just like those had. Maybe more.

He lifted his head. "How do you feel about maple syrup being poured all over your body?"

Her eyes widened. "I feel like I would be *very* disappointed about the no-condom thing we have going on."

Right, no condoms. "I could make you *very* happy in spite of that."

"You have maple syrup experience?"

"I don't. But this is something I feel very good about ad-libbing."

She grinned but shook her head. "I believe you about making me happy, but we've got nine people milling about this campground now, and I get loud."

He didn't know why that surprised him. Actually, it didn't. Piper was loud in bed? That not only fit but totally fired his blood. It also didn't surprise him that she told him that so easily.

"Noted," he said, his voice gruff. "And I can't wait."

She gave him a sexy smile. "You go write and entertain the boys and brainstorm and all of that, and I'll paint and plant some bushes, and we'll have s'mores later."

That sounded absolutely perfect.

He thought about that as he dressed and settled in at the table in the kitchen area, coffee in hand, the smell of bacon still lingering in the air. Who would have thought his perfect day would include the woods behind Drew Fucking Ryan's house and eight teenagers who wanted to climb trees and army crawl through the dirt and leaves and... okay, the obstacle course made sense. And was cool. But the cabin in the woods where he'd slept with, but not *slept with*, his assistant was weird.

Good thing he was very good at weird.

———

The day had been amazing.

He'd finished not just the scene that had been bugging him for almost three weeks, but he'd gotten through most of the next one.

Brainstorming with Matt, Tanner, and Landon had been awesome.

The obstacle course with two teams of four to do relays had been awesome.

The amount of work they'd gotten done on the cabins had been awesome.

And being able to walk up behind Piper, turn her, put his hands on her ass, and back her up against the side of the cabin before kissing the hell out of her was awesome.

When he let her go after long, delicious seconds, she grinned up at him. "What was that for?"

"Because I can. Because Drew Ryan might be watching. And because of how you look in those jeans."

She laughed. "Drew headed out for alpaca duty a few hours ago."

"The kids are gone too," he told her, bending to place kisses along her neck.

She tipped her head so he could get to more skin. "I have a little more work to do, but I'm almost done."

"Great, I'll help."

He was in a fantastic mood.

She simply bent over and grabbed a brush. She handed it over. "Great."

She was about two-thirds done with this side of the cabin.

He let her take the ladder—he liked the view a lot—and he started work on the lower slats.

"So tell me about your brothers."

Her paintbrush paused.

Yeah, he was surprised too.

"It's really bugging you that you didn't know about them, isn't it?" she asked.

It really was. "Yep."

"Why is that, do you suppose?" she asked, resuming the back and forth strokes with her brush.

"Because I'm interested in you," he said.

Her brush paused again.

He rolled his eyes. "That shocks you?"

"It surprises me that you realize that's why you want to know more about me."

"You think I'm an idiot?" he asked.

She looked down at him. "Definitely not."

"Then why wouldn't I realize that I like you and am interested in you and that would make me want to know more about you?"

"I guess I expected you to ignore that and not admit it."

"Why would you expect that?"

"Because I think you've been doing that for at least a year. Definitely since we all moved to Appleby."

He shifted to face her more fully and propped an elbow on the rung beside her knee. "You think I've been interested in you for a year?"

She nodded.

"And that I've been fighting it?"

"Yes. But not consciously," she said. She seemed thoughtful. "Now that you've told me about your mom and how you've seen me as so organized and put together and you thought your ADHD would bug me, I think that you just put me in this space in your head that said, *don't get close*. I don't think you really let yourself think about *wanting* to get close."

He couldn't help the small grin that stretched his lips. She was confident, he'd give her that. "What makes you think my interest shifted a year ago?"

"It might have been longer ago than that."

His smile grew. "What makes you think it was ever more than just 'Hey, she's a great assistant'?"

"You came to Appleby for about two weeks before I did."

"Yeah."

"And you called me three times a day and texted at least twice during those two weeks."

"Well, I probably needed stuff." He hadn't. Not really. Well, not more than a couple of times.

"Yes. Apparently you needed to tell me about how your office smells like cake. And how they think it's weird here that a man would get a pedicure. And that actually the whole side of town where the factory is smells like cake—a separate phone call from the first one about your office. And to let me know that you had decided that you *do* like pineapple on your pizza."

"Granny Smith's has great pizza."

"You've always liked pineapple on your pizza, Ollie."

"I'm sure that's not true."

"It is."

"No. I thought pineapple on pizza was *fine*. But I wouldn't say I *liked it*. Until I had it at Granny Smith's on the Hawaiian Delight."

He watched her roll her eyes and grinned. All of that was true, of course. But going from fine to liking pineapple on pizza was not truly of phone-call-in-the-middle-of-a-workday importance. Which he'd known at the time. But, yes, he'd missed her.

"You missed me," she said.

"I did."

"And not just for assistant stuff."

"Yes."

"Even though you probably weren't admitting that to yourself."

"Right."

"But now you *definitely* like me," she said, giving him a smug look. "For more than assistant stuff."

"After the things you let me do to you last night, I think it's safe to say you're one of my very favorite people in the world," he said sincerely. He definitely wanted to see her react to the reminder of last night.

In true Piper fashion, she didn't blush or avert her eyes. She lifted an eyebrow, gave him a cocky smile, and said, "I would certainly hope so."

He really wanted to kiss her. He loved her confidence. He loved just how *capable* she was. She could do anything, he swore. She had this caring, nurturing side that was edged with I'm-doing-this-for-you-but-I-know-you-know-you're-better-than-this.

This was definitely one way she was different from his mother. Vivian Caprinelli had never been all that *capable*. She'd been, well, frail frankly. So many things bothered her and made her anxious. Not the least of which had been her only child. But she'd always needed Oliver's father there to reassure her and help her and support her. Which was nice, on one hand. Marco had always been there for her. He'd been her rock.

When Marco was around, Ollie had always felt better. Marco would deal with Vivian. Ollie didn't have to. He didn't have to worry about bothering her because Marco would run interference.

Maybe that was why Ollie was so drawn to Piper. She was definitely a rock. She was steady, dependable. Told you exactly what she thought. He knew where he stood with her. He didn't have to walk on eggshells around her. He could be himself because she could handle it. She could handle *him*.

"I think I should warn you," Piper said. "If you get to know me better, you're going to definitely like me more and be even *more* interested."

See? She was handling him. Not dancing around any issues. Not letting him think this was anything other than what it was... her wanting him and pursuing him and drawing him in.

And knowing that she was going to get him.

14

He took a moment, then nodded. "So... your brothers," he said. He knew it was an admission of everything she'd just said.

"Really?"

"Yep."

The only people he knew well enough to know about their siblings were the guys. And Whitney, though that was partly because her oldest brother had been a big part of Hot Cakes when the guys were buying the company, and Ollie had met the man once. He hadn't liked Wes Lancaster much.

But he wanted to know about Piper's family the way he did Cam's and Grant's and Dax's and Aiden's.

"Okay." She went back to her painting, but she had a soft smile on her lips. "The twins are Nathan and Lucas. They're eleven. Nathan is the sweetest kid. All into firemen. Lucas is really quiet and shy. Loves books. And they both love video games." She slid Ollie a glance.

"That's totally my fault?"

"It really is."

"And yours. You're the one that introduced them."

She nodded and sighed. "Yeah."

"Jacob is sixteen," she went on. "He's a pretty typical teenager in a lot of ways. He plays basketball and is way more into girls than into studying."

"Understandable."

She chuckled. "Yeah, you two need to not spend a lot of time alone together."

Ollie grinned, but he liked the idea of meeting her family. Which he knew was a sign he was getting attached. And he probably should *not* do that. If nothing else because if Piper was like her mom or dad at all, then that would be two more people for Ollie to drive nuts.

Still, he couldn't help but think that he'd love to see Piper with her brothers. It had to be a lot like watching her interacting with, and taking care of, Dax, Aiden, Grant, and Cam over the years. She did it without any of them even truly realizing how much she did for them. He knew she'd probably say it was because it had been her job, but he knew it was more than that.

He swiped paint onto the side of the building as he thought about Piper interacting with the four men he loved like brothers.

She loved those guys too. Regardless of how she felt about *Warriors of Easton* specifically, she'd been a huge part of their success in the years she'd been a part of the company. The guys couldn't have done all the things they'd done without her help. She did more than organize meetings and make reservations. When they checked into hotel rooms, there were always things there to make them more comfortable. And they were specific to each man.

She made sure Aiden had feather pillows. She made sure Grant had smoked almonds. She made sure Dax had gummy bears. She made sure Cam had his favorite brand of high-lighters.

As he thought about all of that, Ollie realized she could have just reminded the guys to each bring those things themselves. Or she could have packed them into their carry-ons. Well, except for the pillows.

But she didn't. She'd make sure the hotel staff could provide the items and that they were waiting in their rooms. He wouldn't have been surprised if she'd shipped everything ahead to the front desk to be sure it was all exactly right.

And those were just a few examples.

She did that stuff all the time.

For Ollie there was always a pack of his favorite iced tea, along with multivitamins and a pad of sticky notes.

He realized now that he'd always felt very cared for when he saw those things sitting on the top of the dresser even in a strange hotel room.

She was so good at making them all feel loved even while she wasn't afraid to roll her eyes and tell them that an idea was stupid. Of course, she was always happy to offer suggestions for making the idea *not* stupid.

Even though she didn't love *Warriors*, it had been important to the guys, and they were important to her, so she'd done her part to make *Warriors* successful.

He really appreciated that now that he thought about it.

Piper was a lot like Grant in his life. She was a rock. Someone who kept him steady. He was able to be a dreamer because she kept his feet on the ground. He didn't have to worry about "floating away" or getting lost, because Piper was there for him.

Just like Grant was.

But she smelled a lot better. And he did *not* want to see Grant naked.

"Do you send care packages to your brothers?" he asked. He knew the answer was yes.

"I do. Why do you ask?"

"It's what you do for the people you care about. It's how you show your love," he said. "You do it with all of us. Your kind-of brothers. I figured you for sure do it for your real brothers."

"You've noticed."

"I have. I hadn't really thought about it because it's just what you've always done. Full water bottles just appear on our desks. The mayo is always on the side of Aiden's burgers. You make sure there are always replacement Ping-Pong balls for Dax. You make sure the antacid and ibuprofen bottles in Grant's desk drawer are full." He grinned at that. Grant wrote DAX on the side of the antacids and OLLIE on the side of the painkillers.

He glanced up to find her looking at him with a strange expression.

"What?" he asked.

"I guess..." She shook her head. "I guess I do do those things."

He chuckled. "You don't do them on purpose?"

"Well, I mean, I don't *accidentally* buy Grant antacids, but I never thought of that as a way of showing love."

"I don't think most professional assistants specifically buy cola-flavored Chapstick for their bosses." It was Aiden's favorite.

"I'm sure they do."

"Not without being asked to," he said. He paused, watching her think that over. "Has Aiden ever specifically asked you to get cola-flavored?"

She shook her head. Then said, "I don't think he's ever specifically asked me to buy Chapstick at all."

"So why did you?" He knew why, but he wanted her to realize why.

"I noticed he was almost out one day and it seemed like something I could help him with."

Ollie nodded. "Exactly. You do it without us asking but even without *thinking* about it. You do things like spraying Cam's office with that citrus room spray his mom makes. You had her send it to you, didn't you?"

She nodded, her bottom lip between her teeth.

"And you dust Grant's office every morning before he gets in."

Not because Grant was a neat freak, though he was a little, but because he was allergic to dust.

"Not *every* morning," she said weakly.

Ollie grinned. "Liar."

"I don't go in on the weekends to do it." She paused. "But if I'm in on the weekend anyway, I do."

"I know."

She gave him a smile. "And you noticed all of this?"

"I guess so." He shrugged. "I'll be honest. I didn't give it a ton of thought until now. But it definitely makes us all feel cared for and makes us happier. And healthier. Which makes the business do better and... just all of us do better."

That made Piper do something he'd never seen her do before. She ducked her head with a little smile that almost made her look... shy.

He reached out and tipped her chin up, looking into her eyes. "I'm sorry I didn't appreciate all of that more before now."

"But see," she said. "I don't mind that you didn't notice. If I made your lives a little easier, then I was happy."

She was so sweet. And out of all the adjectives that he would have applied to Piper before now, that was probably not one of them. She was sassy and confident and capable and sharp and bold. But not sweet. She told them all when they were being idiots. She told them when their ideas were terrible. She told them when they pissed her off.

But that made the way she loved them and took care of them even better.

The realization hit him right in the heart.

She could have walked out and landed another job somewhere else easily. Hell, the guys would have given her a glowing recommendation even as they begged her to stay.

She could have just done the basics and still made a great paycheck. She could have kept herself from getting involved and saved herself a lot of headaches, 3:00 a.m. phone calls, and having to dust Grant's shelves.

But she didn't. She told them the truth and kept them in line even while making sure Cam had pineapple juice instead of orange juice at any breakfast, formal or informal, and any number of other little details that really did make their lives better. They seemed like small things, but they all added up. They were all better for the little Piper touches.

He wanted to kiss her but was a little glad she was too far up the ladder to be able to reach her lips. If he started now, he wasn't sure he'd stop, and there were more things to talk about.

"You make our lives so much better, Piper. And it's not just the things you do. It's how you do them. It's that it's so natural to you. You're a caregiver through and through. Even when you're telling us we're wrong, it's because you care."

She nodded.

"You even care about *Warriors*," he teased.

"Well..." She gave him a little smile. "I care because you all care. But I'm not upset that everyone has other stuff now." She frowned. "I'm sorry. I know it means more to you than the others."

"It's just... the thing that brought us all together. That's mostly it," he said. "I love it, but I love what it does for people." He looked at her as his heart kicked. "Kind of like what you do."

She lifted a brow. "*Warriors* is like what I do? What do you mean?"

"You take care of people. Little subtle things that blend into this bigger picture of them being happy and more successful."

"And *Warriors* does the same?"

"It does." He laughed at her look of skepticism. "The game teaches things like teamwork and self-sacrifice and the importance of loyalty over riches. Things like that. But it's subtle. It's built into the stories and the things players encounter as they go through the stories. The choices they have to make, the way they have to work together, the obstacles they have to confront."

"Hmm." She didn't sound convinced. But she didn't argue. She might have looked a tiny bit interested, in fact.

"So what about your oldest brother?" he asked. He still wanted to know everything about her, and they'd only gotten through three-fourths of the other guys she took care of.

Of course, that wasn't true either. He'd watched her today with the kids and Drew. She was constantly making sure everyone had everything they needed and that they were all happy. She'd praised them all for their work, thanked them for doing such a great job, made sure they had plenty of sandwiches and water. She'd even come down to the obstacle course during one of their breaks to check it out—and insisted that Matt pound some nails into the one end of the wooden plank they'd added between two trees to secure it. But she never told them to be more careful or questioned if they should be doing things like putting monkey bars between two trees twenty feet off the ground.

"My oldest brother is Ethan," she said, her voice softening with affection. "He just turned twenty. I'm hoping that he'll come and help run the camp once it's up and going."

"Really? He'd want to come to Appleby?"

She nodded. "I think so. He tried college but it wasn't really for him. So he's been working and living with my parents instead. I think he'd like to get away from home and be on his own a little. Plus, Appleby is really different from Chicago. I think a new place and lifestyle could be good. Teach him a few things."

"Definitely different," Ollie agreed. "Lots of cute girls here though. At least according to my *four* best friends. You know, if he's into that kind of thing."

Piper laughed. "Oh, he is." Then after a moment said, "Ethan is the one who loves *Warriors* the most."

"Yeah?"

"They all do," she said. "Too much," she added quickly.

"Yeah, yeah."

"But Ethan was the one who really got into it first. He broke his leg badly about six years ago. It required two surgeries and a lot of pins and stuff, so he couldn't play any sports and got around at school in a wheelchair for a while. He'd always liked video games but got into it more then. And *Warriors* was his thing. Said it made him a lot less depressed because he could find people to 'hang out with' any time while his friends from school were out being active and he was stuck at home."

Okay, that was awesome. That gave Ollie a definite sense of pride.

"He still has some limitations from that injury," she went on. "Nothing super serious, but he can't run like he used to and jumping and pivoting for competitive basketball was out even after he'd healed and done rehab. He became a lot less active." She was still painting, watching her brush go back and forth, but she seemed lost in thought. "He'd wanted to try to play basketball in college, and I've wondered if that wasn't why college didn't really work out. Because he'd always envisioned himself as an athlete but hadn't really thought about what *else* he wanted to do. When that dream ended, he had a hard time finding a new one."

"You think coming to Appleby can help him figure out his dream?" Ollie asked.

She looked down at him. "I don't know. But I know that when everything you thought you knew ends, and you have to figure out a new plan, you realize the things that you want to hang on to and the things you're willing to let go of."

He stared at her. He felt like she'd just punched him in the chest. It was hard to take a deep breath for a second.

"Is that how you feel about Appleby?" he asked, his voice a little rough.

She nodded. "Yeah. Everything about the company and business and the interactions with you guys changed when Hot Cakes came into our lives and we all moved here. But from that I realized the things that are unchanging. Your friendships and how I feel about all of you and what I'm good at. And that I want to keep doing the things I'm good at. Organizing and planning and pulling big things off and taking care of people."

He swallowed with some difficulty. "You think that's happened to the rest of us?"

"For sure," she said without hesitation. "The guys have all realized that they were ready to bring other people into their lives and add love in. They were ready to look at new endeavors. They were ready to just look at life differently. And that they all had new directions to go in, but that they wanted to stay together, seeing each other, involved in each other's lives."

"I didn't want things to change," Ollie said.

"I know."

"So that makes me, what? Less enlightened than the other guys?"

She smiled. "It just means that you need more stability."

"Like being with a woman I know really well."

She nodded. "And who knows you really well."

He couldn't help his smile. He wondered if Piper had ever

doubted that she'd get him wrapped around her little finger. It didn't seem so.

"Well, writing in the woods is new."

"And building obstacle courses for teenagers is new."

"And painting cabins is new."

"And being friends with Drew Ryan is new."

"I'm not going to be friends with Drew Ryan," he said firmly.

She laughed. "Okay. Well the rest of it is good."

He studied her. Her face, her voice, her scent, her laugh… it was all so familiar and comforting, and maybe he hadn't let himself think of her as someone he wanted to fuck against the wall, and on the table, and bent over a sofa, and by a campfire —okay, he definitely hadn't thought about fucking her by a campfire—but in less than forty-eight hours he was already realizing that it was ridiculous that he *hadn't* thought about that every day for the past five years.

"I really have been a dumbass," he told her.

She nodded. "I know. But you're cute, and you're here now, so I forgive you."

He felt that warm-in-his-chest feeling again. "I think I should be the activities director here at the camp."

She shifted gears with him without even blinking. "Um, no."

"Come on." He grinned at her. "You know that one recommendation to help with ADHD is physical activity and having lots of different things to focus on rather than having to attend to one thing for long periods. In fact, sitting still and staring at a computer screen or a blank piece of paper for long periods is hell. It's been really working for me, and for the kids. So let me do some camp stuff with you. Besides painting."

"No."

"You said yourself that you're not good at the creative,

making-things-up stuff. I'm *awesome* at it. Then you can help me mold it into things that are workable."

She didn't say no as quickly this time.

So he kept going. One thing he'd learned from Dax Marshall was *always* push your advantage. "I've gotten a ton done out here." That would make her happy. "And I think it's because during my breaks I had the obstacle course and the kids to focus on. As much as I like the writing and creating, the parts of my day that I like most are the ones that involve other people."

Piper snorted. "No kidding."

He grinned. He loved the morning meetings with the guys. He loved when Piper was in his office. He even liked the editing process. He liked talking about the stories and plots and characters.

The stuff he did alone was the hardest for him.

"I'm a creator but I'm a teamwork guy. When I put pen to paper, it's a long time until I see the final product. The graphics Dax did always brought it to life for me, and he'd let me see early sketches and stuff as we went along. I loved that stage of the process. But now Dax is doing less of the graphics and design work." Dax was more of a consultant to the other designers now. "The guys with Plus Gaming never show me stuff until it's done."

Piper was listening, her attention fully on him now.

"This is different," he went on. "I can see the paint going onto the sides of the buildings. I see something new for the obstacle course in my head, and then we make it and start using it right away." He could already mentally picture all of the things he wanted to add to the campground. "I'm having fun. And I want to keep doing this. I feel like I've been able to focus and accomplish something here in a way I haven't in a long time."

He could tell that made her soften toward the idea.

Piper really did want what was best for him and wanted him to be happy.

How had he resisted her this long?

"I just worry that you might... go overboard," she said.

They both knew that he *would* go overboard. That was part of the fun.

"I'm so good at going overboard," he said. "I didn't know what to expect being out here, but this is fun. I like that we're doing this together. And I think it's going to be good for me to have something new to do. Like the other guys have."

She narrowed her eyes. "I said that first," she reminded him. "I *know* you need something else."

"Then we're on the same page." He grinned. "And I'll pay for everything."

That definitely gave her pause. Yeah, being a millionaire had its perks.

"I'll pay for all materials and labor costs *and* you don't have to pay me. And I promise it will be kick ass."

She sighed.

"Plus—" He reached up and curled a finger through one of her belt loops and tugged.

She came down the ladder, and he leaned in, bracing his hands on the siderails. "If I go too overboard or screw things up, you can make me make it up to you however you want." He felt her lean closer and he smiled.

"*However* I want?" she asked.

He ran a hand up her back and into her hair. "*However* you want." He kissed his way down her neck, along her collarbone and up to her jaw.

"You know exactly how to get to me, Mr. Caprinelli," she said, her voice a little breathless.

He definitely did. And while he knew she loved the kissing and the promise of being able to get whatever she wanted in the bedroom—which of course she could have without anything more than a simple request—he realized she really mostly loved the idea of him getting involved in the camp and doing something *he* would love.

That was a humbling thought. Even as it made him want her with an intensity that was actually shocking.

"So," he said against her mouth, "can I be the activities director? And can you get your brothers here in a few days?"

"The younger ones are in school," she said.

"Can they miss a couple of days? They could get here Thursday and stay until Sunday."

She pulled back and looked into his eyes. "Next Thursday?"

"Yeah."

"You really have plans to get things together that fast?"

"Of course. Why wait?"

"I..." She shook her head.

It was so unusual for Piper Barry to be at a loss for words that Ollie actually felt kind of proud of himself.

Then she surprised him even further by saying, "Yes, they could miss a couple of days."

"Really?" Piper did not strike him as the type to condone skipping school.

"Sure. They could get their work done ahead of time. And this could be important for Ethan. If you're here and he could meet you, it would make him even more enthusiastic about coming."

"I would have gladly met him any time."

"I know. But having you involved with the camp I want him involved with..."

She trailed off with a little frown.

"What's wrong?" he asked.

"I just..." She swallowed. "You've made this even more important. I didn't expect that. I thought I was into this and was hoping that once you were here you'd help out, but now you're taking this to a new level. You've been awesome with the guys working here, and now you want my brothers here too, and you're just being you, but you've made this into something even bigger."

She gave him a wobbly smile so full of affection that he felt a strange tightness in his chest.

He knew what it was.

Expectation.

Someone was expecting something from him. And now he had to deliver.

Dammit.

People expecting things always made him nervous. Delivering on expectations was not a strong suit of his.

But... this was Piper.

He knew that thought kept going through his mind, but it was so damned comforting. This was Piper. He wanted to deliver on expectations for her more than he'd ever wanted to for anyone else. At the same time, he didn't feel as nervous as usual thinking about that. Because she was patient and forgiving and loving and would understand that him even trying mattered.

"I'm just talking about some camp games and activities," he said.

"But you're excited about this?"

He nodded. "I am."

"That's so great." Her voice softened. "Thank you."

Ollie felt a weird squeeze in his heart at that. She was thanking him for caring about this? But he realized almost instantly that it made sense. He hadn't done that a lot. Or at all. The other guys hadn't really either.

Piper hadn't had stuff that she'd shared with them or needed them to care about.

Except Drew. She and Drew had worked together on some of the farm programming for Dax and the nursing home. Because Drew had alpacas, and Piper had a natural ability to organize absolutely anything and make it work perfectly.

And now this camp.

Drew had been a friend to her that the guys—that *he*—hadn't been.

And rather than jealous, that made him feel a surge of *no more*. Not because he wanted to keep Drew away from her, but because *he* wanted to be someone that helped her get what she needed and wanted.

Everything Piper did was with a pureness of heart that he had to admit was pretty damned sexy.

She dusted shelves and replaced Ping-Pong balls and bought Chapstick. She kept them on their toes and made them laugh but also took care of them and was incredibly loyal, and she cared about things just because they did.

Hell, *he* still cared about *Warriors* in part because of her. He maybe would have quit once Dax and Cam and Aiden and Grant were done. But Piper was still there.

He'd kept doing his *Warriors* work, in part, because he didn't know what else he'd do. But Piper had still been there, making it okay. Yes, she literally *made* him do it some days, but it was also what kept her there.

If he hadn't been writing *Warriors*, he wouldn't have been having conference calls about *Warriors*. So he wouldn't have needed someone to keep track of his conference calls about it.

He'd initially kept writing *Warriors* because of the guys. It had been fun to write stuff for Dax to play with. That Aiden had been able to sell it had just been a perk. He could now live off the royalties and what Plus Games paid to use his name, for years.

But *Warriors* kept Piper in his life.

Until a week ago.

And for a week he hadn't been able to write a word. Until

he came here. To her. Was she his muse? Maybe. Or maybe she was just his *reason*.

Now he wanted to be part of the reason she was excited about this camp and what it could do. He wanted to be here with her when she needed help and when she had successes, the way she'd been there for him.

"I'm in because of you."

She watched him for a few seconds after he spoke. Then she asked, "Are you falling for me?"

To the point, no bullshit. That was Piper.

He took a breath. "No."

"Oh."

"I think I've already fallen."

Her eyes widened at that. And a smile slowly tipped her mouth. "Yeah?"

"I mean, I'm probably not going to be *good* at being in love," he said. "So I wouldn't get your hopes too high. But yeah. You're completely amazing, and I want to be here every day with you, building this thing. I want to meet your family. I want to be friends with your friends. I want to make this even bigger and better than what you have planned. And I want to amaze you even half as much as you amaze me."

Now she really did look dumbstruck and that was absolutely a first. Ollie grinned. He wished he had a photo of that expression right now.

"Oliver." That was all she said. But she looked like she might cry.

And *that* was definitely new and weird.

"Are you feeling totally swoony and lovestruck?" he asked.

"Did you just use the word swoony?"

"I did."

"How do you know that word?"

"I go to conventions that are attended by women of all ages

and where actors, who play superheroes, show up," he told her. He gave her an eye roll. "I've heard the word."

She laughed, the threat of tears seeming to vanish. "Well, yes, I am feeling swoony," she said with a nod.

"Then I think you need to come here, and show me some of those mushy feelings."

She leaned forward, running her hands up his chest and linking her hands behind his neck. "Like this?"

His hands dropped to her ass and he squeezed. "Yep."

"Okay, I will," she said. "But... we don't have any condoms. And we're going to need them."

15

———————

There was a long pause.

Then Ollie pulled away. "I've got this." He started toward the truck.

"What are you doing?"

He jerked the truck door open and looked back at her. "Going to get condoms."

"Now? Just like that?"

He gave a short laugh. "Yeah, just like that, Piper. This is the best sex I've ever had, and we haven't even had it yet."

Then he got in the truck, slammed the door, and started the engine.

Piper watched him pull away from the cabin and go rumbling down the dirt path.

This is the best sex I've ever had, and we haven't even had it yet.

She couldn't stop repeating that line over and over in her mind.

And grinning.

She did wonder, of course, how long it would take him to realize that he didn't have his wallet so he'd be unable to buy any condoms anywhere in Appleby. Maybe he was thinking he was going to go all the way to Dubuque to his hotel room. Without his keycard, of course. The front desk staff would let him into his room without his key or ID. He'd been a permanent guest for the past nine months. In the penthouse suite. They knew who he was.

But surely he'd realize it was ridiculous to drive all the way to Dubuque for condoms.

Right?

He'd turn around and come back for his wallet.

Wouldn't he?

Well, if he didn't, then he'd come back eventually and get his wallet, and then she'd tell him he could get condoms in Appleby. Or maybe she wouldn't.

Ollie was taking this into his own hands. He was solving the problem. He might not do it in the most efficient manner, but he was doing it. That was really, really good.

He just needed the right motivation it seemed.

She couldn't help but feel damned satisfied as she turned and started for the cabin. She really liked being his motivation.

And, hey, he had a fifteen-mile drive into Appleby before hitting the highway to Dubuque. Maybe he'd realize that Aiden, Dax, Cam, and Grant all lived in Appleby and would have condoms. Or might have condoms. Okay, she had no idea if those couples used condoms. Nor was it any of her business.

But they did all have money. They could loan him money to use to go buy condoms in Appleby.

Yeah, he'd figure that out.

Probably.

She had just finishing putting everything away and was in the cabin straightening up when she heard a vehicle pull up in front.

Ollie came through the door a moment later.

He stalked toward her.

"You realized you forgot your—"

He tossed a box of condoms onto the table and backed her up against the countertop behind her. He took her face in his hands and bent to kiss her.

The kiss was hot and hungry, and she immediately melted into it. Gripping his biceps, she arched closer, opening her mouth.

His tongue swept into her mouth, stroking, as his hands ran from her face, down her neck, down her sides, to her hips. He brought her up against his rock-hard cock and she moaned.

"Get naked," he ordered against her mouth.

Then he stepped back and stripped his shirt over his head.

Heart pounding, she pulled her t-shirt off and unhooked her bra, tossing it to the side.

He groaned and lifted a hand to cup one breast, thumbing the nipple, then rolling it between his thumb and finger.

She gasped and let her eyes slide shut.

He pinched harder, and her breath hissed out as pleasure spread from her belly between her legs.

"Fuck. Less clothes, Piper. Now."

She pushed her jeans and panties to the floor.

His eyes were dark and hot as he shed his jeans and boxers, then reached for her.

He scooped his hands under her ass and lifted her onto the counter as if she weighed nothing. Without breaking eye contact with her, he stepped back to reach the box of condoms.

She pressed her knees together, her core aching.

"Oh no, wide open," he said, noticing.

He ripped the box open and withdrew a condom.

"Piper."

Her gaze was on his cock, anticipating watching him roll the condom on. "Huh?"

"Open your legs."

Her eyes flew to his. Dang, this bossy side of him was so sexy. She parted her knees.

"That's it," he praised, his eyes roaming over her body.

She was never particularly self-conscious, but the way Ollie was looking at her right now made her want to stretch and pose, making sure he could see every inch. He was regarding her the way some people looked at beautiful art.

And like he wanted to ravage her.

He tore the condom open and rolled it down the length of his erection.

She wiggled on the counter as she watched, the sight making her hot and needy.

He noticed. "Oh, you like that?"

"Yes."

He stroked himself again.

She licked her lips.

He gave her a slow grin. "Oh yeah. Later."

She gave *him* a slow grin. "Promise?"

"To let you wrap that bossy mouth around my cock? I would love only one thing more."

Her breath caught in her chest she managed to ask, "What's that?"

"To make you come on that counter right now." He stepped forward.

She spread her legs wider.

He cupped her ass and brought her to the edge. "You're fucking fantastic, Piper Barry."

In spite of what they were about to do, his tone was definitely affectionate as was the look in his eyes as he leaned over to kiss her.

She curled her hand into the back of his neck at the base of his hair and let him stroke her and taste her for nearly a minute.

Finally he lifted his head. "You ready?"

"I've been ready for two years, Ollie."

For a second, she wondered if that was the wrong thing to say. Was it too much? Too intense? Overkill?

But his eyes flickered with an emotion that was definitely lust combined with a softer emotion, almost like wonder.

Then he lined himself up and pressed forward, thrusting deep.

And yes, it was absolutely fucking fantastic.

He drew back and thrust again. He was big and he was so damned good.

Piper moaned and wrapped her legs around him, pressing her heels into his ass. He gripped her hips, his jaw tight, thrusting steady and deep, his eyes locked on hers.

Every stroke was perfect, hitting *that spot*. The one she hadn't even known she needed to have hit. But she did. She so did. Again and again and—

"Ollie!" she cried out, feeling her orgasm tightening low and deep, coiling, ready to let go.

"Yes," he said through gritted teeth. "Fuck. Yes."

"I... don't stop..."

"No fucking way."

He gripped her hips tighter and picked up the pace, pumping into her deep and hard.

She dug her heels in and gripped his shoulders. "Ollie!"

And then she shot over the pinnacle.

"Oh damn. Yes, Piper," Ollie groaned. He thrust faster, and the waves of her orgasm went on and on.

She felt his body tighten and his breath catch and then heard her name on a low, sexy groan.

She wrapped her arms around him, and he hugged her close as they caught their breaths and their bodies cooled.

Wow. That had been very worth waiting two years.

"I take back everything I said about calling it a 'magical staff,'" she said against his neck. "It really is."

He gave a chuckle. "You heard about that?"

"You guys are *not* quiet when giving each other shit."

"Fair enough." He paused. "Sorry you heard about that. All of it. Any of it."

She pulled back and looked up at him. "You don't have to be. We weren't together. You didn't say it *to* me or to be mean or anything."

He lifted a shoulder. "Still. Feel like an ass now."

"Don't." She rubbed his shoulder. "Nothing to feel bad about. It was fun. Good, consensual sex between adults. And," she added, grinning up at him, "magical."

He gave a little eye roll. "That was Dax's thing. Not mine."

"Hmm."

He stepped back and dealt with the condom. She hopped to the floor and grabbed her t-shirt again. But she'd just pulled it over her head when he moved in behind her, wrapping his arms around her. "I got a whole box of condoms."

"I noticed."

"So don't feel like you have to get too dressed."

She shivered in his arms. Naked all night with Ollie? Yes, please. "Noted. Where'd you get those so fast?"

"Drew."

Piper froze. Then turned in his arms. "You went to Drew's?"

"Yeah. He was the closest."

"You just went up to his house and said, 'Hey do you have some condoms?'"

"Yeah."

"And what did he say?"

"He laughed and said, 'As a matter of fact I do' and went and got them. Asked how many I needed, and I just grabbed the box and left."

Piper put a hand over her mouth as she grinned. She could picture Drew's face. He knew that Ollie was the reason she'd said no to dating him. He was a good friend. He'd wanted to date her, but when she'd explained that she was in love with someone else, he'd respectfully backed off and remained her friend.

And now, he'd be happy for her. That was just the kind of guy Drew was.

But he'd tease her about it the next time he saw her.

She wouldn't mind.

She wrapped her arms around Ollie's neck and stretched up to kiss him. "I'm glad you thought of that."

His hands went to her hips, pulling her close, and he kissed her deeply. "Me too," he finally said when he let her up.

"Very resourceful of you, Mr. Caprinelli."

"Turns out I *can* be a problem solver." He gave her a crooked grin.

Yeah. Naked all night. That was definitely a plan.

"Need any help over here?" a male voice called.

Ollie wanted to punch Drew Ryan in the face.

Despite the other man coming through with condoms last night.

Ollie had written two new scenes that morning with three obstacle course breaks with the guys. They'd nearly finished painting the outside of cabin three. Now Ollie was helping Piper plant bushes along one side of cabin two. Things were great over here. Without Drew.

He looked over his shoulder at Drew. "Yeah, I could use someone to run to town for me. For more condoms."

Drew smirked. "You lost the box on your way back over here?"

"On second thought, you'd better get me two boxes."

"Okay," Piper cut in. She pushed up from where she'd been kneeling on the ground and wiped her hands together to brush the dirt off. "As entertaining as it is to listen to two men discuss my sex life right in front of me as if I'm not here, I think we could find another topic."

"We're bonding," Drew said. "You're the one who wanted us to be friends."

"You did?" Ollie asked. Why would she want that? He had friends. Four of them. Maybe even five if he counted Whitney, which he probably did now that he thought about it.

"Friend*ly*," Piper said. "I think that's probably the most I could hope for."

"Probably not gonna happen," Ollie told her honestly. Drew Ryan wanted to date Piper. He knew that the other man had asked her out. And kissed her. Sure, Piper had turned him down, but that didn't make *Drew* more likable. It just made Ollie like *Piper* more.

"That's too bad," Drew said. "Because I could use a hand with something that requires a blowtorch, and, for some reason, that seemed like your kind of thing." He was looking at Ollie.

"A blowtorch seemed like my kind of thing?" Ollie asked. "What does that even mean?"

"It means you seem like the type of guy who might like to use fire to melt things."

Ollie thought about that. Dammit. He *was* that type of guy. Presumably. He'd never used a blowtorch. And the only fire he'd ever set outside of the gas fireplace in his apartment in Chicago had been purely accidental, had been put out quickly by the Miami Fire Department, and had cost him nearly a hundred grand. Porsches were not cheap.

"What are you *melting*?" Piper asked Drew.

"Metal," Drew said with a grin. "I'm welding. Need to mend a couple of gates, and then I thought I'd try making a couple of things for the mini golf."

"You think you can make some stuff?"

He shrugged. "I think so."

Piper looked at Ollie. "I swear, Drew can make anything."

Yeah, yeah. But it sounded like the guy had blowtorches. Ollie couldn't deny that was cool.

"You're going to have miniature golf?" he asked Piper.

"I think that seems like a good outdoor activity to include, don't you?"

Not really. He shrugged. "Are you going to make it exciting?"

"Exciting?" Piper asked.

"Yeah."

"Miniature golf isn't exciting as is?"

"No. Not at all," Ollie told her. Hey, she told him when he had bad ideas, right? He could return the favor.

She propped a hand on her hip. "Not at *all*?"

"No. Now, disc golf could *possibly* be fun," Ollie said.

"Frisbee golf?" Piper clarified. "How is that more fun?"

"Well... it's not putting balls through fake castles and shit."

"But frisbee golf is just throwing a frisbee around," Piper said.

"Right. You'd have to make it more exciting than that," Ollie said. That was obvious, wasn't it?

"How would we make it exciting?" Drew asked. He actually seemed interested. If amused.

"Hazards," Ollie said simply.

Piper sighed.

"Like water hazards in real golf?" Drew asked.

Ollie frowned. "No. First of all, real golf blows." Golf was way too slow paced and tranquil for Ollie. He'd hated it all three times he'd played. And he'd sucked at it. "And water hazards in golf are hazards only because your ball might go in and cost you strokes."

"So you mean hazards like..." Drew prompted.

"Like hazards to the players," Ollie said. Obviously.

"I'm not sure we should purposefully add *hazards* to an

activity for kids at a camp where we are responsible for their health and safety," Piper said. Though she definitely didn't seem surprised by Ollie's suggestion.

"Well, I'm not talking about having people shoot poisoned darts at them while they're golfing," he said. Though that would be pretty great. Not poisoned, of course, but the darts. Maybe rubber tipped. Still...

Piper moved to stand in front of him. "You're thinking about how to shoot darts at them, aren't you?"

"No."

"Ollie."

He grinned. "Well, we could have teams. One team golfing and the other team making it hazardous. Darts—rubber tipped, of course—paintballs, dodgeballs."

"No."

"But the team with the darts and balls could climb trees and hide out and wait for the golfers. The golfers could have shields and stuff if that would make you feel better."

Piper put a hand on her hip. "No."

It was always fun to brainstorm with Piper around. More fun when Whitney and Dax and Grant and Aiden were there though. That ended up being like a Team A vs Team B setup as well. The Idea Team against the Practical Team.

He loved making Piper sigh and roll her eyes. Grant too.

"I'm guessing having them walk across a narrow balance beam with hungry alligators underneath on the seventh hole is also a no?"

She shook her head but was clearly fighting a smile. "That's definitely a no."

"Rings of fire?" he asked.

She narrowed her eyes. "To throw the discs through or for them to climb through?"

"Which would you say yes to?"

"Neither."

He laughed. "Then both."

She snorted. "No."

He sighed. "So boring old disc golf, huh?"

"Boring old disc golf."

"You can at least melt metal to make baskets for it," Drew offered.

That was true. Ollie regarded the man who Piper wanted him to be friends with. Drew having alpacas and working with Dax to have a farming program for some of the nursing-home residents who missed getting outside to garden and care for animals was pretty cool. And him letting Piper set this whole thing up on his land was cool.

And he had blowtorches.

Piper finally said, "Go ahead."

Ollie realized he'd been thinking about Drew's offer.

"But we have a lot of planting to do."

"It will be okay." She smiled at him. "I'm just glad you're here, no matter what you're doing."

Because she'd been tempting him all morning by bending over and being on all-fours and just *being* near him in general, and… because Drew was right there watching… Ollie moved in until he was nearly on top of her. "Of course, some of the things I've been doing you've liked more than others."

Her eyes heated and her breath caught.

He loved that. So damned much.

She wet her bottom lip. "Yeah."

Ha, take that, Drew Ryan. Ollie cupped the back of her head and bent to kiss her. He kissed her deep, stroking her tongue with his, wishing he could take a breast in hand, tease her nipple, and make her whimper in that sweet, sexy way that he was already hooked on.

But he let her up after fully tasting her, pleased to see her eyes slightly dazed.

"See you later, then," he said.

She nodded.

He stepped around her to follow Drew to his truck.

"Um, Drew?" Piper called.

"Yeah?"

"Don't let him... hurt himself. You know, burn any vital parts off or anything."

Drew laughed.

Ollie slapped a hand over his heart. "You don't trust me?"

"I remember a call from Miami and a Porsche being on fire—"

"Yeah, yeah, okay," Ollie cut her off. "We'll be fine."

"Well, at least I know he knows how to use protection if you two already blew through a box of condoms," Drew quipped.

Piper didn't respond to that.

Ollie just gave her a wink.

As he was getting in the truck, Drew said, low enough that Piper couldn't hear, "You know, if we *did* want to include some hazards on the golf course—"

"No!" Piper yelled.

Ollie and Drew exchanged a look. Then a grin.

Well, hell, maybe he and Drew Ryan *would* end up being friends.

* * *

Ollie and Drew should definitely *not* become friends.

That had been a miscalculation on her part Piper realized as she continued working.

Drew was a reasonable, laid-back, responsible guy.

Presumably.

But she knew all too well how persuasive Oliver Caprinelli could be.

He was charming and fun and... fun. Ollie was fun. He

could even get Grant Lorre to have fun, and Grant was *way* more serious and gruff than Drew.

Drew had tools. And land. And everyone in Appleby loved him. He could do no wrong in this community.

Ollie had ideas and extraordinarily little inhibition and lots of money.

Together they could turn this town upside down.

Yeah, she'd definitely miscalculated this, Piper decided.

She'd finished planting the bushes along the side of cabin two and was moving to the front when she heard the teens shouting and laughing. She looked over to find them chasing each other around the cabin. Two of the boys had the water hoses out and were spraying the others.

She sighed. Yeah, they'd been working without a break for a while now since Ollie had gone to "work" with Drew. She stretched to her feet and headed in the direction of the water fight.

"Okay!" she called over the noise of the laughter and shouting. They all turned to her, and she barely jumped out of the way of the stream of water from one of the hoses before it doused her.

"Oops! Sorry, Piper!" Tanner called, pointing the hose in the other direction.

"Looks like it's time for an obstacle course break," she said.

They all looked surprised. "You'd let us take a break?" Tanner asked.

"You're already taking a break," she pointed out.

Matt and a couple of the others at least looked slightly sheepish.

"I know you've all been working hard, and you've gotten a ton done when you've been doing it Ollie's way," she said. "So, yeah, you can take a break. But I think it should be at the obstacle course."

"Okay, awesome," Matt said.

Tanner went to shut the water off, and a few of the boys took off running toward the stream.

"Hey," Piper called to Matt and Tanner.

Matt pivoted back. "Yeah?"

"I want to come."

Matt was clearly surprised. "You want to come to the obstacle course?"

She nodded.

"To watch?"

"I want to *do* the course," she said.

"Really?"

"You don't think I can?"

"No. I just..." He grinned. "You're going to get dirty."

She looked down at her jeans, the pale-pink t-shirt with the sparkly *Classy, Sassy, and A Little Bad-Assy* across the front, and the pink-and-blue-checkered flannel she wore over it. She grinned at Matt. "I'll survive."

She liked sparkles. But sparkles were washable.

They started across the grassy field toward the line of trees where the obstacle course was nestled.

Not only had the course and whatever challenges and games Ollie had come up with been working to keep the kids focused in between the breaks, she was curious. She knew they'd added a lot to the course, and she wanted to see it.

Because it made Ollie happy. And these kids. But mostly Ollie.

It was really that simple.

The obstacle course had made him happy, and she wanted to see it and try it out.

And the kids really needed to get back to work, so she could give them an obstacle course break.

Thirty minutes later, she could officially declare that the obstacle course was The Best Obstacle Course Ever.

She was laughing and a little breathless as she and the kids headed back across the field to the cabins. Her pink t-shirt was definitely dirty—you didn't crawl on your stomach through a tunnel made of tree branches and leaves without getting dirty. She'd lost a couple of sequins that she was never going to see again; her flannel had a tear in the left shoulder, and she had a scrape on her right wrist.

And she'd had a great time.

Sure, she'd told Matt he needed to stabilize another plank and instructed Tanner and Kelsey to come back out with gloves and pull out the poison ivy along the one side of the tunnel they had to army crawl through. But she'd also suggested that they wet down one area of dirt to make it actual mud instead and that they should raise one of the platforms a few feet higher to make it harder to jump to.

The kids got back to work, and she happily knelt in the dirt by cabin three to plant more bushes.

She had the front and side of cabin two and three finished by the time Drew drove Ollie back over.

Ollie was laughing as he got out of the cab of the truck.

"No way!" Drew said as he rounded the front bumper.

"Swear to God. But if you want to hear great weird stories, customs agents have some of the best," Ollie told him.

Drew laughed. "I haven't even been outside the US, so not much chance to run into customs agents."

Ollie stopped, clearly shocked. "You've never been out of the US?"

"Nope." Drew shrugged. "Hard to leave a farm for long periods."

"That's it," Ollie said. "We're hiring you some temp help—like those guys," he said, casting a glance at the teens. "Then you and I are getting on a plane to... Ireland," he decided after a second. "Ireland is awesome."

Drew's eyes were wide, but Piper was sure hers were wider.

They'd been gone for just over two hours.

They'd gone from "probably not gonna happen" as an answer to simply being *friendly* to one another to Oliver inviting Drew on an international trip?

She put a hand on her hip. "You are so easy," she told Ollie.

"You had to work for two years, sweetheart." He turned to her with a grin.

She snorted. "I started *working* on you two *days* ago, big shot."

His gaze went over her from head to toe. "What have you been doing?" he asked, taking in the dirt and general rumpledness of her appearance.

"Working. Planting. Oh, and I did the obstacle course with the kids during a break."

His eyes widened as he took that in. "That right?"

"Yep. My time wasn't bad either. But I know I can break it next time."

He crossed the gravel to her. He cupped the back of her head and brought her up on tiptoes and into a deep kiss.

When he let her go, she had to take a deep breath.

"That's really fucking hot," he told her.

She laughed lightly. "See? So easy."

"I'm easy for you," he agreed.

"And Drew," she said, nudging him back. "All he had to do was pull out a blowtorch, and now he's got a ticket on your private plane."

Ollie looked over at Drew. "Well, it's not just anyone who will let me mess with a blowtorch."

"Yeah, Drew doesn't know you very well."

Drew chuckled and came forward. "Be honest with her."

Ollie sighed. "We only used the blowtorches for about twenty minutes."

"What happened?" She really hoped the barn Drew used as a workshop was still standing.

"It's just easier to buy the disc golf baskets," Ollie said.

"Oh."

"It really is," Drew said. "We *could* do it, but the time it would take probably isn't worth the cost savings."

"Especially when we've got other stuff we need to build that we can't just buy," Ollie added.

Drew was clearly fighting a smile as he nodded. "Right."

"What other stuff?" Piper asked suspiciously.

"Other activities."

"We've got activities planned," she said.

Ollie rolled his eyes. "I know. Drew filled me in."

"And you don't approve?"

"They're going to go fishing, right?" he asked. "And swimming. And hiking to look at plants and animals. And they're going to do disc golf and volleyball and cooking classes and arts and crafts."

He said "arts and crafts" the way she said "kale salad."

She crossed her arms. "What's wrong with hiking and volleyball and cooking classes?"

"Piper," he said, squaring up to face her directly. "You've always been totally honest with me when my ideas suck."

"I have never told you an idea *sucked*," she said.

"Semantics," he told her.

"Okay, lay it on me."

"This camp sounds like the most boring thing ever."

"Have you ever been to camp?" she asked.

"No. And I think I'm really grateful for that."

She rolled her eyes.

He gave her a little smile. "The thing is, *all* of this has potential. We just need to... turn it up a little."

Oh boy. When Oliver "turned it up", people ended up wearing parachutes or with arrest records. Sometimes in the same night.

"Ollie—"

"Come on," he coaxed with a grin. "We talked about me being activities director last night. I'm into this."

"I was high on s'mores and sex."

His grin grew. "I can keep you supplied with both."

She couldn't help but laugh.

"We can definitely make all of this a ton of fun," he said.

"You sometimes go a little overboard," she reminded him.

"Yes. And you rein me in. But you never shut it all down." He moved in a little closer. "And *you* were the one who talked *me* into having the petting zoo at the baking competition."

Whitney had *not* been impressed with that. But the town had loved it. "Because the alpacas were Drew's, and I knew you were saying no just because of him."

Ollie nodded. "And you said yes just because of him."

"I said yes because I wanted to make you jealous of him."

"It worked."

Her heart did a little flip. She'd suspected it had worked. No, she'd *known* it had worked, but she hadn't been sure that Ollie realized he was jealous. Or that it meant he cared about her as more than his assistant.

"I'm right here and can hear you, you know," Drew said.

Piper gave him a little grin. "Sorry."

"No, you're not," Drew returned with a smile. "But, anyway, Ollie has some interesting ideas."

"Oh, I have no doubt they're interesting." Oliver was a lot of things but *uninteresting* was not one of them.

"Maybe you should hear him out."

Ollie immediately started shaking his head. "No, I want to *show* you."

"You think I'm going to say no," she guessed.

"Before you see it, maybe," he agreed. "But once you see it all, you'll love it." He paused. "Probably."

She huffed out a laugh. "When you say *it all*, how much are we talking here?'

"I have... a few ideas," Ollie said.

Uh huh. "Okay, how about this. You can add *one* thing to the camp plans besides what I have," she said. "*Then*," she went on as he tried to interject. "If it's awesome and not over the top, or not *too* over the top—" Because, of course, it would be over the top. "—then we can talk about more."

He was studying her, and he slowly nodded as he thought about what she'd offered. "Okay."

Oh boy, that was an easy consent. That definitely made her suspicious too. "But you can't—"

"Nope," he said. "You already said one thing. I know just the thing I'm going to do to show you. This is going to be awesome."

She was not so sure about that. She looked at Drew. "You're going to help him?"

"Definitely."

Definitely? That was also a really fast agreement. "I can help too," she said.

"No, you've got too much going on with the buildings and getting everything organized. Paperwork and stuff," Ollie said.

She laughed. He had no idea what she needed to organize or what kind of paperwork she had to do. But he was excited, clearly. He was into this. He was doing something for the camp. He was getting to know Drew. He was a part of this project of hers.

She stepped forward and pulled him down by the front of his shirt. With her lips against his, she said, "You better not burn these cabins down. If I did all this painting for nothing, I'm going to be pissed."

Then she kissed him.

Man, she *really* loved being able to do that.

He definitely kissed her back. She loved that too.

He cupped her head and tasted her completely before they parted.

"Oh, and Drew's making a campfire dinner for us and the kids," Ollie said.

"He is?" She looked at Drew.

"Yep. Potatoes and sausages and grilled veggies."

That sounded great.

"*On* the campfire," Ollie added.

"That will be great," she agreed with a grin. He was just a big kid.

"And we can do s'mores after," Drew said, turning to head toward his truck.

"Fuck off, Ryan," Ollie said. "You and all those kids better be long gone by s'more time."

"You *told him* about s'more time?" Piper asked.

"I just mentioned that I *really* liked s'mores."

"You called them naked s'mores," Drew said, pulling a cooler from the truck bed.

"Oh yeah, I guess I might have said it that way."

"You guess?" Piper asked.

He didn't look apologetic. "I definitely said it that way. Now that I know he's cool, I definitely need him to know that you're taken. If you figure out that he knows way more about the physics behind catapults than I do, you might change your mind. I gotta keep you... sweet and sticky."

The words and the way he dropped his voice and looked at her distracted her for a moment.

But just *one*.

"*Catapults?*"

He glanced at Drew and then back at her with a grin. "That's a metaphor."

"A metaphor for what?"

He paused. Then said, "For contraptions that launch things into the air."

She closed her eyes. "Drew?"

"Yeah?" She could hear the laughter in his voice even without seeing his face.

"You're the grown-up in the room when you're alone with Ollie. Please remember that."

They both laughed. And neither said anything. Like, "You got it, Piper" or "Of course, Piper" or "Nothing to worry about, Piper."

Yeah, she'd definitely miscalculated this.

But as she opened her eyes and watched Ollie help Drew set up for their campfire dinner, she had to admit that the guy was so damned attractive when he was excited and happy. As he clearly was right now.

She felt her heart squeeze.

He was here. With her. Getting involved in her project.

Yeah, he could definitely put in a catapult. Well, probably. As long as they weren't catapulting *people*.

She frowned. She was going to have to clarify that, she knew.

And she was going to have to be careful not to let on that she'd let him do just about anything as long as he looked that happy doing it.

She was really glad he hadn't been *that* happy about the unicorn-snot soda.

16

———

"I have a confession," Whitney told her a week later.

Piper paused with her coffee cup halfway to her mouth. "Oh boy."

She and Whitney were at Buttered Up. Whitney had asked her to a late breakfast and since everything was going well at the camp and Ollie and Drew were busy from about nine a.m. to four p.m. over in Drew's big workshop inside one of his barns, Piper had agreed. She needed to get back to the campground to make sure the kids got their break—and to work on her time on the obstacle course—but she'd figured she could spare an hour.

"As your friend, I feel obligated to tell you that Oliver is building a volcano," Whitney said. "And I might have been part of the brainstorming for it."

Whitney looked apologetic. But not as if she was joking. At all.

Piper blinked at her. "A *volcano*?"

Whitney nodded. "And before you ask, yes, it will actually erupt. Elliot's been out there for the last few days helping them."

Piper set her coffee cup down without drinking.

Elliot was an engineer for Fluke. He worked as a designer as well, second in talent only to Dax. He was also recently engaged to Max, one of the Hot Cakes employees, and so was working from Appleby a majority of the time.

But the important part was Elliot was an *engineer*. Someone who would know how to make a volcano. Or at least a pretty-damned-realistic fake volcano.

"Does *no one* but me say no to Ollie?" Piper asked.

Whitney laughed. "Grant. Sometimes. Aiden once in a while."

Piper sighed. "I told him he could add *one* thing to the campground, and he decided on a *volcano*? What is *that* for?"

Whitney grinned. "Well, I don't know if this will make you feel better but the volcano is only *part* of whatever they're building."

"Of course that doesn't make it better!" Piper let her eyes slide shut. But even as she took a deep breath, she had to admit that made sense. Of course Oliver would take the "one thing" she'd agreed to and make that one thing multifaceted and huge.

She opened her eyes again. "And you're partly to blame?"

Whitney nodded, cupping her coffee mug in both hands. "I am. You know how Ollie and I get when we start talking about a new plan for something."

They were trouble. That's what they were. The two were wildly creative and they built on one another's crazy ideas until someone—usually Grant—reeled them back in.

"How did I not expect this?" Piper asked.

Whitney laughed. "He's softened you up with sex."

Piper nodded. "Seriously. I've always enabled him in a lot of ways, but man, it's really hard to say no to him now."

But she wasn't *sure* she would have said no.

That was a startling revelation.

It was because of the obstacle course, she knew. And the alpacas at the cake tasting. And any number of other things over the years. Sure, Ollie got a little wild in his initial ideas, but he could be reasoned with and the actual implementation of his ideas ended up being pretty great in actuality. They *sounded* crazy, but he had a way of pulling them off.

There was a part of her that wanted to see this volcano.

Surely it didn't have *real* molten liquid of any kind inside. What were they planning with that thing? How did that fit into camp activities?

And that was a sure sign she was in love with him.

She was a little worried about the idea of a volcano at camp. But she was more intrigued.

Whitney shook her head with a sly grin. "I should have been ready for you to admit that."

"Doesn't it work that way with Cam?" Piper teased.

"Oh, for sure," Whitney said. "But," she added. "*He* is softened up because of me, and the sex, too."

Piper smiled at her friend. They were calling it sex, but they both knew that it was more than that. It was love. Plain and simple. She would have never let another man she'd slept with put a volcano in the middle of her campground.

Of course, she couldn't imagine any of them even considering that.

But that was one of the reasons she was in love with Ollie and hadn't been with the others. His big, crazy, fun thinking was as much a part of him as his sense of humor and his aversion to sauteed onions and his ADHD. He wouldn't be him without it.

"So tell me everything," Piper said.

"No way." Whitney shook her head. "First, I don't know what all from our brainstorming session actually made it into the plan. And second, he wants to surprise you."

"I've been wondering what they've been up to in Drew's

workshop all day every day," Piper said. "You have to give me *something*. Is there a catapult?"

Whitney's pause was enough to confirm that yes, there was a catapult. And to remind Piper that she'd never clarified with Ollie or Drew that they couldn't catapult *people*. Or alpacas.

"You *have* to tell me, Whit," Piper insisted.

"Nope. I want to see your face when you see it all," Whitney said.

"How will you see my face?"

"Oh, we're all invited."

Piper frowned. "Invited to what?"

"To the campfire cookout and reveal of the new campground activities tonight."

Piper leaned in. "Who all is invited?"

"Me and Cam. And Henry and Maggie and Steve," she said, naming Cam's little brother and his parents. "Didi too," she said of her grandmother. "Zoe and Aiden. Dax and Jane. Grant and Josie. Max. Though I think that Elliot has told Max more about it than the rest of us even know."

Piper was staring at her. "Who invited everyone? Ollie?"

"And Drew," Whitney said. "Oh, and all the kids who've been helping you paint and landscape." Whitney grinned.

Piper shook her head. It was going to be a damned party. At her campground. Without her knowing a thing about it.

But... it sounded like fun.

Piper sighed. Dammit, the sex really was getting to her. Okay, the being in love with Oliver Caprinelli was really getting to her. She was more excited about this whole thing than she was nervous.

It had been over a week since they'd first gone "camping" together. They'd been living together in that cabin, laughing, having sex, cooking, acting like live-in boyfriend and girlfriend for all intents and purposes. She'd even gotten used to showering at the next building over, rather than being able to just walk down the hall to the bathroom in the hotel room. She didn't even miss the marble countertops or the shower with the six shower heads. Much.

The cabins were all nearly finished. They were fully painted on the outside and inside. The landscaping was done. Furniture had arrived yesterday. That had been because of her and Matt and the other kids though, with a hand from Dallas and Justin every now and then. Drew and Ollie had been otherwise engaged. Every morning after breakfast Drew came and picked Ollie up and they headed for Drew's big barn-slash-workshop.

And she'd been denied access to the building.

All three times she'd asked and the one time she'd just showed up there.

Ollie had actually picked her up over his shoulder and carried her back to her truck.

That had been kind of hot. And funny. And it had worked to get her driving back to the campground without getting even a peek at what they were working on.

Then, each day Ollie came back to the cabin around four and helped finish up the projects she was working on. They'd talk and laugh and tease and flirt. They'd make dinner, which had included the kids and Drew a few times too. Then everyone else headed out and she and Ollie had their campfire date. They had s'mores most nights. And every night they had fun, dirty, sweet sex. Sometimes by the fire. Sometimes in the cabin. Sometimes both.

"So if you're not going to spill anything else, why did you tell me about the volcano?" Piper said. "And the party?"

"Not going to tell you much," Whitney said, shaking her head. "But I thought you needed a little heads-up. Cam told me Ollie is really into this and I just wanted you to be prepared so..." She seemed unsure how to finish that thought.

"So I don't yell at him?" Piper asked.

Whitney smiled. "I don't think you would yell."

Piper shrugged. "I've been known to raise my voice."

"I guess I didn't want you to be completely surprised and react and... I don't know. Hurt his feelings, maybe?" Whitney grimaced slightly. "Sorry. That sounds bad."

Piper shook her head. "No, I get it. I would *not* have been expecting a volcano. My reaction might not have been perfect."

Whitney smiled. "Cam and the other guys have been amazed at how Ollie's been over the past week."

"Yeah?" Piper had been too, but that was possibly because she was seeing him in an entirely new environment, including his burgeoning friendship with Drew—which was about more than blowtorches, no matter what Ollie said—and because she had been doing dirty things to him with toasted marshmallows. And vice versa. That was *completely* different for them. The guys weren't seeing all of that.

"Definitely," Whitney confirmed. "He's been so focused on the conference calls. He's been enthusiastic and energetic. I think we all expected him to be more distracted than usual because he's doing this camp stuff most of the time, but he's been engaged and on top of the stuff we've needed from him."

Okay, Piper was a little surprised by that. "Really? I didn't even know he was working on anything but the script and now this stuff with Drew while he's been out here."

"He hasn't had a lot to do," Whitney said. "But we wanted some ideas from him about the new commercials we're doing and he gave great input. And I know they needed him to send some stuff in and he did it by the next morning."

Maybe he'd been doing some of it up at Drew's house. She supposed Drew had to take some breaks from volcano building to tend to his livestock and other farm chores. Playing with blowtorches with Ollie wasn't his full-time gig.

Though if she found out Ollie was paying Drew to make that his full-time job, she wouldn't have been shocked.

"What do you think of these?"

Piper and Whitney looked up to find Josie beside their table with a plate of what looked like cupcakes. Kind of. They were brown, but they were triangular in shape and slightly bigger than cupcakes.

Then she realized... they looked like little volcanoes.

Piper knew she had a huge grin on her face as she took them in.

"Ollie told me the party has a volcano theme," Josie said, setting the plate down between Piper and Whitney. "So first I made a big cake and messed around with red Jell-O and different things to look like lava, but it was so messy and didn't really taste that good. Then he called back and said if I could also make it taste like s'mores that would be great." Josie sighed. "Seriously? A volcano that tastes like s'mores too?"

Piper wanted to laugh out loud. That was Ollie. The idea guy. He didn't really think through *how* they'd make things happen, just that he wanted them a certain way.

Josie put a hand on her hip, frowning at the mini volcanoes. "So then I started messing with cakes that would taste like graham crackers, then chocolate cake and trying to get the marshmallow to be runny and come out like lava and..." She blew out a breath. "Here's where I'm at now."

Piper studied the little volcanoes. "So what is this?"

"The volcanoes are made with graham cracker crumbs stuck together like Rice Krispy bars so I could mold them. Then—" She leaned in and pulled one apart. Chocolate oozed out. Like lava. "—the lava is chocolate and you can dip marshmallows in it." She did just that with a marshmallow she pulled out of her apron pocket. "Or tear of pieces of the volcano to dip. Or both. I think having them be individual works best, though, or there will be chocolate lava going everywhere."

She held the chunk of the volcano out to Piper who took it and tasted it.

Delicious. Of course. It definitely reminded Piper of a s'more.

"Yum."

"Yeah?" Josie asked. "It's really simple. But I guess it checks all the boxes?"

"Absolutely." Piper shrugged. "I mean, I guess. He hasn't told me anything about this."

Josie's eyes widened. "What?" She glanced at Whitney. "Crap, was this a secret?"

"Kind of," Whitney said.

"Oh *no*," Josie groaned. "I'm so sorry," she told Piper. "I've been having Zoe and Jane taste the other stuff because they're here, but when I saw you two in here today I thought I should get your input."

"This is great," Piper assured her. "I'm absolutely sure that whatever Ollie has planned will still surprise me."

Whitney laughed at that and Josie nodded.

They both knew Ollie well.

"I won't tell you anything more about the plans," Whitney said. "But he definitely has a theme going."

"And no one's telling him no on anything?" Piper asked. She felt a little flutter of excitement. She wondered what all Ollie would come up with if just left to his own devices.

"Well, I mean, that's *your* job a lot of the time," Whitney reminded her.

That made the flutter in her chest feel more like a jab. Yeah, it was. She frowned but nodded. "What about Grant?"

"This isn't about Hot Cakes," Whitney said. "I think Grant feels like he doesn't have much to say."

"Well, good." Piper realized that response was a little more forceful than it probably needed to be.

Whitney's raised eyebrow confirmed that it had come off a little strong.

"I just mean, maybe we should just let Ollie have some fun."

"With something that could spew molten lava into the air to then rain down on some of your closest friends and their families?" Whitney asked.

Piper hesitated. "Is the volcano actually going to *erupt*?" That could be pretty cool. Except for the molten lava raining down on people. And the buildings she'd just painted.

Whitney laughed. "I don't know much about the volcano other than it's being built. Elliot and Dax have been going out there to help. And I did hear the word *erupt*. At least twice."

"Dax has been coming out to Drew's too?" Piper asked. "You didn't say that before."

"That doesn't make it *less* worrisome does it?" Whitney asked with a smile.

No, it didn't. But it made it sound like an even bigger deal. A bigger, more *fun* deal.

When had Piper started thinking that Ollie and Dax's crazy plans could be fun?

Well, always. Their plans *were* always fun. No one could argue that. But they could be crazy, a little dangerous, and potentially expensive.

But she knew that she'd started thinking about Ollie's ideas differently at the campground. With the obstacle course, in part. That had been totally his doing. She would have never come up with that and while it seemed a little strange, seeing him and the kids using it and then doing it herself, she had to admit that it had been fun and not as off the wall as she might have imagined if he'd just said the words "obstacle course" to her.

Like her reaction to hearing "hazards" and "catapults." She'd immediately jumped to *oh, that's gotta be crazy and dangerous and not well thought out.* But where did that come from?

The label that Ollie had been given before she'd even met him.

"I'm not worried about the volcano," she told Whitney.

"Oh *good*." Josie picked up the plate. "So I can go ahead with making fifty of these?"

"Fifty?" Piper repeated. "He's invited *fifty* people to this?"

Whitney nodded with a grin. "Yep."

"Then... yeah, I guess make fifty," Piper said.

"You've got it." Josie started to turn away.

"But—" Piper said.

Josie turned back.

Piper realized she and Whitney were both expecting her to put some condition on the treats or the party or both.

"Can I have the rest of that one? Since we already broke a piece off?" she asked instead. It really was good. And she was always a sucker for anything s'more.

Josie grinned and picked the little volcano up, setting it on Piper's empty muffin plate. Then she pulled a handful of marshmallows from her apron pocket and put them beside the volcano.

She went back to the kitchen and Piper took another piece of graham cracker volcano and dipped it in chocolate lava.

"You're not worried about the party?" Whitney asked.

Piper met Whitney's eyes. "I was just thinking that maybe we should have let him have acrobats at the cake tasting."

Whitney sat up. "Really?"

"Yeah. I mean, I get that it sounds over the top and crazy, but there are *professional* acrobats, right? They clearly know how to walk on tightropes. And there's liability insurance for a reason. That would have covered us if anything would have happened."

Whitney nodded slowly. "Okay, fair enough. Though I'm not sure acrobats really matched up with a cake tasting theme."

"But it must have when you and Ollie were talking about it," Piper said. "He convinced you of it at one point because you were into it."

Whitney couldn't argue with that. "You're right. He made it make sense somehow."

Piper grinned. "So no, I'm not worried about the volcano party. In fact, I'd love to see what he would do if he'd really just let go. If he was allowed to let his imagination really run."

"Isn't that how he and Dax end up in jail in other countries?" Whitney asked with a grin.

Piper laughed. "Yes. But..." A thought occurred to her just then for the first time. Something that she'd never really realized before but now seemed clear. "The only times he's actually gotten into *trouble*—like jail or the time there was a Porsche set on fire—"

Whitney's eyes got round.

Piper laughed and nodded. "Have them tell you that story at the party."

"Oh, I will."

"Anyway, the only times there was actual *trouble* was when it was just him and Dax."

"Because Dax never says no to him or holds him back, right?" Whitney asked.

Piper thought about that. "Maybe. At least, that's how it seems, I know. That's probably part of it. But maybe it's also because Ollie knows that Dax loves that stuff. Dax loves the high-risk, over-the-top stuff that gives them awesome stories to tell for years after. And he knows they have the resources to fix whatever problems come up. They can buy someone a new Porsche, stuff like that."

"Okay," Whitney said. "I'm following so far."

Piper nodded. "But I think all of that is more about Dax than about Ollie."

"What do you mean?"

"I don't think Ollie would ever put anyone else in a situation like that. I think he picks and chooses how he lets his imagination go depending on who he's with. He's not out of control or some delicate genius who's so in his head he can't be trusted to understand the situations and risks and consequences."

Whitney was thinking about that, it seemed. She nodded. "I know that when he and I brainstorm, we go in some crazy directions sometimes, but, like you said, it all actually makes sense. And yeah, we both have fun with it, but I think he trusts that I'll help hone the ideas."

Piper nodded. "I'm certain he has tons of ideas that he never brings up to Grant and Aiden at all because he *knows* they're too out there."

"Do any of you ever completely shut him down?" Whitney asked.

Piper chewed on her bottom lip, studying the mini volcano. Finally, she confessed, "Yeah. Like the acrobats. We heard the word, along with circus tents, and immediately thought *no way*."

"And now you think you should have let it go?"

"I think it would have turned out better than we were imagining."

"Interesting."

Piper tipped her head. "Is it interesting?"

"It is." Whitney leaned in. "I think you're right. But I also think it's interesting that you're realizing this. As the person who is the most in charge of keeping his feet on the ground."

Piper felt her chest tighten. "I've always thought of myself that way. That's how I was hired. That was one of the things Grant essentially said to me when I interviewed. I've always felt really good about being a part of Fluke that way. Taking care of the guys, but especially Ollie because he really is the imagination behind it all. We need him most in a lot of ways."

Whitney didn't say anything but she was clearly listening intently.

"Maybe it's because it's just been the two of us and we've been spending a ton of time together and I'm seeing him out of his usual environment and the stuff we've been doing hasn't been about *Warriors* much at all, but I'm looking at it differently now."

"How so?"

Piper hadn't given this a lot of deep thought. She'd just been so happy this past week. It had felt so *good* to have Ollie there with her, him clearly happy and feeling productive, him interacting with the kids, and working with Drew—becoming *friends* with Drew—and then all of the domestic things about basically living together. They ate and slept together, talked, did dishes, cleaned the cabin, all very normal activities. And then there was the hot sex. She had to admit that it had distracted her from a lot of thoughts beyond *this is even better than I'd imagined.*

But now that she was pondering everything, her thoughts were rolling—one realization after another—through her mind.

"Like the obstacle course I told you about," she said to Whitney. "He started it. Then when he realized how much the kids liked it, he made it grow. Then when he realized that I wasn't going to flip out and make him tear it down, he *really* made it grow. The thing is huge now and super fun. It's like one of those play structures at the park for little kids, but this can also be for teens and adults."

She thought about how the obstacles had even grown. It had started with jumping and climbing and swinging from one tree to another, but now it included monkey bars and what was essentially a rock wall they had to climb and a mud pit they had to walk across on stilts. Stilts.

There was also a section where they had to avoid bean bags swinging down from tree branches overhead trying to knock them off the narrow wooden beam they were crossing. Yes, the other team was swinging those bean bags at them.

The obstacle course was now done in teams as a relay. Each

section of the obstacle course had to be completed before they could move on to the next section. Points were given or subtracted for various things and the whole thing was also timed.

So the "hazards" he'd talked about with the disc golf had become a part of the obstacle course. And there were others. In one section, the other team threw dodge balls—they were *very* soft balls, without Piper even having to insist on that, and weren't designed to knock anyone over—but if you got hit, you lost a point.

There was also a ring of fire.

It wasn't real fire. It was a ring that glowed bright orange and to complete that section, the "warrior"—yes, they'd decided to call themselves warriors—had to throw three spears through the ring.

It was no surprise to Piper that the number of teens coming to the campground every day to "help" had grown and she now had so much help they were way ahead of schedule with getting everything ready for camp the first weekend of June.

"But even though the obstacles and the course have grown and seem a little over the top, it's not. It's fun and safe, at least for kids the age these are at, and he's just done it and then I come in behind and do a few things like tie things down tighter or have them nail things more securely or add a net under the highest tree. Just little things. So instead of saying no to it completely, he just did it and then I "fix" whatever needs a little extra fixing."

Whitney took all of that in. "That's all really nice, actually. Ollie's got to feel good about all of that, right?"

"I hope so."

Piper hadn't really thought about what she was doing. She never mentioned that something needed "fixed." She knew he was aware. He'd never commented on it either. He'd never protested. And it hadn't kept him from continuing to add to the course.

"I have held him back before though," Piper said. "Like with the acrobats. For instance."

Like the unicorn-snot soda. Dammit.

"Can I be honest with you about something?" Whitney asked.

"Of course."

The women hadn't known each other for long. At least not compared to the other women in the Fluke circle. Zoe, Jane, and Josie had been friends for years. Zoe and Josie since childhood. Piper and Whitney weren't as close as the guys. The five men they both knew and cared about were closer than some brothers.

But Piper knew that Whitney wanted to be friends as much as Piper did, and they both felt their friendship growing.

Spilling their guts and honest opinions was the way to get closer.

"Your tendencies to be perfect and to always have the right answer are amazing and very appreciated in the office," Whitney said with a smile. "But on a personal level they can be very intimidating."

"I don't always have the right answer," Piper protested.

"Yes, you do. Or at least, it really seems that way. I think it is fine, good even, for you to mess up once in a while."

Wow, she really hated the term "messed up" in regard to her own stuff.

"So you *do* think I messed up pulling him back on the acrobats," Piper said.

Whitney laughed. "I think it's okay for you to learn something new about Ollie and about yourself, Piper."

Piper sat back in her chair, probably looking a lot like Ollie had that day he'd come to find her, sulking about muffins. And missing her.

Her annoyance softened thinking about that.

Yeah, it was okay to learn something new about him and herself. In fact, it was great.

"You're right," she told Whitney. "And I'm definitely looking forward to this volcano party."

Whitney looked proud of her. "Great. And just so you know, you not only have to act surprised when you get there, but you have to spend the day at Hot Cakes with me pretending that I came up with a brilliant way to keep you busy so you didn't go back to the campground before they got all set up."

Piper laughed. "I can do that. Do I need to train the new girl?"

"Actually, she's doing pretty well. I mean, she's only working for me and Aiden and Grant, really, so she's fine. I was thinking we could do mani-pedis actually."

Piper laughed and nodded. "Nothing weird about taking care of you all."

"Guess not. But, don't worry, Dax comes in often enough to keep things a little weird."

Piper laughed. She missed being around all of the guys, she had to admit.

She'd always wanted to get Ollie to herself, and the camp really was a passion project, but now that it was coming together and she and Ollie were on a new, awesome path, she had to admit she was feeling a little Ollie-ish... like she was going to soon need a new challenge and would want something *more.*

Oh no.

She groaned internally. Dammit. She and Ollie were clearly an opposites-attract couple. Right? *Right?*

Or did they have that constant need for *more?*

17

Ollie was nervous.

He never got nervous.

Annoyed, pissed, happy, excited, jealous—apparently—yes. But never nervous. He didn't love getting on stage at Comic Con, but that was more because it took a lot of energy and he didn't want to let people down. The people who came to see the guy who created their beloved *Warriors of Easton* and who built him up to be a particular way in their minds, for instance.

But he never got nervous.

Tonight he was.

Because Piper was pulling up in front of the cabins at the campground and was about to see what he'd created.

He never got nervous about the things he created.

Of course, he mostly created things—story lines, characters, settings—in a fictional world he'd entirely made up and could manipulate in any way he wanted to, and that other people had found far more intriguing and "brilliant" than he ever had. First Dax, then Aiden and Cam and Grant, had declared his creation special long before he'd ever thought so. Which meant he'd never been in a position where he'd created something with the hopes that others would like it.

Wow, that sounded really dumb when he thought about it.

"Hey," he greeted Piper as she approached from her car.

She was the last to arrive, as planned. He wasn't sure how Whitney had been able to leave Hot Cakes and get out here before Piper did when Whit had been the one stalling her in Appleby all day, but Whitney had pulled it off. All of their friends, Cam's family, the kids who'd been helping at the campground for the past several days, even Drew, Dallas, and Justin were all here already, gathered around the volcano, waiting for the unveiling.

Ollie felt a surge of excitement.

The volcano. It was done and he couldn't wait to show Piper.

It was symbolic as much as it was just damned cool in general.

It stood about twelve feet tall and had a twenty-foot radius. It just *looked* cool. But it was also functional. In more than one way.

It was also something he'd imagined and created without worrying about Piper thinking it was too much. Three weeks ago, he might have hesitated. He would have thought she'd be skeptical about putting a *volcano* behind her campground. But she'd showed him over the past week or so that she could roll with things and she trusted him more than he'd realized.

She'd not only been fine with the obstacle course, but she'd been *doing* the obstacle course herself at least once a day. She'd told him it was fun and actually a decent workout.

He'd put her up on the kitchen table and kissed and licked every inch of her after she'd said that.

When she'd bragged, clearly pleased, about breaking her own time record on the course two days ago, he'd carried her to the bed and made her come twice.

Having Piper on board and excited about his creations was a surprising aphrodisiac and he was addicted. She'd always been supportive and, of course, an important behind-the-scenes part of Fluke, but she'd never been *enthusiastic* about *Warriors* or specific things he made. This was different. And he loved it.

This party was going to be great, but he couldn't wait to have her alone and make her call him her volcano god before he let her come tonight.

Maybe he'd fuck her against the volcano.

A jab of heat and happiness rolled together hit him in the gut.

"What are you grinning about?" she asked as she stopped in front of him.

"Glad to see you."

"I'm glad to see you too." She gave him a little smile that he couldn't quite decipher. "Sorry I was gone all day. Whitney needed help at the office."

Whitney had been stalling her so that he and Drew, Dallas, Matt and the other teens could get tonight set up. He shrugged. "No problem."

"Since we didn't get to have dinner together and our usual campfire time, I was thinking we could maybe head inside and have a little fun with this." She held up a bag from Buttered Up.

"And what's that?"

"Cream-filled cupcakes with *lots* of frosting. Zoe assures me they can be very... *sweet*."

Ollie had definitely heard Aiden's very smug innuendos about those cupcakes, so Ollie knew exactly what she was talking about. And his body responded.

But they had a campground full of people.

And a volcano.

Damn, he was definitely torn here.

And that was an absolute certain sign that he'd fallen for

this woman. There wasn't another person on the planet who could make him want to skip out on a party with a huge, glowing, heated, looks-pretty-fucking-real volcano that could even erupt.

"I would love that," he said sincerely. "I would *really* love that. But I... had another plan."

"Ooooh, well, if you want to do more with the melted marshmallows, you know I'm in," she said with a playful smile.

He definitely did. How did he get rid of fifty guests? And hide a volcano?

It was actually amazing that they'd kept this a secret so far anyway. Everyone had parked up at Drew's and he'd driven them in groups out to the campground.

They'd all been extremely impressed with how the camp was turning out and he couldn't wait for Piper to hear all of their praise. She didn't think she was creative? Well, maybe not in the way he was, exactly—making shit up when there were no actual rules anyway—but he hoped this camp and everyone's response to it would show her that she wasn't just the woman behind the scenes dotting I's and making coffee for the creatives. She helped make things happen.

And *that* was what made him say, "Frosting and cream filling and marshmallows are going to have to wait."

"Oh?" She tipped her head to one side. "Why?"

"Come on, I'll show you."

He took the bakery bag from her and set it on the porch step. He hoped the frosting and cream would still be good later, but they always had marshmallows and chocolate if not. Lots of both actually. Josie had done an amazing job on the dessert volcanoes.

Ollie took Piper's hand. "Close your eyes."

She did without hesitation or question.

Which made him narrow his eyes.

That was *way* too compliant. She wasn't usually so trusting when he had something up his sleeve and she had no details.

"Open your mouth."

She did it.

Oh yeah, something was up.

"Stick your tongue out," he told her.

There was just a tiny pause then, but she still did it without question.

He reached up and took her tongue between his thumb and finger. "What's going on?"

Her eyes flew open and she instinctively tried to pull her tongue back in.

"You know something, don't you?" he asked.

She shook her head.

"You do too. Who spilled?"

She shook her head again. Then sighed.

He let go of her tongue. "You know about the party."

She swallowed and nodded.

"Who told?"

"I'm not telling on anyone."

He sighed. It didn't matter. The party was happening. And there was a volcano. "Okay, come on." He took her hand and they started around the side of the cabin.

Everyone in the field behind the cabins had stayed quiet all this time. But as soon as they saw Piper, a chorus of "Surprise!" rang out as if they'd been hiding behind furniture in a living room at a surprise party.

She laughed and looked up at Ollie.

He grinned down at her. "Welcome to the kick-off party for the most fun camp ever."

"You've never been to camp," she pointed out. "How would you know if this was the most fun?"

"Your brothers assured me that it is."

"My bro—"

The entire crowd of friends had moved toward them but Piper's four younger brothers were at the front and reached her first, circling her and giving her a big group hug.

"Oh my God!" She embraced them all at once, lifting her face to Ollie's.

The look of surprise and joy in her expression made Ollie's chest tighten and he could feel his own grin stretching. That look right there was one he wanted to be responsible for over and over again for this woman.

The realization hit but it didn't feel as stunning as he would have expected.

Piper had been making his life easier and happier for five years. It might have seemed like little things inside of her overall job, but her working to find ways to make the tasks that were difficult or annoying for him easier or more pleasant meant a lot. Mixed with things like making sure he had coffee exactly the way he liked it really did make his life happier. And the way she took care of his friends, people he felt closer to than he did his own family, made him understand what it was to be loved.

Watching Piper take care of people, being one of those people, had taught him more about love than anything he'd learned from his own parents.

And he wanted to love her and make her happy in return.

Damn, he really hoped she liked his volcano.

"I can't believe you guys are here!" she told her brothers, still clearly a little stunned. She was laughing and had already hugged them each individually as well.

"Ollie called us and asked if we could miss school," one of the twins—Ollie thought it was Nathan—said. "Mom said yes, so here we are."

"He sent a private plane for us," Jacob, the sixteen-year-old, added. It was clear that had impressed them all.

Ollie wasn't going to lie. He wanted Piper's brothers to like him. And he wasn't above using *Warriors* and private planes to do that. At least at first.

"I'm so glad you're all here," Piper said, suddenly sounding choked up. She looked at Ethan. "I really wanted you to see the camp in person."

"It's really great," her oldest brother told her. "I've never seen anything like it."

A little crease appeared between her eyebrows. "Really?" She looked up at Ollie. "The activities, you mean?"

Ethan nodded. "Well, the whole theme really. I mean, the cabins are great," he added quickly.

Ollie had been sure to give them all a tour of the camp, not just describing the activities he, Drew, Dallas, Elliot, and Dax had been working on, but the buildings and grounds as well.

Piper laughed. "They're just typical camp cabins." She met Ollie's eyes. "But I'm guessing there's nothing typical about the activities."

"It's really awesome," Ethan agreed.

Ollie felt a surge of pride. But he wanted—no, he *needed*—Piper to feel the same way about what she was about to see.

And yeah, he was nervous about it.

"Piper, this is *sooooo* awesome!" Henry McCaffery had pushed to the front of the crowd, along with his two best friends, Hunter and Jack, who had tagged along tonight.

They were the same age as Piper's twin brothers and they'd been friends within about two minutes of meeting.

"Hey, Henry," Piper greeted. "What's soooo awesome?" But she shot Ollie a grin.

"All of this!" He looked over his shoulder. "I can't wait to come to this camp!"

Yes. Ollie was shocked by how much he loved hearing Henry say that.

But yes, he wanted Appleby kids here. He wanted this whole thing to be great for the town. Piper had envisioned it as a place for city kids to come and appreciate nature. But this little town, and his best friends' affection for it, had gotten to him. He loved the idea of Appleby kids wanting to be here and having the time of their lives here too.

"Well, then I need to give Ollie a raise," Piper told Henry.

"You do! Have you *seen the obstacle course*?" Henry asked.

"Oh, I have. I've *done* the obstacle course," she said. "My best time is ten minutes and eighteen seconds."

Henry grinned at her. "I challenged Zoe. I'm so gonna beat her."

Piper laughed. Henry's older siblings, Zoe and Cam, were great with him. As were all of their friends. "I can't wait to see that contest," Piper said. "We should get prizes."

"*More* prizes?" Lucas asked.

Piper looked up at Ollie. "Oh, there are prizes?"

He gave her a "please" look. "Of course there are prizes. How could there not be prizes?"

She nodded with a laugh. "What was I thinking?"

"Come on, guys!" Henry said. "We need to practice."

Nathan and Lucas started across the field with Henry, Jack, and Hunter.

"What are they practicing for exactly?" Piper asked.

"Their team is going up against ours," Jacob said with a grin.

Piper lifted a brow. "Oh?"

"Teams of five," Jacob said. "Of course."

Ollie wasn't sure Piper would understand why *of course* there would be five people to a team.

"So, Ethan and I've been put with some of the other guys who've been working out here on everything." He nodded toward the cluster of kids, including Matt, Tanner, and Landon. "Lucky for me, the cute blond wants to be on my team."

The cute blond was Aspen, Jane Kemper's stepsister. She was... a handful... for Jane and Jane's sister Kelsey, but over the past few months she'd become a lot nicer and she and Kelsey had been spending more time together. She'd, apparently, been jealous of the time Kelsey was spending out here working at the camp, and with the cute boys, and had joined them the last couple of days. She'd been thrilled to be invited along to the party tonight.

Piper shook her head. "Well, don't get distracted when you're up there in the tree branches and jumping over mud pits, okay? The closest ER is about thirty minutes away and I don't want you bleeding all over my car interior."

"Got it," Jacob said with a grin.

Ollie was again pleased by how go-with-the-flow Piper actually was. He truly believed that if one of her brothers ended up hurt and bleeding, she'd simply wrap him up, give him an ice pack, and drive him to the ER. She wouldn't freak out. She wouldn't lecture or yell. But she might make him scrub her car the next day if he dripped blood on her seat.

Piper was waving and grinning and saying hi to the rest of the crowd.

"Hey, before you all get busy on the obstacle course again, we're going to light the volcano," Ollie told the kids.

Jacob stopped mid-stride and turned back. "Oh awesome."

Piper heard him and pivoted to face him. "*Light* the volcano?" she repeated.

He narrowed his eyes. "You emphasized 'light' and not 'volcano'."

She pressed her lips together.

"You knew about the volcano too?"

Whitney was beside Piper and she coughed. Josie turned to Grant and pretended to be in the middle of conversation with her husband.

"Wow, you guys," Oliver told them.

"You should take it as a very positive sign about the way she feels about you that she knew about the volcano and still showed up tonight," Whitney, ever the saleswoman, said.

Ollie looked down at Piper. She grinned up at him and nodded. Okay, that was a good point.

"Josie's s'mores volcanoes are very cool," Piper said.

"There's also a bread volcano full of marinara that you can dip pepperoni-cheese sticks into," he told her.

Her eyes widened. "I'm definitely going to need to see *that*."

He laughed. "Big volcano first." He was excited about this damned thing.

Piper looked out over the party. The crowd was milling around three fire pits that Drew and Dallas had assembled earlier that day. There were long tables set up with the food and drink—bright red "lava punch" included—and lawn chairs and benches made of hay bales with wooden planks laid over them.

She frowned. "I don't see a volcano."

"Come on."

He took her hand and started across the party site, telling everyone to follow them as he passed them. The little crowd headed out into the darkened expanse between the party site and the stream where the obstacle course started. They'd put up tall lights out there that would soon be replaced with lights like those found on baseball fields for permanent use, but they'd turned them off before Piper arrived to maintain the surprise-party feel.

But the obstacle course would absolutely be able to be used at night as well. In fact, there were some really fun things they could do with glow sticks and glowing paintballs and "night walkers" to change the course up from day to night use.

"Okay, everyone, gather around!" Ollie called to the group as they got to the site.

If they squinted and peered about fifty feet ahead they would be able to make out the outline of the volcano. Everyone but Piper had already seen it though. But it hadn't been dark enough to light it up until now so no one had gotten the full effect.

"Ready?"

Everyone cheered, lifting their glasses, and whistling and clapping.

He grinned and turned toward Drew, who was carrying a lighted torch toward him. Piper's eyes were wide as he took the torch.

"Any last words? Warnings?" he teased.

She shook her head. But just as he started to turn away, she grabbed the front of his shirt. She pulled him down and kissed him. In front of everyone. While he was holding a torch and about to light a volcano. That he'd built on her campground. Without permission.

Yeah, he was in love with her.

He cupped the back of her head and deepened the kiss for just a moment.

Until the "ewwww!" and "Oh, come on!" and "Let's go already!" started up from the kids.

He lifted his head and looked down at her.

"Go light something on fire," she told him.

So he did.

He touched the torch to the bottom of the volcano where they'd laid the coals. It was a lot like lighting a grill. Except that Elliot had taken it a step—or ten—further. The heat from the coals started a chemical reaction that not only heated the entire structure but also made it start smoking and made the other stuff—Ollie had no idea what it was—start to bubble and expand and would eventually boil over the top and spill down the sides like lava.

Ollie didn't know anything more about what happened inside the volcano than that, and he didn't need to. Elliot was in charge. He'd assured Ollie the whole thing was nontoxic to the humans, plants, and animals around and that a good hosing down or rainstorm would clean it up, and that's all Ollie needed to know.

Everyone *oohed* as the structure began to glow from the bottom up. The lights inside turned the dark, almost-black cone to a warm brown with an orange glow emanating from the top.

The smoke began to billow from the top and one of the kids declared it, "Super *cool!*"

Ollie looked over at Piper and saw her watching with a bemused expression. She looked a little confused frankly. It definitely wasn't the awed expression he'd been expecting.

She was standing with her brothers and Henry, Hunter, and Jack. Henry was, as usual, talking. She was nodding absently. It seemed that her brothers were also adding to the conversation here and there.

Then the lava began to spill over the top and ooze down the sides.

Again people *oohed* about it and another kid just shouted, "Yes!" in reaction.

That was exactly how he felt about it.

He figured they could light it every night after dinner and the kids could gather around. He envisioned them sitting on benches, watching the volcano and discussing times that they'd done something they didn't think they could do or something tough that had happened to them and what they'd learned from that situation.

The volcano in *Warriors of Easton* was a major challenge moment and when the characters managed to get to the top as a team, they were greatly rewarded.

He knew that this couldn't be about *Warriors*, but when Piper had shared what her brothers had learned and loved about camp, he hadn't been able to stop thinking about how similar it was to what people told him about playing *Warriors* and how the fandom worked.

People from around the world connected in the game and found a place to belong. They learned about people with backgrounds different from their own. They sometimes met and played with someone from a country on the other side of the globe which would inspire them to look that country up and learn more.

There were tons of message boards and forums where fans got together and talked and those conversations often went in directions outside of *Warriors*.

Inside the game, they learned about teamwork and loyalty and sacrifice and people commented often about how, while it was an online game, the stories pulled them in and made them think about real life differently.

He knew, of course, after nine years of the game existing and being both praised and critiqued, that there were plenty of people who felt it was ridiculous to think a simple video game could actually make a difference in people's lives. But he'd gotten the email and letters and talked to hundreds of people at conventions telling him it was true.

It was what kept him writing the stories even when he didn't want to.

But right now, looking at Piper's face taking it all in, he wanted *her* to know and understand it. It was one of the reasons he'd made sure her brothers could be here.

Piper said something to the boys and they all grinned and ran off in the direction of the obstacle course. She watched them go. Then she turned and headed... for Dax.

Ollie watched her as Cam came up beside him.

"Pretty great, man," Cam said.

"You think?" Ollie asked absently.

"Definitely. Looks just like Mount Frenzy."

Ollie looked over. "Don't most volcanoes look alike?"

"I mean—" Cam lifted a shoulder. "So this isn't supposed to

be Mount Frenzy? Henry told me that you made it so a kid could climb it and then throw black diamonds from the top to their teammates to carry to the stream for safe passage from the water nymphs." He looked in the direction of the stream. "I know that's part of the obstacle course. Though Henry's really hoping you put some kind of challenge between here and the stream."

Ollie chuckled. "Okay, maybe it slightly resembles Mount Frenzy."

In *Warriors of Easton*, Mount Frenzy required all five of the teammates to climb together to collect the black diamonds and they had to carry them back down while volcano wolves—wolves made of lava—and fire spirits tried to stop them. If the warriors were able to keep possession of the diamonds, the gems made their passage to the next level easier by illuminating dark paths, healing any wounds, and shrinking obstacles.

But yeah, this part of the course *might* have been inspired by that.

"It's cool. I'm glad you've been able to help Piper with all of this," Cam said.

Ollie had barely taken his eyes from his girlfriend. Yeah, she was his girlfriend. For sure. But he was wondering about her idea of how much help this really was now. She was talking to Dax and Grant both. Dax was giving her a look that said whatever she was asking him about was a surprise and Grant now held his hands up in the universal sign for "it wasn't me."

"Yeah, I think maybe I need to go help Dax and Grant right now actually." He nodded in the direction of the threesome.

Cam looked intrigued. "I'll come with you."

"You *swear*?" Piper was asking Grant as they came up behind her.

"I didn't know about it," Grant told her. "Dax was the only one of us who was involved."

"You know I didn't talk him out of anything," Dax said with a snort. "That's not my thing."

"But then... it was me." Piper's voice was softer and she sounded upset.

"Talked who out of what?" Ollie asked.

She gasped and swung to face him. "Ollie!"

"Hey." He moved in closer. "Who talked who out of what?"

She pressed her lips together.

"She's worried that—*oomph*," Grant started and stopped when Piper swung a hand and whacked him in the stomach.

"I just..." She blew out a breath, looked around, then reached for Ollie's hand. "Come here."

She started pulling him away from the party and toward their cabin.

He let her lead him away. What was going on?

As soon as they hit the porch to the cabin he tugged on her hand, swinging her around. "Piper, what's going on? Are you okay?"

She shook her head. "No."

Concern knotted his gut and he frowned, stepping in close. "What's wrong?"

The lamp beside the sofa inside the cabin was on and the soft light came through the window and gave them a little illumination out here.

"Why isn't the volcano bigger?"

He blinked at her. That was definitely not what he'd been expecting her to say. "Um, it's just... a good size."

"It should be bigger."

"It should?"

"Shouldn't it?"

He looked at her carefully. The shadows still made it hard

to read her expression clearly. "Why do you think it should be bigger?"

"It's supposed to be Mount Frenzy, right?"

He hadn't been expecting that either. At all. "I thought you didn't play *Warriors*."

"I don't. But that's what Henry and Nathan said."

Ollie nodded. "I'll admit it does bear a little bit of a resemblance."

"Most volcanoes don't have black diamonds at the top, do they?" She crossed her arms.

He tucked his hands into his front pockets. "So the kids filled you in on Mount Frenzy." He wasn't sure what she was getting at here but she was upset, it seemed.

"They did. But even before that, I was expecting it to be bigger and just... more."

"You had expectations for my volcano?"

"Of course I did."

"And they were that it would be bigger and, what else?"

"Shouldn't it at least *really* erupt?" she asked. She dropped her arms, seemingly exasperated. "I mean, it's short, Ollie. And it just kind of... *oozes*. And it's not even that hot!"

He stared at her.

"And if it's supposed to be Mount Frenzy, shouldn't it be big enough that more than one kid can climb it? Isn't the point that the teams have to scale the mountain *together*? Henry said that all the major challenges in *Warriors* have to do with teamwork. That there's no way to get to the top of Mount Frenzy by yourself. Unless you have..." She frowned as if trying to recall what Henry had told her. "Some spell to make you fly. But those are really rare and only for..." She frowned again. "Searchers?"

"Seekers," Ollie supplied.

"Right, only Seekers can use those spells and they don't last very long and if you do use that to get to the top you might end up stranded there and you can't even really get *down* from

Mount Frenzy alone. Plus you can't take as many diamonds as you can with five people so getting across the..." Again she frowned.

"The Moaning Barrens," he filled in. He felt the corner of his mouth twitching, trying to curl into a smile. But he wasn't entirely amused. She was upset and he didn't completely understand why, but it made him curious and feel like hugging her and also a little upset himself. She didn't like his volcano.

"Moaning Barrens," she repeated with a nod.

"But I'm probably going to add the Infernal Prairie," he said. "The field seems more like a prairie than a barren wasteland."

Even in the faint light, he could see her eyes round. "You can't just change barren wastelands to a prairie."

"Why not?" He could, literally, do whatever he wanted in *Warriors*. That was really good for a guy who had a hard time making plans that were too long-term. If he needed six seasons, instead of four, he just added two more. If days needed more hours, he added them. There weren't a lot of rules in *Easton*.

"There could be a period of fertility," he said, thinking out loud. "Lots of rain. Some wind creature could bring seeds. Or a goddess could come along and reclaim the wasteland from the ghouls. Or someone could cast a spell over the lands. That would take a lot of points from someone and I'd have to come up with why they'd want those lands to be productive, but I can come up with something."

She was staring at him now.

"You would change *Warriors* to match up with the campground?"

Oh... well... He shrugged. "It would make it more fun for the kids here."

"Are you turning my camp into a *Warriors of Easton* theme park?"

Now he did let his lips curl. "Not really. I mean, theme park indicates rides and stuff. But this could be a training camp. If we add archery and some fencing and things like that to the physical aspects of the obstacle course, it could fit.

"But we can also have them spend time in other team-building activities and time in groups learning and talking about courage and loyalty and empathy and leadership.

"In *Warriors* everything is done in teams of five where each person has a specific role and they master their talents and learn about how those gifts fit into the bigger picture and how everyone has a place and plays an important role. We could do something like that here."

He took a breath. "Drew said that there are some teachers and counselors that might enjoy being a part of something like this in the summers. So the camp would include physical activity but it could also include mental and emotional aspects as well."

Piper's mouth was actually hanging open now.

Ollie took a step forward and cupped her face, pressing his thumb under her chin to close her mouth.

"We can't call it *Warriors of Easton*, of course," he told her. "We sold the trademark and everything. But we can still incorporate the important parts of *Warriors*. I've already bounced some things around with Cam. He said we can call it a warrior training camp and hint that it's like *Warriors of Easton*. With my name attached to it—and Dax's... he said he'd love to be involved—people will probably infer a lot. But Plus Gaming can't come after us if we don't use the exact name or logo or anything."

She still didn't say anything.

"You building a camp is amazing," he told her. "I love what you want to do here and I wanted to add to it."

Finally she wet her lips. "You made it *a lot* more."

"I did." It was kind of what he did. And for the first time he felt a niggle of *uh-oh*. "It still has everything you wanted it to have. All the physical activities—they'll still swim and stuff." He paused. "Okay, they might not fish. Fishing is *really* boring."

"They don't have to fish," she said softly.

He grinned. He dropped his hand from her face but slid his hand down her arm to link their fingers. "Good. But everything else—the physical activity and the friendship building and learning about other people and teamwork and all of that is definitely still here. It's just..."

"Turned up a bit," she filled in.

He nodded. "Yeah. Turned up. It's got some flair now."

"Yeah." She blew out a breath. "It sure does."

"Is that a good thing?" He really couldn't tell what was going through her head.

"I think so," she said slowly. "But, Ollie. The volcano should be *bigger*."

"Yeah, why did you think that before even hearing all these plans?"

"I completely expected you to have built a gigantic volcano that even you and Dax could climb. And that it would actually *erupt*."

He laughed softly. "We can't have actual hot liquid spilling out on kids." He paused. "Can we?"

"Well, can't it at least be *warm*?" she asked. "Not hot enough to cause burns of course, but does that stuff in yours now even get warm?"

"A little. But no, not really."

"It should be warm. And it needs to look more like lava. And come out faster. It needs to be something that they have to actually climb around and avoid. Or it should be slippery or *something*. It has to be at least a *little* hazardous."

He stared at her. He was freaking *marveling* at her right now. She *wanted* hazardous? That should not be a turn-on, he knew. And it wasn't that she was now entertaining the idea of putting little kids in danger that was getting to him. It was that she was on board with his crazy idea to turn her camp into a warrior training camp. It was a little out there. He knew that.

But it was different and fun and dammit, he'd rediscovered his creativity and enthusiasm while working on it. His writing had never been better and getting his hands on things like an actual Mount Frenzy had focused him and excited him in a way he hadn't felt since the early days of writing *Warriors*.

"Let me get this straight... you are insisting on a bigger volcano with more hazardous lava," he finally said to her.

She nodded. "If you're going to put a volcano in the middle of a campground and call it a warrior training facility then the volcano better be *big* and at least slightly problematic."

Problematic. Piper was asking him to make something *more* problematic. He felt his grin growing.

"And I think that—"

He cut her off with his mouth on hers. He wanted to hear everything she thought. He really did. He wanted to brainstorm and talk all of this through.

But right at this very moment he *needed* to kiss her.

She'd said she wasn't good at the brainstorming part. She wasn't the creative that could come up with ideas out of the blue. She couldn't take the idea of summer camp and turn it into a crazy-fun warrior training camp. But once *he* did, she could absolutely add to it and embellish it and point out areas that needed to be different or better or changed. Like the volcano.

This was going to be perfect. This camp was going to kick ass. They were going to be an amazing team.

But first he needed to kiss her.

And as she gave a little moan against his lips and arched closer, he knew he had to do more than kiss her.

This was a celebration. The camp was the epitome of how their personalities and energies and talents fit together.

He needed to fit together with her in every way. Right now.

Their friends were all busy with the party. There was an obstacle course and tons of food to keep them occupied for a little bit. There were enough people out there that they might not even notice that he and Piper were gone.

He started backing her up toward the cabin door.

She didn't resist for even a moment.

She walked backward, kissing him, tugging his shirt up his torso. He reached behind her and pushed the door open. As she stepped across the threshold, he grabbed the bottom of his shirt and stripped it off. Their mouths momentarily separated, she took him in.

As always, she looked at him with a combination of lust and love that made his gut knot and his whole body tighten with want. He wanted her body, but he also wanted that look on her face and every bit of emotion behind it. Always.

"Take your clothes off."

"There are a lot of people outside."

He crossed to the lamp and switched it off. That way no one would be able to see in the windows. "I don't care."

She didn't either, apparently, because she started stripping.

By the time he'd backed her up to the bed, they were both naked. They tumbled to the mattress together. He kissed her long and deep as his hand stroked from her shoulder to her hip.

"God, I love how you smell," he told her gruffly, dragging his mouth along her jaw to her neck. He kissed his way to her ear. "I love how you feel. How you sound."

She arched into him as he licked along the soft skin just behind her ear.

"I especially love how you sound when you're telling me that my crazy idea should be even bigger and crazier."

He felt her stiffen against him for just a moment. He started to pull back, but she wrapped her arms around him and kept him close, hooking a leg around his thigh too.

"I love how you've been this past week, Ollie," she said softly. "You've been so happy. So open and enthusiastic and... unleashed."

He thought about that word. *Unleashed*. He had been. He'd been outside, no tie around his neck, the writing flowing, his creativity not just rolling but actually *seeing* things come to life.

It had been like how he felt when he saw Dax's graphics on screen. When he saw a story make it from his head to actual colorful, moving scenes on screen. But this had been even better. He'd been *making* these things. The volcano of course, but also the slide that mimicked the Forgotten Falls waterfall and carried warriors from one side of the stream to the other after they survived the Hermithill Chasm—which, of course, he'd have to rename.

They'd also added a rope bridge to mimic a perilous invisible bridge in *Warriors*, a tunnel that was similar to the Precarious Pass in *Warriors*, and a spot where participants would have to fight off gigantic scorpions. The scorpions were fiberglass and Elliot was still working on the mechanics but it was basically a big dart board where warriors had to shoot arrows to get the scorpion head to retreat so they could pass.

The whole thing was just so cool. And they had even more plans.

He'd really enjoyed every minute over the past couple of weeks. And this woman was so much of it. Coming home to her each night had been heavenly. Keeping everything a secret from her had been hard because he knew that she'd help make it even better. She'd think of things he hadn't considered. She'd help him figure out how to incorporate the leadership trainings. She'd figure out how to get the word out about the camp.

And, best of all, she'd look at him with that familiar what-am-I-going-to-do-with-you and you're-amazing and I-want-to-tear-your-clothes-off-and-ride-you-in-your-office-chair.

Yeah, he hadn't realized what that last look actually was

until recently, and he didn't have an office chair out here, but they'd absolutely made do with... just about every other surface present in the cabin and just outside the cabin. And now that he knew what that look meant, he wasn't sure how he'd missed it for the past two years.

He was never going to get over it now.

"Unleashed, huh?" he asked, stroking his big palm down her thigh and then wrapping it around her knee and bringing her legs apart.

"Yeah."

Her breath caught as he started kissing his way down her neck to her collarbone and then to the upper curve of her breast.

"I like that word." He swirled his tongue around her nipple.

The tip drew tight, begging him for more attention. He licked and then sucked. She moaned and arched closer, her hand in his hair, pressing him closer.

"I do too," she said, her voice breathless. "I like you unleashed. I like you when you can do whatever you want, whatever you feel. No one should hold you back, Ollie."

He moved his attention to her other breast, licking and sucking that nipple as well as he teased the first with his fingers. He knew attention to her nipples made her hot and wet faster than almost anything and he needed her hot and wet. He needed her to *need* him the way he needed her right now.

"You're amazing." Her voice was ragged and her hips were lifting against his torso where he lay across her, as if seeking more pressure and friction.

He was going to deliver on both of those.

"You need to just let go," she went on.

He kissed his way down her stomach, one hand still teasing a nipple while the other stroked her thigh. He lifted her leg even higher and wider, making room for his shoulders between her thighs.

She gasped, knowing exactly where he was headed. She did nothing to stop him though.

"Tell me more," he said against her belly button. "Tell me how you want me to let go, how I should be *unleashed*."

"You need to be free to just run with all of your ideas and enthusiasm," she said. "You don't need people telling you to be careful or to rein it in or to take it down a notch."

Her voice was thick but she was obviously able to form clear thoughts.

He didn't want her forming clear thoughts. While he appreciated her sentiments, he wanted her thinking of nothing but his tongue and hands and cock. Able to only utter his name and maybe a couple of *mores* and a *harder* or two.

He moved lower, spreading her legs, and kissed his way up her inner thigh.

"Piper?" he murmured against the soft, sweet skin where her thigh curved into her pussy lips.

"Yeah?"

That answer was definitely more breathless.

"I'm going to unleash some enthusiasm on you right now, okay?"

"Oh God," she choked out. "Yes."

He very enthusiastically licked over her clit and then lower, tasting her fully. He licked and swirled as she writhed against him. He held her thighs open as she arched against him, gasping and chanting his name. Her hands fisted the sheets next to her. He teased, talking dirty to her as he took her closer and closer to the crest. Then he slipped two fingers into her wet heat as he sucked on her clit and she came, bucking against his mouth, calling his name louder.

If anyone was on the porch or just under the window on this side of the cabin, they'd hear.

And he hoped they did.

When she'd come down from the high a bit, he kissed back

up her body, unable to stop stroking his hands over her soft skin and curves. "I am most definitely enthusiastic about that."

She rolled toward him, wrapping herself around him. "I appreciate your enthusiasm there very much."

He took her mouth in a deep kiss, sure that she could taste herself on his tongue. She kissed him back, her tongue meeting his, stroke for stroke. That was hot as hell.

Mouths still fused, he rolled to reach for the drawer in the table beside the bed. He found a condom without looking.

She plucked it from his fingers before he could open it. Pulling back, she gave him a sly, seductive look. She tore it open and tossed the package to the floor. Then she reached for him. She circled his cock with one hand, stroking up and down, nearly making his eyes cross. He instantly went from incredibly hard to painfully hard.

He'd been hard since she'd told him his volcano needed to be bigger. His need for her had only grown as she'd insisted that he should make it a true Mount Frenzy that could be climbed, and then listened with the awe he'd been wanting and needing as he'd described his ideas for the camp.

This was so much more than physical need. So much more than lust. He could have put a camp like this together with someone else, he supposed, but it wouldn't mean this much. Doing this with Piper, being able to surprise her and go beyond her expectations and give her something to be awed about, hearing her say he should go for it, big and bold, was so much more than he'd even known he needed.

Creating *Warriors* and then building it into an empire of sorts with his best friends had been the best thing in his life. Hands down.

Until now.

Doing this with Piper was even more than that. Because she would steady him. And she'd grow *with* him. The guys had outgrown him. They still loved him, he knew that. They wanted him to succeed. They'd help him however they could. They'd always be there. But they had lives that had branched off from him.

Piper's life was intersecting with his. The branches from here would be *their* branches.

That thought made the strongest need he'd ever felt surge through him. He needed this woman on every level and she needed him too. Not for *Warriors*. She barely knew anything about the game. She needed *him*.

"Piper." He grasped her wrist. "Now."

She must have heard something in his voice or seen something in his expression, because her lips parted and her eyes rounded and she started rolling the condom down his length.

The second it was all the way on, he rolled her to her back and braced himself over her.

"You asked for unleashed," he reminded her.

She nodded.

"You ready?"

"So ready."

He lifted one of her legs, spreading her wide, then thrust, sliding deep.

They both groaned and Ollie felt the pleasure coursing through him from the soles of his feet to his scalp.

"God, girl."

"I know." Her fingers dug into his back. "This is so good."

"So. Fucking. Good."

He started to move, his thrusts as slow and deep as possible.

But soon she was lifting against him and encouraging him to go faster.

"More, Ollie. More."

He wanted to give her more. More of anything she wanted. Anything she needed. More of everything.

He picked up the pace, thrusting harder.

"Yes!" Piper wrapped one leg around him, her heel digging into his ass.

He loved that she liked it hard and he could go for it without worrying about hurting her or scaring her off.

He went for it, pumping into her hard, fast, deep. The knowledge that he could just *let go* was incredible and intensified everything and he was soon barreling toward climax.

"Piper, honey—"

"Yes! Ollie!"

She came a second later and as her pussy milked him, Ollie felt the waves washing over him and he surrendered, coming hard as well.

He relished every second, holding himself over her as the ripples of physical and emotional pleasure washed through him.

Finally, he sagged to the mattress beside her, pulling her up against his side, his arm over her stomach, their legs tangled.

Piper was breathing hard and they just lay together, their hearts thundering.

It was nearly five minutes before she spoke.

"I'm sorry."

He gave a soft laugh and kissed her shoulder. "Nothing to be sorry about there."

He heard her swallow.

"No. I mean... I'm sorry for... making you hold back on the volcano."

She had her hand resting on his forearm where it was draped over her stomach. She rubbed back and forth.

"Holding me back on the volcano?" he repeated. "What are you talking about?"

"I know that you would have wanted to build a huge volcano that spewed... like red candy liquid all over every three hours or something and Grant told me that *he* didn't talk you out of it and Dax, of course, didn't and that... leaves me. I'm the other one who pulls you back from stuff and who talks you out of big ideas and... I'm just sorry. I've been thinking all night about how often I've done that over the years and it's a lot."

She paused and took a breath.

He started to respond but she went on.

"I know that's what I was hired for. It's how it was set up from the beginning. And it's what I'm good at. I've been doing it for my brothers forever. I was praised growing up whenever I could manage the boys or control them. And then whenever I could keep you on track or rein you in, it was a source of satisfaction. I knew that Grant and Aiden, and even Cam to some extent, appreciated that. I made things easier on them. And I took pride in that. I felt like I was contributing to the business by keeping the 'delicate genius' focused and working and not causing headaches."

Her voice sounded tight now.

Just like Ollie's gut felt. He didn't respond as she paused now. He didn't know what to say.

She wasn't wrong. She'd been hired to keep him on track and out of trouble. That had been the entire purpose for Grant putting the ad out to hire an assistant.

At first, Ollie had balked at it. He'd been slightly insulted actually, even as he acknowledged that he did need some help.

But it had taken only about a week—maybe more like three days—for him to realize that Piper gave him comfort and... relief. He could relax with her around because he didn't have to try as hard to keep his shit together. She was there to help him. And she did. She helped him so much. With a smile that was, at first, friendly and, over time, turned affectionate. And her sense of humor and the bright colors she wore and the way she smelled and just the way she made everything easier for them all. She made things *better*. Piper made everything better.

They all breathed easier when she was around. And when his friends were happy and more relaxed, that helped Ollie too.

"You *were* contributing by doing that," he finally said, his voice gruff.

"Maybe. Kind of. But I shouldn't have been so rigid about it. I should have realized that I was holding you back."

"I never felt like you were holding me back."

But something niggled in the back of his mind.

"Liar," she said softly.

He tightened his arm around her, suddenly feeling like she was pulling away. She wasn't. Not physically anyway, but the urge to hold her close was strong.

"I never resented it," he said after a moment. "I never felt like you were doing anything but keeping me, and the company, safe."

Her hand stopped moving on his arm. Ollie felt his gut tighten. Trepidation. That was definitely what he was feeling.

"But I was holding you back. I was listening but I wasn't really paying attention. I watched you with the guys. I listened to what they worried about. *I* worried too. I wanted to make things comfortable for you and help you be more productive. I found red folders and set alarms and nagged." She pulled in a long breath. "They weren't the ones I should have been listening to. They sold Fluke. They sold off *Warriors*. *Warriors* was *yours*, Ollie. You created it. Without it, none of the rest would have happened. But they said, 'let's sell' and you went along. Just like when I say, 'yes you have to do this conference call' or 'you have to quit goofing around' or 'get back to work.' We all talk at you a lot, and you listen—mostly—but *we* don't listen much."

He frowned. That all *sounded* true, he knew, but it didn't feel right. Exactly.

"It wasn't until we came out here and *I* let down a little that I realized all of this," she said. "It wasn't until the whole project was mine and not about Fluke and I didn't have to do a certain job for other people, that I relaxed and really *saw* you and heard you. And then I realized what you really need."

She paused. Ollie stayed quiet. He had no idea what to say. The sense of trepidation wouldn't leave him though.

She rolled toward him. "I used to imagine myself as the person who was holding onto the string and you were the big, bright balloon that was trying to float away. I thought of myself as the thing keeping you tethered."

He swallowed.

"But these past several days, out here, I started thinking of myself as more of a parachute. Your feet are up off the ground, nothing keeps you down, but when you take those big leaps, I'm there to make sure you get back to earth safely and softly."

He felt his chest tighten. He liked that metaphor. So why couldn't he shake the ball of dread in his stomach? "I like that. I've felt that out here too. You've let me go. You've trusted me. You've secured the wobbly things. You've tightened a few loose screws. Literally and metaphorically. But you've let me do my thing."

She gave him the tiniest of smiles.

"And you haven't said no about anything."

"I said no about the rings of fire. And the alligators."

"You haven't said no about anything I was serious about."

"But..." She wet her lips. "The thing is, in your head I did."

He frowned. "What do you mean?"

"Even if I didn't say no out loud, I've gotten to you. Me holding you back has become a habit. You could have—would have—built an enormous volcano, but something held you back. And it wasn't Grant. Which pretty much leaves me. And my voice of reason in the back of your mind."

"Your voice of reason is necessary, Piper. I love it. I need it. It makes me feel... relieved. Comforted."

She shook her head. "That volcano should be bigger, Ollie."

"So I'll build another one. A bigger one."

"But I hate that you didn't in the first place."

He started to speak again, but she lifted a hand and covered his mouth.

"I thought I was in love with you. I thought I was the perfect woman for you."

Ollie felt his heart squeeze. "Piper—"

"But how could I love you if I was holding you back? If I thought my role in your life was to keep you tethered?" She lifted her hand to his cheek, rubbing the palm over his beard.

He'd let his beard grow while he'd been out here at camp and he liked the new look. It felt less buttoned up and expected. He also knew she liked the feel of it on her skin. Like the skin of her neck. And breasts. And inner thighs.

He rubbed his cheek against her hand. "Your role in my life is exactly what it's always been. To be my partner in making sure the ideas are big, but realistic and safe and good."

"But that's not what I've done." She looked genuinely sad. "I don't think your ideas should be *realistic*. You specialize in amazing. That's what you do. You write an amazing, fantastical world that means so much to so many and it's definitely not *realistic.*"

She was still cupping his face, but he could feel her pulling back emotionally.

"You took a simple campground and made it into a warrior training camp." A tiny smile curled her lips. "I would have never thought of any of this. You started from disc golf and got to a *volcano* in a week's time."

"We started on the volcano after just a few days," he said. Though he wasn't sure why.

She nodded. "Exactly. My ideas for this camp were very realistic. They were very straightforward. The usual camp-type stuff. And my brothers have been to camp before and *loved* it. But this? *This* made them light up. Even Ethan. This is exciting to everyone from the eleven-year-olds to the twenty-nine-year-olds."

"Well, if you're talking about Dax, it's not like he's a typical twenty-nine-year-old."

She smiled again. "True. But I could tell even Grant thought this was all amazing. This is beyond anything my brothers have done at camp before. And you have plans to make it even *more*. And it's not just the camp," she added when he started to reply. "It's everything you do. From wanting to add acrobats to a baking contest to the gag gifts you get the guys at Christmas to… how you kiss." She sighed. "You do everything with this extra energy and this bigger-than-life feel and…"

He wanted to respond. He wanted to kiss her now that she mentioned that. But he needed her to finish her thought. Even though he knew he didn't want to hear what she was going to say.

"You need someone who encourages that. Who appreciates that. Who doesn't shake her head and roll her eyes and try to put your life and ideas into folders and onto schedules."

He frowned. "You appreciate it all. That's what you're saying, right? That you think this is all good and amazing? That you've seen that over this past week?"

"Yes."

He braced himself for the "but."

She swallowed hard. "But how can I say I'm in love with you and we should be together when I've really *just* gotten to know you? The way we've been for the past nine days out here at camp has been new. It's not how we've been for the past five years. Or even the past two when I thought I was in love with you. This way of being together is new."

She was right. He knew that. She'd told him she was in love with him eighteen days ago in his office. At the time, he'd rejected the idea, thinking that was crazy. Even as a part of him had grabbed onto it and been unable to let go of it.

Now, hearing her say that maybe it *wasn't* true, that she couldn't be in love with him, sent a bolt of panic racing through him.

He wanted her to be in love with him. He wanted her to want to be with him.

Of course, he did.

Because *he* was in love with *her*.

But that had happened over the past nine days. As he'd gotten to really know her. He'd learned about her family and her "real" side—yes, the one that wore blue jeans and tennis shoes—and that she could put together a plan for a kids' camp as easily as she could pull together a big community baking contest.

And maybe most importantly, he'd truly realized that she didn't take care of him because of *him,* because she thought he was a dumbass who couldn't find his own way home (even though the first time he'd driven back to the hotel in Dubuque from Appleby, he'd ended up on the wrong highway going the wrong direction for nearly thirty minutes, before he stopped and called her and she'd given him the address for his GPS). She took care of him because that was *her.* She was a natural-born caregiver.

She was attracted to him. Obviously. Sex with Piper was the best he'd ever had. Turned out, really knowing and liking the person you were naked with made sex really, really good. Loving that person and trusting them and being able to be himself completely with her made it phenomenal.

But, still, she had a point.

He'd gotten to really know her over the past nine days out here together. She'd let him be himself and he'd found his passion for *Warriors* again.

She was just figuring this all out. Who he *really* was, what it was like to be with him, how they fit.

"This is interesting," he finally said.

"It's *interesting*?"

"It is."

"Which part?" she asked with a frown.

"The part where *I* actually fell in love with *you* first."

Her eyes widened. "What?"

He nodded. "I'm in love with you. I've fallen in love with you over these past nine days. Our history over the past five years has been a part of it, sure. But I've definitely fallen for you, for real, since coming out here."

Her eyes got shiny as if she was on the verge of tears. She blinked rapidly. "But I haven't been who you need me to be."

"You have though. I've been free to do everything I need to do, everything I want to do. I've dreamed and planned and created." He reached up to cup her cheek now. "And then I come home at night and we talk and laugh and make love. It's been perfect."

"But it's not real life out here."

"There's nothing out here that we can't have for real all the time, Piper."

"I still told you to be careful and told Drew to watch out for you and I made the kids redo parts of the obstacle course." She shook her head. "I can't just let you be you. You deserve that."

"*I* deserve someone who doesn't care if I set something on fire?" He narrowed his eyes when she started to reply. "And you *know* the chances of me setting something on fire are good."

She pressed her lips together.

"And all you did on the obstacle course was make it better. You made them secure some unstable parts. *That* is exactly what I need. I need to be able to *do* big, fun, crazy things while having someone there to make it all stable."

She was blinking fast again.

"You are my parachute," he said, stroking his thumb over her cheek. "That's exactly what you are. You are the reason I can even consider jumping in the first place."

She just stared at him, her breathing a little ragged.

The sound of his phone ringing suddenly erupted in the quiet.

He frowned. Everyone he knew was here at the camp. Well, mostly.

He let it ring again.

"Get it," she urged, nudging him back.

He sighed and rolled, getting up and going to grab his pants from the floor a few steps away. He pulled his phone out of the pocket and looked at it. It was Cam.

"Yeah?" he answered.

"We have a little problem. Where are you?"

"Close. What's up?"

"The volcano... broke."

"What do you mean it *broke*?"

"Well, you and Elliot really should have told us that there was a weight limit on it."

"What did you guys do?" Ollie asked. He was torn between laughing and rubbing the middle of his forehead—the way Piper and Grant often did when *he* said things like "we have a problem."

"Dax and Aiden were racing to the top and..."

"Never mind. I'll be there in a minute."

He disconnected and turned back to Piper.

She was still in bed, the sheet covering her curves but lots of bare skin and tousled dark hair highlighted against the white linens.

He knew what he had to do. He had to show her, in a big, Ollie-like way, that he was *fine*. That he was going to be able to do and be everything he wanted to do and be, with her right by his side. That she absolutely did not hold him back. That he knew she'd be there to cheer him on and support him and, yes, love him even as she made sure his landings were safe and soft.

Had he been held back the past few years? Yeah, he had

been. Not just because of her. But he hadn't been *fully* go-for-it, dream-big Oliver. Not the way he wanted to be. Not the way she wanted him to be.

He'd wanted to make good decisions and choices for his friends' sake, for their businesses' sake. He'd wanted to do his part to make Fluke stable and solid. And that meant *Warriors* had to consistently be good so it would sell well. The safest way to be consistently good was to not take too many crazy risks.

He'd saved the risks for his personal life and free time. Wading in the Roman fountains, sky diving, rock climbing.

But now... he was free.

The guys weren't dependent on Fluke entirely anymore. *Warriors* wasn't central to their lives and their financial security anymore.

And for the first time, he realized that was awesome.

He'd been bemoaning that fact—to himself anyway—since they'd sold to Plus Gaming, but now he could see that it took all the pressure off. He didn't have to worry about his friends. They were all good.

Now he could take some real risks and dream big.

"The guys broke the volcano," he told Piper, stepping into his jeans and then crossing to the bed. He put a knee on the mattress and leaned in. He took her face in his hands and kissed her deeply. "I'm going to go check on what's going on, but I'll be back."

She nodded. She almost looked relieved at the interruption.

Well, if she thought she could just call this a breakup and they'd be done, she was very wrong.

"I'll come back out too," she said as she slid to the other side of the bed to get up. "The party's not over and we should be out there."

"Piper."

She looked over her shoulder at him. "Yeah?"

"I love you."

She pulled in a quick breath.

Yeah, he could relate to the surprise, and pleasure, those three words could send through you when you weren't used to them yet. "I…"

She didn't have to say it right now. She'd said it a lot before he'd been able to say it back, when he was still figuring things out. And if she wasn't sure right now, or had to work through some things, that was fine.

He knew how to prove to her it was all going to be great.

He needed to show her he wasn't holding back, he was going to be unleashed, and he knew just where to start.

And he'd make her fall in love with him for real.

"It's okay," he told her gruffly. "We've been working on this for five years. You can take your time with that."

She looked sad before she gave him a little smile. "So you're going to be the grown-up now? The patient, reasonable one?"

He grinned and shrugged. "Should we try it?"

"I mean… I suddenly want a *bigger* volcano in the middle of my peaceful, basic kids' campground so… stranger things have happened."

Ollie had to admit, he was feeling good about things as they dressed and headed back to the party.

Even though the woman he was now for sure in love with was not in love with him after all.

19

He was gone.

Piper awakened alone the morning after the party and she was relieved to find that Ollie wasn't in the cabin.

They'd come to bed separately. Not completely on purpose, but she'd been happy to avoid further conversation about how she wasn't the right woman for him after all.

Their guests and the cleanup from the party had kept them up until late. Ollie had worked with the guys to get the volcano guts cleaned up and the outer shell dismantled and hauled up to Drew's workshop.

Piper had needed to get her brothers and their new friends —Henry, Hunter, and Jack as well as Matthew, Tanner, Landon, and a couple other guys who'd helped with the camp—settled into other cabins for the night. It was a great chance to have kids "trying out" the camp. They were going to sleep in the cabins, shower and use the bathroom building facilities, and she and Drew were going to see if the bigger kitchen in the cabin they'd decided would house the counselors could handle breakfast for everyone. Then Henry's mom and dad were going to come get the younger kids and the teens were going to head out. Tomorrow Piper was going to take her brothers to the airport for the private plane ride home.

Piper rolled over and stared at the ceiling. She didn't want to get up.

She finally had a camp full of kids and she should be eager to see what they thought of the cabins and if the showers were working and she should get started on pancakes.

But she didn't want to get up and face the first day where she realized Ollie could do better than her.

She was still reeling from the fact that she couldn't actually be really in love with Ollie. And the confusion that came from that realization because, *dammit*, it really *felt* like she was in love with him. And the feeling of sadness that she couldn't be what he needed.

She was an organizer. She wasn't the creative type. She was a planner. She was careful. She tightened the loose screws, as he said, literally and figuratively.

And she was keeping him from building volcanoes.

The knock on her cabin door roused her.

She blew out a breath and threw the covers back. "Just a second!" She pulled on yoga pants and a hoodie over her tank and padded to the door.

Drew was on her porch.

"Hey." He didn't give her his usual big smile.

"Hey. I can be ready to make breakfast in ten minutes," she told him, pulling her fingers through her hair.

He frowned. "Oh, uh. We already did that."

"What? You already did what?"

"We already did breakfast."

She looked behind him, then behind her, then at the clock over the kitchen sink. She felt a jolt of surprise. "It's ten a.m.?"

"Yeah."

She looked back at Drew. "I slept through breakfast and everyone leaving?"

"Yeah."

She peered at him. "What's going on? Why didn't you wake me up?"

"Ollie said not to."

Even the mention of his name made a pain stab her under her ribs on the left side. "He helped with breakfast?" she guessed.

"Yeah."

She narrowed her eyes. Drew wasn't really a one-syllable-answer kind of guy. "Why do you look like you need to tell me something that you don't want to tell me? Was everything okay? Did the kids hate staying out here? Did someone get bitten by a snake or something?"

Drew's shoulders relaxed and he actually smiled. "No snake bites."

"Okay, then what's going on?"

"Breakfast was great. Though Ollie thinks your pancakes are better."

She nodded. "I'm sure they are."

Drew's smile grew. "The kids loved staying out here. The showers worked. Everything is great."

"But?"

"Ollie left."

Her heart kicked hard. "Left?"

"Yeah. He took my truck to Dubuque."

She took a breath. "He went back to Dubuque." That could mean a lot of things.

"To the airport."

Okay, that was more specific. "Did he say why?"

"Said he had something he needed to do."

She took another deep breath. Then nodded. Ollie did stuff like this. This wasn't the first time he'd just left and told them all why later. "Okay."

Drew didn't look convinced. "Really?"

"This is... Ollie." Yes, they all enabled him with that excuse to an extent. But the truth was, it just *was* Ollie. He didn't plan ahead all the time or think through consequences, but he had good intentions and big dreams.

He also had the money, resources, and connections to not end up penniless on a dark street in a strange city alone in a storm. Or something.

Probably.

She thought about their conversation the night before and made herself breathe deep again. Twice.

She didn't want to hold him back. She wanted him to be *him*. Fully. Unrestrained. Without any voices whispering in his ear about being careful or worrying.

She wanted to be his parachute. The thing that made it safe for him to jump.

She didn't think she'd really been pulling that off the way she should, but that was what she wanted. And he seemed to think she was that.

"Yeah, it's okay," she nodded. She focused on Drew. "I'll make sure it's okay."

"I got the impression he didn't want you to know what he was up to."

"Oh, I'm sure that's probably true," she said.

He'd told her he loved her. He'd insisted she was what he wanted and needed.

He wasn't upset. He was planning something.

Probably something really over the top.

The volcano had energized him. Everything she'd said about it not being big enough and crazy enough had been true.

She'd driven out to the campground excited, anticipating something huge and excessive. Something wildly imaginative.

She'd been disappointed. She wouldn't deny it. That volcano had been kind of cool, but it had not been an Ollie volcano. She'd had a knot in her stomach from the second she'd seen it until, well, right now.

Holding him back had never been her intention, but it's what had happened and she hated it. She might have hurt his feelings a little bit last night, but if it pushed him to go bigger and be confident, then it was okay.

She didn't need to know what he was doing exactly. She just needed to be sure he had a soft landing spot when he came back down to earth.

"I've got this," she assured Drew.

"Anything I can do to help?"

She really liked Drew. He was a good guy. She probably needed to set him up with someone.

"Maybe keep my brothers busy for just a little longer while I make some calls and take a shower?"

"They're down at the obstacle course," he said. "I'll go check on them."

They didn't really need checked on, she knew. But it would make Drew feel like he was helping her. "Thanks."

Piper swung the door shut and went straight for her phone. She dialed Dax's number. "Are you with Ollie?" she asked when he picked up.

"Uh, no."

"But you know where he is?"

"Yes."

Dax's short answers were as unusual as Drew's. She rolled her eyes. "You don't have to tell me what he's doing. But if he's going to Chicago, he's not going to have any food at his apartment and the heat's been turned way down all winter and the place will be freezing. He might not have linens on his bed either."

"Oh... right."

She shook her head. "I'll have the building manager turn the thermostat up and have food delivered and see if his previous housekeeper will stop by before he gets there."

"How did you know that's where he was going?" Dax asked.

She thought about that. "I'm not sure." She frowned. "I guess because that's one place he'd go alone. And he only goes to New York or San Francisco when he needs inspiration, and he's not stuck on anything right now."

Dax gave a little laugh. "You really do know him."

"I've been paying attention."

Dax hesitated, then said, "I offered to go with him. He was adamant about doing this on his own."

That was unusual. Ollie didn't really go on adventures alone. Maybe this wasn't an adventure.

But she didn't think this *wasn't* an adventure. He was happy. In love.

Her heart squeezed and her breath caught at that.

She'd been mostly ignoring that he'd said that. Because it was unfair to think that he'd fallen for her just when she'd realized she wasn't good for him.

But he'd said it. He'd told her he'd fallen for her. And it hadn't sounded crazy. They'd gotten to know each other. He'd spent real time with her, listening to her, getting to know more about her, being around her outside of the office, without her functioning as his assistant.

They'd essentially been dating for these past nine days. And he'd fallen for her.

That made sense.

Dammit.

But if he thought he was in love, he wouldn't just run off on some spontaneous adventure in an attempt to entertain himself or blow off steam.

Ollie's previous adventures hadn't been about being bored or having too much time and money on his hands or because he was allergic to responsibility or consequences.

Those were the way he could take chances and let his imagination go without it negatively impacting *Warriors* or Fluke. And his friends.

She knew that. Now.

But he now had this camp. This was a place where he could let his imagination run free. And she was sure this mattered more.

Imagining Mount Frenzy and then *making* it happen in real life, not even on a computer screen but in real 3D-touchable-actuality and having other people ooh and aah over it had to be better than wading in the fountains in Rome.

"How long will he be gone?" she asked.

"He just said a couple of days. He wasn't specific."

Specifics weren't Ollie's thing. "He's going to stay in touch with you?"

"Yeah."

"Okay."

"Really?"

She shrugged though Dax couldn't see her. "Yeah. I mean, I quit my job and basically broke up with him last night. I guess I don't have a lot of say here."

"Uh, okay." Dax clearly wasn't sure how to respond to this.

Ollie had told him not to tell her what he was up to. Fine.

"I'll make those calls to Chicago but then... I guess he's all yours," she said.

"I've got him," Dax assured her.

They disconnected and Piper just stood in the middle of the cabin for nearly a minute. She looked around. Now what?

None of what Ollie did should be her problem now.

But Ollie had *never* felt like a problem.

Sure, she got headaches once in awhile and she would name them after him but... she hadn't really meant it. Or she had, but she hadn't wished it was different. Or...

Piper plopped down on the sofa and frowned at the wall.

She had wished it was different, she supposed.

But there were only two ways to make that different. Either change Ollie. Or change how she reacted to Ollie.

She thought about that.

She'd tried to change Ollie over the years. Not *really*, but she'd tried to hone his behaviors. She'd tried to help him be more, well... manageable, she supposed. The alarms and sticky notes and folders were supposed to help him get the things done she thought he needed to do on a timeline that she thought he should follow.

The breeze lifted the light curtains at the window and she glanced in that direction. The edge of the volcano was just visible from this window.

She blew out a breath.

That volcano had turned into a crazy symbol of everything. Every way that Ollie was larger-than-life and bright and unexpected and seemingly chaotic, and yet underneath it, he was really passionate and powerful and impossible to actually contain.

Sure, sometimes he wreaked a little havoc, but it was just his nature and you could worry and keep a wide berth, or you could get close and appreciate the power and beauty and maybe, if you were really good, you could even find the diamonds that would make your journey easier.

She'd learned about the volcano and diamonds in *Warriors* from Henry and her brothers. She'd been intrigued that there was so much to it all.

Layers. Depths. To the volcano. To the game. To Ollie.

Wow, she really sucked at being in love with someone.

How could she be in love with him when she was just now realizing his layers?

She groaned and let her head fall back onto the cushion behind her.

What else didn't she know? What else could she discover about Oliver Caprinelli?

Suddenly she sat upright.

Warriors of Easton.

She'd never played the game. The game that the man she claimed to be in love with had *created*. Literally from the very first spark of an idea to the fully fleshed-out, elaborate, internationally beloved world it was now. The game that meant so much to him.

Yeah, she *really* sucked at being in love with him.

But she could fix that now.

Twenty minutes later, she had downloaded *Warriors* onto her computer and her brothers were gathered around teaching her and coaching her through it.

They talked over one another, corrected one another, argued about the details of everything from the Rabid Arctic Rabbits to the Prickly Burr Grass, but Piper just absorbed it all with a smile and an I-should-have-done-this-a-long-time-ago feeling.

Dang, she kind of sucked at being an awesome older sister too. Why hadn't she just played with them before when she knew how much they liked it? Or even just sat with them while they played and learned?

She thought she knew so much. She thought she was always right.

Turned out, she had a few things to learn too.

Four days later, Piper got off the elevator on the top floor at Hot Cakes where the executive offices were and stomped past the receptionist's desk. *Her* old desk.

"Excuse me?" the girl sitting there asked. "Can I help you?"

Piper glanced at her. Oh right, they had a new assistant.

What was her name again? Did she even know? "No, I just need to talk to... all of them."

The girl's eyebrows went up. "All of them?"

"Yes, Aiden and Grant and Cam and Dax."

The girl looked surprised. "They're in a meeting."

Her surprise was probably that Piper knew Dax was here. He didn't work here anymore. No one came to see him at Hot Cakes.

"I know," Piper told her.

It was the time of morning the guys all gathered for their daily meeting. Even though they didn't really need to gather for a morning meeting. But it had been a tradition for as long as Fluke Inc. had existed—before there had been an official Fluke Inc. in fact—and it had continued even after it was no longer necessary for actual business.

It was exactly why Piper was here right now at this specific time.

"I'll need to ask them if they can be interrupted," the new girl said.

Piper really wanted to just sweep past her desk and go stomping into their meeting. But the girl was doing her job and didn't know that Piper could walk into any meeting the guys would be having.

She nodded. "Let's go ask them then." She gestured toward the door to the conference room.

Piper wasn't wearing an "office outfit." She was in blue jeans, a t-shirt that said, *Speak your mind even if your voice shakes*, one of her favorite quotes from Ruth Bader Ginsburg, and her tennis shoes. But she was wearing her office attitude. She was here to get some business taken care of with the men of Hot Cakes.

Their new receptionist knocked on the door—something Piper would have never considered doing—and waited until

Aiden called, "Come in!" She then opened it slightly and said, "There's someone here to see you."

"Who is it?" Aiden asked.

The girl looked back at her.

"It's me, Aiden!" Piper called.

"Definitely let her in," Aiden said.

The receptionist pushed the door open and Piper gave her a smile as she stepped past her and into the conference room.

Grant, Aiden, Dax, and even Cam, who often attended via Zoom since he worked from home where he could hang out with Whitney's grandma, Didi, were seated around the far end of the table.

Aiden had his laptop open in front of him. They all had coffee cups, but no one had water. She would need to mention that to... what's-her-name outside. They needed to drink more water and if she just put it in front of them they would.

"Piper," Aiden said, clearly surprised to see her. "Hi."

"Good morning."

"Everything okay?" Grant asked.

"Nope." She moved to stand at the opposite end from where Aiden was sitting in his usual place at the head of the table.

Grant frowned. "What's wrong?"

"We need to talk about Oliver."

They all shared a look. Aiden glanced down at his computer.

"He's fine, Piper, I promise," Grant told her.

"Oh, well, he'd better be." She propped a hand on her hip. "I'm trusting him and you all that that's true. Or that you've taken care of anything that's come up. That's not why I'm here."

They all looked at each other again and Grant leaned in to rest his forearms on the table.

"Okay, why are you here?" he asked.

"To tell you all that, while I've been part of the problem and I'm certainly not perfect, *you* all are part of the problem too.

And that from now on, Oliver is going to talk to *me* about ideas and plans for *Warriors of Easton*. Not you."

That clearly surprised them. Even Cam, whose perpetual posture was leaned back with one ankle propped on his opposite knee, sat forward.

"What problem?" Aiden repeated.

"The Ollie problem."

"There's an Ollie problem?"

"Yes, there is. We've all messed up loving him."

Aiden's brows arched. "We have? How so?"

"I've been playing *Warriors* over the past four days," she informed them.

She'd actually been playing nearly nonstop. Things at the camp were mostly done. She'd taken her brothers to the airport two days ago. Ollie was gone. She didn't have a job anymore. So she'd had plenty of time to sit on her couch and get lost in the world of *Easton*. She hadn't showered at all yesterday. She'd only stopped to eat a peanut butter and jelly sandwich when her stomach refused to be ignored any longer.

The damned game was addicting.

It was amazing, actually. It was exciting and fun and unique, and success did, indeed, rely on teamwork and good communication and trust and loyalty and making tough decisions for the greater good rather than individual success.

Her brothers were the other four in her five-person team and who had been, she had to admit, pretty amazing too. Even though it had been more online than in person, she'd felt closer to them and as if they'd laughed and talked more while playing together than they had in a very long time. Maybe ever as a group.

She'd been wrong. About *Warriors* and about Oliver and about... a lot of things.

Like her not being good for him.

She had more to learn and she needed to make some

adjustments, but she could be good for him. She *wanted* to be good for him.

In fact, she was now convinced that she was the person who could be the *best* for him.

Forever.

"Well, that's... great," Dax said of her playing the game. "Right?"

"No." She frowned at him.

She blamed him most. He'd been right there in the midst of it all. He'd seen the stories as Ollie created them. He'd turned them into the moving graphics. He'd *known* what was happening, practically in the moment.

"Well, yes," she amended. "It's good that I've been playing because I needed to know the game. I needed to see that side of Ollie for myself. I needed to understand it and appreciate it. And if I hadn't, I wouldn't have seen what's been happening. What you all"—she pointed a finger at each of them, one by one—"let happen."

"What did we let happen?" Cam asked, frowning as if legitimately confused and concerned.

"The game has gotten progressively suckier over time," she said. She pointed at Dax. "And you know it."

Dax looked completely shocked. He held up his hands. "Hey. I just design what I'm asked to design."

"Bullshit," she said. "You're his best friend." She dropped her hand. "You should have told him that he could do better."

This was another reason *she* was perfect for Ollie. He needed these men. He loved them. But he needed someone who would stick up for him and protect him. Even if the people she needed to kick in the ass were these guys.

"What do you mean it's gotten suckier?" Grant asked. He also looked legitimately concerned.

"The first two episodes were *amazing*," she said.

Each year they released a new "episode." It included new

adventures. New lands. New obstacles and enemies and quests. Last year they'd celebrated their tenth.

The first two were the ones Oliver wrote before he'd even met the guys. Before they'd decided to turn it into a video game. Long before Fluke Inc. was a thing.

"The third was pretty great too," she said. "But they've slowly been getting worse. Less exciting. Less bold. Less twisty and over the top. And the last two? Pretty freaking boring," she said bluntly.

"And you're blaming us," Aiden said. It wasn't stated as a question.

"Yes."

"Why?"

"Because you've—*we've*—been holding him back."

"How so?"

"He wanted to make the game successful for *you* all. You were the ones that wanted to turn it into an online game in the first place. That was never *his* dream. Then it became huge and you were all in on it, so he knew he needed to keep delivering. To make you all money, but also because it was your company too. You were all proud of it and out there working hard for it. So he... pulled back. Made more safe choices."

She'd seen it so clearly as she'd played straight through the episodes. It had been like reading a book where the main protagonist got more and more conservative and worried and careful.

"Then," she said, when Grant opened his mouth to respond, "you sold. You sold the whole thing to Plus Gaming. You took his story, you built it up, you made him think that you were all in it together, made him make choices to keep it safe and productive for you *all*, and then you sold it. That's when it *really* started to suck. When he had to make choices for a big corporation and a bunch of people he didn't know and couldn't trust to care about it as much as he—and you all—did. People he didn't know would trust him to make wild choices and to push the envelope."

She felt tightness in her throat as she looked at the four men she considered close friends. No, more than that. They were like brothers. She loved them. And she was damned disappointed in them right now.

"And as he was making those choices, none of you stopped him. None of you pointed it out. None of you said, 'Ollie you don't have to pull back and be careful. Do your thing. We're here. We've got your back,' and so he was on his own."

They were all staring at her. But none of them said anything.

"So," she said, pulling herself up straight, "you don't get any more say in it. I know you've all moved on to your other stuff in your own lives. But *I'm* going to still be in Ollie's life and I'm going to be sure he follows his heart and lets his imagination loose and isn't held back at all from here on out." She took a breath. "You're all fired as consultants to *Warriors of Easton*."

There was silence for nearly ten seconds.

Then Cam said, "I thought you quit as his assistant and broke up with him as his girlfriend."

She nodded. "I did."

"So how's all of that going to work?"

"I'm going to be his *personal* consultant. Not for Fluke or Hot Cakes. Just him."

"I assume I'll be helping to draw up that contract?" Cam asked. He seemed mildly amused now.

"No, thanks," she told him. "The contract is really easy. We're just going to help each other out with whatever the other needs. And," she added, "I wouldn't want to put all the sexual favors in writing. In case we'd accidentally leave one out."

Again, there was a long moment of silence. Then four big grins stretched around the table.

"Thank you for your time." She pivoted and started for the

door. She loved these men and she hoped their relationship would survive this, but if she had to pick between being their friend or Ollie's... everything... she'd choose Ollie every time.

"Piper." Aiden's voice stopped her.

She turned back.

"We haven't washed our hands of *Warriors* or of Ollie. But if you, or Ollie, think we've been holding him back, we're really sorry and we're going to stop doing that."

She gave him a nod. "It wasn't just you. I did it too. I tried to make him more careful and responsible. But that was actually the opposite of what he needs. He needs people who will tell him to go for it and help him make whatever he's doing big and bold and badass."

Dax gave her an affectionate grin. "I think you're the perfect partner for him if bold and badass are the goals."

She smiled. She really was. "Thanks."

"And we'll be there for him too," Grant said. "Though feel free to let us know if you think we're holding him back at any point in the future." He gave her a smile that said he knew very well she *would* let them know, even if he hadn't asked her to.

"It will be my pleasure," she told him.

He gave her a wink.

An actual *wink*. From Grant Lorre.

Yeah, their relationship was going to be fine.

She smiled at him. "Tell Ollie that I can't wait for him to get home."

She was 99 percent sure Ollie was on Zoom on Aiden's computer at that very moment.

20

———

"See? I need her," Ollie said from Aiden's computer screen where he'd been on Zoom the entire time Piper was chewing his four best friends' asses. On his behalf.

"Of course you do," Aiden said.

"We've always known that," Grant agreed.

"She's amazing," Dax added.

"Thank God you didn't mess that up," Cam also inputted.

Ollie couldn't agree more. With all of it.

"So as I was saying—" He grinned widely as Aiden turned the computer back around so he could see all of his friends. "Plus Gaming is willing to sell it all back to me. But the bastards are gouging me on the price."

"I'll call Frank," Aiden, their best negotiator said. "They won't have anything at all if you walk."

"I don't want to walk," Ollie said. "At all. I want it all back."

He never should have agreed to the sale in the first place. He realized that now. But it was going to be okay. He wanted *Warriors of Easton* back. Every bit of it. The stories, the logos, the trademarks for the merch, every single file and sticky note associated with it from day one.

330

He was going to go forward with it. On his own.

Well, him and Piper.

He'd barely slept over the past few days. He knew he'd been gone longer than he'd expected, but this was all taking a lot more time than he'd planned on and he was getting frustrated and antsy with all the paperwork and the obstacles Plus Gaming was throwing up.

They didn't want to lose a cash cow. Of course. But they couldn't do this without him and he knew he had to at least *act* like he was willing to walk way.

The truth was, all of his plans hinged on getting *Warriors* back. He couldn't do any of it while they owned the name and trademarks and he'd be damned if he was going to share this with anyone else.

Except Piper.

This was the big, unleashed, over-the-top dream that she'd encouraged him to dream. He wanted to present this all to her as proof that with her in his life he felt the absolute opposite of held back.

But he had to get the business part of it all over with so he could get back to the fun parts.

He should have known better than to just pack a quick bag and jet off to Chicago by himself. The business and negotiations and paperwork were not his thing. But then, neither was thinking about how he shouldn't just pack a quick bag and jet off to Chicago by himself.

He needed his friends.

"You don't have to walk," Cam said. "The whole thing hinges on you."

Ollie made himself focus on this conversation instead of all the ways he'd screwed this up by just waking up, kissing Piper on the forehead, and getting on their private jet to Chicago and not taking time to plan it out.

"Well, that's very flattering, but they own forty-nine percent of *Warriors of Easton*," Ollie said. "I own the other forty-nine percent. And someone else, I don't know who, owns the remaining two percent. I can't just do anything I want."

Cam had worked it all out that Ollie remained an owner of *Warriors*. He'd convinced Ollie that he not only deserved that, but it was in his best interest for long-term stability in working with Plus Gaming. He'd tried to get Ollie 51 percent but Plus Gaming had balked.

"But you can," Cam said.

"Not with less than the majority."

"But you can if you have your forty-nine percent and my one percent."

This came from Dax.

Ollie frowned. "Wait... what?"

"Well, the one percent was actually my mother's," Dax said. "You know she's a huge fan. And when Cam came to me and said that we needed another investor, I asked her and she jumped at the chance."

"What are you talking about?" Grant asked.

"When we were negotiating the sale, Plus Gaming would only agree to equal shares with Oliver," Cam explained. "I knew that it was a bad idea to make it fifty-fifty and potentially lock up decisions because no one had majority say. I convinced them to have two percent of the company go to outside investors to keep it fair."

"So Dax's mom owns one percent of the *Warriors of Easton*?" Aiden asked.

"Yep," Cam confirmed.

"But who has the other one percent? If Plus Gaming gets to them—"

"Your mom," Cam told him.

Grant stared at him. "What?"

Cam shrugged. "Your mom owns the other one percent. Her son has convinced her over the years to invest and has taught her to manage her portfolio. I told her *Warriors* had one percent for sale and she grabbed it immediately."

Ollie took in Grant and Aiden's expressions. They were clearly surprised... and impressed.

"Wow." Grant shook his head. "She's never said a word."

"They've both made a lot of money from the investment," Cam said, looking smug. "And I get the impression they both love being part owners."

"So that means..." Ollie said, wanting Cam to fill in the blank.

"It means, you and Dax's mom and Grant's mom together own fifty-one percent of *Warriors of Easton*."

"So..."

"So we talk to the ladies and tell them what you want to do going forward. Then we go to Plus Gaming and explain to them that we're going to be making a bunch of changes and if they don't like it, they should just sell off their forty-nine percent to you."

"That's what I want," Ollie said.

"Then we make the changes crazy shit they'll never want to take on."

"We can do that," Ollie said.

"We can definitely do that," Cam agreed with a laugh.

Ollie felt a sense of relief seep through him. Yes. This was going to be okay.

"Then that just leaves two more tiny details," Ollie said.

"What do you need?" Grant asked.

God he loved these guys. They were there for him. They didn't own *Warriors* anymore and they didn't operate Fluke like they used to, but they were still there for him. Their friendships were solid. They always had been. They always would be. But things would change. He'd go on with *Warriors* more on his own. They'd be there to help, but he'd do things his way now.

With Piper.

Piper would be there. That wouldn't change.

As long as he could get back to Appleby and show her his big grand gesture before she wrote him off as too much trouble and decided a nice alpaca farmer might be just what she needed.

Good thing he and Drew were friends now too. He would absolutely remind Drew of the bro-code and not dating a friend's love interest.

In fact, he might text Drew right now. He pulled out his phone.

"Ollie?"

He looked up at the computer. Oh right.

"What two tiny details?" Grant asked.

He frowned. He could only remember one of them right now. But it was not-so-tiny. "I don't have enough money to buy out their forty-nine percent on my own."

The guys all grinned.

Aiden nodded. "I think we can help out with that."

"Yeah?" Ollie had expected the answer, but hearing it made his throat tighten.

"Fuck yeah," Dax said. "Let's own *Warriors* together again."

"Definitely," Grant agreed.

Ollie breathed out. "Okay. Awesome. So…"

"We'll be there in a couple of hours," Aiden said, rising from his chair.

"Oh. You're coming to Chicago?"

"Absolutely," Cam said, also pushing back from the table. "But you're buying the deep-dish pizza."

He sat back with a huge sigh of relief and a big grin. He would buy all the deep-dish pizza in the city.

Well, except that he was going to need all his money to buy back *Warriors of Easton.*

And maybe to buy a diamond ring.

"Happy birthday, Piper!" Whitney said.

Whitney, Piper, Zoe, Jane, and Josie all lifted their barrels full of hard cider and bumped them together over the tabletop at Granny Smith's.

Piper grinned. "Thanks, girls." She looked at Whitney. "I can't believe you knew it was my birthday. Did you look in my personnel file?"

Whitney had called last night and said Piper *had to* shut off *Warriors* and come out with the girls tonight.

It was a regular practice for the four other women to get together but Piper was not usually one of the gang. Tonight though, she'd known it was a good idea. She'd been out at the cabin alone for six days now.

She'd been "hanging out" with her brothers and Drew had stopped by every day to check on her, but she knew that playing hermit wasn't a good long-term plan. She did, however, take back all the things she'd said about how online relationships weren't as good as in person. They were different in many ways, but she felt closer to her brothers after the last few days of playing *Warriors* with them than she had in a long time.

Whitney took a sip of her hard cider and shook her head. "Nope. Aiden told me."

Piper was surprised. "Really?"

"Yep. In fact, this is all on the guys," Whitney said, indicating the drinks and the food on the table that included some of the bar's famous "apple-tizers" including quesadillas with apple, cheddar, and bacon filling; apple and butternut squash bruschetta; and an apple and gouda flatbread.

Piper smiled. Her ex-bosses were pretty great. Then she frowned. "They didn't want to come along?"

"Oh, they're in Chicago," Josie said. Then she jumped slightly and frowned at Zoe. "Ow."

Zoe smiled at Piper. "They were... busy tonight."

Piper set her little wooden barrel full of cider down. "The guys are in Chicago?"

"I didn't know you weren't supposed to know that," Josie said with a little grimace. "I didn't want you to think they didn't want to be here."

"Why would them being in Chicago be a secret?" Piper directed that to Zoe, who had clearly kicked Josie for her slip.

"Because they're helping Ollie with something," Zoe said.

"I knew Ollie was in Chicago," Piper pointed out.

"But you don't know what he's doing in Chicago."

"True." And she didn't know why it was taking so long. It had been six days. What was he up to?

But the guys were there now. That meant...

She sighed. "He got into trouble with something?"

The other women all lifted their barrels to their mouths.

Uh-huh.

"You forget that I know him really well," she told them. "He needed them to come because he got in over his head. Did he end up in jail?"

Jane was the first to set her mug down. She was grinning. "No to jail. Yes to over his head."

Piper regarded the other woman. Her fiancé was the one who most often encouraged Ollie in his over-his-head endeavors. "Did *anyone* end up in jail?"

Jane laughed. She clearly knew exactly what Piper was getting at.

"Nope. No jail for anyone."

"Did the fire department need called for any reason?" Piper asked.

"No," Jane said. "No sirens of any kind have been used. No cop cars, no firetrucks, no ambulances."

Well, that was something.

Piper studied the women around the table. Which of them

would be the easiest to get something out of? Zoe was stubborn. Jane was fierce. Whitney was so used to dealing with the asshole misogynists she called Dad and Grandpa that she could out-cool anyone in any situation without blinking.

That left Josie. The sweet one. The optimist. The romantic.

Piper leaned in, her eyes on Josie. "I miss him," she said. "I know I said that I didn't think I was the right woman for him, but I was wrong. I need to make some changes, but I want to be there for him and help him with all of his dreams."

Josie's expression softened and she smiled brightly, her eyes growing large. "Oh," she said, putting her hand over her heart.

"No." Jane leaned over and covered Josie's ears. "Close your eyes. Don't fall for it. She knows you're the weak link."

Piper sat back with a huff as Whitney and Zoe laughed.

Josie groaned. "I *am* the weak link. I want *everyone* to be in love."

Piper couldn't help but smile. "Well, no worries there. I am definitely in love."

"I am so glad to hear that."

She gasped and swung around, nearly sliding off her stool at the sound of the voice behind her.

Ollie was there. Grinning at her. He was wearing jeans, tennis shoes, and a *Warriors of Easton* t-shirt. He hadn't shaved the beard either.

God, he looked so damned good.

Piper launched herself off the stool at him.

He caught her... mostly... stumbling back only a step, hugging her tightly.

Their height difference made the whole thing awkward and she ended up on tiptoe with her arms around his torso while he grabbed her hips.

But their mouths met easily.

The people and noise and tables and chairs and the smell of cider and pizza all faded as they kissed. One of them, or maybe both of them at the same time, deepened the kiss. Tongues tangled. Moans mingled. Hands began to wander.

Someone cleared their throat as her hands slipped under his t-shirt and his hands dropped to her ass.

They pulled apart. But stood grinning at each other.

"I can't believe you've been gone for six days."

"I'm sorry I've been gone for so long."

They spoke at the same time.

Then grinned at each other some more.

"Happy birthday, Piper."

She pulled her gaze from Ollie—God, she really loved that beard—to smile at Grant. "Thanks."

"Happy birthday, Piper," Aiden added.

Cam and Dax echoed it as they all grabbed stools and dragged them to the tall table to join their girls.

She gave a happy sigh and looked back to Ollie.

He looked like he was going to be sick.

She frowned. "What's wrong?"

"It's your birthday?"

"Well, yesterday was."

The I-might-be-sick look intensified and she considered stepping back.

"Are you okay?" she asked.

"Fuck no, I'm not okay." He let her go and shoved a hand through his hair. He looked miserable. "I missed your birthday."

"Well..." She chewed on her bottom lip for a second then said, "You've *always* missed my birthday, Ollie."

"Mine too," Cam said, just before he bit into a quesadilla.

"Mine too," Grant added, as the waitress set ciders and beers down in front of the guys.

"A large Squealer," Dax requested of her. Then he looked at Ollie. "Mine too. Except that time we were in Madrid and I reminded you of it."

Ollie sighed.

"You didn't get me anything for my birthday either," Jane told him. Grinning widely.

"Yeah, okay," Ollie told them. "I get it."

"But Piper sent me a dozen strawberry cookies from you," Jane said.

"You knew they were from Piper though?" Ollie asked.

Jane laughed. "Of course."

Ollie looked down at Piper. "Good try, I guess."

She grinned. "Jane just knows better because of Dax. I've been making you look good for five years with everyone else."

He gave her a small smile and stepped closer again. "Yeah. I know." His smile faded. "I'm so damned sorry I didn't know it was your birthday."

"I'm not upset."

"You should be."

"Why? You gave me a surprise volcano party the other night."

"Well, it wasn't exactly a *surprise*," he said, shooting a glance at Josie and Whitney.

"You brought me the *best* clam chowder I've ever had from Boston when you were last there for a convention. And that was no small thing. Getting seafood chowder from Boston to Chicago took some sweet-talking and some money."

He shrugged. "It was amazing chowder."

"It was." She put a hand to his face. "I would rather have surprise volcano parties and amazing clam chowder for no reason other than you thinking I would like it than a planned birthday celebration anyway."

"Hey," Jane and Whitney both protested.

Piper sent them a grin. "From *him*. Planned girls' nights for my birthday are awesome."

"Well, you're coming to girls' patio nights at my mom's from now on," Zoe told her.

Piper felt her heart flip. That was a big deal. It meant she was truly part of the group. The other four couples got together at Zoe and Cam's parents' house for dinner once a week—sometimes more—and the girls gathered on the back patio with drinks for girl talk while the guys did the dishes.

She looked up at Ollie. "What do you say? Group dinners at Maggie's?"

He nodded. "Yeah. Definitely."

Her whole body felt like it flipped then.

He'd avoided those because he didn't think he was good with attachments.

He was changing his mind.

"Why don't you *surprise* her now with what we were doing in Chicago?" Dax asked, picking up a piece of bruschetta.

The apple-tizers were nearly gone now that the guys had joined them. It was a good thing Dax had ordered pizza.

Piper pulled Ollie closer to the table and climbed back onto her stool while he took the one next to her. "Yeah, what was going on?"

"I'm sorry I just took off."

"I wasn't shocked," she told him dryly.

He looked a little abashed anyway. "I thought it would be a quick trip and I could get right back and tell you all about it."

Her lips quirked. Of course, he'd thought it would be quick and easy and then it hadn't been. "It's okay. I knew Grant and Dax and the guys would be there for you."

He reached for her hand and linked their fingers. "You would have been too."

She nodded.

"I noticed the stocked fridge and the fresh sheets."

She smiled. "I couldn't let you starve."

"I would die without you, Piper. And I know that sounds a little romantic, and I mean it that way too, but I seriously think it's possible that I might literally die without you taking care of me."

Everyone at the table laughed. And no one argued.

She leaned in and kissed him. "I will never let that happen."

"Good. Because... I need you to help me keep *Easton* alive too."

She sat back, confused. "*Easton*?"

"Yep."

"Is it dying? I've played to the end. Oh my God, Ollie! Are you planning something in the next episode? The one you've been writing? If you do something to *Easton*, *I* will kill you. You can *not* have an earthquake or swarm of locusts or something come in. No. I won't let you." She looked at Dax. Then Grant. Then Aiden. Then Cam. "You guys! Say something!"

Grant shook his head and popped an apple slice into his mouth. "Nope, I'm on his side. Completely."

That surprised her enough that she paused and just stared. Those words had never come out of Grant Lorre's mouth before.

"Completely?" she finally asked.

"Yep."

"Because you've talked him out of the really horrible idea he initially had that led you all to jump on the plane to Chicago and rush to stop him?" she asked.

"Nope."

She turned to face Grant more fully. "So Ollie had an idea, and you are fully on board without question, without any revisions?"

"Yep."

Piper looked at Josie. "I'm so sorry."

Josie frowned. "For what?"

"That your new husband is having a stroke."

Josie grinned and snuggled up closer to Grant. "He's fine."

Piper shook her head. What the hell was going on?

"Piper."

She looked back to Ollie. He seemed highly entertained.

"You've been playing *Warriors*?"

She nodded. "With my brothers. And I love it. Though we do have to talk about how things have been progressing lately."

"Oh?"

"You've been slacking."

Surprise flickered in his eyes briefly, but then he nodded. "I have. I've been too careful."

"Exactly."

"I've worried too much about not letting others down and I've let myself down instead."

"We've been holding you back though."

He shook his head.

She nodded.

He sighed. "Okay. Yeah, maybe a little. But it's my fault too. I *let* that happen. I didn't push back."

Okay, maybe there was a little fault on both sides. She nodded again, her throat feeling a little tight.

"And," he went on. "I finally understand that I'm not letting down the important people—the guys... you—if I'm doing something I'm passionate about and that makes me proud and happy. Because you all love me."

She felt her smile spreading and her heart swelling in her chest. God, she was so glad he realized all of that. Especially the part about her loving him. "I do," she said sincerely. "I love you so much."

He leaned in. "I love you too. But fair warning—I'm done with holding back and being careful. I'm going all in. Full on. Totally unleashed. On everything."

Her heart gave a hard beat and she felt a rush of adrenaline. It was the words, but also the look in his eyes. He was excited. Enthusiastic. Motivated. He looked like the guy she'd met five years ago. Before she'd covered him in a pile of sticky notes.

"And I promise to stay out of your way," she told him.

He shook his head. "That's not what I want. I want you right there with me. My parachute."

She pressed her lips together. She wanted that too. More than anything.

Suddenly a little ding rang out and Ollie looked down at the watch on his wrist.

Piper stared. Oliver Caprinelli had a *watch* on his wrist.

"What's that?" she asked.

"A watch." He looked at her, clearly amused. "But it also shows me my emails... one at a time. And texts. And a bunch of other stuff. Like the alarm feature that's really easy to use." He grabbed her hand. "Come here. I have something to show you." He started for the door.

They stepped out of Granny's and into the parking lot. Their friends were right behind them.

Ollie pulled her around the edge of the building and then looked up at the sky. He pointed. "There!"

Piper looked up. And gasped.

There was a small plane flying overhead, pulling a banner that said, "Piper, Will You Marry Me?"

She swung to face him, her mouth hanging open.

He grinned, clearly proud. "I wanted a sky-writer, but there isn't one nearby. This guy does banners, though, and I figured that was pretty over the top too."

"Ollie—"

But that was all she got out before he dropped to one knee and held up a ring box. "Piper, marry me. Please. I need you. I need you to help me dream, to push, to go for it all. And to help me land safely and softly."

She felt the tears spilling over her lower lashes and she wiped them away as she grinned down at him.

Oliver Caprinelli. Genius. Pain in her butt. The love of her life.

"Yes, I will absolutely marry you, Ollie," she said, her voice wobbly.

He rose and pulled her into a big hug. "Thank God. There's so much ahead and I want you with me for all of it."

She squeezed him tightly. "I knew I'd get you to fall in love with me," she said against his chest.

He laughed. "Well, I was already partway there when you kidnapped me to the woods. Even if I didn't realize it."

She leaned back, grinning. "Kidnapped, huh?"

"Or something." He bent and kissed her.

It was sweet and short, but it made her stomach flip and her toes curl.

He lifted his head. "And I'm definitely not destroying *Easton*," he said. "I bought..." He looked at the other guys. "*We* bought *Warriors* back. It's all ours. We can do whatever we want with it now."

Piper's heart beat hard again. Really hard. Her ribs almost hurt with how hard it was suddenly pounding. "What?" She looked at the other guys. They all nodded.

"Ollie is the majority owner," Grant said. "But we're all back in. It's ours again."

Piper felt tears stinging her eyes again. "Oh my God."

Aiden smiled at her. "Why didn't you tell us you thought selling was a bad idea when we did it?"

She sniffed and turned to face them, her arm still around Ollie. "That wasn't my place to say."

"It was," Aiden said.

"It was," Cam agreed. "You should have told us what you thought."

"You would have listened?" she asked.

"We would have," Grant said with a nod. "Especially if you had told us how Ollie was feeling about it."

She looked up at the man she was in love with. She smiled, then met Grant's gaze. "Well, no worries. I will be telling you exactly what I think and how you should all be treating Ollie from now on."

Grant chuckled. "Yeah, we know."

Ollie's arm tightened around her. "What do you think about expanding the camps? Making them actual *Warriors of Easton* camps and putting them in multiple locations?"

Piper didn't know if she was going to survive her heart pounding like this, but she nodded enthusiastically. "Yes. I love that."

"And I have an idea for a book. An actual novel. Maybe more than one. Maybe a whole series. I could expand on the *Warriors* universe, take known characters and backstory and history, but delve more into their personal stories, maybe give them more in-depth relationships, explore more of their thoughts and feelings and reactions to the adventures and challenges."

Piper gripped him tighter. "Oh my God, Ollie. Yes!"

"And I want to expand the camp. Make it even bigger. And then do it again in other locations. Have *Warriors of Easton* training camps all over the country. They'll be places where kids can come together in real life and get a little dirty and actually be physical and meet new friends face-to-face instead of just behind the screen. *Warriors of Easton* can come to life in so many ways."

"Oh wow!" Whitney's eyes were wide with excitement. "Yes! Will you cosplay at the camp? Have them do costumes and stuff?"

"I don't know," Ollie said. "Maybe."

"Oh, you could make actual costumes *at* the camps," Whitney said. "I know there are a ton of people who are so creative about using very regular items and doing it on very low budgets. That would be such a cool thing to include so that the kids could take those ideas back home and continue with them. You could open up the whole world of cosplay to all these people."

"That's great," Dax agreed. "I know the head designer for *World of Leokin,* Kiera Connelly. She's big into cosplay. Her best friend, Sophie, does a lot of costuming. We could talk to them."

"How cool," Whitney said. "I'd love to know more about it. I could maybe get into some... costumes."

She glanced at Cam with a look that even made Piper feel a little warmer.

"I'm in. Let's do it. Call her now," Cam said, pointing at Dax.

They all laughed.

Piper blinked, making another tear roll down her cheek.

Ollie noticed immediately.

In spite of the fact that he was wrapped up in brainstorming and his two biggest enablers, Dax and Whitney, were right there, he noticed Piper.

He lifted a hand and brushed the tear away with his thumb. "What's going on in that amazing head of yours? You know I can keep you fully supplied with all the folders and sticky notes you'll need to keep this all on track right?"

She gave him a wobbly smile. "I'm trying to break my sticky-note habit."

"Oh no, you can't. I need it. I need you."

Her heart *thunked.* "I need you too. Exactly the way you are."

"Good." His grin was huge and he pivoted to face her fully. He took both of her hands in his. "So here's the proposal. We'd like you to be the new CEO of Fluke Inc."

Those words just hung in the air between them for several seconds.

She heard them. She repeated them to herself.

But they made no sense.

"Piper?"

"You... I..." She frowned and shook her head. "Aiden is your CEO."

"I'm the CEO of Hot Cakes," Aiden said. "And I'm a consultant at Buttered Up and I'd like to stay on as a board member for Fluke, but I've got my hands full." He smiled at her. "Fluke needs someone who's completely focused on what's next for *Warriors of Easton* and"—he glanced at Ollie—"taking care of our delicate genius in the manner to which he has become accustomed."

"Do you mean the way she's 'taken care of him' recently?" Dax asked, a mischievous grin on his face. "Or always?"

"Both," Aiden said with his own grin.

Piper shook her head, trying not to smile. That would only encourage them. She focused on Ollie. "I don't know."

"Aiden will be on the board. Whitney too. Grant will still be CFO. Cam will still be our attorney. Dax will still consult. And I'll still be the creative heart and soul that keeps everything going." He grinned. "But we need a leader who can keep us organized, get shit done, and who can take us to the next level. That's you, Piper. It's always been you."

Her heart rate picked up. She'd been thinking she needed a new challenge. Something more. Her gifts were organizing and planning. She didn't come up with the big ideas, but she could lay foundations that Ollie could build on and she could add on layers to what he did. She felt excitement start to bubble in her veins. Could she run Fluke and more specifically help grow *Warriors* into something even bigger and better?

Oh, yeah she could.

"I would absolutely demand more money and benefits," she said, just because she could.

"We are definitely going to talk about your *benefits*," he said, his voice just husky enough to send delicious tingles down her spine.

She worked to look remorseful. "I'm very sorry, Mr. Caprinelli, but our personal relationship will have to end."

He frowned. "Excuse me?"

She nodded. "We won't be able to sleep together anymore. It would be inappropriate."

"How so?"

"Well, if I'm CEO, then I'll be your boss."

There was a beat of silence. Then laughter erupted.

He gave her a slow grin. "And to think that I was going to have Knight Arnott fall for a beautiful, feisty warrior who turns out to be the princess of a neighboring land."

"You were, huh?"

"It was going to be a really awesome love story."

She tipped her head. "In the game or in the novel?"

"Novel."

"So would there be on-the-page sex scenes?"

"These are kids' books."

"You should totally write two versions—one for the kids, one for the adults."

"Now, see, that's CEO thinking right there." He grinned.

"You write me a romance novel complete with some really steamy scenes and we can renegotiate how we spend our outside-of-work time," she told him with a grin.

"No way," he said. "I'm going to need inspiration."

"You do still have that big leather office chair..." she said thoughtfully.

"They don't have leather office chairs in *Easton*," Dax said.

She laughed. "True."

"They will have," Ollie declared.

"How will that work? They'll just stumble upon random chairs left out in the woods?" Dax asked.

"I'll make it work," Ollie said.

And somehow, Piper believed that he would. She lifted a shoulder. "But I'll be wearing my dresses and skirts again if we're at the office together. You've never been *inspired* by those before."

He lifted his hand and cupped the back of her head, pulling

her in until their foreheads touched. "Well, I don't know if you were aware of this, but I can be kind of a dumbass sometimes."

She laughed softly. "I've never thought you were a dumbass."

"I have," Cam said.

"Same," Grant agreed.

Ollie just lifted a middle finger to them both, his eyes locked on Piper's.

"Never leave me," he said.

Her heart squeezed. "Okay. And *you* never leave me. At least, not for more than like four days at a time."

He laughed. "I'll take you with me from now on."

"Awesome." She squeezed his thigh.

"How do you feel about wading in Roman fountains?"

"You know, I might just be into that."

"How about a few hours in a Roman jail?" Dax asked.

"Maybe even that," she said.

"Oh God, he's going to turn *her* into a dumbass," Grant muttered.

She lifted her middle finger to Grant too.

The CFO of Fluke Inc. chuckled. "Does that mean you're taking the CEO position?"

She lifted her head from Ollie's, looked around at all of their friends, and then back to Ollie. And nodded. "Yes. On one condition."

"Yes, we can get married next weekend at the camp," Ollie said.

Her heart and stomach flipped, her nipples tingled, and her toes curled.

"Okay, two conditions," she amended, her voice a little thick. She *really* wanted to marry him next weekend at the camp.

"What's the second?" he asked, grinning, but clearly curious.

"That we also start a *Warriors of Easton* energy drink line and the first one is called Dragon Spit."

It only took him a second to catch her up in a huge hug, lifting her off her feet, and say in her ear, "That *Warriors of Easton* romance novel just got a lot dirtier."

21

One year later...

That *Warriors of Easton* romance novel became a *New York Times* bestseller.

Coming in right behind the children's version on the list.

Thank you so much for reading *Gimme S'more!* I hope you loved Ollie and Piper's story!

So what's next?

Be sure you haven't missed any of the Hot Cakes series! Then head down to the Louisiana Bayou for more sexy, crazy, small-town fun with Paige, Mitch, and all the Landrys!

The Hot Cakes Series

Sugar Rush (prequel)
Sugarcoated
Forking Around
Making Whoopie
Semi-Sweet On You
Oh, Fudge
Gimme S'more

<u>**The Boys of the Bayou**</u>

Small town, hot-country-boys-with-Louisiana-drawls, crazy-falling-in-love fun!

My Best Friend's Mardi Gras Wedding
A fake relationship, small town, rom com

Sweet Home Louisiana
A sexy second chance, small town rom com

Beauty and the Bayou
A beauty and the beast, wounded hero,
small town rom com

Crazy Rich Cajuns
A sexy opposites attract, nerdy hero,
small town, rom com

Must Love Alligators
A fish-out-of-water, nerd heroine,
small town rom com

Four Weddings and a Swamp Boat Tour

A friends-with-benefits, small town, rom com

And join in on all the FAN FUN!

Join my **email list!**
http://bit.ly/ErinNicholasEmails

And be the first to hear about my news, sales, freebies, behind-the-scenes, and more!

Or for even more fun, join my **Super Fan page** on Facebook and chat with me and other super fans every day! Just search Facebook for Erin Nicholas Super Fans!

If you love sexy, funny, small town romance and, well, hot kitchens and baked goods ;) you should also check out my **Billionaires in Blue Jeans** series!
Triplet billionaire sisters find themselves in small town Kansas for a year running a pie shop...and falling in love!

Diamonds and Dirt Roads
High Heels and Haystacks
Cashmere and Camo

Find all my books, including a printable book list, at
www.ErinNicholas.com

ABOUT ERIN

Erin Nicholas is the New York Times and USA Today bestselling author of over thirty sexy contemporary romances. Her stories have been described as toe-curling, enchanting, steamy and fun. She loves to write about reluctant heroes, imperfect heroines and happily ever afters. She lives in the Midwest with her husband who only wants to read the sex scenes in her books, her kids who will never read the sex scenes in her books, and family and friends who say they're shocked by the sex scenes in her books (yeah, right!).

Find her and all her books at
www.ErinNicholas.com

And find her on Facebook, Goodreads, BookBub, and Instagram!